As a young man I remember thrilling to the phantasmagorical novels of A. Merritt, like Ship of Ishtar, and the novel She by H. Rider Haggard, the fantastical story of an immortal white Queen. Brinckman, owes a huge debt to H. Rider Haggard, as he tells the tale of a modern woman from Ottawa who, as a neglected and abused child discovers the novel She, and interprets and adopts a passage from the novel, which she takes to mean that it's alright to kill anyone who stands between her and what she desires. At twelve she kills her drunken mother's abusive boyfriend, and lets her mother take the rap and go to prison. At fourteen she kills two girls, a former close friend and the girl who broke up their relationship. Her father is a member of a motorcycle gang, and she quickly learns about keeping books for the club as well as the intricacies of money laundering. She eventually steals half her father's assets and rips off the Hells Angels for some twenty million dollars. Faking her own death, she heads for a Caribbean island where she discovers an isolated tribe that immediately worship her as the reincarnation of their long dead leader. As with Kurtz in Heart of Darkness, absolute power corrupts and the girl, now known as Ayesha, becomes involved in voodoo and her subjects in cannibalism. The melodramatic happenings are told in a calm narrative voice and the pace is excellent. The downside is that Brinckman tells a little too much about a multitude of subjects, ranging from voodoo rituals, to turning cocoa leaves into cocaine, to money laundering. Still, this is an entertaining novel.
W.P. Kinsella (Books in Canada)

"The battle between good and evil is a tale as old as storytelling itself. And the debate over whether one can exist without the other - or whether the two are actually one in the same - has been raging for nearly as long... The author uses the good-evil conundrum to spin an entertaining and thought-provoking tale of death and deception.

"Such as wide swath requires a lot of infilling, and it's here that the book benefits from Brinckman's extensive research. While too much information can mask a weak narrative, this isn't the case with "Ayesha." In fact, the rich descriptions are a welcome respite that allows to the story line to settle in the readers' mind and build anticipation for the events ahead - of which there are many."
Gordon Isfeld (Midwest Review)

This is the story of a woman who commits a number of murders, steals $20,000,000 from the Hells Angels, and ends up queen of a forgotten tribe on a tropical island. As a young girl she reads H.Rider Haggard's She in a dusty library and begins to worship the immortal queen, Ayesha, She who must be obeyed.

The protagonist is a woman who lives by ethical principles, induced from Ayesha's vegetarianism and penchant for removing people who are in the way. These ethics she believes to be essential for all mankind if current life forms on the planet are to survive human population explosion. She believes Ayesha could be a manifestation of Gaia.

However her ethics, thousands of years older than contemporary ethics, religious or secular, conflict with them, and with today's principles of justice, so she is doomed. (English philosopher, John Gray's book *Straw Dogs*, is quoted in the frontispiece: "Ideas of justice are as timeless as fashion in hats"). Her life might be considered a tragedy in the classic sense. The psychiatrist at the conclusion of the book considers her a psychopath, a condition he describes definitively in the Prologue. I don't agree: she lives by a set of ethics that could save the planet if adopted by all mankind. In her inevitable doom, she could be compared to Jesus, who today would probably be diagnosed schizophrenic.

A philosophical novel inside a fascinating adventure story.
Review posted by Dashiell on Amazon.com

JOHN BRINCKMAN

AYESHA, MY QUEENDOM COME
A Novel

CANADA • IRELAND • TRAFFORD PUBLISHING • UK • USA • SPAIN

1/06

© Copyright 2004 John Brinckman.
All rights reserved. No part of this publication may be reproduced, stored in a retrieval system, or transmitted, in any form or by any means, electronic, mechanical, photocopying, recording, or otherwise, without the written prior permission of the author.

Note for Librarians: a cataloguing record for this book that includes Dewey Decimal Classification and US Library of Congress numbers is available from the Library and Archives of Canada. The complete cataloguing record can be obtained from their online database at:
www.collectionscanada.ca/amicus/index-e.html
ISBN 1-4120- 3776-X
Printed in Victoria, BC, Canada

Offices in Canada, USA, Ireland, UK and Spain
This book was published *on-demand* in cooperation with Trafford Publishing. On-demand publishing is a unique process and service of making a book available for retail sale to the public taking advantage of on-demand manufacturing and Internet marketing. On-demand publishing includes promotions, retail sales, manufacturing, order fulfilment, accounting and collecting royalties on behalf of the author.
Book sales for North America and international:
Trafford Publishing, 6E–2333 Government St.,
Victoria, BC V8T 4P4 CANADA
phone 250 383 6864 (toll-free 1 888 232 4444)
fax 250 383 6804; email to orders@trafford.com
Book sales in Europe:
Trafford Publishing (UK) Ltd., Enterprise House, Wistaston Road Business Centre, Wistaston Road, Crewe, Cheshire CW2 7RP UNITED KINGDOM
phone 01270 251 396 (local rate 0845 230 9601)
facsimile 01270 254 983; orders.uk@trafford.com
Order online at:
www.trafford.com/robots/04-1564.html

20 19 18 17 16 15 14 13

To my brother Roddy

CONTENTS

Prologue _____ 1

Portrait of Ayesha _____ 12

I. Hattie _____ 13

II. Alice _____ 67

Map _____ 68

III. Aleysha: Hubris _____ 119

IV. Aleysha: Nemesis _____ 215

V. Susan _____ 269

Epilogue _____ 311

Acknowledgements _____ 313

Note on Pronunciation: The name Ayesha has three syllables, the first and third are accented, the middle barely pronounced thus: eye – e – sha

The brain within its groove
Runs evenly and true;
But let a splinter swerve,
'T were easier for you
To put the water back
When floods have slit the hills,
And scooped a turnpike for themselves,
And blotted out the mills!

Emily Dickinson

Ideas of justice are as timeless as fashion in hats.

John Gray, Straw Dogs

As individuals we go our separate ways while the ineluctable forces of Gaia marshal against us.

James Lovelock, *The Revenge of Gaia*

PROLOGUE

Theodore McLeod, a deputy inspector of the Drug Law Enforcement Branch, Royal Canadian Mounted Police, Station A, Ottawa had taken voluntary retirement with a big severance bonus at the age of twenty-nine. Four months later, pondering his future, he walked south along a beach on the west coast of the island of St. Anthony, or St. Antoine, as some still call it, in the West Indies. He was on the last day of a winter holiday. He wore an unbuttoned white dress shirt and a red bathing suit of the boxer-shorts variety, a white hotel towel was tossed lightly over the shoulders of his tanned athletic body, and he dripped with gold jewelry.

A brief affair with a woman, one Hattie Brading, had led to his early retirement. That it had resulted in a spectacular drug bust was not considered in his favor. There were powerful people who thought that he had informed Hattie and her father that they were under surveillance, allowing Hattie to escape. In fact he had had no idea that her father was in drugs and what little he had told her was completely wrong. His colleagues in the DLEB who thought that all undercover agents were corrupt suspected him of a low form of treachery: trading secrets for sexual favors. Then the woman had been murdered, her decapitated body found in a lake and identified by her father. The only suspect had fled with a great deal of stolen money.

"An officer of the RCMP," Superintendent Wood had told him, "is not expected to play the role of Mata Hari and trade secrets in bed, no matter how successful the outcome. It's undignified. A constable might be forgiven, a junior corporal, perhaps, but a deputy inspector! In my view, you were promoted too young and were indiscreet. I don't for one second, myself, suspect you of any kind of betrayal. It is thought best, however, that you resign from the force. Because I believe you innocent of any wrongdoing, I will see to it personally that you get a large severance bonus and letters of recommendation."

"It was not in bed," said Theodore, although he was not sure. That he and the woman had gone to bed together, he did not consider important. Nor did he consider it germane that he had been in love with the woman because he considered that sort of infatuation akin to lust. But it must have been love, or why did he feel such terrible grief when he heard the news of her death? It was an emotion independent of the remorse that he felt for being indirectly responsible. She had been murdered and her killer, a Korean named Song, had gone scot-free. Theodore had accepted early retirement, not as punishment for being involved in a scandal, but as punishment for not knowing how to go about getting the man.

He had a half-baked notion that a man who was wanted for murder and had just stolen $20,000,000 from the Hells Angels – the exact amount was unknown – might head for an obscure West Indian island. Because St. Anthony had a rugged coastline and few beaches, there were not many tourists, and Theodore had come here with a picture of Song and was making inquiries. Of course, it was just an excuse for an unemployed man to take a holiday; he knew that. No Koreans had settled on the island, he was told. It was suggested by one sarcastic black police officer that he try the island of Chechu Do off the southern coast of Korea, a Korean wouldn't stand out there.

Theodore should never have been a deputy inspector in the first place. A lot of his success was due to luck. His first week on the job as a constable in Medicine Hat, Alberta, a report had come into the station that an armed bank robbery was in progress downtown. Without waiting for his partner, who was in the can, Theodore had run out, leapt into the RCMP police car, and with red light flashing and siren screaming, raced downtown. He found the getaway car stopped at a red light, three of the bandits yelling at the driver to get going.

"But it's a red light! It's a red light!" the driver shouted back at them and then at Theodore as he pulled his squad car in front, cutting them off. They were still shouting at each other as they politely got out of the car so that Theodore could put the handcuffs on. It turned out that they were just kids who had been drinking. They had one broken gun between them and no ammunition. Nonetheless, *The Medicine Hat News* had acclaimed him a hero, with the headline "Lone Mountie Captures Armed Gang."

A few other lucky breaks and he drew the attention of the Drug Law Enforcement Bureau, who were looking for undercover agents. Without having laid eyes on him, they asked for Theodore and got a tall, broad shouldered, blonde young man with honest, candid blue eyes, who might have been sent by central casting to play Sergeant King in one of those old Mountie movies. The supervisor took one look at him and muttered that he had cop written all over him.

"Not necessarily," said Theodore. During a brief career in minor pro hockey in the States, he had developed envy for major leaguers with their gold jewelry and alligator boots. He saw his chance and talked the DLEB into it.

Outfitted with lots of gold jewelry, cowboy hat, Texas pants, and alligator boots, he developed a swagger, a slouch, and definite attitude. He went high profile and worked expensive bars in western Canadian cities. He let it be known that he was looking for dope, and when offered it, he would say, nah, my people are looking for something bigger than that, five hundred thou minimum. He was something of an actor and enjoyed the role. It worked; there was something about him that crooks trusted. He contributed to the entrapment of three major drug dealers. Concerned that his cover had been overworked, the DLEB moved him to a desk job in Ottawa. He had to get his hair cut and leave the gold jewelry at home.

The DLEB had never asked for the jewelry back, due to some administrative oversight. He never wore it at home, but what the hell, he was on holiday, why not? So here he was at six o'clock, walking along a tropical beach, thinking of a drink and dripping with gold. On his left was a large hotel of Palladian grandeur, built of glimmering new white coral, where he could not afford to stay, but in which he liked to drink. Above him on a terrace, he could see the tops of green beach umbrellas, and waving palms. Beneath them, he thought, will be Michael, and rum punch, and the swimming pool. He carried a credit card in his bathing suit pocket.

Just before turning up the inviting staircase, he noticed a woman some sixty feet away wearing large opaque dark glasses, a black bikini under a beach robe and a large straw hat shading her long red hair walking north towards him, close to the sea. It was her striking figure that got his attention; it was familiar. The breasts were a bit fuller, and a shade lower; the waist perhaps thicker, the legs maybe shorter. It could not be Hattie. He could not make out the woman's face, shaded under the hat. He looked at her for a moment but she gave no sign of recognition.

Hattie! I see her everywhere, he reflected ruefully. But if I am looking at the breasts, it must have been lust, not love. I shall try to cure my longing with that thought. But what is the difference between love and lust? Both cause an ache in the heart. There is an Arab saying that women want the body and the soul of a man, whereas men merely want the body. He knew now that lust could extend to the soul of another. Hattie had the soul of an angel and if there was a heaven, her soul would be there now, with other winged cherubims and seraphims, forever beyond his reach, considering his own likelihood of going to the other place.

He turned and went up the steps. Putting the woman out of his mind, Theodore sauntered across the empty dance floor and sat down. Immediately, a bright young black man in a well-cut white jacket stood before him with a big smile. Theodore looked at him for a moment.

"You always look so clean, Michael," he said. "Why is everything down here so clean?"

"We're getting some pollution now, Theodore," said Michael with pride. "Lots of cars on the road nowadays in St. Anthony, but the east wind blows the stuff away. That wind comes straight from Africa. Three thousand miles. On the other side of the island tiny particles of sand drop out of the sky. Carried here from the Sahara desert. The lord giveth and the lord taketh away." He laughed.

"But why on the other side and not on this coast?"

"I don't know, Theodore. The other side of the island has powerful forces, gravitational and otherwise. But it's probably got something to do with the mountains."

Theodore ordered a planter's punch and, realizing that he had not seen a newspaper in four days, set out to see if he could find one in the hotel lobby. He had almost arrived back at his table, glancing through *The Globe and Mail* – not a great deal of interest in it, the

Sens were winning, well, they always won in February – before he noticed a stranger sitting at it. Just then Michael came back with his drink.

"Thank you, Michael."

"I beg your pardon," said the stranger, a large bearded man, starting to get up. "I didn't know the table was taken."

"No, no, stay where you are. There's room for us both."

"In that case, let me introduce myself, my name is Bernard Levinson. I'm from Chicago."

Neither offered to shake hands. Theodore examined his new companion briefly. A florid tropical shirt covered an enormous chest and tufts of gray hair showed where the top three buttons were undone. Not for display purposes, thought Theodore, but simply to make room. Direct curious black eyes looked out from black-framed spectacles and a wide mouth over a heavy jaw curved in a friendly smile. Probably an American poet, he thought whimsically. Looks like Ginsberg.

"I'm Theodore. Theodore McLeod."

"People call you Ted, then? Or Theo?"

"Never."

Bernard looked at him questioningly.

"See, it's a family name. My dad insisted. There was a teacher in grade one called me Ted and Dad went to the school, took the teacher aside, and told her my name was Theodore. I told Dad that some of the kids then started to call me Theo. He said any kid calls you Theo, you beat him up. So I did."

Bernard laughed a great booming laugh. "Theodore it is. You're a Canadian?" Theodore nodded, impressed. "I am a student of accents. You can't be a hockey player, wrong season, you'd be playing. Let me guess, you're a mining promoter."

"Huh? Oh, the jewelry." He laughed. "The gold belongs to the horsemen, really. It's not mine. Should give it back to them sometime. I'm a retired police officer," said Theodore with an engaging grin. "Drug law enforcement."

He was being indiscreet but he didn't care. The blue sky above, the palms waving overhead, and the first swallow of good Martinique rum warmed his blood, banishing discretion. He had been discreet long enough; fuck 'em.

"But who are the horsemen?" asked the American. "Oh, wait a second, the Royal Canadian Mounted Police. The Mounties. You were a Mountie." He paused. "You're a bit young to retire."

"Had to. Scandal." Theodore told him the story. "Mounties have to be above suspicion. Like Caesar's wife. That's what they told me. Anyway, I got a big severance. Thinking of setting myself up as a private detective back in Winnipeg. Maybe fix traffic tickets. I dunno. What do you do?"

"My work is not that remote from yours. I'm a forensic psychiatrist."

"You go to court?"

"Sometimes."

Theodore thought this over for a moment. "Tell me something. In the States you prove pre-meditation to convict on murder in the first degree. In Canada we prove intent. Is there a difference?"

"I can't see that there's a difference. Scientists now think we have three brains, one on top of the other. The neo-mammalian brain sits above the mammalian brain and beneath that is what we call the reptilian brain. Each, believe it or not, has its own subjectivity. Our society, I suppose, has been more or less aware of this all along. Where intent or premeditation is involved, the higher neo-mammalian brain's subjectivity has been involved. One is fully guilty. Sometimes, although guilt is proven, we are lenient with crimes of passion, where the middle brain has taken over, and with crimes of impulse, where the subjectivity of the reptilian brain has temporarily taken control. The accused's peers, the jury, make these judgments. Psychiatrists do not come into it."

"Where you come in, is to get the fully guilty off because you say they are crazy. I've seen you guys in the movies, and once in a courtroom, get a psycho off scot-free. Sorry, did not mean to be rude."

"Not at all, You've given me an opportunity to explain a misunderstanding of the law that the movies have spread. Movies muddy the distinction between insanity and mental illness. Mental illness and mental disorder are terms we doctors use; insanity is a cultural and legal concept. What we are sometimes able to do is to convince a judge or jury that the accused is legally insane: one, because of a mental disorder, the defendant did not understand that what he or she was doing was illegal; two, because of a mental disorder, the defendant did not know what he or she was doing; or three, because of a mental disorder, the defendant was compelled to commit the crime by an irresistible force."

"And psychopaths suffer from a mental disorder and get off?"

"No, but you have put your finger on one of the most intriguing questions in psychology, and a particular interest of mine. The term, psychopathy, now psychopathology, was invented by a German psychiatrist in the nineteenth century to describe a condition where an offender commits shockingly anti-social acts, without exhibiting evidence of delusions, psychotic behavior, or even emotional instability."

"The Anthony Perkins character in *Psycho* exhibited plenty of all three."

"Ah, but Norman Bates, the *Psycho* character, was not a psychopath. That film did a lot to confuse the meaning of the term. He suffered from delusions and various disorders – he was insane by any definition and was sent, quite properly, to a hospital for the insane."

" I don't get it. So the genuine psychopath is not insane?"

"Nowadays many doctors and sociologists call it a social disorder."

"Okay, here's another question. What's the difference between a sociopath and a psychopath?"

"In my opinion, none. The choice term depends on who is doing the treatment. I use the term psychopath because I am a psychiatrist. I don't quibble over the term. My interest is in how they got that way and if it can be undone by treatment. Some may be born that way. There is evidence that there might be a genetic cause for it. There's a German neuroscientist, a Dr. Birbaumer who thinks it may be just that certain parts of their brains, parts involved in feeling emotions involving sympathy for others, receive less blood from the arteries. So there might be innocence to their cold bloodedness.

"But in most cases they choose a strategy that is totally selfish early in life because of something that happened to them. Genes probably have something to do with it. They are often abused as children, their parents not accessing a conscience either. But research has shown that a large number had not been injured in childhood but began with fantasies. These I find particularly intriguing – the ones who have not been abused – but act out their fantasies."

"I suppose schools and neighbors nowadays learn about the abused kids and do something about it."

"That's true. Steps can be taken to take them out of an abusive environment if we are lucky enough to find out about it. But that is not always the case."

"When it is not – when you don't learn about the abuse or they have not been abused, the fantasy kids – can you spot them early?"

"That's a good question. They are very good at secrecy and misdirection, turning on the charm, saying they're sorry when they are not. Girls are better at this than boys. Women psychopaths are harder to spot. Teachers, parents, doctors try to educate them, boys or girls, to prove to them that selfishness is a bad strategy, that it doesn't work. Trouble is, for some it does work."

"Yeah, they get rich, I know. Without breaking the law in many cases. What you say about women is interesting." Orphaned as a child, he reflected for a moment on the goodness of the two aunts who had brought him up. "I have never run into an evil woman."

This remark caused Bernard to smile. His new friend idealized women. He reflected for a moment on the story Theodore had told him. The lady in the lake, he mused, might not have been Hattie, suppose it had all been a set-up by one of his favorite subjects, the omega-type female over-controlled psychopath. He had never met one and had only read about them. I am a bit like a butterfly collector, he ruminated, I do not have one in my files, so I am a bit obsessed by them. He then dismissed the thought: police would have run DNA tests of course.

He noticed Theodore looking at him as if expecting an answer. "Oh, women can be evil alright, I'm afraid. And you have put your finger on the essence of the matter – the existence of evil. There is an American writer, Janet Malcolm, who says that the concept of the psychopath is an admission of failure to solve the mystery of evil."

Theodore thoughtfully repeated the phrase. "The mystery of evil."

"How about another planter's punch? You seem to have finished yours, let me get you another. Michael, would you get us two more?"

Michael had been standing a little away from the table, hand on chin, listening to their discussion. "But Theodore, the mystery of evil is that what you calls evil, maybe is not evil to some, but good? Who knows for sure what is the difference?"

Theodore didn't answer. Michael gave him a long look and left for the drinks. Theodore said, "I don't know how to answer that. In wartime all sorts of atrocities are committed by people who consider themselves virtuous."

"Like us Americans?"

"I didn't say that."

"I think that what Michael is getting at is a philosophical problem. Nowadays most people in our culture tend to accept that others may have very different values."

Bernard asked him, "So, Michael, what you mean is what is good to some people might be evil to others? One man's meat is another man's poison, something like that?"

The waiter looked directly at Theodore. "What I mean is that in the Voudon religion, good cannot exist without evil and evil cannot exist without good. You must not confuse them but you cannot always tell them apart."

"Michael," asked Bernard, "is it true that Voudon is still practiced in the mountains?"

"It is the religion there, but it is still practiced here in Le Havre by a few. You can visit an *hounfour* and witness it. There's a charge and you have to be introduced. I know people there. For two gentlemen interested in the existence of evil and good, I would be glad to arrange it."

"When? I'm leaving tomorrow," asked Theodore.

"There's one tonight."

The two men looked at each other.

"Why not?" asked Bernard and Theodore nodded.

Ayesha

'Like the vampire dust at the end of Christopher Lee movies, blowing away only to reassemble itself at the outset of the next film, She could come back. And back. And back'

Margaret Atwood

From the Introduction to the Modern Library edition of She by H. Rider Haggard. Copyright O .W. Toad Ltd. Used by permission of the author

HATTIE

1

Hattie Brading grew up in Vanier, formerly Eastview, an old district of Ottawa, now in the process of being gentrified, but then almost a ghetto, surrounded by opulent suburbs. Many of the old brick and wood frame houses of Vanier were divided into flats, and the rents were low. She had been born in Boston where her mother had fled to get away from her father, but they were later reconciled. Her father offered generous child support if the child took his name. Henry "The Bear" Brading had been a member of the Bandits, an Ottawa motorcycle club, before he disappeared, leaving her mother to raise Hattie on her own. Louise LeBlanc was out a lot while Hattie was growing up, drinking and carrying on. She worked in bars and collected welfare. She was good looking and addicted to alcohol and drugs.

Hattie spent a lot of time at her grandmother's apartment. Her grandfather was dead. There were a number of photographs of him in the house. In none of them did he smile. Her mother and grandmother did not get along. When she was with her mother her grandmother would turn up from time to time, complain vociferously in French about the condition of the apartment and her mother's way of life. She would then physically seize the child and take her home. Her grandmother looked after her in a way that was cloying, fussy, and irritating, but she did look after her. Hattie was fed, her laundry was done, and she learned to speak French. She slept in her grandmother's double bed. Her grandmother was old, her clothes were musty, and she had bad breath. Hattie did not like her.

The only thing she liked about her grandmother's flat when she was a bit older were the videos. The television was an old black and white set with poor reception and they never watched it. But with the video machine, the picture was almost perfect. Her grandmother had a collection of old black and white movies that included almost every film Katherine Hepburn had ever made. Hattie and her grandmother would sometimes watch these all day when she was not at school.

From time to time her mother would turn up sober and affectionate. She moved frequently complaining about the landlords and whenever she got a new flat, always in Vanier, she would try to turn over a new leaf, and come and get Hattie back. Soon she would start drinking again, there would be a new boyfriend and quarrelling would commence. The boyfriends were usually kind to Hattie at first, but she didn't respond and they tended to ignore her. She was occasionally slapped when her mother wasn't home. She learned to stay out of the way and be silent. Her mother never beat her; punishment was to be sent to her room for long periods without food.

She went to the local public school, entering junior kindergarten at the age of four. There she made a close friend, a pretty little girl named Phyllis. Sometimes, when living with her mother, she was picked up after school by Phyllis's mother, who had been to high school with Louise. They lived in a small house with a yard and a dog and Hattie became attached to the family. Phyllis had several brothers and sisters. It was warm and friendly there; everyone was good to her. In the winter they all went skating on the Rideau Canal.

On Sundays, when Louise was hung-over, Hattie would go over early to Phyllis's house and go to an Anglican church with the family. Hattie had a good voice and enjoyed the hymns but the rest of the service she found boring. Her favorite hymn was William Blake's Jerusalem and she learned the words by heart.

When Hattie was eight Phyllis found a new friend, a girl named Margot, who lived up the hill, just across Lindenlea, the street that firmly divided the Town of Vanier from its opulent neighbor, the Village of Rockcliffe. The two girls had met at summer camp. Phyllis dropped Hattie like a hot potato. The two new friends passed Hattie in the street and pretended not to see her. Hattie was so hurt that she withdrew from the world and became for a time almost autistic. Margot had pretty new clothes; Hattie's mostly came from garage sales and were chosen, usually, just because they fit. She tried to convince herself that it had something to do with her clothes, but if it were just that, then would Phyllis have ever loved her in the first place?

When it first happened she went on a long walk by herself in Beechwood cemetery. It was September and the leaves were turning and beginning to fall. She sat on a bench and watched them swirl on the grass chased by a light breeze. She stared at the solemn beech trees and saw faces in the bark formations on the trunks. The wind rustled the dry leaves and the faces seemed to whisper to her, *people are no good... shee ... ahshee...* She could not quite make out the words. *A...shee, look around you, the only good people are the dead ones...shee....* The trees and the wind seemed to call her by name, but it was not her own name, it was another name, ashee, something like that. Two squirrels approached and sat looking at her kindly. Or so she thought. She dug a half-empty package of peanuts out of a pocket and fed them. Then the tears came, at first gently and then copiously. These are my friends, she thought, the animals and the trees. She dried her tears with a handkerchief and left the park.

She began to spend her time in the central Ottawa library. She read science fiction and old novels of the more fantastic sort, which she picked at random from the shelves. No one guided her reading; she tended to pick out older books for the illustrations. When she was nine, she read H. Rider Haggard's nineteenth-century novel, *She*. The personality of Ayesha, the immortal white queen, deeply impressed her. One passage gave her a strategy for life. Ayesha had decided that a rival must die; Holly, the man who through whose eyes we see her (it is written in the first person), objects on moral grounds. What then is her sin, he asks, and the queen replies, "Truly, O Holly, thou art foolish. Where is her sin? Her sin is that she stands between me and my desire." That made sense to the young girl and she adopted it as a moral maxim. She began to pray to Ayesha. That is the name the wind and the trees had called to her the year before in Beechwood cemetery, she thought.

She made changes to the Lord's Prayer to fit her new beliefs: *Ayesha, who art in Heaven, hallowed be thy name, my queendom come, my will be done on earth as it is in heaven, give me this day what I want, lead me not into trouble I cannot get out of, deliver me from people who would make me good, I will not forgive those who trespass against me, as you do not forgive those who trespass against you, for ours is the queendom, the power and the glory. Amen*

She said this prayer at night before going to sleep and it was a comfort to her. She repeated the phrase "my queendom come" to herself when things did not appear to be going her way. One day, the little girl thought, my queendom will come. She identified with Ayesha and became like the queen, a vegetarian.

Her grandmother died when she was nine. She sat and watched. *Ayesha, my queendom come.* Her grandmother seemed to be having some kind of fit, groaning and thrashing about in bed as they watched Katherine Hepburn in *The Philadelphia Story* with Cary Grant and Jimmy Stewart. The old lady could not get out of bed and cried out to Hattie to call 911. Hattie did not move. She just sat there in her wooden chair by the bed. When all was quiet, her grandmother dead, and the movie over, she called 911.

From then on she lived permanently with her mother, who made a real effort to get her life together for Hattie's sake. They had a new apartment, this time without a live-in boyfriend. Her father surfaced for a while; he never said why he had left nor why he came back. He was not good at showing Hattie affection and she liked him for that. He brought her presents that amused her: they were suitable for a girl much younger than she was. Hattie thought that he only wanted to get back with Louise, but she was wrong; it was just that he didn't know how to go about making friends with her. Then he disappeared again.

When Hattie was twelve, Louise became involved with a new boyfriend, Tom, who did not live with them but hung out at their place. He would often arrive with a case of beer – he had a key – when Louise wasn't home. On mornings when he slept over, he would get up around ten, drink what beer there was in the fridge and then go out and get some more. He was quite kind to Hattie, but he would stare at her a lot, and touch her unnecessarily. Sometimes when they were watching TV together, he would put his hand on her head or her knee and caress her. This she did not like, and if he continued she would head for the library. She learned to be nimble and stay out of his reach.

She was a strikingly attractive and precocious girl at twelve. She had long black hair and emerald green eyes. Even at that age men stared at her long legs in the street and searched her chest with their eyes for signs of development. She groomed herself with care; what clothes she had were always clean and she ironed them herself. But she was not interested in dresses; she dressed like a boy.

Tom bought her a dress but she refused to wear it. One December afternoon, Tom, quite drunk, cornered her in the kitchen, turned her around and began to forcefully put his hands were they were not wanted. *Ayesha, my queendom come.* She picked up a kitchen knife that was in a drawer in front of her and plunged it over her shoulder through his ribs and into his heart. He collapsed gasping on the floor, the knife in his chest. She stared at him for a moment and then checked his pulse. She could not find one. She held a mirror to his mouth as she had seen done in the movies. Satisfied that he was dead, she wiped her fingerprints off the handle and went into the other room to watch one of the Katherine Hepburn videos that she and her mother had inherited.

When her mother finished work at four that afternoon, she didn't come straight home, but had some drinks with a friend in another bar. When she found Tom she was rather drunk. She attempted to remove the knife, which resulted in a sudden torrent of blood. She collapsed in hysterics. Hattie called 911.

The police concluded that Louise had stabbed Tom and Hattie did not dispute the conclusion. The poor woman was covered with blood, and it was later established that her prints were on the handle. No one ever found out that Hattie had been home all the time. Louise thought Hattie had just walked in the door coming home from the library when she was calling the police.

It never occurred to anyone that Hattie had done it. Louise thought that Henry had killed Tom, but the police established that he was out of the country. Even her lawyer thought that Louise was guilty and fought long and hard for her, as lawyers do for guilty people, innocent people being notoriously hard to defend. While arguing her innocence, he also made sure that it came out at the trial that Tom beat Louise regularly, which was what Hattie had told the police and the Children's Aid. It was not true, but she was pleased with her mother for believing in her innocence and thought that it was the least she could do. The court was sympathetic to Louise and she was sentenced to the minimum sentence for her crime.

Children's Aid put Hattie in a foster home. She hated it. The home had a few pets for the children: a dog, a cat, a canary, and an aquarium. Hattie didn't like any of the people there, kids or adults. She liked the pets and formed the opinion, which she held all her life, that animals were honest and good and people were not.

Henry Brading moved back to Ottawa four months after Tom's death, and he applied for custody. He and Louise never married but she had put his name on the birth certificate. Hattie told the Children's Aid that her father was a good man and that she loved him very much. In fact she didn't know him at all; except for one brief period, he had been away all her life. She told the court how much she had loved the presents he would bring her, and at the hearing she broke from her place and threw herself sobbing on her father. It was the first time that anyone had seen her cry. She had never faked tears before and was so pleased with her performance that suddenly, with her arms around Henry Brading's neck, she broke into a broad and winsome smile. The court decided in Henry's favor.

So Henry, who worked in a motorcycle body shop specializing in customizing Harley-Davidsons, gained custody of his daughter without it being revealed that he had never severed his connections with the Bandits. He was quite active in certain of the club's criminal activities but kept a low profile, never wearing club colors in public. He was on his way to becoming the richest member of the club. The Bandits had a hierarchy of seniority, president, vice-president, and officers of different ranks such as ride captains. But Henry never accepted any office.

The police were convinced that he was a tough customer who had gone straight. When consulted by Children's Aid, the Ottawa police had given him a clean bill of health. The reason for his two long disappearances was that he had disposed of important enemies of the Bandits, but he had never been suspected of a crime by the police.

While away he had made interesting and important connections in Florida and Texas. He returned to Ottawa with a mission:

to use the Bandits to become the number one drug dealer in the Ottawa valley. He was aware that having custody of a child was good for his image in the community, so his motives for seeking custody were not simply paternal. He was impressed with her performance at the hearing, indeed, he was the only one present who was not taken in. He began to admire her, not for her beauty, nor her charm, but for her cunning.

Henry Brading bought a modest house in Manor Park, which lies below the Rockcliffe escarpment, not far from the headquarters of the Royal Canadian Mounted Police. They moved into the house together the day she came to live with him. Henry bought two highly trained giant schnauzers, named Rommel and Goering, who moved in with them. These she both loved and respected; taking care of them was one of her chores. The dogs obeyed her commands and she could take them for walks without using a leash.

"I don't expect you to give me any trouble," Henry told her the first night. He paused and looked at her. They were sitting in the dining room enjoying their first meal together over the brand new maple dining room table. He had made a fettuccini Alfredo dinner – she had made it clear that she would not eat meat. They didn't speak again until dessert; neither had much use for small talk.

"I know who killed Tom," he said over ice cream, looking her straight in the eye. "It's okay. He was a shit. And Louise, well, maybe prison will dry her out."

Hattie looked back at him for a long moment. Without batting an eye, as if she had not heard the last statements, she replied, "I won't be any trouble to you, Bear." Bear is what Louise had called him and it came to her naturally. She would not have been comfortable with Dad or Daddy and neither would he. They understood one another. Hattie didn't love her father; she hardly knew him. She had never loved anyone except Phyllis and certain animals. Her feelings for her mother were ambivalent. But she respected Bear; she had not had any respect for her mother or grandmother.

She watched re-runs of *Father Knows Best* and modeled herself after the mother, usually wearing an apron when her father was home. She kept house, but Henry did the cooking. He would make vegetable casseroles and steaks or chops for himself. They ate very well when he was home. When he was not, like Ayesha, she ate fruit and raw vegetables. She looked after the dishes and laundry, dusted, and vacuumed. She walked and fed the dogs.

They didn't have any unnecessary conversation. They watched TV together sometimes. Hattie preferred to read. He taught her to play chess. The fourth game she won, Henry giving her some opportunities. She was soon his equal and for a while they were even. She was aggressive with the Queen. She would bring it out early and was dangerous with it. Henry learned to concentrate on trapping the Queen. If he succeeded, she became dispirited and he would usually win. To get her over this, he made her learn by heart a famous game: Lewinsky versus Marshall. It ends with a brilliant move by Black (Marshall) who sacrifices the Queen. Four White pieces can capture the Black Queen, which has put the White King in check, but each leads to checkmate. White (Lewinsky) resigned and it was said that spectators rained gold pieces on to the board. This brilliant move got her over becoming depressed on losing the Queen.

She began to win almost every time. Henry bought chess books for them to study and they solved chess problems together. He did not like losing, but it was more than that: it was essential for his future plans that she learn to cooperate with him; to think of him as a partner rather than an opponent.

She read the sequels to *She* and enjoyed them. She recognized that the books were fiction, but this did not diminish her regard for Ayesha. She felt that Rider Haggard was akin to an Old Testament prophet who had had an epiphany. In this, although she did not know it, she was not far apart from Carl Jung, Sigmund Freud, and in our own day, Margaret Atwood. She continued to say her adaptation of the Lord's Prayer and get strength from it. Ayesha remained a religion for her, although she respected what Ayesha herself had said in the book when Holly tried to convert her to Christianity: "The religions come and the religions pass, and civilizations come and pass, and naught endures but the world and human nature."

Henry's girlfriends would sometimes come for the night, but they were always gone by breakfast; if he stayed over with a girl friend he was always home for breakfast. This was probably a rule that he had adopted long before Hattie came on the scene, but it helped her feel secure. He showed her no visible affection, but she felt that she was the number one female in his life. He never hugged her or kissed her, but they were, in their peculiar way, a close little family.

She had turned thirteen in May and her father decided to put her in a private girls' day school, Elmwood, in neighboring Rockcliffe. He thought that she might be better protected there from the notoriety following her mother's trial than in a high school. Mrs. Austin, the school principal, was sympathetic. Henry Brading wore a suit and tie to the interview, Hattie a dark dress. She pretended that she was Katherine Hepburn and made a good impression. The interview took place in August a few weeks before the school term was to begin.

The principal spoke to her class on the first day and told them that they must not prejudge her because of what had happened, nor because she had been a ward of the Children's Aid Society for seven months. The other girls were impressed by the lurid details of her past. Hattie played a genteel Katherine Hepburn during her entire stay at Elmwood except while playing sports, which she did with ferocity. Because she was always demure, even standoffish, and did not seem to be aware of her striking good looks, they accepted her. But she did not make friends and discouraged anyone who appeared to want to be her friend. She had been burned once and that was enough.

Her father ordered her to work hard and she did. She had always been good at school, but now for the first time she worked. She had a flair for mathematics and became interested in computers, which were just being introduced to the school. She learned to restrain her superior natural strength at sports. Uncomfortable with both her notoriety and her good looks, she aimed at lowering her profile. She was a good skater; when she was friends with Phyllis she had spent hours on the Rideau canal skating with her family. The one sport at which she permitted herself to excel was hockey, perhaps because she played goal and wore a mask.

Henry Brading usually drove her to school and picked her up. But often she was driven by Charley, a blond long-haired bearded biker Henry had known since childhood, in a black pick-up truck, which often carried a cut-down Harley in the back. This added to her reputation. The principal didn't like it but said nothing. Charley was chatty, he amused her with jokes, and smoked cigarettes. He always offered her one and she sometimes accepted. But she was careful to put it out as the truck turned up the road to the Village of Rockcliffe Park. She liked Charley; he didn't flirt with her and treated her like a boy.

She told Charley that she played goal on the Elmwood hockey team. So he built a small rink in Henry's backyard and spent hours taking shots on her and teaching her the importance of positioning. He taught her to be a butterfly goalie: one moment her legs were spread in the splits, and then as quick as the snap of a butterfly's wings, she was back standing up, her legs together.

"I'm teaching her to keep her legs together," Charley joked to Henry one day, but Henry, who kept Charley around largely for entertainment, was not amused. He saw that his daughter's figure was attracting men's eyes. On her fourteenth birthday, he presented her with a knife that came with a sheath that could be attached either to her belt or to her calf just above the ankle. He taught her to use it.

"Next time you might not be standing close to a kitchen drawer," he remarked.

Margot, who had stolen Phyllis away from her, went to Elmwood and was in her class. A big, talkative girl, Margot tried to influence the other girls against her, but did not have much success. Margot and Hattie never spoke. Hattie pretended that she had never seen her before, but Margot was not fooled. Once or twice she caught Hattie's green eyes looking at her and sensed the malice behind them.

The first time that Henry had to go out of town they discussed getting a babysitter. Henry preferred not to get one; he had an office in the basement and although he kept it well locked up, he did not want a stranger in the house. He did not know any women he trusted. Hattie didn't want a babysitter either, and convinced her father that she, Rommel, and Goering, could manage on their own.

So if he were away overnight, Charley, who lived nearby, would drive over on his bike to check on her. He would help himself to one of Henry's Heinekens and watch TV for a bit. He never stayed more than half an hour.

The next fall she began her second year at Elmwood and played on the school's minor bantam hockey team. She was by far the better of the team's two goalies. The school also had an intra-mural league; they played on the Ashbury College artificial ice surface. One afternoon in February, in a game in which Margot was a forward on the opposing team, Hattie made a series of good saves on her. On the next shift Margot crashed the net, knocking Hattie down. The net came loose, Margot's helmet came off, and Hattie slashed her across the face with her stick, knocking out her front teeth, giving her a concussion, and breaking her nose. The coach took Margot to the hospital.

There was quite a fuss made over this incident. Margot's father telephoned Hattie's father and threatened him, not having any idea what sort of man he was. Henry paid him a visit and Margot's father joined his daughter in the hospital. No charges were laid. An incident of this sort, or anything remotely like it, had never happened in the history of Elmwood School.

Henry regretted what he had done. That sort of reaction was the kind of thing he was trying to put behind him. Hattie refused to go back to Elmwood, recognizing her father's predicament, and also that life might be awkward for her there in the future. So the principal was spared the decision of whether to suspend or expel her.

Hattie didn't go back to school at all that year. She took to dressing gothic but did not hang out with other dropouts; she spent her time at the library. She did not embrace body jewelry or tattoos. One day, she told herself, I will not be me but someone else and I will not want any telltale identification.

Hattie turned fifteen in May and they moved to a larger house in Rothwell Heights with a view of the Ottawa River. Henry gave her an aluminum canoe for her birthday. That spring and the following summer, Hattie spent most of her time on the river. She loved it. *'The Ottawa is a dark stream, the Ottawa is deep, great hills along the Ottawa, are wrapped in endless sleep,'* she would chant to herself as she paddled.

Like most great rivers, and it is a great river – the Ottawa pours a greater volume of water into the St. Lawrence River every year than all the rivers of western Europe combined pour into the Atlantic – wide and slow in places and narrow and rapid in others. The source of the Ottawa in western Quebec has never been found; people have perished trying to find it. There is an endless maze of streams, ponds, swamps, and lakes, that change the direction of their flow from time to time, rendering the source as unknowable as the human heart.

The river narrows into rapids a mile west of the cliff on which the Parliament Buildings stand and tumbles furiously over a short wild waterfall known as the Chaudiere, after *chaudière,* the French word for copper boiler. Above these rapids the river is so wide and slow it forms a lake, Lake Deschenes. Here and in Brittania Bay people sail their boats. Below the Chaudiere the water widens again; it is muddy and there is a current. It is downstream of the Ottawa sewage plant and not much used for boating. Then it is joined by the Gatineau, a mighty river in its own right, near where Hattie paddled her canoe, about five miles downstream from the Parliament buildings.

There was a little cove with unpainted rickety boathouses, on whose wharves men would sit and drink beer. No one really fished anymore: there were only pike and carp to be caught by trolling and they had an unpleasant flavor. Henry rented one of these boathouses for a fast outboard he used from time to time for trips to the Gatineau, Lachute, and other places on the north or Quebec side of the river. This was where Hattie kept her canoe.

The river was nearly a mile wide at the boathouse and on hot summer days she would bicycle down there, take her canoe out to the middle of the river, strip, and sunbathe out of sight, lying down on the bottom of the canoe. After about half an hour or so she would rouse herself, get back in her jeans and top, and paddle hard against the current to get back. Not many people swam here, but Hattie kept a bathing suit in the boathouse, and would dive in for a quick dip to cool off. She would shower when she got home.

Margot was still smarting from the incident in the rink. She had to have expensive and painful dental work. She and Phyllis conspired to do Hattie a mischief; they were not sure quite what. That summer they found out where she lived and would hide in the woods and spy on her. They made a game of following her, which they did with stealth; Hattie never noticed them. They knew about the canoe and, with the aid of binoculars, established that Hattie sunbathed naked. What a neat trick it would be, they decided, to sneak up on her in an outboard, when she was probably asleep, tip her out of the canoe, and then make off with it, leaving her to swim back to the boathouse naked and pull herself out of the river in front of all the beer-drinking old men.

For this caper they borrowed an outboard that they found pulled up on shore upriver. They did not know who owned it and did not bother to ask. They dawdled for about half a mile upstream, until they saw Hattie paddle out and strip in a channel between two long, thin, deserted islands. They approached and about a hundred yards away cut the engine. Hattie had good ears and she had heard the boat approaching. When the engine was cut, she was tempted to take a look, but she was suddenly convinced that someone was sneaking up on her. She lay absolutely still on the bottom of the canoe, listening. *My queendom come*, she prayed.

She was just able to hear someone slipping into the water, and heard Phyllis whisper, "Margot, don't forget to grab the painter."

What a couple of oafs, she thought, and waited. When the moment was ripe, she rolled out of the canoe, firmly planted her right hand on Margot's head, and held her underwater. Phyllis dove in to the rescue and seized Hattie by the throat. There was a terrible underwater catfight. Hattie was bitten, scratched, and half drowned. She drew the knife from its sheath on her calf and stabbed both the girls, one in the back, the other in the chest.

When she realized that they were dead, she hauled the bodies to the shore of the island feet first, one by one, letting the river carry away their blood. Both had been stabbed in the heart and she watched as the river stained incarnadine, first three, then six, then twelve, then twenty feet downstream. Hattie was not the first murderess to marvel at how much blood the human body held. As she stood there watching the gentle Ottawa take care of it for her, she thought of Lady Macbeth: "Who would have thought the old man to have so much blood in him?"

She swam back for the canoe, letting the outboard drift away on the current. She cut the two painters from each end of the canoe, found two suitable large rocks on the shore of the island and tied them to the girls' feet. Using the canoe with one hand to give her buoyancy, she swam out with the bodies, one by one, to the deep water between the islands, and sank them. She had read somewhere that bodies can fill with gas and become buoyant; they might break free, she thought, so she gave each a few stabs in the belly before letting go. She imagined their bones, stripped of flesh, gut, and cartilage by the sharp teeth of the pike and the soft mouths of the carp, collapsing over time on the river bottom.

She got dressed and paddled the canoe back to the boathouse. No one had seen what had happened. In fact no one knew that Phyllis and Margot had been on the river that day. Their bicycles were found in the woods near the place where they had borrowed the outboard, but no one made a connection. A serial rapist was active in the Ottawa valley that summer and the girls' disappearance was attributed to him.

In the fall Henry found a private business school that would accept a gifted fifteen year- old, so that she could help with his business. She was to learn accounting and computer programming and quickly became adept at both. She became friends with a couple of older computer nerds at the school; she liked them because they were interested in hacking into places they were not supposed to go. She learned a lot from them and worked with them on developing a virus. It was in the form of a file attached to an email. They used different email messages, usually something appealing to lust or greed, such as one that stated:

> WIN $1,000,000 IN HOSPITAL LOTTERY
> OPEN ATTACHMENT AND PRINT FREE TICKET.

The file contained a program that would instantly delete everything in the computer's memory or hard drive. The virus was traced to the school's computers and the boys were caught but they did not squeal on her. Hattie kept the virus file. She didn't use it for some years, but she followed anti-virus programs as they were developed, and amused herself by overcoming defenses against them.

She tried out for and made a AA Bantam Greater Ottawa Hockey League team called the Panthers that was having goalie problems. She was the only girl playing in the league at the bantam level. Charley was one of the coaches and arranged for the tryout. He had been a center for the Major Junior Ottawa 67s and had been considered an NHL prospect, although a bit small for professional hockey. He got into trouble not just for fighting, but for not stopping when told to by the referee. After an incident in which he used his stick on the ref, he had been banned from playing in organized hockey for life. He wore his old 67s jacket to the Panthers practice. He had sewn the badge and colors of the Bandits onto it. He was popular with the parents and the kids for his knowledge of the game and his good humor. No one held it against him that he was a member of the Bandits.

Hattie quickly established herself as the number one goalie on the team. She was taller than most of the boys on the team, as girls often are at that age. Her long legs and arms were a big asset in goal. She arrived dressed to play, Charley carrying her hockey bag that held only her helmet, gloves, skates and pads. She put these on and went to watch the goalies in whatever game was being played before theirs. She didn't use the changing room. The boys liked her the better for that; they could be free with their language and jokes.

A good goalie makes all the difference to a hockey team and it didn't bother the boys that she was a girl. In fact they revered her. If there was the slightest hint that a player on another team might be roughing her up, a fight broke out. They would take penalties for her and the coaches didn't object. She brought the team closer together. The boys called her The Princess and indeed there was a regal aspect to her aloofness, her beauty, and her play.

She enjoyed the role of princess, the boys' reverence, their regard for her beauty, and the admiration the crowd felt for her play. She treated Charley a little bit like her personal servant. This amused him; he didn't mind playing that role. She was Henry's daughter after all, and was he not a Bandit chieftain? If she sensed that she was going too far, she would mollify him with a dazzling

Katherine Hepburn smile. He was protective of her during her teen years, keeping an eye out for her at all times. She was kept well away from the Bandits. Few of them knew she even existed.

The Bandits were incorporated and members were shareholders. The profits from certain activities such as the sale of club colors and badges, and the wholesaling of marijuana, belonged to the corporation. But members also operated within the Bandits as independent businessmen. Henry Brading was by far the most prosperous of these.

During his sojourn in Florida, Henry had hung out with a motorcycle gang, establishing his credentials in the usual ways, and had become respected enough to be one of the elect few who were taught to manufacture amphetamines, or cook crank, as they called it. On his return he was the only member of the Bandits to have this skill, and the only members to whom he taught it worked for him.

He loved motorcycles and was good at customizing them, a skill he had brought to a high level during his travels. When he returned to Ottawa he began working at a little garage in the country south of Ottawa. He would drive his choppers around town and show them in places that bikers hung out. He would sell them and sometimes get a custom order. He was bringing in a lot of business, as he pointed out to George, the owner, and he asked for a half interest in the business. He paid for it with an undated interest free note and the transaction fell into the category of offers that cannot be refused. Six months later he owned the whole shop and property, but George was content because he was soon making more money working for Henry than he had when he owned it.

He hired Charley, who was also a good body shop man, to work at the garage and kept George on as mechanic. They started to make amphetamines in the garage. Henry wouldn't touch the stuff, but Charley and George were users. They would sell it in bike bars and to other Bandits, gradually building up a network as the original Bandit customers began to deal themselves.

Cooking crank in the garage was all right at first. There are several ways to make meta-amphetamine. The simplest is to just mix methylamine and phenyl-2-propanone, neither of which can be bought in Ontario without a permit, and other legal chemicals in a bowl. Methylamine is used in dyes and pesticides; phenyl-2-propanone is used in photo processing. He and Charley would steal it or get someone else to steal it for them. This was sometimes expensive and Henry didn't like being dependent on thieves.

The volume of the business they began to do made stealing the ingredients increasingly impractical and dangerous. They also sold LSD, which Henry got from his contacts in the States. And then there were the others, the synthesized 'magic mushrooms,' Quaaludes, and later, Ecstasy. It would be more profitable to invest in a plant and synthesize all these products.

Not far from the garage was an abandoned cheese factory in a deserted hamlet. The wooden buildings around were rotting and falling down but the factory itself was solid. It had been built of brick with a corrugated roof and had water from its own well. Henry bought it and kept the dilapidated look. This worked well for a couple of years.

Cash was rolling in. He and Charley had trouble knowing what to do with all the cash. Some of it they just stashed. Charley liked to gamble and tried to set himself up as a bookie. But he didn't hedge his bets intelligently and tended to get fleeced by more experienced gamblers.

Hattie heard them talking about their problems and offered to help solve them. Henry had been waiting for this moment. At this point she had been in business school for two years and she had figured out how to launder money. They began to buy real estate, small businesses, and country properties. On one of these, near Alexandria, there was an abandoned mine, and they moved the lab there when Hattie was twenty. She visited the place after it was set up, but prudently never went there again.

2

In early youth Theodore McLeod had distinguished himself as a hockey player but not in any other way. He had dazzled in Midget, shone in Junior, but showed only a dim light in minor pro. He had been drafted 347th by the Ottawa Senators and ended up briefly with their farm team in Binghamton. He could skate, handle the puck at times, and had a powerful if inaccurate shot. He was a big tough boy who could give and take checks. He had a strong sense of justice and was enraged by any hint of spearing, tripping, or even elbows. He would fight. He got too many penalties, lacked concentration, and made mistakes. When he was told that he was not going to the NHL, he quit. He returned to Winnipeg at the age of twenty-one with no marketable skills. He spent his time in the beer halls playing pool and trying to pick up girls.

"Such a big handsome boy, such charm, but really no good at anything, what are we going to do with him?" asked his aunt Moira.

"I keep telling you," replied her sister Jean. The two of them had brought him up. He was an orphan; Theodore's mother had died in a car accident. "There's only one place for a boy like Theodore: the Mounties."

Theodore's father and grandfather had been Mounties and both had distinguished themselves. The sisters had ruled it out for Theodore earlier because he was always in so much trouble at school. But the connection was a strong one: Theodore's father had been killed by a mad killer in a shootout at a farm in Saskatchewan. Theodore senior had been approaching the farmhouse with a white flag of truce when he was shot dead.

"We should ask them to give Theodore a chance. They owe the family."

So this was done. He was given an interview, made a good impression, and was accepted. And six years later came his promotion to the rank of deputy inspector and his transfer to Ottawa. It was thought that he had a future.

A city of snobs and spires is the way an early-twentieth-century writer once described Ottawa. There have been changes. The spires are dwarfed now by hotel and office towers, but the centers of power are still beneath them. The old lumber barons have given way to high-tech millionaires, and the lumberjacks to computer wizards. The computer printers of the civil servants of Ottawa consume paper by the ton and the cities of Ottawa and Hull, once paper producers, have become net consumers.

"Welcome to paperwork," said Theodore McLeod's new boss, Chief Superintendent John Wood, Officer in Charge, Drug Law Enforcement Branch, shaking his hand.

"Toilet paper performs a more useful function and bears an imprint of no lesser significance," he declared, gesturing to the steep white stacks of paper that weighed down a long table against a wall of his office. "Someone in personnel, or human resources, or whatever they call themselves nowadays, noticed that we had an undercover man in Winnipeg who was good at his job. Naturally he has to be brought here to shuffle paper around. It will be your job to read all these goddamn things. I don't have time to read them. I glance at them sometimes. But they must be read by someone in the DLEB and that person, for now, is you. They have all been acknowledged, but they need to be replied to in such a way that the writer feels his concerns are being addressed.

"They're written by MPs, MPPs, senators, mayors, and the general public. Everyone who thinks he or she knows what is wrong with the Drug Law Enforcement Branch of the RCMP, and that, as you can see, is a great many people. I made the mistake of telling the Minister over the telephone that I don't read the goddamn things. Excuse my language. Somebody opens them, passes them to someone else, and they end up in my office. So I was given a special assistant with first-hand knowledge of drug law enforcement – that's you – to reply to them. Some of them are email print outs so you reply by email."

"Suppose I don't know the answer?"

"Oh, ask around, and if no one knows the answer, wing it, make something up."

"Do you speak French? No? We'll put you down for that. Go to school at government expense. Why not? You've earned it."

I think I am going to get along with Wood, thought Theodore to himself. Everyone in Winnipeg is scared of him. He's irascible, but I can see what makes him angry: bullshit. I don't have much use for it myself.

At the time Theodore McLeod moved to Ottawa, Hattie was twenty-four. She worked for her father, looking after the Bandits' money and properties and managing the money laundering and offshore banking. Henry was not involved in stealing cars, selling weapons, contract hits, and a number of other activities that kept many members of the Bandits gainfully employed, but he was often asked to launder the profits.

As a rule, the Bandits did not trust each other with cash, but Henry had the ability and skills – actually it was Hattie who had the skills, but the Bandits did not know that – to take a lump sum of cash and turn it into either a legitimate bank account or a hard asset, such as a dry cleaning franchise or a piece of real estate. They would do this for other Bandits for a commission. Henry and Hattie, in a very discreet way, would sometimes lend money to people who couldn't borrow elsewhere, a practice known to the police as loan sharking. Hattie kept the books and Henry could provide up-to-date accounts on request. Actually, Hattie had developed programs that kept several sets of books, but Henry didn't know that.

She lived in a rented apartment in the Sandy Hill district and owned a VW minibus with space in the rear for her large dog, a white-throated salt-and-pepper male giant schnauzer named Manson. She and Manson ran together for half an hour every morning and most afternoons. In addition, they went regularly to an obedience school to keep their relationship taut and disciplined.

When Louise was released from prison, Henry had found her a small apartment and kept her supplied with booze and drugs. Hattie had persuaded her mother to take out a large life insurance policy when she got out of prison. Hattie paid the premiums; if her mother got back in her old ways she could put her out of her misery and benefit at the same time. She would wait and see if her mother was happy or not. What happened was what she had expected. Louise had become totally addicted to crack while in prison. Henry had arranged – out of kindness really – to see that she got all she wanted. Hattie did not really approve but she was not consulted.

After she got out, Louise got back on vodka and drank it until she was about to pass out. Then she took crack to stay awake so that she could drink more vodka. Drunk she would often call Hattie and complain that Hattie had ruined her life. She had got it into her head that Hattie had been the one who had killed Tom. As this was true, Hattie did not mind the complaint so much, but the constant phone calls and the crying and the yelling were tiresome.

One evening when her mother was quite drunk, Hattie gave her an overdose of tranquilizers instead of the crack she was asking for. She went home after her mother was fast asleep. The next morning she telephoned a neighbor and asked her to look in. There was no trouble with the insurance company: death by misadventure. Hattie was the beneficiary.

Hattie was a goalie coach in her spare time. She and Charley had a hockey school; she ran the goalie coaching as a separate department. She demanded absolute concentration, believing that concentration was the most important element of good goaltending, given that the reflexes and necessary athleticism were present. Those whose attention wandered were punished, by being made to do push ups, or laps around the rink, in their heavy equipment. She was always fair, and the young goalies admired her. When she demonstrated positioning against the shooters that the school employed, she would wow her students with her flamboyant butterfly style. She and Charley ran a month's summer camp, and in the winter ran classes for all ages on Sundays on two separate adjacent rinks. In addition Hattie acted as goalie coach to a few individual teams that could afford to hire one.

She went out on the occasional date, but in general found young men of her own age insipid and frivolous. Occasionally she would take one home and make him perform cunnilingus naked on his knees as she stood over him. When she had come, she would quickly leave the room to shower and then emerge with Manson at her side. If the young man was still amorous, his ardor would quickly dissipate at the sight of the dog, and he would leave. Hattie enjoyed the thought of his balls aching all the way home. On rare occasions when the man revealed a cock of impressive girth and height, she might yield; she respected power in all its forms. But she would never date him again.

The summer Hattie met Theodore, she had just begun a relationship with a man who thought he was her boyfriend; in fact she was not at all interested in him. It was something her father had set up. Henry was proud of his daughter; he believed that there was nothing she did not understand in the field of money laundering, computer hacking, and offshore banking.

A business meeting had been called in Montreal to discuss Lachute, a town on the north shore of the Ottawa, which the Angels considered their territory, and where the Bandits were doing business. The Angels wanted the Bandits out of Quebec altogether and began by demanding Lachute. The alternative was war. Henry conceded Lachute because it was close to Montreal, but told Deacon Kane of the Quebec Hells Angels that in no circumstances would the Bandits allow the Angels to move any further up the Ottawa valley.

The two men stayed up late drinking beer celebrating the successful negotiations. The Deacon boasted about his Korean computer wizard, Song "Angel Eyes" Hang-sen, who operated out of the Lennoxville headquarters. Henry deliberately let it slip that his daughter was learning computers and was looking after the Bandits' money. She was learning money laundering, he said, but was having problems. Deacon felt confident that Song, who after all was Asian, would be more than a match for Hattie, who after all was only a woman and a woman from the rustic Ottawa valley at that. He took the bait. This turned out to be the major mistake of Deacon Kane's life – like many men before him he had underestimated the power of a woman.

"Song would be glad to share his knowledge with your daughter," he said to Henry, relishing the idea that Song would be able to get access to information about Henry and the Bandits' business, and maybe do some hacking and stealing as well.

"It would be much appreciated," responded Henry, looking at the Deacon with the sly caginess that sixteen Heinekens can produce in a two-hundred-and-seventy pound man. It was Henry's plan that Hattie find out everything about the Angels' business, and maybe do some hacking and stealing as well. So it was arranged that the two would meet. Hattie was to take a room at Hovey Manor, an old and fashionable inn in North Hatley, near Lennoxville, one weekend in early August and Song would get in touch. Then they could arrange their own agenda.

"The Angels think that you are just learning computers and money laundering and all that stuff you do that I don't understand," Henry told Hattie. Henry hinted that a little vamping might be in order. He had never made such a request before out of respect for his daughter's virtue. Nor had Hattie ever done any vamping; but she quickly saw the opportunity. She would make Song fall in love with her.

Theodore met Hattie in August of that year through hockey. Not knowing many people in Ottawa, most of his evenings were free, and he thought he might try his hand at coaching. He called an old friend from Winnipeg, a government lawyer who coached a boys' team in the Greater Ottawa Hockey League. The coaches were mostly fathers, but there was a AA Peewee team looking for an experienced defensive coach. He met the head coach and got the job. It was a volunteer position, two practices and two games a week. He figured that it would keep him out of the bars on those nights, anyway.

The man who had coached defense the year before had moved to Toronto with his family, which included the team's best goalie. The team was almost desperate for a replacement, so Theodore volunteered to find one. He looked up hockey schools in the yellow pages, made a few phone calls from his Sandy Hill flat – he had found an apartment in a converted large old house – and found himself talking to Hattie. She did know of a goalie of the right age, who played in the girls' league. The boys' league would be tougher but Hattie thought that she could make it.

So she took the girl to a practice and there she met Theodore. The girl was good and the team wanted to sign her; Hattie promised to bring the mother to the next practice. The only problem was that the girl's mother was single and worked as a nurse – she would not be able to drive her daughter to games and practices most of the time. But as it turned out they also lived in Sandy Hill so Hattie agreed to drive the girl when the mother could not.

Theodore was smitten by Hattie. Soon they were driving to from and the hockey rinks together. Hattie found him attractive; he had an engaging self-deprecating candor that was new to her. What she disliked in attractive men was testosterone-charged egotism. This quality seemed to be completely missing from Theodore's personality, but she sensed the testosterone was present. He seemed a bit ingenuous, and Hattie, being of the opinion that all Mounties were simple-minded, was not surprised when he told her that he was with the RCMP. When he asked her to join him for a drink one evening, after dropping the goalie off, she accepted partly because she found him attractive, and partly because she thought she might find him useful.

This drink became customary whenever they drove the girl. They each bought their own; Hattie insisted. When he told her that he did office work for the DLEB, she concealed her interest. She was sure that they had a file on the Bandits. Perhaps she could get him to find out what was in it. Attracted to him, she decided to try out her new vamping skills on him. This time it might be more interesting from a sexual point of view.

One night he asked her back to his apartment for a drink and they became lovers. Hattie demanded certain things from men: good looks, simple-mindedness, humility, skill at cunnilingus, and a big cock. Theodore passed all tests. But Hattie, in the course of vamping him, began to feel a real affection. She found one day that she was no longer faking a sweetness toward him; inadvertently, she had opened up a part of her heart that had been dormant for a long time.

Weekends Hattie spent in North Hatley with someone else. She told Theodore her father was ill and she had to look after him. He never doubted her.

One night, while in bed, lying quietly beside each other after lovemaking, she brought up the subject of the Bandits. Charley, her partner in the hockey school, she said, was a member. At least he wore their colors. But surely he was not up to anything bad? She was worried about it.

"I could probably find out for you," said Theodore. "We'll have a file on them at the office. Would you like me to check on your Charley?"

"Could you? Oh, of course you're with drug law enforcement. Of course you could." Hattie was silent for a minute. "There's something else. My father has a cousin, Henry Brading, who was once a member, or so my father says. I would hate to think of our name being in the police files. Could you look while you're at it?"

"For you, my dear, I would search the prime minister's office."

Theodore reported back a few days later that indeed the Bandits were bad dudes. Charley was in the file and was suspected of being involved in the manufacture of drugs. "They have a plant somewhere. Everybody's been looking for it, the Ottawa police, the Ontario Provincial Police, and us. No Bradings in the file. You have no family black sheep, not on our files, anyway."

That night Hattie stayed over. Previously she had always gone home after sex. But she had picked a bad night, for she was being watched, and shortly afterward all hell broke loose.

If Hattie and her father were laundering the money of a Bandit who died a sudden death – which was not uncommon – Henry would stall for a while when someone came forward to claim it, to see if the relative had any clear idea of what was owed. If not, he and Hattie would expropriate as much of the money as they could. On one occasion Henry was asked to launder some money for one, Angelo Pacifico. Angelo had suddenly acquired $30,000 in cash that was hot; he confided in Henry and asked him for help. He told Henry that no one knew about the money but him. It also happened that Henry had an ancient score to settle with the Pacificos so instead of laundering the money, he lured Angelo to a secret rendezvous, killed him, and took it.

But Henry didn't know that Angelo had an associate, one Leonardo Battaglia. He considered half of the money to be his. Battaglia was not upset by Angelo's death because he figured he now had a claim on everything that was left after Henry's cut. He questioned Henry about the money; Henry stalled; Leonardo pressed. To the Bandits Henry was the money-man; they never spoke directly to Hattie. Henry, stalling, made the mistake of giving him Hattie's phone number. She would think of something.

"Call the office," he said. "Tell them you need information on Angelo's estate."

"Tell who?" asked Leonardo.

"Whoever answers the phone," said Henry.

"Give me a name."

"I don't know who'll be there. You don't need a name. I'll call ahead." Henry walked away to avoid further questions. He called Hattie to tell her to expect the call. "Stall him, find out how much he knows. We may have to give him half, less our thirty per cent draw down."

"You shouldn't have given out my phone number."

"I know, he was pressing, I had to give him something. Sorry. It was a mistake."

It was Hattie's practice to answer the telephone with a simple "Hello." It was not her way, or her father's, to ever give out more information than was necessary.

When Leonardo called, he immediately asked, "What's your name?"

"Who wants to know?"

Long pause. "Leonardo Battaglia, cousin of Angelo Pacifico." Then a shot in the dark. "You're Hattie, Henry's daughter, right?"

"Maybe."

"You looked after Angelo's money?"

"I help Henry in the office part time."

"And where is the office?"

"You ask a lot of questions."

"Listen up, Hattie, Angelo is dead. Our money is missing. I have a right to ask a lot of questions."

"How much do you think was there in the first place? Angelo was told what our cut is. How much do you think is missing?"

"Thirty grand."

"You've got to be kidding. You'll have to speak to Henry."

"You guys are giving me the runaround." He hung up.

Leonardo had the phone number traced to Hattie's apartment. Then he decided to conduct a little surveillance, thinking it might be useful to get something on her. Some of the Bandits knew that Henry had a daughter who had grown up and had a consulting business of some kind. A few, including Leonardo, knew that when she had lived at home, she had helped her father in the office. Charley would be asked about her from time to time. He maintained that she did no work for her father and that she and her father were not on good terms.

One night Leonardo saw a man pick her up at her apartment building. She was waiting just inside the entrance. He followed as they picked up the goalie and went to the arena. Leonardo watched the hockey practice from high up keeping out of sight. He followed them home, watched as they dropped the girl off, and went to McLeod's apartment. He was still sitting in his car, drinking coffee and smoking cigarettes, when she left the flat with the man at 8 a.m. They kissed and walked off in different directions. Leonardo followed the man. Two days later he called Henry.

"Guess what, Henry. When I spoke to you before I knew two things: one, that someone killed Angelo. I am not sayin' that you had anything to do with that. And two, I knew that he had just handed $30,000 in cash over to you. Maybe someone thought he still had it on him when they snuffed him. Now I know two more things: one, that dame you put me on to at the so-called office is your daughter. And two, she's sleeping with a horseman and not no ordinary horseman neither. He's a big shot in the DLEB."

Henry settled with Leonardo for $15,000, but not before Leonardo had called a meeting of key members of the Bandits' executive to discuss Henry's daughter's connections to the Bandits and to the RCMP. He insisted that the meeting be held at Henry's secret lab. Leonardo wanted to know where it was and figured that the executive might want to know too.

A few days after Leonardo Battaglia first surveyed his apartment, Theodore learned that all the branch files had been transferred to a central computer. The file he had looked in for the Bandits was an out-of-date paper file. So, obtaining the password from a colleague, he looked up the Bandits on his computer.

There were some photographs. He was looking them over when suddenly the gates of hell opened widely. There she was, a stern and businesslike Hattie, carrying what looked like a laptop, leaving a suburban ranch-type bungalow. The house was identified as belonging to Henry "The Bear" Brading, a member of the Bandits, suspected of being at the center of the biggest drug distribution network in the Ottawa valley. Hattie was identified as being his daughter. There was not much on her in the file. She worked as a business consultant and a few clients were listed: a dry cleaning franchise distributor, whose ownership had been traced to a series of Ontario numbered corporations; a frozen meat locker establishment; and a real estate holding company. Ownership of these assets had proved impossible to establish: there was a chain of numbered corporations ending up in the Bahamas. She was suspected of laundering money and loan sharking. He printed out the page with her picture, folded the paper and put it in his inside jacket pocket.

His intimacy with Hattie was dangerous for them both. Theodore pondered the alternatives and decided he would tell her what he had learned at the practice that night, sever their relationship, and tell Wood about it in the morning.

That morning Hattie had a rare visit at her apartment from her father. She was working in her office in the second bedroom in her flat when he buzzed her from downstairs.

"Hattie, let me in!"

She buzzed him up. When she opened the door she could tell from his face that something was very wrong.

That night Hattie and Theodore talked little on the drive to the rink and on the way back. They drove in Theodore's big gray Chevrolet. After the girl hopped out, grabbed her bag from the trunk, and said good night, he turned to her.

"Hattie, we have to talk. I had a look at another file on the Bandits. You're in it. And your dad." He took the sheet of paper with her picture on it out of his pocket and passed it to her.

She looked at the picture and passed it back to him. "Okay. Your place."

When they got to his flat, he poured them each a stiff malt whiskey. They sat in his den. The room was dark, one lamp in the corner of the room on a plain, heavy, dark, maple desk, inherited from his father. They had made love on the sofa a number of times. Theodore switched on the ugly overhead light to better study her face. Neither of them spoke, each waiting for the other to begin.

"Ah, Theodore, the bright light stuff. Switch it off." He did. "Okay," Hattie said after about a minute and a half. She got up, sat down at the desk, found a blank sheet of paper and began to draw. "I'll give them to you. Here's a map. It shows exactly where the lab is, in an abandoned mine not far from Alexandria. At four o'clock Friday afternoon, there be a meeting there. The president of the Bandits, the vice-president, my father and I, a guy named Leonardo Battaglia, and a couple of others. Big shots in the Bandits, I don't know exactly who, they didn't tell me. You'll also pick up the guys who work there. Be careful. There's probably an arsenal down there. And, of course, drugs and uh – a generator, a vacuum extractor, that sort of stuff."

She got up, gave the map to him and smiled down at him. "If you go in person, be careful. I don't want you shot."

"But what about – us?"

"I dunno." She stroked his head. "We don't have time to think about us. Maybe you can visit me in jail. Just make sure the cops don't fuck up. I would take not less than thirty. Surround the place. Go at four thirty on Friday. Oh, and go easy on Bear, my dad, he doesn't have anything to do with it. He's at the meeting 'cause of you and me." There was silence as he studied the map. She thought,

I've never done this before, stroked someone's head, just dogs. About time I got out.

"Okay." He looked up. The candid blue eyes of the Westerner looked into inscrutable green. "So you were using me?"

"Ah, Theodore." There was a long pause. "I just thought, what the hell, I would ask you. What you told me turned out to be bullshit anyway. They did have something on us. No, I liked you, I really did. One reason I liked you is that you are so stupid."

Theodore noticed the past tense. "I never said I wasn't stupid." He smiled at her. "Did you ever hear me say I wasn't stupid?"

"No. Never."

"Okay, then. You'll be there? At the lab?"

"What do you think the big meeting is about? It's about us. I was being watched by a Bandit the night I stayed over. I have to be there. But I don't expect to be prosecuted. Is that a deal?"

He held her gaze. "I can't promise anything, but that is the way it usually works."

"I'll take my chances." They both knew she was not going to be there.

"How come – "

She cut him off. "No more questions." She picked up her bag and her skates, which she had brought in with her.

"I'm walking home. *Au revoir.*"

He got up and kissed her, a long tender kiss on the mouth, and she left. He went to the window and watched her hail a cab. I wonder what she's thinking, he mused, right now. She was thinking it could not have worked out better if I had planned it: this thing has been dropped into my fucking lap.

It never occurred to her that she might miss him.

3

Hovey Manor is situated just south of the village of North Hatley, on the west side of Lake Massawippi in the Eastern Townships, a hundred miles or so east of Montreal. The flat plain of the St. Lawrence valley rises into the Appalachians about fifty miles from Montreal. It is not far from Vermont, home of the Green Mountain Boys who took Fort Ticonderoga in the first victory of the American Revolution. The English-speaking population of the Eastern Townships is largely their kin. The topography is similar to that of Vermont but the landscape is gentler: green mountains, rich farmland and deep lakes. When it was first sounded Lake Massawippi was found to be bottomless in places. A powerful underground river carried the lead away. In the mid-nineteenth century a man on a sleigh driving a team of horses went through the ice while crossing the lake. His body was never found. The body of one of the horses emerged that spring, battered and torn, in another lake altogether, seven miles to the west.

One Saturday in August, a couple of weeks before she met Theodore, Hattie had sat on the terrace of this old inn overlooking the lake, enjoying the view. She could see Vermont in the distance and the waiter told her that the most distant mountain was in New Hampshire. She sipped a glass of white wine and waited for her first meeting with Song "Angel Eyes" Hang-sen. Everywhere she looked the world was green and she felt at peace. I am in love with this green earth, she reflected. She had driven from Ottawa in her van. Manson, at her feet, looked up at the sound of the Harley coming to a halt in the gravel parking lot.

For Song it was love at first sight. He had found her intriguing over the phone and what he saw as he walked onto the terrace did not disappoint him: long legs stretched out in black tight-fitting denim, bare feet, sandals kicked off, a bare midriff, a red top supporting a high firm bosom, a cascade of black hair. He could not quite make out her face behind large-lensed dark glasses, shaded by an elegant wide brimmed straw hat.

Manson remained prone. He growled at Song as he introduced himself. "Should I try to make friends?" Song asked.

"Best not," said Hattie. "He mistrusts strangers who try to make friends with him. Better to ignore him. He'll watch us, and once he sees that I accept you, he will."

"What's his name?"

"Manson. After Charles."

"You're kidding."

"No. It's better, believe me, that people be scared of him as soon as they hear his name than that they find out later how scary he can be. I'm no fan of Charles Manson. Marilyn Manson, now, has an interesting slant on things, but I didn't name my dog after him." As she said this she put her hand down and caressed his head.

"You know, it is about one hundred thousand years ago that wolves and humans formed their partnership. At first it was an equal partnership. The wolves taught us to work in teams – no other apes do that. And as we evolved together, we lost some of our powers, such as smell, and they lost some of theirs, such as brainpower. We did the thinking a lot of the time; that is why wolves are smarter than dogs as a rule. And at some point we took over total control of the food supply, and then bred them sometimes as toys, toy poodles and Pomeranians. Kind of shabby treatment of a partner, but what do you expect from a human? Their society is completely hierarchal, all that Alpha male stuff?" Song nodded. "We learned a lot of that from them. Manson here," she paused, dog and mistress exchanged a glance, "he considers me number one female in the world, and himself number one male. He won't back down from man or beast. He will kill and enjoy it." She paused. "Look out there at the green earth, there are owls, weasels, foxes, raccoons, and wolves out there who kill for what they want and feel the pleasure of it. One eats, say a fish, in a restaurant, one is not connected to the kill....enough, am I boring you?" Actually I'm warning him, she thought, but he won't pick up on it.

"Not at all," said Song, totally fascinated by the woman and the dog, and not picking up on it.

He would have liked to join her in a glass of white wine and felt suddenly gross carrying the bottle of Molson Ex he had picked up at the bar on his way through. He was not wearing club colors but a pearl gray silk suit. The Angels always wore suits when they went to Hovey Manor. They were the only customers of the inn who did, like professional hockey players who stand out from their fans because they dress like gentlemen off the ice.

From the first phone call from Song, she had tried to play dumb. She was certain from what her father had told her about him that he wrote his own programs or code as she did. These she wanted to learn, as well as the tools and computer languages he used. As it happened, he had brought his laptop along. He encrypted his work, as Hattie did, on CDs that were used to transfer it to the club's mainframe computer. Both of them had written utility programs for themselves that automatically encrypted everything, copied the encrypted information to a CD, and destroyed the original. There was nothing at all on the hard drive; he had a CD in his pocket.

There were two differences in the way they operated. Hattie had written a program that kept some deposits off the books. If the Bandits suddenly asked for all their cash assets she would be in trouble. Song was scrupulously honest, and the files on his CDs were identical to those on the club's main computer. He never saw the cash; it was moved according to his instructions, by members acting as messengers. Hattie handled the cash herself and this sometimes meant trips abroad.

Song never suspected for a moment that Hattie was a threat. The Deacon had told him that she was learning computer programming and money laundering. He was to help her and at the same time learn all he could about the Bandits' affairs. If he saw a feasible opportunity to hack into the Bandits' system and steal some of their money, he was to report to the Deacon before proceeding. Now that he had met her he dropped all intentions of doing anything of the sort. All he could think of on first meeting was that he wanted her to come back to his cottage.

"Let's have our drinks," said Song, "and go somewhere else. This is not a good place to talk."

"Where?"

"I have a cottage on the lake. I'll take you on my bike."

"Okay." If there was one thing Hattie did not like, it was hanging on to the waist of some macho man as he drove his hog and showed her off to the world. But if a girl's gotta vamp, a girl's gotta vamp, she said to herself.

"What about Manson?" Manson had not moved since Song had arrived nor had he taken his eyes off him. At this mention of his name, Hattie observed a slight movement of his long tail. Schnauzers generally have their tails and ears cropped as puppies. Hattie had specifically ordered the kennel not to do this to him.

"He's accepted you. I think he was touched by your concern." She smiled. "Don't worry about him. He'll run along behind."

"Yeah? I won't go fast."

"You can go up to fifty kilometers," said Hattie. "He loves to run."

"It's on the other side of the lake. We have to go through the village."

"He'll be okay. Don't worry. He'll focus entirely on us."

They got up. Hattie was the taller by two inches. She went to her room, got her laptop, a bathing suit and towel and Manson's dog food and bowl, and met Song in the parking lot.

Song was not a typical Hells Angel. He was slightly built and good-looking in a way that was almost pretty. He was a keen motorcyclist and had joined the Seoul chapter of the club while studying computer science at university. He had done his compulsory two-year army service and was adept at Tai Kwan Do, as are all male Koreans who learn it as part of their military service. After working for two years at the Bank of South Korea, he was sent to Montreal to improve his English at a language school.

He turned up one day at the Hells Angels Montreal clubhouse wearing the colors of the South Korean chapter. He was polite and sensitive and the Angels were not sure what to make of him at first. He did not have a bike and tended to hang around striking up conversations. He wanted to improve his English and rather got on the nerves of the French-speaking members. One afternoon he tried to start a conversation in English with a huge Angel, Roger Gervais, who, as it happened, was not in a good mood.

"*Parle francais, calice, maudit tête de riz gâteau!*" declared the huge man and suddenly started to pick Song up by his shirt collar. Roger quickly found himself hitting the floor face down which amused several of his pals. Roger got up and went for Song again. Same result. This time Roger himself was amused.

"Hey, angle eyes, you teach me dat, and you get to keep your life, okay?" Song did teach Roger some Tai Kwan Do and the two became friends.

Among those witnessing this encounter was Eric, an Angel who was working on transferring club financial data to a new computer. He was having some problems and when he found out that Song was a computer programmer, he asked him some questions. Song answered them as well as he could, but said it would be easier if he had the computer in front of him. The next time he came in Eric told him that the club had talked it over and they wanted Song to go to Lennoxville and help Eric.

Song went on the back of Eric's bike and after working with Eric on the computer, gave his opinion that the club needed some new programs. He offered to write them and teach Eric to use them. He told the Angels that he could also show them more secure ways to bank offshore. He also told them that their encryptions needed updating.

"You know, Eric," he told him, "there are codebusters and cryptobrains that could get in here. This stuff gets obsolete very fast. Your security walls are out of date. I can fix it for you; I have done it for banks."

The next time that he was in the Montreal clubhouse, Eric said, "Hey, Angel Eyes, come on outside." They had taken to calling him Angel Eyes, a more respectful nickname than Roger Gervais's racist "angle eyes", *angle* being French for slant. He led Song outside to the yard and showed him a brand new red Harley Davidson.

"What do you think?"
"Nice bike."
"It's yours for $6,000."
"I don't have any money, just enough for school."

"Don't worry about that, pay us when you can. Dollar a week would be okay. They want you to take over my job for a while, which is fine with me, as long as you teach me stuff."

Song took the offer and did valuable work for the Angels. He kept paying his dollar a week. When he attempted to pay more, his money was refused. When the time came for him to return to the bank in Korea, the Angels didn't want him to go. They offered him a weekly cash salary to stay and he accepted, working out of the Lennoxville headquarters.

Most of the year Song lived in an apartment in Montreal; he could get *gimche* and other Korean foods there. He didn't like North American food. He had taken the cottage for the summer and had been working for the Angels full time for about a year when he was assigned to work with Hattie.

The cottage was set back about forty feet from the lake. It was unheated but there was a wood stove and a woodshed with an ax and chopping block outside. An old farm had been subdivided into narrow lots that extended about a quarter of a mile from a gravel road through woods to the lake. Song's rented cottage was on the lot where the original farmhouse had stood; the foundations survived about two hundred yards from the shore in a little clearing in the woods. They passed it to get to the cottage, the bike bouncing on the dirt track and Manson bounding along behind them.

The cottage itself, a two-bedroom bungalow, was fairly new. When they got there Song proposed a swim and Hattie was all for it. Neither was anxious to get down to business. Hattie wanted to make sure that Song was thoroughly in thrall and figured that her appearance in a bathing suit would help. And she had something to set up in her room in the hotel; she wanted the business sessions to take place there. For his part Song was waiting politely for her to ask for help.

They swam; Manson came in with them. He always swam towards Hattie, his great clawed front paws paddling furiously. She had to be agile to avoid getting scratched. Song had a canoe that came with the cottage. He had never used it, he didn't know how to paddle a canoe. He ran, practiced Tai Kwan Do, and lifted weights for exercise. Hattie offered to teach him to use the canoe. Song suggested that they paddle into North Hatley and have dinner there.

"What about Manson?" he asked.

"He'll stay and guard your house. He likes being a watchdog. It's his job." She called Manson to the front door of the cottage. She gave him his dinner in the bowl she had brought with her and a saucepan full of water.

"Stay," she commanded firmly, using the word only once. He didn't move as they walked to the dock; he lay down before the front steps and assumed the role for which he had been trained: guard dog. Whenever Hattie came to the cottage that summer, Manson took up this post and would not move from it unless called.

They paddled to North Hatley with Hattie in the rear doing the J stroke. She taught Song to keep his back straight, to kneel in order to lower the canoe's center of gravity, and to do a steady light stroke. He had excellent command of his body and caught on quickly. He set the pace and the canoe moved along smartly. In the village they had ice cream cones and strolled about.

Song was glad to have company and thrilled to be in the company of a woman whose looks drew glances. In Montreal he had Korean friends but in the townships he knew no one but the Angels, and he had not made personal friends among them. They respected him for his loyalty to the club, for the work he did, and for his skill at Tai Kwan Do. He was polite and showed consideration for others; these qualities were egregious in the Angels' herd, but they forgave him. He was Korean after all, and couldn't help it. His Tai Kwan Do made him potentially dangerous and that made him acceptable. To be dangerous was the supreme quality they all admired and shared. They considered him their possession, like the computer itself. They were proud of him, but felt no inclination to socialize with him. He had casually invited some of them to drop in at his summer cottage but none of them ever did. For his part he was not that fond of their company. He didn't like the way they treated women and was not keen on drugs. He liked scotch.

So Hattie was company. He couldn't talk to his Korean friends in Montreal about his job. She was a colleague; they did the same work. He was looking forward to tomorrow when they could discuss it. But first he wanted to get to know her; perhaps he could persuade her to stay over. They had dinner in North Hatley. They chatted about food. He told her about the Korean food that he missed. They discussed movies and then computers and programs. She mostly listened and seemed in no hurry to go back to the inn.

"Do you like malt whisky?" he asked after dinner.

"I do."

"I have a collection at home."

"Let's go then but don't forget you have to drive me home."

"If you think me even a tiny bit –" he paused, looking for a word.

"Squiffed?"

"Squiffed!" he laughed. "You have such wonderful words in English for drinking. If you think me squiffed, we'll get a taxi to take you home."

It was still daylight when they walked back to the canoe. He warned her, "I think my place is bugged. I'm not sure. I don't care really. I don't even care who's doing it. But we can't talk business there."

They took glasses, a few bottles of malt whisky, and a bottle of spring water out to the clearing near the old house. Song had a barbecue there and a picnic table. They sat on the table with shot glasses between them and compared the malts, taking a drink of water between whiskies to clean the palate. Song took large swigs of whisky and small sips of water; Hattie took small sips of whisky and large swigs of water.

The sun went down and a gibbous moon sailed overhead. Song lit a fire. They talked about Scotland while they drank its whisky; Song revealed a longing to travel.

"I would love to get away," said Hattie. "From everything."

"Where would you go?"

"Anywhere." She got up. "Right now I'm going into the woods to pee." Coming back, she stepped on something. It looked like the lid to a large wooden box. "What's this?"

He came over. "It's the cover of an old abandoned well. No water there now. I suppose there was an underground stream that changed its course."

He took off the lid. There was a square black hole, about sixteen inches across, lined with old wood. He picked up a stone and dropped it. After a moment there was a clink. He looked at her and they both made the calculation. They said in unison, "About forty feet."

They went back to the whisky. Song drank a lot. He was trying to get up his courage to kiss her. "Hattie," he said after a long comfortable silence, "I feel as if I've known you a long time."

Hattie was gazing in the direction of the abandoned well. "Me too." She smiled at him. "We have a destiny, perhaps."

He told her that he was not happy working for the Angels, but that he did not think he could quit; he knew too much. He had saved some money and wanted to travel.

"How much have you saved?" Hattie asked.

"About $50,000."

"Not enough."

"Tax-free!" He laughed foolishly. He was a bit drunk. "And you and I know how to keep it that way."

"That's true. But it's still not enough. Maybe I'll come with you, I'd like to keep traveling forever. I've saved some, too, but between us we haven't enough to travel for long."

With this little speech, Song's heart raced. There was a long silence. "I want to go back to the inn," she said suddenly.

"I don't want you to go. I was hoping you might stay. And I don't think I should drive you."

"You can call a taxi. Remember?" she smiled at him, gave him a kiss on the cheek, and got up. They went back to the cottage and got her things. He called the taxi and, carrying a flashlight, he walked her up to the road. Manson stayed very close to Hattie. He started to put his arm around her but there was a growl from Manson and he withdrew it. When they saw the cab, he waved the light as arranged. Just before getting in, she kissed him full on the lips.

"About staying over. Maybe some other night. Okay? Good night." Song went back to his cottage in a state of exhilaration.

After breakfast the next morning, Hattie changed rooms. She had no reason to suspect that her bedroom in the inn was bugged, but there was no point in taking a chance. That Song was unhappy with the Angels and wanted to travel was encouraging. He seemed successfully hooked and vamped. Perhaps she could draw him into a conspiracy; nothing enhances romance better than a secret. He was not a bad-looking boy: the spider is attracted to the fly.

The inn was full, but a room on the top floor in the original older building had just been vacated. It had exposed beams and rafters and looked east at the same view she had admired from the terrace. There was a large table where they could set up their computers side by side.

All of her work was encrypted and then put on CDs. There were two 64-bit keys: one for encrypting and another for decrypting. She carried her encryption keys on her laptop; a combination of typewriter characters or letters typed in sequence opened the computer, her utility program then produced the keys, and enabled her to unlock the encryption, and read and work on her material. This meant that the CDs could be unlocked only by her own computer. She supposed that he worked the same way, but his keys could be 128-bit. Regardless, he could not possibly have them memorized. His keys had to be stored somewhere. Probably, like her, they were on his computer, which required a lengthy password to open.

To accomplish her objective she needed to learn his password – the key to the keys as it were – have physical possession of his computer, have physical possession of his CDs, and be familiar generally with how he operated, with his codes and programs.

She figured that Song would instinctively turn his screen away from her while he typed in the combination that unlocked the decryption key, and she would gaze politely out the window at distant Vermont. She had rented a tiny video camera in Ottawa that was easy to conceal. Positioning it so that it would look down over his shoulder, focusing it, setting the zoom, adjusting the position of the table, and taping it in place on a roof rafter took almost an hour.

She went downstairs and was in the lobby looking at a newspaper when he drove up. She went outside to greet him but did not kiss him. She walked briskly ahead of him to the front desk, ordered coffee sent to the room, and, beckoning him, went up the stairs first, giving him a good rear view of the lower part of her body. This is where the eggs are kept, and few sperm-carrying males can keep their eyes off it while climbing stairs. They went along a narrow passage to the older building.

In the room she sat down in her chair, showing a bit of cleavage. She was not wearing a bra; this was business. She didn't want Song's attention to be entirely focused on their work. *Ayesha, my queendom come*, she prayed. He put his laptop down on the table in front of the chair she drew up for him. She sat at right angles to him and could not see his screen unless he turned it towards her, but her camera could.

She was certain that he had been assigned to obtain information from her computer. She was curious to see how he was going to go about it. For his part, he had already decided against retrieving information from her computer as the Deacon had requested. She had achieved her goal: he was falling in love with her and in his passion was going to make all sorts of mistakes that were to cause the Angels grief.

He had perceived that Hattie understood more than she let on, but he flattered himself that she was playing ignorant because she liked him, and wanted to spend time with him. And he knew she was cleverer than she let on; again he flattered himself that she hid her cleverness because she was afraid it might put him off. In fact Song liked clever women; he decided that when the time came, he would tell her that.

The night before there had been a hint that they might conspire to rob the Angels and run away together. He planned to drop a hint today to the same end and see if she picked up on it.

They got right down to business. Laundering money was something the Bandits had worked out, she told him; going offshore was what she wanted to learn about. She told him the Bandits had no contacts and that she didn't know where to begin. Song had two years experience in international banking before he came to Montreal and gave her a short course in things she already knew.

"Can you transfer funds electronically?" A dumb question.

"Of course," he replied, smiling at her artlessness.

Hattie looked puzzled. She leaned forward exposing extra cleavage. "Show me how," she said. She looked to see if his keyboard was a Western one. It was.

As it happened he had some fund transfers to put on a CD, which later that day he would take to Lennoxville. He slid the CD into his laptop and turned it an additional fifteen degrees away from her, just as she had anticipated in setting up her camera. He typed for half a minute or so. Gazing out the window into the distance, she listened carefully as he typed, using two fingers, what she estimated was well over a hundred and characters. He knows it by heart, probably a long sentence, even if it's in Korean it will be written in the Western alphabet. She had focused the camera with great care, but could not be certain she would be able to read what he typed on the screen.

He then turned his laptop so that she could see the screen. His utility program had automatically decoded the encryption. What she saw were electronic bank forms. "For security reasons the procedures are complex," he said. "It is just a matter of learning and remembering the steps. There are public encryption keys and IDs to enter. Taken one at a time, it's easy." He proceeded with a transfer, then smiled at her and repeated, "Easy."

"Public encryption keys? How do you remember them? Or do you have them written down?"

"The banks send me their public encryption keys for me to use when sending them confidential material. I keep them on the CD, encrypted, of course, with my own encryption keys."

"Encryption keys now, are they hard to crack?"

"Hard but not impossible. It was originally calculated that it would take a hundred years to crack an RC5-64 sequence. Then they held a contest, there's people called codebusters who specialize in it – and it was done in two years. You have to set up a large computer to run all the combinations. Think about it. A binary digit is either 0 or 1, as you know. The key length is 64 bits or binary digits. Two to the power of 64 gives you the number of possible combinations from which a key can be created. There are people who feel insecure with that and are going with 128 bits, 256, even. Now I have both a private encryption key and a private decryption key of my own on my laptop, they are the only things I keep there. I go with 64 bits. I change it once a year or so. I use it to encrypt and decrypt everything on the CD that holds the bank info."

It was as she had thought and hoped. She pretended to be puzzled. "But then anyone who stole your computer could find the keys and read your CDs?"

"No. I have a password of over a hundred letters that has to be typed in order to get my computer to open. Only Eric, the guy who works with me, and I know what it is. And we have it memorized. It's not written down anywhere."

Hattie did her best to look impressed and resisted the temptation to glance up at her camera.

Back in Ottawa that night Hattie slipped the videocassette into a special cartridge and played it on her VCR with some trepidation. It was a long English sentence. She could only make out the words in the middle of the text; the words at the edges were illegible. She could not make out any punctuation at all and the punctuation would probably be part of the key What she saw looked something like this:

xxxxxxxxxxxx fell from Noon to dewy Eve a Summers day
xxxxxx xxxxxxxxxxxxx like a falling star

She stared at it for a full minute and then a bell rang. It's Milton, it's the fall of Satan from heaven, it's from *Paradise Lost*. In her adolescent years in the Ottawa library she had taken an interest in Satan and a librarian had steered her to *Paradise Lost*. Milton's seventeenth century English had fascinated her. It was difficult at first, but she had persevered and found it the most beautiful thing she had ever read. She had identified with Satan: he had led a revolution because God was a despot and was thrown out of heaven for it. Some critics believed that Milton himself, a supporter of the dictator Oliver Cromwell, had sympathy for Satan. The Hells Angels certainly identified with Satan but she doubted that many of them carried a copy of *Paradise Lost* in their hip pockets.

Hattie had a copy of Milton in her apartment. She got it out and quickly found the passage:

> *from Morn to Noon he fell, from Noon to dewy Eve, a Summer's day, and with the setting Sun, dropt from the Zenith like a falling star,*

She counted out the letters for the passage and matched them to the illegible letters. It was a shade too long; she wondered about eliminating punctuation. The Hells Angels had dropped the apostrophe from their original name; they didn't go in for punctuation. The commas had not been visible on the videotape. There was only one way to find out: open up his computer while he slept.

The next weekend she stayed with Song at the cottage. He spent the afternoon demonstrating the programs or codes that he had written for the Angels, and they went over bank transfer procedures. Neither mentioned the possibility of conspiring together. Each was waiting for the other to bring it up.

After Song had made a Korean dinner they took the canoe out to the middle of the lake. They didn't wear their life jackets, but used them as cushions. It was dead calm. She stretched out, facing him, while he paddled. He had become proficient. Sound travels clearly over calm water so they spoke softly. They were watching the sunset when Song proposed that they rob the Angels and run away together.

Hattie agreed. "But let's work out the details tomorrow. It is too beautiful right now to talk of money."

"The other night there was a terrible storm," said Song. "I dreamt of us being out on the lake together in the canoe. It was a nightmare. You saved my life. A neighbor told me the next day that if a black cloud comes over Lake Massawippi, watch out."

She stripped that night under the moon in the clearing by the old house, and asked Song to take a bottle of Avon bath oil, of the kind that acts as an insect repellent, from her bag and rub the oil all over her. This led to him satisfying her on his knees, while she stood and gazed at the moon. He is quite good at this, she thought. In fact he used the tip of his tongue to write love letters on her clitoris in his native Korean. She did not reciprocate, but relieved him later with her hand. She told him that she was a virgin and wanted to marry him.

That night Song again drank a lot of malt whisky. They danced together under the moon. Hattie encouraged him to get quite drunk and then led him to bed. When she was sure he was completely passed out, she explored the house, found his CDs, and set up the computer. In one of his drawers she found a little nickel-plated automatic handgun. She checked it out, made sure it was loaded, and put it back exactly as she had found it.

She knew that all his banking data was on one CD. She slid it in. What she saw was incomprehensible so she typed in the quotation from Milton. Nothing happened. Then she tried it without punctuation. Presto, the CD was legible: the Milton quote had opened the decryption key and put his utility program to work, which in turn had decrypted the CD. She had the keys to the banking kingdom of the Quebec chapter of the Hells Angels Motorcycle Club – provided that she could steal his laptop and the CD.

The next day, in the woods by the ruins of the old house where Song had his barbeque, they talked about what they were going to do. Song thought that she might look down on him for betraying the Angels and felt he had to justify himself in her eyes. He told her about murders that some of the Angels were involved in and the contemptuous way some of them treated women.

Then, being Song, he felt bad about speaking ill of them; they had helped him in many ways. "Some of them are okay, though. Some don't commit any crimes at all. They just like to wear the club colors. It is a famous motorcycle club, after all. Eric, the guy I work with on the computer, is a decent guy. He doesn't commit any crimes. He likes to read poetry, English poetry, old-fashioned stuff that nobody reads."

Like Milton, Hattie thought, I didn't think it was Song; he wouldn't be familiar with English literature. Still, it was stupid of him not to check to see if the poem was well known. "So, how much are we going to take?" she asked, getting down to business.

"Nearly all banks now report large deposits to the authorities. We will not be able to steal a large sum," Song told Hattie. "The Swiss banks are certainly out of the question."

"What about Cyprus?" asked Hattie, testing him. "I've heard that there's a bank there that's tame."

Song shook his head. "Cyprus is no good now. The Angels use a number of banks and transfer relatively small sums on a regular basis. No one notices. You and I will not get away with stealing a large sum. Period. I can move $20,000 to ten different banks. I have already set up the accounts. $200,000 max is what we steal. Plus I doubt if the Angels will come after us all that hard for $200,000. Probably look at it as severance pay."

Hattie said nothing. Several years before in Switzerland she had helped a Russian move $200,000,000 out of his country and then back in again. They had met at the hotel she was staying in. She had got drunk a few times on vodka with him and his wife. Hattie had helped him as a favor; she had not asked anything in return. When he set up his secret bank within a bank, she used it almost exclusively. He was now a billionaire. Hattie could move any amount she wanted with impunity. Shady banks that will accept stolen money will also steal it themselves if they are sure the depositor has no legal recourse. But Russian crooks have a sense of personal honor in one respect: they might steal from governments, corporations, enemies, and strangers. But they never forget a favor; if a Russian is your friend you can trust him absolutely.

It was now early September and they decided to make their move in the next two weeks.

When Hattie got home on the night she said *au revoir* to Theodore, she had work to do. She planned to liquidate most of the assets that belonged to her father and the Bandits, and to transfer them through a series of untraceable transactions to her Russian bank. She would make the transfer next Friday just before the meeting, but she first had to put what she was taking into cash.

She called Song from a pay phone. "I'm in serious trouble with the horsemen and the Bandits," she said. "We have to leave tomorrow. I'll explain when I see you. I'll be there at two in the afternoon. We'll take the first plane to anywhere in Canada early tomorrow morning from Dorval, paying cash. There's one to Halifax, I know will have empty seats." Song agreed to this without asking questions.

Hattie had an American passport in the name Alice LeBlanc. She was born in a hospital in Boston and this was the name her mother had given her at birth. She was never told that she had an American birth certificate; nor was her father. She had found it among her mother's papers after her death. Louise LeBlanc had somehow also obtained a Canadian birth certificate in the name of Hattie Brading. Hattie never knew why or how her mother had two different birth certificates in two different names, but she applied for the US passport from an address in Switzerland she had acquired for Alice LeBlanc. The American authorities had no other records of this particular Alice LeBlanc; she wrote to them to state that she had been taken to Europe as a baby.

She had spent a month in Switzerland two years previously as a goalie coach. This was when she met the Russian banker. She had opened Swiss bank accounts for Alice with money acquired from her mother's life insurance policy. The existence of this bank account helped establish her new identity.

Hatties's Russian friend now spent most of his time in New York. Before she left for the townships she telephoned him there on a private line. She told that him that she would be transferring large sums later in the week to accounts that she had already set up.

"How large?"

"Ten to twenty million," she said. "I don't know yet for sure."

He laughed. "I know that you are a better accountant than that. I'll draw my own conclusions. Confidentiality will be a priority. I appreciate the business. There is a little island in the Pacific you will never have heard of called Nauru. The inhabitants are rich from bird dropping deposits that they have been selling for years for fertilizer. But it's running out, so they have gone into banking, and we have found them very cooperative. I suggest US treasury bills and short-term Euro paper. I think the US dollar vulnerable.

But we won't speculate too much on exchange rates: just maintain an international portfolio of short-term paper."

Hattie concurred. The transfers from the Bandits accounts would total about $3,000,000 and she would make them from Paris at roughly the same time that the police would be descending on her father's lab at the old mine near Alexandria.

Ever since she was a young girl Hattie had wanted the easy power that belonged to the rich. She wanted money not so much for the material goods it could bring, but for its power – power over people like waiters, hairdressers, sales clerks in shops, real estate agents, lawyers, stockbrokers, bankers, friends and lovers. And money would also give her the power to do good. She was not one to devote her life to doing good for its own sake. She coveted the power implicit in *noblesse oblige*: the power to do something good, perhaps, for animals, for the green earth, for third-world impoverished people.

Three million dollars was not enough. Her father already had a small fortune when she started to take over his affairs and it was growing exponentially. She had worked hard for him, often sacrificing life's pleasures to increase his assets. She knew that she would inherit, but she was impatient. She had no quarrel with her father but she needed to get out from under his wing.

She had a Power of Attorney and that summer had liquidated some of his real estate without his knowledge. Not all of it; he was her father after all. She would leave him roughly half his net worth. He owes me half, she thought.

Late the next morning Hattie left her apartment for the last time driving her VW van. She took very little; it had to look as if she was planning to return. She took Manson with her, along with her laptop computer, her American passport, a bundle of cash, and clothes for a weekend. She picked up a large frozen food locker in Vanier. It was heavy so the attendant helped her load it. She stopped once at a feed store outside the small Ontario town of Hawkesbury, where she picked up two bags of quicklime.

She arrived at Song's cottage about two. He was curious about what had happened. They took the canoe out on the lake where they would not be overheard. She stretched out on the floor of the canoe. Song stopped paddling and turned around to face her,

"I've been working with a hockey team, I told you about the school. Well, it turns out that one of the coaches is a Mountie with the DLEB. He and I have been socializing a bit. He didn't know about my connection to the Bandits. As for me, I just wanted to find out what they had on the Bandits so I asked him to find out if they had anything about my partner in the school, an old friend of my father's, and if they had anything on my father. I never told my father I was doing this, but one of the Bandits found out I was seeing this guy. Now the Bandits have their balls in a bloody knot. The rest you don't have to know about."

"Did you sleep with him?"

"Oh, come on, Song. Just like a man. Did I sleep with him? Here we are, me in real trouble, you and I about to run away together and, I hope, get married, about to go on the adventure of our lives, and you ask, did I sleep with some guy." She was genuinely outraged; she had told Song she was a virgin and he had not believed her! Then she laughed at herself, at the absurdity of her outrage, and said to him gently. "The answer is no, you are my boyfriend, you know that. Listen, today let's try to relax, we'll do our work later. Leave in the morning in my van. Abandon it somewhere and take a taxi to Dorval."

Song was mortified. "I am so sorry. I know you are a virgin."

"Forget it."

"What about my bike?"

"How about we take an extra $15,000 and get you a new one in Vegas?" This is where Song had planned to go first to hide out – it's North America's hideout capital. Something like ten per cent of the population there is hiding out and using false ID. It's where you go if you want to disappear.

That afternoon she persuaded Song to sell all of the Angels' short-term securities, both in Canada and abroad. They kept most of their money in treasury bills. "We won't take it," she said, "but we'll make it clear that we could have, maybe then they'll leave us alone. We'll just take two hundred grand, hope that they consider it severance pay or something, as you said. Today is Tuesday. They won't know you've sold all this stuff until the delivery date. But the cash will be there; we just won't touch it. It's like we're sending them a message that we're letting them off easy."

These transactions required voice confirmation. Some eight different dealers, some in New York, some in Montreal, were involved. They all knew Song; the accounts were with numbered companies. The dealers had no idea who the principals were and didn't care.

"It looks like we're going into real estate," he told them. "Don't ask me. Right now my people want to be in cash. On delivery put the cash in the bank account you have on record."

In the evening they went to the clearing as they usually did and Song grilled a steak over the barbecue. Hattie had a veggie burger. They drank wine. They didn't go out on the lake that night. There was a storm warning.

After dinner she stripped, he performed, and then he lay back supine under the black sky, his head not far from what remained of the fire, and she went down on him. She had never done this before for any man and told him so. As he came he turned his head in ecstasy to the left and she took his little nickel-plated automatic from her bag, brought it up to the base of the back of his head, to the medulla, shot him, and then spat out his semen. He died instantly. He never opened his eyes. She wrapped his head in his shirt to cover the bleeding

Naked, she went over to the well and removed the lid. She picked up his body and dumped it down the well. She scattered embers where there might be blood.

She called Manson to come from his place at the front door, and when the dog came bounding up to her, she kneeled down and shot him too, through the head, speaking to him gently as she pulled the trigger, "I cannot leave you here, dear Manson, good dog, all alone, without me." She carried his body over to the well and gently dropped it down. "Shabby treatment, I know, but to leave you behind would be worse. Brave dog, I will mourn you later."

Hattie got the two bags of lime from the car and poured the contents down the well. She burned the empty bags in the fire, went to the cottage for two buckets of water, and poured them down.

She went to her van and opened the frozen food locker that she had picked up in Vanier. Inside was the frozen headless body of a woman. The body had thawed out sufficiently that she was able to get a set of fingerprints on a glass which she placed on Song's kitchen table with a drop of whiskey inside. She put the body in the canoe. She cleaned the container and put it in Song's cabin. The dead woman had been an illegal Albanian migrant, of roughly her build.

One of the Bandits was running an immigrant smuggling gang. Hattie and her father had provided a safe house on a tree farm Henry owned. The woman had attempted to hang herself in the barn and someone in the gang had called Charley, who told Hattie. They wanted the woman out of there. She had learned that she was to be sold, drugged, as a prostitute. Hattie asked for a detailed description of the woman, and then told Charley to tell the smugglers to leave her hitchhiking on the dirt road that went past the farm at a certain time. The woman was told that Hattie was taking her to the States. Instead Hattie had drugged her and drowned her in a pond. She had cut off the head with an axe. There had been a lot of blood and she saved some in a jar that she placed in a cooler in her van. She then buried the head; the body she put in a frozen food container to await its role in her disappearance.

The frozen food locker building in Ottawa belonged to her father. It was mostly used by a couple of Bandits who had a cattle rustling business. Hattie provided money laundering services for both the cattle rustling and the immigrant racket.

Hattie went back to the van for the jar of blood that she had collected when she murdered the Albanian. DNA can be found in the white cells of blood. She had kept it in her fridge at home and the night before had deliberately spilled a little on her hands, wiped them with Kleenex that she tossed in a wastebasket. Then she washed her hands and took care that when she dried them she slightly stained a white hand towel on the rack by the bathroom sink. She made sure that there was nothing else in the apartment from which her own DNA could be extracted. Nor did she leave any of her own fingerprints anywhere, not in her apartment, nor in Song's cabin, nor in her van. Her finger prints were not on file anywhere. Now she emptied the jar over the chopping block beside Song's woodpile and then turned the block upside down. Right side up the blood might wash away with the rain. The fact that there was not as much blood as might be expected from a decapitation could be explained by rain. Still naked, she carried both of Song's twelve-pound dumbbells to the canoe, and tied one to each of the dead woman's feet using catgut, which would dissolve in the water after three weeks or so. She calculated that when the body thawed it would fill up with gas and break free.

    The night was black and it started to rain heavily. The lake was calm; she was in the eye of a storm. She didn't want to be seen; Hattie always counted on a little bit of luck; risk fed her adrenaline. It was a dark night and no one saw her. The wind was building up. It came in squalls, mostly from the south, to her left and away from the shore. The spare paddle and the life jackets lay on the bottom. About a hundred yards out, she dumped the body and the dumbbells. Then she capsized the canoe, gave it a push towards the far shore, and swam in.

    Hattie dried herself and got dressed. From the cottage she took the two computers, Song's and hers, and an overnight bag of his, packing his toilet kit and a few of his clothes. She took the CD with the bank information and a black plastic garbage bag from the kitchen. She left her own things. She put on Song's helmet and leather jacket with the Angels' colors.

    She got on the bike in the pouring rain. There's a black cloud over Lake Massawippi tonight, that's for sure, she thought. If someone saw me they couldn't swear it wasn't Song. She drove through North Hatley slowly in the pouring rain, gunning the engine in neutral from time to time. She wanted the departure of Song's bike to be remembered. *Ayesha, my queendom come.*

    Alice LeBlanc had a reservation on Air France on the night plane from Dorval to Paris. She put all of Song's things except his laptop and the CD, in the black garbage bag and threw it in a dumpster at the airport. She left the motorcycle in the parking lot. In the washroom she put on a red wig and blue contacts. Sitting in the first class lounge with the laptops and no other luggage, Alice read *Le Figaro.* Thursday she would watch the Angel bank accounts from her hotel room in Paris for cash; Friday it would be gone. Everything is going to be hunky dory, she thought, from now on. Then she thought of Manson and wept.

ALICE

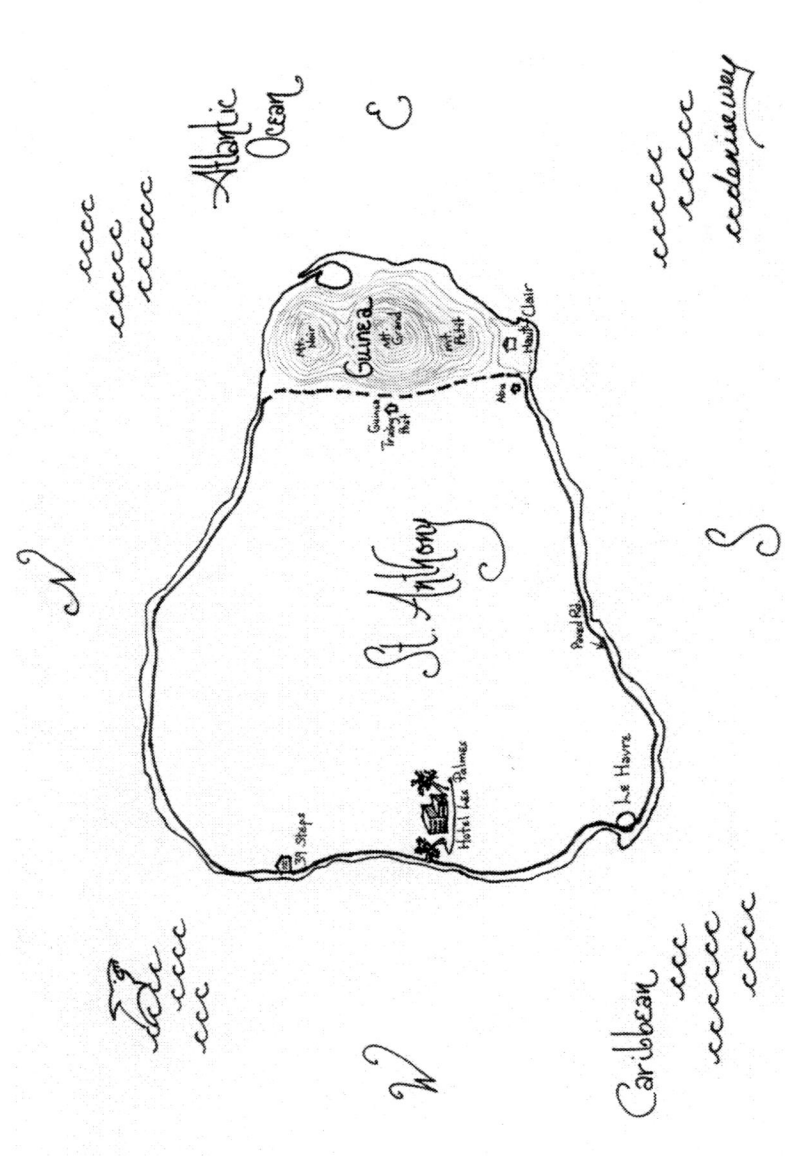

4

The island of St. Anthony has its rugged eastern coast on the Atlantic. On the western side its cliffs look down on the placid Caribbean; sandy beaches are few. Most of the beaches on the Caribbean side are stony, the coral not yet turned to sand so the island, which covers about two hundred and fifty square miles, does not attract many tourists. It had once been a French possession, and passed into British hands during the Napoleonic wars. The northernmost of the Lesser Antilles it is a hundred miles or so north east by east of the tiny island of Sombrero. French planters had grown mostly sugar on the western plain of the island and this remains the principal export crop. The base rock is coral, which is a limestone, and the soil is suitable for large plantations. The eastern fifth of the island is mountainous and barely accessible by land or sea. Slaves would occasionally escape and if they were able to reach the mountains, all attempts to recapture them ended in failure.

Two years after the French Revolution, in 1791, the slaves rose up in Saint Domingue, at that time the richest jewel among French colonial possessions, its trade greater than that of all North America and the Spanish West Indies including Cuba combined. For twelve years the French fought bitterly to put it down, losing sixty thousand soldiers before giving up.

The slaves in St. Antoine, as it was called then, rose up at the same time, apparently by coincidence. Most of the slave population of St. Antoine was born in Africa. The French planters imported thousands of adult slaves every year, this being more economical than waiting for children to grow up. But there were children; there were female slaves and marriage was encouraged in certain circumstances, and in all circumstances after the British outlawed the slave trade in captured colonies in 1804. The slaves came from different tribes, but learned to speak a common language, a variety of Creole. They were united by a secret society known as the

Leopards. It was this society that organized and led the revolt, although they did not begin it.

The French were engaged in a difficult campaign to put down the slave revolt when the British arrived. A French fleet that was in the harbor of Le Havre, the island's main port on the southwest coast, took to sea to fight and was completely destroyed by the British fleet under Admiral Hood in 1798. The British landed a combined force of marines and sailors of the Royal Navy under cover of darkness, and took the fort guarding the harbor from the rear. At dawn the British fleet sailed into the harbor and commenced bombarding the town. The French surrendered the island.

The British, in turn, tried to subdue the revolt, but were forced by the strength of the resistance, their own losses from disease, and strategic problems due to the Napoleonic war, to a negotiated peace. The Leopard Society, under the command of a woman, Zena, a *mambo*, or sorceress, negotiated freedom for her army – including the women and children who were with them – but not for the considerable number of slaves who had not been part of the revolt, or for those who had been captured during it. The almost inaccessible mountainous eastern side of the island, which, except for the southeastern tip, was not considered suitable for large scale planting, was given to the army and their followers, as a reservation by treaty, much as Indian reservations were established in North America. This area covered about fifty square miles of land. They called their land Guinea, and considered it an independent nation, but to the international community it was British territory. When the island received its independence in the twentieth century, Guinea was specified in the constitution as land reserved for the Leopard Society. Its members did not have the vote, but had the right to citizenship if they left the reservation. If they left, the Society would not let them return.

Zena, who was reputed to have the blood of ancient Nubians, became queen. She was chief priestess in the practice of Voudon, made the laws, presided over major disputes, and decided punishments for crimes. She selected one of her daughters as an apprentice. The queen did not marry and this strengthened the matriarchy. She would mate with one of the Leopards from time to time, and when babies were born the father was seldom acknowledged.

When the older woman died, the younger would seamlessly take her place.

Normal monogamy prevailed elsewhere in Guinea. A small band of Arawak Indians had fled to the mountains to escape their cannibal enemies, the Caribs, and had stayed there when the French disposed of the Caribs, to avoid being enslaved. They had welcomed the escaped African slaves and intermarried with them long before the Leopards arrived. These people accepted Zena as their queen and shared their magic and medicine with her.

The Society forbade trade with whites. The people bartered among themselves but were forbidden to trade with the people of St. Antoine, except at a trading post, run by the Society. Zena and the Leopards believed the slave economy was based on a surplus, that the surplus was created by slave labor, and enjoyed by a few rich white men. They thought that if they produced a surplus the whites might come and enslave them again.

The people were also forbidden to trade with foreign ships. There were only two places on the east coast were a ship could land. One was a lagoon where the rim of an ancient volcano rose thirty to forty feet above sea level and the sea had entered through a single narrow gap. The gap was almost invisible from a few hundred yards out because the two edges or points of the rim, which formed the gateway to the entrance, overlapped. A ship could enter if the pilot knew the approach; but the Leopard Society forbade ships to enter the lagoon. There was a second place where a ship could harbor further south.

Coral had invaded the cove or lagoon inside the ancient volcano and the interior was white. White coral reefs inside, teeming with fish, were an hazard to any ship that might enter. The cove was almost round in shape and about a mile in diameter and resembled a Pacific lagoon. There was a white sandy beach along the shoreline. The fishing was excellent. The Guinea people never had to take their boats out on the open sea.

The lagoon would have been attractive to tourists, but the Society did not want tourists. A few years before Alice came to the island, a tourist boat, attempting to enter, had been caught by a huge wave and crashed against the cliff. There were no survivors and no bodies. It was assumed that everyone had been eaten by sharks; a few suspected that some of them had reached shore and met another fate. A rented helicopter from St. Anthony airport investigating the accident had landed in the lagoon. A few bits of wreckage had drifted in but none of the Guinea people had apparently observed the accident.

This led to a political incident. The Leopard Society's official representative in Le Havre, Henri Cantave, a prominent lawyer, called on the prime minister of St. Anthony, now an independent nation and a member of the Commonwealth, and objected to the helicopter landing. The prime minister was told that if it happened again, the helicopter would be destroyed. Cantave explained that the people of Guinea were concerned about tourists coming by helicopter in the future, and also reminded him that the people of Guinea had exclusive fishing rights in the cove by the original treaty. The prime minister assured Cantave that further tourist excursions would not be permitted, the public reason being concern for the safety of the tourists, but that Guinea might have to make an exception for search or rescue missions. If the Leopard Society objected to this, he suggested that it form its own coast guard, knowing full well that it did not have the resources to do this.

The Cantaves were a unique family. They came from that class of mulattos who had been engaged in commerce and the professions in Le Havre since before the British conquest. When the British took over the island, most of the French planters had already left it. Most sold their plantations to British settlers rather than return. They feared another slave rebellion, which they thought would be led by the Leopard Society from its stronghold in the east. This never happened, in part because the British honored their treaty with the Guinea people. The mulatto class, who had always been discriminated against by the French, welcomed the British. The British were glad to have allies on the island and allowed them to prosper. The British settlers who took over the plantations found them useful for business. Speaking Creole and French, they learned English and dominated the professions.

What was unique about the Cantaves was that the head of the family was a member of the Leopard Society. He looked out for the interests of the reservation. The male head of the family would often marry a daughter of the queen of Guinea. Henri's wife, Yvonne, was a younger sister of Saba, the current queen and chief sorceress of Guinea.

Alice LeBlanc, formerly Hattie Brading, met Narcisse Cantave in Paris on her fourth day there. She had chosen Paris because of its size – strangers are seldom noticed in big cities – no one knew her there, and she spoke French.

The plane arrived in the early morning. She had had a long day and slept well in her first class seat. A taxi took her to a commercial hotel in the suburbs. In her room she bleached her hair and dyed it red. Since her gothic teen years, she had always worn jeans, T-shirts and pullovers. To reduce the chances of being recognized she was going to dress with *parisienne* elegance; she could afford to and looked forward to it. She planned to enroll in a modeling school and change her walk and posture. She had to do something about her accent; she had noticed that *les parisiennes* did not warm to it. This did not bother her personally, but she did not want to give away the fact that she was Canadian. She wanted to pass as a provincial or a colonial, perhaps a West Indian.

She finished her electronic money transfers from the Bandits by four o'clock Eastern Standard Time on Friday, the hour the police were due to swoop down on her father and the Bandits at the underground establishment outside Alexandria, Ontario. She took approximately $3,000,000.

This done she slid Song's CD into his laptop and entered the password from Milton. His utility program automatically unlocked the encryption and all the data on the banking CD were available to her.

But the process had some added complications; Song had been cagier than she thought. Fund transfers are subject to elaborate protection mechanisms and each bank required a procedure that was not on the CD. Perhaps Song had kept them in his head. Alice was going to have to do some hacking. Hacking is not necessarily illegal, nor unethical. A hacker is a programmer who is good at solving programming/communication problems that others find difficult. It requires good knowledge of how computers work under the hood; it requires knowledge of registers, communication protocols, timing errors, message queues, and so on. She ordered a thermos of strong French coffee from room service and worked around the clock.

When Alice finally laid her head on the pillow on Saturday evening she had stolen over $20,000,000 in US funds from the Quebec chapter of the Hells Angels Motorcycle Club. She had not slept since the Thursday night flight from Montreal, and she felt that she had earned it. She deposited the whole amount in her friendly Russian's bank within a bank on the remote Pacific island of Nauru. When she had finished, she obtained a Hotmail email address in Song's name, using a Las Vegas hotel address, and sent both the Bandits and the Angels the virus file she had developed with her nerd friends at computer school. Both were attached to an email that read: "Funds have been transferred. Please open attachment for details."

She had not left her room, but had ordered food along with the coffee from room service. On Sunday she used the newspapers to find a large furnished flat in the IVth *arrondissement*. She bought a simple black dress in the hotel boutique and moved in that afternoon, paying three months rent in advance in US dollars. She bought groceries and made herself comfortable. She watched French television and worked on her accent.

Monday morning was a bit tense. The transfers from the Angels accounts would not go through on a weekend, but would be postponed until a business day. So she went shopping. Alice would wear high heels – Hattie had never worn them. So the first stop was a *chaussure*. She took her time and bought four pairs, and then went shopping for underwear, blouses, and a dress.

Walking along the Faubourg Saint Honoré she noticed the Hermés shop on the corner. Hermes was the god of thieves, she remembered, and as probably the biggest thief in Paris right now, I must go in, and so, dazzled by the brilliant silk scarves in the window, she did. *My queendom come.* The young man who served her was Narcisse Cantave, a native of the island of St. Anthony. He was struck by her good looks and found both her nationality and her personality mysterious. She gave an impression of icy self-confidence yet seemed to be playing a role. She was clearly not used to shopping and was a stranger to Paris. She was fluent in French but her accent was odd. And she was a little unsteady on her high heels.

He presented, with successive flourishes, about a dozen scarves that he thought would go with her white skin, blue eyes, and red hair. She was a long time making up her mind. When he gently suggested that she take them all, he was rewarded with a dazzling smile of pure delight, which had two distinct consequences. He perceived that she was not used to having a lot of money, and he fell in love with her.

"You're from the islands," she said as he wrapped the scarves and tucked them into a Hermès shopping bag. "I like the way you speak French, it has a soft musical sound. I find the Parisienne accent a bit pompous."

They chatted a bit about Creole and languages in general. She told him she was American and had learned French at boarding schools in America and Switzerland. She said she wished that she could speak French like him. She was already carrying a number of parcels and Narcisse asked if she would like the scarves delivered.

"If you bring them yourself."

Wondering if she was serious he gave her a long look; the look she returned was inviting. "It would be after six," he said.

Alice gave him her address and turned and left the shop. When she got back to her flat she checked on the bank transactions: they had all gone through without a hitch.

Narcisse Cantave, as the second son of Henri, would not inherit anything. It was the custom among the mulatto families of Le Havre to leave everything to the oldest son. This was something they had picked up from the British to preserve family fortunes. Narcisse was to learn a profession. Although the language of St. Anthony was English, the Cantaves were brought up to speak both French and Creole as well. His father wanted him to be a doctor and he had been studying medicine in Paris at the University of Paris. When Hattie met him he was twenty-five and he was no longer at the medical school. He had quarreled with his family and was studying psychopharmacology at night.

He did not visit St. Anthony often. He felt like a poor relation and found the lavish life style of his actively gay older brother, a lawyer in his father's office, annoying. His mother thought the inheritance practice unfair, and tended to favor her handsome younger son, whom she missed and wanted home. But he could not afford to return until he completed his degree in medicine, which he stubbornly refused to do.

His maternal aunt was Saba, queen of Guinea, and chief *mambo* of Voudon. He and his brother Philippe had spent their childhood summers with his aunt's people in the mountains. Here he had witnessed strange things: people cured of disease while in a trances; people cured of illnesses by potions made of different herbs mixed and cooked with odd things, fishes, toads, spiders, human bones. These medicines often worked and he wanted to know why and how.

Philippe didn't like it in the mountains and stopped going when he was about thirteen. Narcisse continued to spend his summers there right up to the time he went to France. Saba's daughter, Zena, who was being trained to succeed her, was four years younger than Narcisse. He and Zena spent a lot of time together. She had a crush on her cousin Narcisse, but he thought of her as a little girl and never noticed.

Narcisse agreed to his father's plan to study medicine in Paris because he wanted to learn if the magic of his aunt could be explained by modern science. During his third year at the Sorbonne he abandoned the plan to become a doctor and concentrated on studying psychopharmacology. When he told his parents on their annual visit to Paris, neither was pleased for different reasons.

"You are here to study Western medicine," he was told by his father. "And when you have completed your studies, you are to return to Le Havre to practice it."

"You are not initiated," his mother told him in a private conversation. "If you are to learn about these things, it should be from our people. There is more to it than Western science can comprehend with its materialist philosophy. It is mistaken and dangerous to look for explanations of Voudon magic in Western books and laboratories."

His father made it clear that his funds would be cut off if he persisted. They quarreled. After that visit Narcisse continued his studies with no financial help from home. He started working at Hermès and studying science at night. He had fantasies about the rich women he met at the shop; perhaps he could meet one who would support him and his studies. Lovers do not meet for the first time by chance; they are looking for one another.

Alice had suggested that Narcisse make the delivery himself because he was good-looking, she liked him, and she wanted to learn to speak French as he did. She was thinking of keeping a man; she liked the idea of having a lover who was dependent on her for money. And the West Indies was high in her list of places where she might settle down. At the moment she was still a fugitive and Paris was a good place to hide. When the body was found, the Angels and the police would stop looking for her, and she could leave Paris. She wanted to go somewhere exotic.

She felt confident that her father would identify the body as hers; they had been partners in crime for too long not to know each other's minds. On seeing the body Henry would know it was not Hattie's and that Hattie had put it in the lake. He would already know that Hattie was still alive somewhere, that it was Song who was dead. Two days after robbing the Bandits and the Angels, she put $150,000 in one of her father's secret bank accounts. She estimated that his lawyer's fee would be $50,000, and that the payments to the two junior members of the Bandits who had undertaken to take the rap if the lab was discovered were $50,000 each. The neatly calculated amount and the fact that it arrived two days after the Bandits' accounts were cleaned out would let him know for sure that she was still alive.

Henry would have figured out that the money she had stolen from him personally was roughly half of what she could have stolen and that she probably thought this fair. He would identify the body as Hattie's and have the remains promptly and quickly cremated. And he would tell no one, not even Charley. When he learned of the theft from the Angels he would expect her to cut him in. He would expect her to get in touch with him by the time he got out of prison and this she intended to do. She was in the driver's seat now; she had brought her father to heel. He would not be in prison for long. There was not enough evidence to convict him of anything serious and they had a first-class lawyer.

When Narcisse arrived at the apartment with the parcel, she offered him a glass of white wine from a bottle of Pouilly Fuissé chilling in a wine cooler. They talked about the Caribbean and its food. When she told him that she did not eat meat, he offered to cook her a vegetarian West Indian dinner. Then they went shopping together. She paid for everything; he didn't seem to mind.

After dinner they made love. She found him satisfactory, but this didn't stop her from literally kicking him out of bed in the middle of the night. Narcisse was surprised and hurt after giving what he had thought was a good account of himself. But she gave him a kiss at the door; she just had to let him know who was boss, she told him. She didn't see him for a few days.

She spent her time shopping and sightseeing. Late one night she dropped Song's laptop into the Seine. She missed Manson, and was surprised to find that she missed Theodore. When she saw something that delighted her, which happens to people often in Paris, she found that she wanted to share her delight with her horseman, as she had always thought of him. She was lonely.

She breezed into Hermès one morning and invited Narcisse Cantave to lunch. Over the salad, Narcisse declared his love for her. They spoke French; it is a good language for such declarations. There was much about her that he did not understand; she was a woman of mystery to him, he told her. Her refusal to eat meat puzzled him, and even more when she explained it.

"I don't think much of human beings," Alice told him, switching to English. "They have this quaint idea that they are the center of the universe. Science and religion encourage this bizarre notion. I would sooner kill a human than a pig. And eat one, too. Animals have dignity and should be allowed to keep it; human beings have very little. *Après moi.* And there are so many of them, humans, I mean. The population grows like a tumor and is choking the life out of the planet Earth."

"Killing Gaia, are you familiar with James Lovelock's theory that all life on earth is symbiotic?"

"Yes," she said, and thought to herself, but it is more than that, the rocks, the sea, and the air are part of it, and I know her by another name, Ayesha, and it is not just a theory. She is divine but I am not going to discuss that with a scientist.

"And you think not eating meat helps matters?"

Alice poured herself a second glass of wine and warmed to her topic. "Reasons for not eating meat fall into three categories. First: the environmental. It is estimated that it takes 80,000 liters of water to produce a hamburger. You have to take into account the rainfall that is diverted to feed the cattle, the ground water that is pumped up for them to drink in winter, and to wash their stalls. Same with pigs and chickens. Land was cleared to make the fields where previously there was forest. The forest supported a biomass of animals equivalent to the cattle on the fields, but the forest absorbed the carbon dioxide that the animals produced. Now it goes into the atmosphere and contributes to global warming. Then there is the animal waste that runs off the fields and into the streams, where it joins the pig and bird manure from the factory farms. Second, there is the effect on your own health. People who eat meat suffer from heart disease, arthritis, and gout, not to mention developing a tolerance to the antibiotics that they are constantly absorbing with the flesh of the animals. When they need an antibiotic to fight off an infection, it won't be as effective. The animals are overcrowded and stuffed with antibiotics to prevent disease. Third, there is the suffering that the animals themselves endure." These were opinions she had always kept to herself, but she was beginning to think of Narcisse as her personal property, and she felt she could do what she liked with him, even bore him. She looked over at him. "*Après moi*, we lose our own dignity if we don't respect that of the animals. Sorry, I am being a bore."

"No, not at all, my dear, I think you have me convinced. I shall have another salad for my entrée and think over what you have told me. But what good will it do if I, little *moi*, give up meat? I am just one person."

"I don't know what ethic guides your life, but I find Kant's Categorical Imperative useful. 'Act only according to that maxim whereby you can at the same time will that it should become a universal law.'"

Alice had drunk a couple of glasses of white wine rather quickly and was on her third. She was happy. Here she was in Paris, rich and free. And she had found a companion she liked. She was revealing more of her private thoughts to her new lover than she ever had to anyone. "Things we used to think of as evil are now virtues. Suicide, for example; those who have the slightest interest in doing away with their lives, should be encouraged, even assisted. Personally, I despise suicidal people; I stand ready to assist them. War has always been an effective way of dealing with excess human population. Wars should be fought and people killed. Ideally, and perhaps I am an idealist, both sides should lose roughly the same number of people. The way the Americans fight – from the air with few casualties – I would say, aside from being cowardly, is not what war is about. From the point of view of the biosphere.'

She looked at him, eyebrows raised, a half smile on her open lips, as if saying, surely you can see that. Then fell into deep thought. After a moment she said, "What were once considered sexual vices are today virtues. Buggery for example – not that, I – by the way," she looked over at him. "Because it does not result in childbirth. Nor does homosexuality, nor masturbation. The Jews in the Bible preached propagation and forbade these things, and the Christians took this up. But with the human population exploding – they are now virtues."

Narcisse nodded. "I assume, dear Alice, that you are pro-choice."

"Of course. There are many people wandering around today that should have been aborted." Her eyes fixed on another table behind Narcisse. He turned and saw a fat couple attacking plates of *longe de porc à la julienne.* He looked back at her and smiled.

"And then there is the stupidity of making infanticide a crime. If a parent cannot provide for a child, he or she should have the right to take its life. Unwanted children grow up unloved and often turn psychopathic, whatever that word means." She was thoughtful for a moment. "And today – après moi – murder is a virtuous act: kill your enemies. And anyone who gets in your way is your enemy. Killing has always been human nature. History is about killing, as is most of Shakespeare, most of our drama, our films, our novels."

She stopped. I am talking too much, she realized. She looked over at Narcisse. He seemed more fascinated than shocked.

"But you – Alice – you wouldn't kill anyone?"

"I was just trying to shock you. No, Alice LeBlanc never killed anyone, not Alice, she has no enemies. It's just that today we need an ethic that legitimizes reducing the human population. Killing one's enemies, for example, or even just people who get in your way. We are the killer ape after all – it is our nature, not to kill is to betray our nature and to betray our planet – for if we don't control our population, who will?"

"How do you feel about suicide bombing?"

"Suicide bombers are almost always people who have been dispossessed by an enemy. It's an act of vengeance and would be okay with me – but it's – it's inelegant, I can't accept it. I suppose I am too – too – fastidious perhaps. Besides I can't square it with Kant. Killing specific individuals, I can." She gave him a dazzling smile. "That works for me."

"I am not at all sure that Kant would agree."

"Oh, he would have to, I think, by the laws of reason on which he bases his ethics. But I don't really wish to discuss Kant anymore. I have been a bore long enough. Not today anyway. It's too nice a day." When she switched to English she had gone to into her pure Katherine Hepburn act, a role she had used to misdirect people all her life. This time, for a change, she was playing the role to tell what she believed to be the truth. Narcisse, who rarely saw her in any other role, was pleased that she was speaking English, and revealing herself. It was a sign to him that she thought of him as a lover rather than as a teacher. She was silent for a moment, pensive. "I am in love with this green earth. I am going to leave Paris soon and go somewhere where everything is green."

"My island is green. And I will take you there, one day. But Alice, to go back a bit, you don't really mean that you would eat human flesh?"

Alice thought for a moment before answering. "No, dear boy, I didn't mean that. I meant that to eat a ham is as repellent to me as eating a human thigh. In a number of ancient cultures a man was expected to eat the flesh of his father on his death. So that the father lived on in the son. It was a sacred thing. To these people, burying the body of one's father or mother in the ground was repugnant and disrespectful."

"Where did you get such a notion?"

"It's in Herodotus." She smiled at him. "Don't look at me like that. As a girl, quite a young girl, in fact, I was fond of the dustier sections of libraries."

Narcisse found that he had lost his appetite and was toying with his salad. "On our island there are a people who are rumored to have been cannibals, a long time ago, but not so long ago as Herodotus. But I don't think their reasons were ritualistic. I know that in circumstances of starvation perfectly normal human beings have resorted to cannibalism. I can't imagine eating a human for sacred purposes."

Alice looked at him for a moment. "Are you a Christian, Narcisse?"

"Brought up a good Roman Catholic with a liberal lacing of Voudon."

"Then you remember the Last Supper? Take, eat, this is my body, drink, this is my blood, et cetera?"

"No, no, Alice, you go too far."

"They thought, they hoped, they could ingest his wisdom. Did you ever take communion?"

"Alice, where did you get this idea?"

"In the dustier parts of the library. I would go there to masturbate. There were interesting illustrations in the old Victorian novels. The idea about the body of Jesus being eaten, I got that from a Welsh writer named George Borrow. It's a very old idea, two thousand years old, less, oh, how old was Jesus when he was crucified? Thirty?" She ordered coffee. "Maybe you can't stand my conversation, but you like me in bed. Tell me, do you really enjoy working at Hermès? There must have been another reason for coming to Paris."

He described his situation candidly. His father had cut him off and he wanted to take up the study of psychopharmacology full time. He wanted to leave his job at Hermès and didn't have the money to do so.

"I would be proud to assist a man on such a mission," she said. "That would be something to do with drugs?"

"It's a specialty. Drugs that affect mental states," he replied. He told her about his mother's side of the family and the powers of the Voudon religion.

"I have always been interested in drugs that affect mental states, as was my father before me. It can be profitable and I think you should continue your studies." Then she thought she had better change the subject. "I would love to go to the races. Isn't there a famous race track near Paris? Longchamp or something?"

"Indeed, I used to go."

"Do you drive?"

"Oh, yes, I had a little Peugeot before Papa cut me off."

"I would like to have a chauffeur and just tell him, Narcisse, to the races, take me to the races."

"How about a black chauffeur?"

"For a black chauffeur, I think a red car, or burgundy. But you're not really black, Narcisse, you're more the color of brown sugar."

"Here they call me a *noir* but there is cream in my coffee, as they used to say in the good old USA. I don't think the expression is politically correct nowadays. Our family is mulatto. On St. Anthony, there are three categories of people classified by color: white, black, and, as you put it, brown sugar. And of the three on St. Anthony, it is best to be mulatto. We control government, dominate the professions, and most of the small businesses. We do not subscribe to this American notion that there are only whites and blacks. It's more of a cultural than a racial thing anyway. As in the US. There are three cultures on our island, no four, maybe five." He was thoughtful for a moment.

"I want to go to St. Anthony. If it is green you say."

"All year round. And I would love to take you. But, right now, Alice, I must get back to work."

"Why don't you quit your job when you get back to the shop? Tell them you have found a sugar mummy. Then we'll buy a car, I will hire you as my chauffeur, and you can pursue your studies. I won't be very demanding except in bed. How much do you earn? I'll double it."

When he told her she offered him double what he was making and he accepted. Alice paid the bill for lunch, the first of many. She never got around to buying the car. That afternoon they took a taxi to Longchamp.

———∞∞———

On the south side of the island of St. Anthony, within the boundary of the reservation of Guinea, there was a fertile plateau of about eight square miles, cut off from the western plains by a steep cliff and from the rest of Guinea by the steep sides of Mont Petit. A good part of the plateau had once been a coffee plantation. A small band of people lived a subsistence life there. They were so cut off from everybody else on the island that no one gave them a thought.

They were descended from the old coffee plantation slaves and Carib Indians. In the eyes of the British and, later, the independent government of St. Anthony, they were Guinea people. The Leopard Society did not think so and ignored them. Ethnically they were quite different; they spoke an African language, Abu and they were rumored to be cannibals. An English missionary had gone to live with them in the nineteenth century, and letters to the Anglican bishop in Le Havre indicated he had stayed there at least five years, and then nothing more was heard from him. The Abu had denied any knowledge of him to an inquiring young cleric. An American couple, anthropologists, who had gone to live with them in the 1920s had simply disappeared, reportedly drowned.

The original French owner – he had owned the whole plateau – had his slaves cut steps in the rock face on the east coast to provide access to the sea. There was a cove there, about eighteen miles south of the lagoon, sheltered from the ocean, and a beach where they kept dugout canoes for fishing in the open sea.

The planter's name was Gilbert Dusseault. He had made his fortune in the slave trade. With a labor force of three to four hundred Abu slaves he brought with him from Africa, he cleared a good part of the plateau and planted coffee beans. He and his overseers were cruel to the mostly male Abu. A few Carib women worked in the house and lived in a separate building. These he used as concubines from time to time. It seemed he was infertile for he had no children by them, nor did he have any children by his beautiful Russian wife, Aloyshovna.

The Abu came from the southern part of the Slave Coast in West Africa. Dusseault worked them hard, often to death, causing him to go frequently to the slave auctions in Le Havre. He only bought Abus, believing them to be good workers. And aside from a propensity to suicide, they were. He also enslaved the Carib Indians whom he found living on the plateau. He appointed certain Caribs as overseers; they ate better than the others and had access to the maids' quarters from time to time. Once the Caribs were trained, he dismissed his original white overseers and he and Aloyshovna were the only white people on the plantation. The Abu, not being given any meat by their owner acquired a fondness for human flesh from the Caribs. This taste was satisfied occasionally – with the help of the overseers – by a slave from the plain below. Sometimes an overseer would lead an expedition by sea to the other side of Mont Petit and they would kidnap someone in Guinea. If Dusseault knew what was going on, he did nothing about it.

The coffee plantation prospered. On the edge of Mont Petit, high enough to overlook the sea and facing south, Dusseault built a great house, almost a palace, which he named Château Haut-Clair. From then on the whole plateau was known as Haut-Clair. He and Aloyshovna entertained a lot. The governor, other officials from Le Havre, visitors from France, and the owners of other plantations were invited to stay for a few days at a time. There were some thirty bedrooms. He had imported some African animals and pheasants from England, which they shot for game. The entertainments provided by the slaves were extravagant, featuring gladiatorial combat and, it was rumored, sexual displays involving wild animals.

Aloyshovna was not happy. She was kind to the slaves and interceded often on their behalf. At the time of the uprising she was killed, not by the Abu, but by her husband.

The Abu believed her to be someone unique, a *mambo* blanche, a white sorceress. Nor did they believe she was dead. Some in St. Anthony said that she rose from her grave and led them in revolt. Others doubted that she had ever had a grave. The slave rebellion on the island of St. Anthony began at Haut-Clair. It was bloody; Dusseault and the overseers had guns and many Abu ran right into the bullets believing their white queen would protect them. In the end they overwhelmed their oppressors. Gilbert Dusseault's body was nailed as if crucified to the front door. The overseers were eaten. The news of their success spread across the island and the Leopard Society commenced its own long-awaited rebellion.

When the British made their treaty with the Leopards they did not even know that Haut-Clair existed. It was made part of the reservation through clerical and cartographic errors. When they did hear about the place, they sent a small survey party under an army lieutenant to investigate. The lieutenant returned alone with a tale of cannibalism of such horror that no one dared go near the place again. The British were glad the property was on the reservation and not, strictly speaking, in St. Anthony, according to the map.

They realized that sending the expedition in the first place had broken their treaty with the Leopard Society. Haut-Clair was not their responsibility. Everyone pretended that the place did not exist and it went back to wilderness.

A small number of the Abu had survived and interbred with the Caribs. They kept to themselves and spoke their own language. The Leopard Society forbade the Guinea people to cross Mont Petit to the south. The Arawak in their blood and their culture still hated and feared the Carib in the Abu blood and culture. From time to time the Abu traded small quantities of coffee with a poor, white, goat-farming family who lived at the bottom of the western cliff. This family prospered as a result and anxious to keep the trade to themselves spread stories about Haut-Clair to frighten others away. Aloyshovna's ghost walked the house at night, they said, wailing and screaming in Russian. There were man-eating lions on the plateau, they said, and the Abu were cannibals. For two hundred years the situation didn't change.

No heir ever claimed the Haut-Clair plantation. Dusseault was extravagant and at the time of his death was in debt to the merchants of Le Havre. A French banker in Le Havre held a mortgage on the property. He had left St. Antoine at the time of the rebellion, selling the mortgage to a mulatto connected to the Leopards, Henri-Robert Cantave. In the nineteenth century, Narcisse Cantave's great-grandfather had consolidated the debts, buying them up, paying some five cents on the dollar. The Cantaves obtained the title to Haut-Clair in the law courts of St. Anthony. Their motive was to protect the Guinea people from an outsider taking over Haut-Clair. The head of the Cantave family was the only member of the Leopard Society permitted to own property.

But the Cantaves were not permitted to run the plantation for profit nor had they any intention of doing so since any trade beyond barter was forbidden. In the eyes of the Leopards the mulatto population of St. Anthony were no better than white people; the Cantave family was an exception, being related to the Guineans by blood. Under their preemptive ownership, Haut-Clair remained as before, the great house falling down, and the Abu squatting in what was now jungle. The Cantaves were not interested in Haut-Clair and never visited it.

In the mid-nineteenth century, a steady stream of gold coins and other kinds of treasure began to arrive in Paris, brought there annually by the Cantaves on behalf of the Leopard Society.

"They found the treasure you see, the pirates' treasure," explained the old Frenchman Alphonse Latulippe, a friend and business associate of his father's, to Narcisse Cantave one night at dinner a few months before he met Alice. He and his wife, Marie, would have Narcisse to dinner several times a year.

"Your great-grandfather turned up one day at my grandfather's bank with gold coins and jewels. Not a fortune. But the whole cache must indeed have been a fortune. The Leopards would send some every year, always brought by a Cantave. We turn it into bank notes and it's used to buy mostly bales of silk. Pure silk, good stuff. And steel needles and silk thread. Oh, and knives and tools. Every year for over a hundred years, a shipment has arrived in Le Havre and is sent straight to the trading post, marked paid. There is no duty, of course, on goods going directly to Guinea."

"I always marveled at their clothes. Both men and women wore silk: shirts, blouses, sashes, dresses, and pajamas, all in such brilliant colors. I knew they made their clothes themselves, but I never knew how they paid for the silk."

"It is a secret."

"So the old stories of pirate treasure were true. But why are you telling me this now?"

Latulippe did not reply to this question right away. "You probably know this story but I will tell it anyway. It seems that in the sixteenth century, a pirate ship about to be dashed to pieces against the cliff, found itself suddenly at the entrance to the lagoon, managed to go about, and sailed into a safe haven. For about a hundred years they used it as a base, and then were gone, as suddenly as they had arrived. Captured by the British, I suppose, and hung. All this was rumored. It was never proven that pirates had made a base there. But the discovery of the treasure, which is a secret, shared only by the Leopards, of which your father is a member, and my family, proved it. Before the reservation was established there were reports that fishing boats from Le Havre found the remains of the pirate settlement, and a graveyard, mostly dug up, the bones, it was rumored, used in African potions. Perhaps the escaped slaves finished them off. No one knows.

"I am telling you all this now at your father's request. He and Philippe think you are something of a playboy. That this interest in – what is it called?"

"Psychopharmacology. Good lord, if there is a playboy in the family it is my brother, Philippe."

"Ah, but Philippe follows the profession his father chose for him, play he may in his spare time, but Henri tells me he does his work conscientiously. But in your case, in their eyes this interest in psychopharmacology is an excuse not to settle down and become a doctor. I tell them in vain that your interest is serious, that you are a scholar. Also I tell them that I think you would have a good head for business, if given an opportunity."

"It's not just that they think my interest is frivolous, they do not approve of the field that I have chosen – my father and Philippe do not approve of my studies."

"Nor does Yvonne. For different reasons. Nor do I really, but perhaps you could continue them on the island."

"There I agree. It is absolutely necessary that I continue them on the island. But how? I would need a laboratory. I have no money."

"There might be a way. Your father is going to leave Haut-Clair to you in his will."

Narcisse was silent for a minute. "Interesting. But what could I possibly do with it? It is useless to the family because of the prohibition against commerce."

"The situation has changed – the treasure has run out. Having got used to an annual revenue, there is some dissatisfaction among the people. Particularly among the women. They want their silk. The Leopards are considering making an exception to the rule of no commercial production in the case of Haut-Clair. Their own people would not be involved. They are interested only in a royalty in the form of a tax. After all, there is no need for slave labor today; the plantation could be mechanized.

"Because of the connections you have on your mother's side, they might permit you to put Haut-Clair back into coffee. There are squatters there, your father tells me, known as the Abu, who harvest coffee from wild trees there. Some of it makes its way to Le Havre.

"The whole property is about 2000 hectares or eight square miles. I am told that most of it is arable. Even with half of it in coffee trees – 1000 hectares – you would be a wealthy man. You would be able to continue with your studies on the reservation once it was set up. You would need a good agronomist to run the place. The Leopard Society will take some of the revenue, this has to be negotiated, but the government of St. Anthony cannot tax you under the original treaty. Your brother Philippe has looked into it."

"But this would take capital. And how could I raise capital? The situation is so unclear. And there's something else – you say there are squatters who trade in coffee. I have heard of them, savages, everyone says. But surely they have rights. Can the Leopards speak for them?"

"All you need is an agreement with the Leopards. The squatters there, the Abu, they have no rights, according to Philippe. You might employ them. They know something about harvesting coffee beans after all. When you have your agreement with the Leopards – and that will take diplomacy but you will have your father and Philippe to help you – you will find that whereas they would not work for you themselves, they have would have no objection to your exploiting the Abu. They don't like the Abu. As for capital, I think it might be raised here in Paris. I cannot promise anything, but the bank will help you. A lot depends on you making a good presentation to investors I can introduce you to. By the way, your father is not well. You have heard?"

"No. That is news. No one told me."

"I think it is one of the reasons he wants to settle Haut-Clair on you. He thinks he has not long to live and he wants to provide for you. He has had a heart attack. He seems to be alright and is resting at home."

Alice enjoyed having a kept man. It seemed to her a better arrangement than marriage; she didn't like to be equal partners with anyone. She had managed to break free from a dependency on her father. In her relationship with Narcisse Cantave, she was not domineering; it just felt good to have the power over him that her money gave her.

As for Narcisse, he also enjoyed the relationship. He was attentive in little matters; his mother had brought him up to be courteous. He kept his independence and his flat and went back to his studies as a full-time student. She never bought a car and the chauffering job never came about. They took taxis everywhere. He was earning his pay by tutoring her in the Creole patois of St. Anthony. A Creole lilt to her French would help her lose her Canadian accent; he suggested that the best way to acquire the accent was to learn Creole. Language lessons need a topic, and they often focus on the customs, history, and geography of the country whose language is being studied. So Alice learned a lot about St. Anthony.

Narcisse knew that Alice was rich; perhaps she could be persuaded to invest in the plantation. That would save him making presentations to Parisian financiers – he was not at all confident that he could do this well. So he did his best to make St. Anthony sound like paradise to Alice. Furthermore she was experienced in business, in accounting, with computers, and had managed farms, or so she said. This gradually came out in conversation. Maybe she would invest in the plantation and run it as well. She did not seem to intend to stay in France. That's why she didn't buy a car or a flat, she told him. She appeared to be waiting for something to happen.

As indeed she was. She bought the Montreal newspapers every day and one day in November it was there. BODY OF HEADLESS WOMAN FOUND IN LAKE announced a headline. This was a relief. It was two months since she had sunk the body; she concluded that catgut took longer to rot in very cold water. And two days later, the papers informed her that a positive identification had been made by the father of Hattie Braden. This was also a relief; everything was going according to plan.

Not long after this Narcisse received news that his father had suffered another heart attack; he might die. Despite their recent differences Narcisse loved his father and wanted to make peace with him. He also wanted to hear from his father's own lips why he was leaving him Haut-Clair. When he told Alice he was flying home, she asked if she might come along. "I don't think this would be a good time to meet your family," she said, relieving Narcisse from saying it. "But I'd like to take a good look at the island. Perhaps rent a house."

"And a car."

"Yes, of course, a car," she laughed. "You would have time to chauffeur me about a bit? Not every day, but I would like to see you once in a while. And see all over the island? I don't suppose we could visit Guinea?"

They were just finishing dinner in Narcisse's flat. It was time to drop the hook. "Well, there is one place we might go," he said slowly. "An old plantation, deserted for almost two hundred years. It actually belongs to my family now. And I have only just learned, a few months ago, that my father is planning to leave it to me."

"But have you seen his will?" asked Hattie, rather too quickly. She is interested, he thought, I believe I have caught myself a fish, a large and beautiful fish. He told her the story of the plantation, everything that he knew about it, and the potential deal with the Leopards. He did this in an offhand rather skeptical way.

"The problem is, it will require a lot of capital," he said. She didn't reply.

But when they took their seats on the plane, Alice traveling with all her material goods – she was not planning to return to

Paris – he found that she had brought along a little book entitled *The Cultivation of Coffee* published by the ARC-Institute for Tropical and Subtropical Crops. She opened it and began to read before the plane took off.

"Just in case you decide to put the whole place in psychopharmacological crops," she said. "Not that I am counting any of your coffee beans before they get planted. Just curiosity, that's all. You might need some capital if you do get the place and, in case, just in case, you ask me to invest, I would like to know something about coffee. I managed my stepfather's vineyards before I sold them, you know." She looked at Narcisse directly.

"Did you? You never told me that. But you're quite right, coffee is a psychopharmacological crop," he replied. Then suddenly, he exclaimed, "Your eyes, they're green!"

"The blue were contact lenses. Purely cosmetic. And my hair, you know is black." She took off the Hermès scarf she was wearing and the long black tresses fell onto her shoulders.

Narcisse looked at her for a full minute. "You know," he said, "had I known that, I would have picked out a completely different selection of scarves."

Alice went back to her book. Half an hour later she said, "Coffee trees take a long time to come to maturity, you know. You don't get a full crop until around the sixth year. I wonder what Dusseault grew in the meantime."

"He continued his slaving, I expect."

Hattie had another book with her that she did not bring out. It was written in Spanish and published in Peru. It was titled *La Cuidar y Cultivada de Coca Planta*, which translates as "The Care and Cultivation of the Coca Plant."

5

Paul Cantave, sitting in his old Morris, was in line to take the next passenger at the Le Havre airport when he saw his cousin Narcisse emerge from the airport with a strikingly beautiful white woman. She was wearing a cashmere suit and a white silk ruffled blouse and was evidently a Parisienne. He was about to move up when the uniformed dispatcher signaled him to stop and the Cantave black Cadillac pulled up in front of him. He watched Narcisse kiss the woman, say a word to the dispatcher, and get in as she stood back. He was signaled to come up.

"Les Palmes," said the dispatcher leaning into the window, and opening the rear door. Narcisse's companion got in. Narcisse had recommended Les Palmes as the best hotel on the island, and it was a good ten miles north of Le Havre. Alice felt that it was important to distance herself from the Cantaves.

It was a late afternoon in early December. The threat of hurricanes had past but it was still the rainy season. The relative humidity was nearly one hundred per cent, and the temperature ninety degrees Fahrenheit. The sugar cane was growing tall on both sides of the narrow dirt road that crossed the island toward the northwest coast and Les Palmes. The land was flat, the sky gray and drizzling. It is not paradise, thought Alice, it's rather depressing in fact. Alice took a map of the island out of her briefcase and oriented herself.

They were driving on the left hand side of the road. The taxi had to slow down behind donkey carts from time to time. She enjoyed the wild acceleration as Paul geared down to pass, the Morris brushing the sugar cane as the right wheels cut close to the ditch, mud flying, and a sharp curve of the road looming ahead. After one such incident she laughed aloud. He turned around and laughed with her, looking straight at her and not at the road for a long moment.

"You like my driving, madame? My name is Paul and I do tours of the island." His accent was more American than West Indian but he gave the word madame a French pronounciation.

"Very much. You have a certain *panache, comme nous disons en français.*"

"Panache!" he laughed. "But we don't speak French here, madame, not anymore. Not for two hundred years. They still teach it in the schools. In the mountains, in the Guinea reservation they speak Creole. Panache! That is the first time my driving has been described as having panache." He laughed. Yet he pronounced madame and panache with a good French accent. "But you're not French?"

"No, American." Alice was studying her map. "They don't let tourists into Guinea, eh? Suppose I wanted to see it. Is there a way of getting permission? Would you drive me?"

He turned around and looked at her seriously, demonstrating an alarming skill at steering the Morris with one finger while not looking at the road. "No, they don't want tourists. They are kind of down on Western civilization, generally, to tell you the truth. It's third world and they want to keep it that way. There are no roads. You see, St. Anthony is really two islands fused together, one was made by volcano, suddenly, and the other by coral, slowly, rising not from the ocean floor but from the side of the volcano. Live coral builds on the skeletons of those who had lived below. For a long time there was sea between the two. Then the coral slowly filled the gap. But it never rose as high as the volcano. So there is a steep cliff the length of the island, from the south coast to the north.

"Above it, in the mountains, live the Guinea people. They don't mix with us. There is a government school near the trading post where the children can go if they want, but for the most part their parents won't let them. There is one place where the cliff can be climbed and the trading post is there. Some go to the school and then leave the reservation. If they do that Queen Saba won't let them back in."

"I heard that there was a plantation there in the days of the French, a long time ago. There must have been a road."

Paul was silent for a minute. "That's in the south, cut off from the rest of Guinea by a mountain, Mont Petit, and cut off from the plain by the cliff. He had lots of slaves, that old planter. He cut steps into the cliff, I think. Don't know really, never been there. No one goes there. I don't think there was ever a road. His beasts of burden were two-legged. It is all grown over now. But you wouldn't want to go there, even if there was a way."

"Why not?"

"Nothing to see there, it's jungle. There are some squatters who aren't very friendly. And the old wreck of a plantation house is supposed to be haunted: 'woman wailing for her demon lover.' There's rumors of hyenas, even lions, and stories that the Abu, the squatters, are cannibals. Just stories, but the people in St. Anthony believe them," he laughed. "True or false, you can't get there by car."

"If you're trying to make it sound unappealing, you're not doing a very good job."

"Well, if you decide to do a tour of the island tomorrow, we might try to get in on foot, but it would be quite a climb. Wear a good pair of boots, if you have such things."

He thinks I am a Parisienne flibbertigibbet, Alice thought, just the impression I want to make, but I'm not sure I like it. They turned north onto a paved road. Suddenly the sun came out, there were palm trees, and on the left white sandy beaches. They drove for about a mile in silence. There were elegant villas in between villages with wooden houses, and booths dispensing drinks to laughing people in brightly colored clothes. Hattie was suddenly happy. This was more like it.

Les Palmas, a three storied building in the French Planter West Indies style, with deep verandahs extending the across its front on the two upper floors, appeared on the right. There was a broad white beach on the left, and in splendid glory the sun was preparing to set over a green sea. Paul pulled the Morris into a wide portico. An old white-coated man opened her door, and a lad was already unloading her luggage when Alice stepped out.

She paid Paul in American dollars the sum they had told her to pay at the airport, and gave him a good tip. He gave her his card.

"Welcome to St. Anthony, madame. I will drive you anytime anywhere." He watched her give a slight start when she saw the name Cantave. "I saw Narcisse with you at the airport. He's my cousin. His father, my uncle Henri, is in hospital. I suppose that's why he's here. He didn't notice me. He had eyes only for you. He looked at you like he used to look at a bowl of ice cream when he was a boy. By the way, need anything, something to smoke, anything, anytime, give me a call." He got back in the Morris, and drove off with a wave.

Interesting guy, thought Alice, he has already figured out that I'm no lady. Beautiful girl, Paul thought, that Narcisse has found himself as he drove back to the airport, but there is something mysterious about her.

Les Palmes was an old hotel. It was difficult to tell how old from the outside; coral buildings soon acquire a gray patina that gives them an ancient appearance. The interior reminded Alice of Paris. The carpets and upholstery were worn, even shabby, but everything was elegant and French. There was no elevator. The boy carried her bags upstairs. She had a bedroom and a sitting room on the second floor looking west over the ocean. The sitting room had a door opening onto the long veranda that ran the length of the building. She tipped the boy and asked him to bring her a rum punch. She sat outside sipping it, watching the sun set. Just as it went down there was a little bright green flash on the horizon and then the phone rang.

"Did you see the little green flash?" Narcisse asked.

"I was just looking at it."

"I thought you'd be watching the sunset. It happens every night when it's clear. I knew your room was on the beach side, so...."

"How's your father?"

"He's not good, but it looks like he will survive. He's still in hospital. He thinks he's not going to make it, but the doctors think he will. They don't want to move him and they are bringing in a surgeon from Texas to perform a bypass operation. He thanked me for coming. He was tired. He told me to come back tomorrow. There's something he wants to talk to me about. Haut-Clair, I suppose."

"I suppose." Alice was thinking, I might have to hasten him on his way. Perhaps I can trap one of those hyenas and release it in his room. Smiling at the thought, she said, "Met a cousin of yours, Paul. He was my driver. Said you look at me like you used to look at a bowl of ice cream."

"Paul? I haven't seen him since we were kids. I didn't notice him. Well, there are no secrets on this island, not for long. But Paul's okay, he used to look out for me at school when I was a little kid. His dad is a doctor, but a drunk or something. So Paul's driving a taxi now."

"He's a cheerful fellow. I liked him. He wants to take me on a tour of the island. But you are going to do that."

"I'll have to tell my mother about you. Right now I'm phoning you from the pantry. Wait until I do, she'll have you to tea or something. Not tomorrow, I better spend the day with her. I'll tell her tomorrow and she'll probably ask you the next day. Meantime, yeah, tour the island with Paul. Give him my regards, tell him I'm sorry I didn't see him. Too busy looking at the ice cream. Don't let him have any licks, save it for me."

She hung up. Suffering a bit from jet lag, she decided on an early dinner. Tomorrow early, she would go for a swim and then tour the island.

The moment she woke up, Alice put on a bathing suit and went straight to the beach. For about half an hour she floated in the Caribbean. It was the first time she had been in the sea and the extra buoyancy of the salt water was a surprise to her. Then she ate a slice of mango and a brioche in the elegant oval dining room.

After breakfast, she called Paul. "Narcisse said to say hello. He thinks it a good idea you give me a tour of the island. He's tied up with the family."

"Okay. How about I get a Land Rover? I can borrow one. It'll cost a bit more, but maybe we can get closer to Haut-Clair. Still want to go? Got boots?"

"I've got running shoes. Yes, if it won't take too long. I want to see the whole island, or is that too much for one day?"

"Depends on how much time we spend at Haut-Clair. I'll get the Land Rover. We'll see how close we can get, anyway. I suggest that you get the hotel to make up a picnic lunch. For two, if that's okay. They do good picnics at Les Palmes."

It was a sunny day. Paul picked her up at eight-thirty in a Land Rover as promised. The roof was down and Alice had him put it up. She told him she didn't want to get a sunburn, but she really wanted to avoid drawing attention to herself. St. Anthony was a small community. She knew she could become the object of gossip; the Cantave family were well known on the island. And although Hattie Brading was officially dead, there was always the possibility of meeting a tourist from Ottawa on the island who knew her. She was not going to take unnecessary chances, but she was damned if she was going to have red hair and blue eyes for the rest of her life.

Alice got in beside Paul. "Do you mind? This way you might have your eyes on the road once in a while."

"Can I still steer with one finger?"

"If you prefer your passenger white-knuckled."

Paul laughed and they drove north, then gradually northeast, and then east, following the coast. They went inland at one point to tour an old sugar mill with a windmill that was no longer used; it had been supplanted by a diesel engine. Paul noticed that Alice asked a lot of business questions: the price of gas to run the turbines and other machinery, the duty on farm machinery, the cost of labor, and so on.

She could see Mont Noir long before they came to it. As they got close its cliff towered over the plain. She had her map out and looked at it. "There were three volcanoes, eh? So you know something about geography, Paul?"

"I took some geography at college in the States, madame."

"What you said before about St. Anthony being two islands grown together, it's visible now. By the way, please call me Alice. So where were you at school?"

"I was at Boston College for three years, Alice, but had to withdraw. Dad lost his money. I had a student visa. Know what I did? I joined the United States Navy. The fact that I was a British subject from a Caribbean island was not a problem. I learned to fly a helicopter. At Boston College I studied science; it was a pre-med course. Both me and Narcisse were supposed to be doctors."

"Narcisse chose not to be a doctor, while you had no choice."

"I don't know that I was cut out for it. I'm like my dad, too fond of a good time. To get back to the volcanoes, usually when lava breaks through the earth's crust, it does so at one point and you have one huge volcano, as in Grenada, erupting from time to time. Here we had four, all at different times, thousands of years apart."

"I see only three mountains, oh, that lagoon on the east coast that's open to the sea, that was a volcano."

"That's the oldest. The next oldest, Mont Petit, is the one in the south where the island narrows. Mont Grand and Mont Petit are really one mountain, with two peaks. You see the elevated plain just south of it, that's Haut-Clair, but I don't think they call it that on the map, we'll get as close as we can to it this afternoon if you like. It belongs to the Cantaves, perhaps you know that." Perhaps that's the reason for her interest, he thought, glancing at her.

"Guinea is a reservation," Paul continued, "as in where you folks in North America stuck your Indians. The African slaves that ran away joined the Arawak Indians up there, what was left of them, who had ran away first."

"That's interesting. The French enslaved them first?"

"No. The Caribs enslaved them, the ones they didn't eat. The Caribs were cannibals. The Arawak ran away from the Caribs who landed on the west coast and took the island over. Before the white man or the black man arrived."

"What happened to the Caribs?"

"The French tried to enslave them, but that didn't work for reasons that aren't clear. I think maybe they were –uh – intractable. Didn't take to slavery. Perhaps there were simply not enough of them. And they were susceptible to European diseases. I don't think any pure Caribs survive. Then the French were offered African slaves by Portuguese traders. But Dusseault, he took the Caribs off the hands of the rest of the planters. About that time the slave trade was drying up. The British put a stop to it. It's one of the reasons, our people, the mulattos, equivalent to what you call métis in Canada, liked the British."

I have Indian blood, Alice was thinking, my mother was part Cree – when the nickel dropped. "Canada!" she cried out. "What makes you think I'm from Canada? I'm American."

"Sorry, your accent. And your way of turning a statement into a question by adding eh at the end. Like you're looking for agreement before continuing the conversation. That's Canadian, eh?"

She reflected for a moment. She had not spoken English much in the last two months except to Narcisse Cantave, and with Narcisse she maintained her Katherine Hepburn act. But with Paul for some reason she had let down her guard and was herself. She said, "Listen, Paul, you spent too much time in Boston. 'Fowah tickets to the Gahden to see Owuh."

"Or," Paul laughed, "Hey, Nomah, hit it hahd, hit the ball wicked hahd."

Alice laughed too. "My mother used to make fun of the Boston accent. Just because I don't talk like that doesn't mean I'm Canadian. I'm from upper New York state. Actually, I was born in Boston." Which was true.

"Okay, okay, you're an American. You want me to continue talking or you bored?"

"Continue. It's interesting. I don't think Narcisse knows all this. He told me a lot about St. Anthony, but some of this is new to me."

Paul parked on a lookout on the north coast and talked.

"So with the slave trade drying up, it became essential to the slave owners to breed slaves. But there were not that many African women. Dusseault kept the Carib women to work in the gardens and the house, and the men he used as overseers – that little bit of power made them happy. At the time of the rebellion, the Abu killed the overseers and married the women. So both the Guinea people and the Abus are of mixed Indian and African blood, but of very different cultures. The Caribs were cannibals. And that is where the Abu got their alleged cannibalistic habits."

"So the other Africans north of Mont Grand met up with the Arawak?"

"Yes, and they also were short of women."

"Who owns the land in Guinea?"

"There is no private property in Guinea. Or put it this way: all the property belongs to the Leopard Society. The Cantaves are in with the Leopards. The head of the family is a member and is their lawyer. My dad's a doctor, he is not a member, nor will Narcisse be. Philippe will take over from Uncle Henri. My dad was too fond of rum and after my mother died got into writing drug prescriptions for himself. He's okay now, but he doesn't have much of a practice. He lost most of his patients as well as his money. He's not well either, bad heart like Narcisse's father. I don't know who's going to go first, my dad or Narcisse's." Paul was silent. They drove up to a village. Paul stopped the Land Rover beside a cafe. "Want to try some of the local coffee? From Haut-Clair?"

At the back of the cafe there was an open terrace overlooking the sea. The northern mountain, Mont Noir, loomed up on the right. The chairs and tables were plastic but clean. A faded umbrella in the center of the table provided shade. The coffee was good.

"Where do you get your coffee?" Alice asked the slender teen-aged girl who served them. "It's really good."

"I roast and grind it myself, madame."

"But the beans, where are they from?"

"From the trading post five miles south of here, madame." The girl looked at Paul, expectant, grinning.

"Oh, my line." He and the girl laughed. "Thing is, Emma, Alice already knows where it's from. Emma and I have the same conversation once or twice a week. Whenever I bring a tourist. It's island coffee, Alice – "

"From Haut-Clair," Alice finished the sentence for him. "It's shade grown, no fertilizer, that's why it's so good."

"Correct. The Abu pick and dry the cherries in the sun. They remove the green beans and barter them to the trader at the foot of the cliff, and we buy from him," said the girl and smiling at Paul went away.

"You know her well?"

"Emma's my daughter. I was very young. Then I went away to school. My dad helped her mother and then, when my dad went broke, Henri Cantave helped the mother. He's a good man, Henri Cantave. He bought her this place. I send them money. It's cool. It's the way it is here – men are expected to support their children, but no one gets married – nothing exceptional. Actually the mulattos, people like the Cantaves are supposed to get married. I'm kind of a black sheep. Downwardly mobile, I think it's called."

"Where's the mother?"

"She's around. Tends to avoid me for some reason."

"You were talking about your uncle and the Leopards."

"The British property laws we have in St. Anthony do not apply in Guinea. So our great- grandfather was considered by many to be wasting his time and money getting clear title to a place on a reservation that did not recognize such titles. But the title is older than the treaty, if that means anything. The reason he did it was that he did not want anyone else to get the title. And remember he was a Leopard. The Leopards are the law in Guinea. Anyway it would cost hundreds of thousands to put it back as a coffee plantation, not counting the house. Commerce is forbidden in Guinea, so it would be pointless to restore it."

The last was said rather tentatively. It was almost a question. Why would Alice take an interest in a place that was going to Narcisse's brother? But then, he thought, I suppose she's just curious.

"So how come in St. Anthony the oldest son always gets everything?"

"Before the British came here the mulatto class was not accepted by the French. Many were well off, some owned plantations, but the French wouldn't let them, for example, walk in the parks, the governor wouldn't receive them. The British were different. They needed the mulattos as allies – you know the British, always pragmatic. All that exclusiveness went out the window. They gave them full rights as citizens; they could acquire passports. So they learned English and became anglophiles. There's a man I know who sent his son to Eton. One of the customs that was picked up was *seniores priores*. Fortunes would remain intact. Look what happened in Haiti – all the property is divided equally and the farms are so small everybody is poor."

"You were wrong about me being Canadian, but my mother's grandparents were farmers in Quebec. The families were large, but the one who inherited was always the best farmer. There was never any argument. By the time the family had grown up, always one son, could be the oldest, the second, third, or fourth had established himself as the best farmer. It was a very old custom; it was seigneurial. The lord or seigneur who owned the land would choose the best farmer in the family. That meant the land was more productive. When the British came the seigneurs left; the British gave the property rights to the peasants in most cases – to their amazement. But the British allowed the *canadiens* to keep their old laws and the family continued the custom of passing the farm to the most productive. The other children had to leave the farm and become priests or whatever. Many went to New England and worked in the factories there. The best farmer won the competition. Here in St. Anthony the British took over from the French, so it should have been the same."

"Well, on that basis, in our family the most competent happened to be the oldest, in my father's generation and in Narcisse's. Philippe, for all his strange lifestyle, is a bright boy. And as for the plantations, the French owners left. Englishmen and Scots took over. And, of course, those who worked the farms were slaves. They had no rights at all."

"Of course. I see. Still, the British system seems fragile."

"Fragile? How?"

"Well, suppose the second son was the most competent. Wouldn't it be better for the family and the property if he took over? Suppose he considered the older brother to be in his way? And suppose, knowing that, he decided to do something about it."

"Like what?"

She smiled. "Oh, I don't know. Murder."

"You look at things in a funny way. It is all a question of law. We – uh – tend to live within the law here, Alice. Besides, Philippe is competent, Alice. He's a hard worker. He's the right guy to look after things, I like Narcisse, but his head is in the clouds. When you know someone well as a kid, you know him forever. People don't change."

"But do you think it fair? To you? Who had to drop out of university? While Narcisse pursues his … his …arcane studies?"

"My father lost his money, that had nothing to do with Narcisse. I play the hand I'm dealt, Alice. Don't you?"

"Sure. But I don't play unless I'm dealing."

They were silent. Paul was thinking this is one tough chick that Narcisse's got himself, I wonder if he knows it. Knowing him, probably not. Alice was thinking of the cards she had dealt Theodore. I wonder if it helped his career, a coup like that. She said: "So that is Mont Noir. I wouldn't say it was beautiful. It looks forbidding, as if it didn't want visitors. A sheer cliff for the first, what, three hundred feet?"

"In places it's higher. It's not quite sheer, but it's too steep to climb unless you had special equipment. Between Mont Noir and Mont Grand, the cliff is lower and slopes. There's a way down. We'll go south from here, drop in at the village and the trading post. There's stuff for tourists at the trading post. African stuff, voodoo dolls and stuff. Then we'll see if we can get close to Haut-Clair. There must be a path that the coffee traders use. And steps."

The road skirted the cliff. On the right the sugar cane grew taller than Alice had seen it before, eight feet in places. Rainfall off the mountain, she thought. The cliff on the left gradually diminished and as they came up to the village she could see people in brightly coloured dresses coming down the slope with baskets on their heads and others going up.

"Voodoo dolls you said? Do they practice voodoo in the mountains?"

"Voudon is their religion, I don't really know, but I think it's pretty close to what goes on in Haiti. They don't use the dolls though, these people were from West Africa, from Guinea mostly, the pricking of dolls with needles and stuff, they don't do that. I have to tell you that it's the good citizens of St. Anthony who run these booths and make the dolls for tourists. The booths take money. The Guinea people won't use money."

The village stood on a little hill. There was a Catholic church, a school, and old wooden houses, similar to what Alice had seen in other parts of the island. They reminded her of the Gatineau, of summer cottages, and then she realized it was probably Canadian siding with that characteristic groove at the top. She was reminded of what she was taught at school, fish and lumber for sugar and rum. But wasn't it triangular? Africa fit in there, somewhere, oh yes, slaves, slaves from Africa. But what did the Africans get in return for their slaves? She couldn't remember. Paul went to get cold drinks at the little boutique that sold sandwiches and souvenirs for tourists. There were two other taxis and several tourists were inspecting handicrafts. She could see the primitive dolls.

To the west was a view of field after field of tall cane. She imagined herself suddenly on horseback, whip in hand, as powerful black men cut the cane. If any of them slackened she would ride over, give them a lash on their shoulders. It would have been exciting, she thought, like driving a motorbike at high speed on a curve, close to the edge, because of the danger; these black men outnumbered the whites and hated them. If they rose up, they would kill, so they must be kept down with the lash. Down, down, down with each stroke of the whip, for if they rise up, we're dead. And on this island they had risen up.

Paul came over with the drinks. He's a good-looking man, she thought; he resembles Narcisse but has a stronger face. Mulatto was originally an Arab word; she had looked it up. The planters, she supposed, would take the better-looking black women as mistresses. Did the white women, as second-class citizens themselves in those days, feel some sympathy for the blacks? Did the white women sometimes take handsome black men as lovers? That would have been risky and exciting. But if there were a baby would she be able to keep it? Perhaps it would be smuggled out of the house by the black women and brought up by them. If the white parent was a man of property the child might be recognized and given a start in life. But the mulatto child of a white woman would seldom be recognized. The mulattos probably became the middle class on this island through their own efforts, she reflected. They had a richer gene pool, it occurred to her, than either the whites or the blacks.

"A penny for your thoughts?"

"Sorry, I was just wondering what it was like in the days of slavery."

"Not much fun, I expect, for anyone."

"I don't know. I think I might have enjoyed it."

Paul gave her an appraising look, and grinned. "Yeah, you...you probably would have. Come into the trading post for a minute. It's barter, the Guineas won't use our money, but they'll use gourds."

The traders from Guinea were all women. They were dressed in brilliantly colored silk robes, tied around their bodies like saris, but in several different ways, with some women baring a single breast. Looking at them closely she could see, or thought that she could see, the Indian blood in their features. Near the front of the store was a well and the women used a communal ladle to drink from a bucket. They didn't barter for soft drinks. They sat on benches patiently waiting their turn. Whenever someone came out of the store someone else would go in.

It was a long narrow building. Alice could see a closed black van drawn up at the rear with the words Black Mountain Trading Post written on its side. She took a look inside the shop. A worn wooden counter ran the width of the shop behind which were three clerks fetching and receiving goods. When a barter was not equal value gourds were used as change. Transactions often took a long time, but everyone seemed to enjoy the process and was patient.

Alice had asked the hotel for a picnic lunch for two, which they shared at a picnic table outside the trading post. Then they continued their journey south. On their left was Mont Grand, more formidable and blacker than its northern neighbor. Mont Petit, the smaller peak that was part of the same mountain lay immediately to the south. The sugar plantations were smaller here and the cane not as tall. Then there was just scrub, and then forest, with the occasional clearing and small farm with goats. They stopped before one such farm. There was no one about.

"This is where the Abu barter their coffee beans from Haut-Clair. It's their currency. I'm going to go in and ask about a way up there."

A fat middle-aged white man came out of the store with Paul and came over to the Jeep. "You don't want go there, ma'am. They's wild animal up there and wild people, too. And ghosts, too. There ain't none of we ever go there, and us the coffee merchant for them. You axe me the way, me'll tell you, but don't say you was not warned. Beside, govment don't permit it. You'll see a sign."

"I see a path over to the left," said Alice. "Is that the way they come?"

"It be the way. You go, I can't stop you, but you been warned."

Paul got back in the Jeep and, waving goodbye to the coffee merchant, they drove along the path. "That family somehow has a monopoly on trading with the Abu. And robbing them. No one can do anything about it."

They were not able to drive very far before they had to stop, get out, and start walking. They were in thick forest now. After about five minutes they came to a sign that read: GUINEA RESERVATION. Then below: KEEP OUT. And in smaller letters: By order of the Government of St. Anthony. They stopped; the path was suddenly steep.

"Someone's coming," Paul whispered.

A girl of about sixteen with a basket on her head stepped out of the woods. She was bare breasted and wore a tattered pair of blue jeans. When she saw them she was startled, even terrified, dropped her basket, turned, and ran back the way she had come.

Alice went over and looked at the basket. "Coffee beans," she said. "Look what she dropped. Green coffee beans." She picked up a handful and put them in her pocket.

"I think we should go back," said Paul. "Can't go around frightening the natives. And you read the sign."

"She didn't look very different from the Guinea people," said Alice. "Except for her clothes. They're poor, these people. She seemed to be afraid of us."

"Of you. She didn't look at me."

"Is it because I'm white? You'd think that she'd seen a ghost or something."

Paul stopped in his tracks and looked at her for a full minute.

"What's the matter?"

"Come on. Next stop the museum in Le Havre. There's something there that may explain this."

They walked back to the Land Rover and drove back to the road. They were now not far from the sea and they joined the coast road going west towards Le Havre. From quite far away they caught sight of a huge cruise ship in the harbor.

"Good for the taxi business, cruise ships, but not for the island. The tourists don't spend much money and the ships take on about a million gallons of fresh water."

"Say, Paul," said Alice. "Drop me off at the museum. I may spend some time there and I want to walk about Le Havre. I'll take another taxi back to the hotel. You go pick up a fare."

Both felt a bit relieved with this arrangement; they had fallen into an easy intimacy, but each needed a break from the other. The museum was in the center of the small city of Le Havre.

"I want to show you something upstairs," he said. "Then I'll split."

When they entered the museum Paul hurried up the stairs, he seemed to know where he was going and was anxious to settle something in his own mind. They went into a small room that had been set up as a period bedchamber from the days of the French regime. The furniture was elegant in the Empire style and looked valuable. Paul went straight to a glass case against a wall. Among a number of small objects set out on green velvet was a portrait painted on ivory in a gold locket on a necklace. They both stared down at it.

It was of a young woman in a formal gown. She had ivory white skin, green eyes, and long black hair that she wore down around her shoulders. Her body was turned a bit away from the artist at whom she was looking intensely. The resemblance to Alice was striking.

"Would you like me to unlock the case so that you can have a closer look?" asked a polite voice behind them. Unnoticed by either, the attendant, a bespectacled middle-aged woman, had followed them in. Alice nodded and the case was unlocked. She picked up the locket and held it close with forefinger and thumb.

"Who was she?"

The woman answered. "Look below, you can just make out the lettering."

"Aloyshovna. She must be Aloyshovna Dusseault."

"But how did it get here?"

"We don't know," said the attendant. "There was a fire some years ago. We don't know the provenance of half the things in the museum."

"Her skin is paler and whiter. But it could be you," said Paul.

O, Ayesha, my queendom come.

"But the girl in the woods, she could never have been here, could she? She could never have seen this picture."

"The Abu maybe have a picture of her themselves. They worshipped her. Aloyshovna was supposed to have had a black baby.

They tried to get it out of the house before Dusseault saw it but failed. He tried to kill it with a knife and one of the Carib maids stabbed him in the neck with a hatpin while another ran off with the baby. Before he died, he used his knife on Aloyshovna. That sparked the revolt. The Abu then went after their overseers and it spread to the rest of the island. That was how the great St. Antoine slave rebellion began. I'm going to leave you and go to the cruise ship. Eighty dollars would do." She gave him a hundred.

"There's one more thing. The child lived. That was seven, eight generations ago. Think about it. The Abu are a small community; they intermarry. By now all of them are descended from her."

"How do you know all this?"

"My grandmother told me. My mother's mother. She was an Abu who ran away. So yours truly, Paul Cantave, related by blood to Saba, queen of Guinea, is descended from Aloyshovna, too. Oh, and something else she told me, I just remembered, there was a book, they had a book with her picture in it, a picture of Aloyshovna. A book in English, none of them could read it, except the chief, he's the only one who can read. An old missionary left the book – he taught the chief to read and gave him the book."

"Just one book?"

"Think so, if there were any others, they probably burnt them for kindling."

"And the missionary?"

"Who knows? Probably they ate him."

6

Alice swam early the next morning, and after breakfast bought a large-brimmed sun hat. She determined to stay out of the sun as much as possible. Narcisse telephoned to invite her to lunch to meet his mother, the Cantave chauffeur would pick her up. She sat on a chaise longue on the verandah outside her room with coffee, her copy of *La Cuidar y Cultivada de Coca Planta,* and a language dictionary.

The upstairs veranda was open, an arrangement designed to enable guests in old-fashioned tropical hotels to promenade in the shade and mingle socially. A Peruvian gentleman, who had a suite down the hall, strolled along the veranda toward Alice. It was early in the winter season the so hotel was not crowded and the two were alone. The hard soles of his white shoes clicked on the floor, giving Alice enough time to put down her book, but not enough time to conceal it.

"*Buenos dias, senorita,*" said the Peruvian.

"*Buenos dias, senor.* I don't speak Spanish, I'm afraid."

"You read it, I see," he replied. "Ah, but you should learn to speak it. It's easy and it's fun. We make jokes in Spanish all the time, with so many words the same, we make puns, we sit in cafes, drink coffee, and make jokes while you Americans take our money. If you can read it you can learn to speak it. It's much easier than French. My name is Hector Gonzales-Prieto, and I hail from Peru. May I sit down?"

"Please. I am Alice LeBlanc, please call me Alice."

"You are reading a Peruvian book." He paused. "About the cultivation of the coca plant. Forgive me, I observe the literature that beautiful young women are reading. It helps me when I go to introduce myself." He paused again. "I know that book and I know a little about the plant. It is native to our country. Our Indians chew the leaves for stamina and it enables them to climb great mountains. But you, my dear, are not, surely, planning to climb any mountains." He was short and fat, wore an elegant white suit and a little black moustache that appeared to be waxed at the ends. He sat down without asking.

"Shall I order coffee?" asked Alice.

"Please."

She went into her sitting room and rang room service. On her return, she brought her other book *The Cultivation of Coffee.*

"I am more interested in coffee," she said. "The coca plant book, well, that's just to satisfy a curiosity."

"I know a lot about the coffee tree, senorita. Whether you are interested in the cultivation of the coffee tree or the coca plant, you should come to Peru. Come as my guest. I will teach you all about both of them. My nephew and I have a little experimental farm. We have interesting new varieties that might do well in a climate such as St. Anthony's."

The coffee came and they talked mostly about the weather in different climates and altitudes. Alice was not charmed by Hector, but it was clear to her that he was knowledgeable in areas that interested her. After about half an hour she looked at her watch.

"If you will excuse me, I have to change. There's a car coming for me at twelve. But we'll meet again. Adios."

I don't believe in coincidences, she thought as she changed. A narc? No, that did not add up.

The suburban hill northeast of Le Havre where the Cantaves lived was – to Alice's senses – a vast garden. Bungalows and ranch houses were sheltered under tropical pines, royal palms, magnolias, tamarinds, and flowering cordear and flamboya trees. Almost everything she saw, from the bougainvillea and mandeville vines to the flowering cacti, poinsettia, and viburnum would have struggled with an Ottawa November and perished utterly by mid-December. The bougainvillea vines flowered in a rainbow of colors, cascading with a brilliance that quite took her breath away. It was curious to reflect that the same French admiral, Louis Antoine de Bougainville, who had brought this vine from the Pacific to these islands, had negotiated the peace outside Montreal that enabled her French ancestors to keep their language and religion. Heliconia, begonia, and hibiscus were everywhere and the scents of purple anis, lady-of-the-night, lemon jasmine, and others exotic to her northern nostrils blended with the faint salt of the clean ocean air.

The Cantave house was set back from the road and had a long driveway. Narcisse was standing in the shade of the portico and stepped out to open her door. He kissed her gently on the cheek.

"That hat! I like it, but it is an impediment to kissing," he said. "Come, let me show you the garden."

They strolled about the garden and Narcisse showed her his mother's orchids. "It is her favorite thing in life, next to her family, the orchids," he said.

"It's beautiful here, Narcisse, you do live in paradise."

"Well, Paris has a few things that we lack, perhaps, but beauty we have. I must warn you that my mother is going to ask you a lot of questions about yourself. She has it in her head that we are to be married. I suppose she got the idea from me."

"An odd way to propose, Narcisse."

He went down on his knees. "Alice, marry me, please."

It was her first proposal. She said, "Yes. If you give me Haut-Clair."

"It shall be done. Really, we are engaged then? Well, I must do something about a ring. Come and meet my mother."

They entered the house, crossed a hall, and then passed out again to a large flag-stoned patio. As Yvonne got up, her mouth was smiling but her eyes were not. She held out her hand.

"Welcome to St. Anthony, Alice. You have come at a bad time for us, I'm afraid."

Yvonne offered Alice a rum punch, which she declined, asking instead for water. They had lunch outside on the patio. The table was set with cut flowers from the garden in crystal glass vases on a white tablecloth. The flowers took care of the initial conversation. A maid in a black dress and white lace apron waited on them. They talked about Henri. The family had sent for a specialist from Texas to perform a bypass, perhaps several. The cardiac surgeon would decide.

Narcisse had told his mother that Alice ate only fruit and vegetables and she was treated to some island vegetables, such as eddoes and doved peas that were new to her. They took care of more conversation. Yvonne then began asking direct questions about herself. She told Narcisse's mother that she was born in Boston and educated privately in Europe and America. She had lived most of her life in upper New York state and Detroit, she said. She was vague about her parents. Both were dead, she said, in fact, she had no living relations. Her stepfather had been a banker. After his death she had managed his vineyards and then sold them.

"When can I meet Narcisse's father?" she asked to draw the subject away from herself. "Now that we are to be married." There was a long silence.

"Mama and I are going to see him this afternoon," said Narcisse looking over at Yvonne.

"I didn't know that it had been decided," said Yvonne looking back at him.

"Just now," said Alice, "while admiring your orchids."

"Well, I think that Henri, anyway, will be pleased," said Yvonne. "It does not look like Philippe is going to marry. Henri wants an heir, a grandson. We'll tell him this afternoon and perhaps you can see him tomorrow."

A clumsy abortion when she was a teenager after clumsy sex while drunk with a computer nerd had left Alice infertile. If there was ever to be a time to mention this, it was not now.

That afternoon Paul's father, Robert Cantave, was at the hospital visiting his brother when Narcisse and Yvonne arrived. They were both told about the engagement.

"Paul likes her," said Robert. "He gave her a tour of the island. Says she is beautiful and rich and tough, one of those hard-boiled American women, but you know where you stand with her. He said she is direct."

"Her mother's family were Franco-Americans, I think. A Quebec family who settled in Massachusetts." said Narcisse. "Her parents were divorced but now they are both dead. Her stepfather was a banker, and he's dead too. She uses her mother's maiden name."

"I would like to meet her," said Henri. "Sad that she has no living family. Poor thing, she has money, but no family. But Narcisse is going to change that."

"Poor thing!" burst in Yvonne. "Poor thing indeed. She has no heart, that one. I think we should get a private investigator to find out who she really is."

"Mama, of course, she has a heart. She is quite sensitive and often lonely. You will come to love her, I know."

"It is a sad thing, Yvonne, when a child has no family," said Henri. "When can she come to see me? Could she come this evening? I am quite curious. And I don't know how much longer I am going to be with you."

"Now, now, Henri, your doctor and I both think that after the bypass operations, you'll be right as rain. The surgeon from Texas will be here tomorrow," said Robert. "But I really think you have had quite enough visitors for one day. I think you should wait and meet Alice tomorrow."

"No. Tonight."

Robert knew better than to argue with Henri when his mind was made up. "Alright, alright. I am not your doctor. But then I suggest that the rest of us leave you now to rest."

On returning to the hotel, Alice visited the hotel library and picked up a medical encyclopedia, which she took to her room. She studied it for about twenty minutes and then slept. I will swim later, she thought, when the sun is not so strong. The phone rang at about four.

"Could you go to the hospital today? At five?" asked Narcisse. "My father wants to see you today and alone. It's a private room, Number 302."

"Yes, I'll go. Is there anything I should know? Do you go in for marriage settlements, pre-nuptials and so on?"

"Sometimes. I don't know what he wants to see you about, but it's probably something like that. You'll have to excuse him, he's a lawyer, you know, he can't help it. And he seems convinced that he is not going to be with us long. The doctor, on the other hand, is optimistic."

"I'm looking forward to meeting him. I don't think your mother liked me very much, but that's okay. You are her darling, I could see that, it's normal, you are rather a charmer."

"I'll pick you up at the hospital at, oh, a quarter to six. Don't stay long, you mustn't tire him. We'll have a date, go out to dinner."

"Good, I look forward to that. Oh, by the way, I keep forgetting to ask you, has your father said anything to you about Haut-Clair?"

"Yes. It's to be mine. An old family trust runs out when Papa dies. It's his to leave to someone and he's left it to me. He said, that with the help of Alphonse in Paris, and Mama's sister in Guinea, maybe I could make something out of it, and out of myself. We talked about me continuing my studies while an agronomist runs the place. He's okay about that. Actually, that might be something he wants to talk to you about, where you might fit in."

"I have managed vineyards in the past. I told you that."

"I know. I pretended to my father to be more interested than I am, but I've been thinking that you could run the plantation and I could concentrate on my research."

A little laboratory for Narcisse, we'll have to see about that, said Alice to herself as she hung up, it would keep him busy and out of the way. I am beginning to think that I want him quite out of the way, once we are married. She sat down and thought for a minute about Henri Cantave. Probably he just wants to know if I've got money. Everything she owned was in that hotel room except her fortune, which was in US treasury bills, short term Euro and Sterling paper, twenty three million dollars worth, all in an obscure bank on a remote Pacific island, administered by her Russian friend, who kept in touch by email. Not interesting investments to her mind. She was an entrepreneur at heart and liked risk. She had no confidence in stock markets; she did not like investments that she couldn't control.

She put her bank statements, her birth certificate, and her passport in the straw beach bag, and put on her hat. She picked up a taxi at the hotel entrance without looking out for Paul.

Alice arrived at Room 302 on time and spent three-quarters of an hour with Henri Cantave. Narcisse came to the room to pick her up. He noticed that his father looked tired and they made their goodbyes and left.

Henri Cantave then made two phone calls. The first was to Yvonne; he told her briefly that there was no need for a private investigator. He thought Alice an ideal woman for their son.

The second call was to his older son, Philippe, who was now running the family law firm. He told him that Narcisse was to be married to a very rich woman, who was prepared to invest in Haut-Clair. Her involvement in Haut-Clair was to be kept confidential. Her assets were liquid and in her own name. Because of the size of her fortune, he asked Philippe to draw up a marriage contract, deeding Haut-Clair to her and on her death to her oldest son. In the event of her dying without issue, or of divorce, the plateau was to revert to the Cantaves.

"Are you sure, Papa? I think we should talk this over, but I will draw up a draft and we'll go over it. I think you are worrying too much about things, Papa. Everything is going well at the office. Try to keep your mind blank or think pleasant thoughts of your garden, which you will soon see again. Relax, stretch your muscles, and relax."

When he got this call, Philippe was at home changing for a dinner party he was giving that evening. All the guests were men. He was a tall, willowy, attractive young man, fond of clothes, food, drink, and other young men. His father's request seemed unorthodox to him. It was customary on the island to make a settlement on the bride. On marriage, without a contract, all property belonging to the bride or groom were to be owned jointly by the couple. This arrangement went back to French civil law, which still applied on St. Anthony. The bride was usually offered a cash settlement or the title to a house, in exchange for giving up her rights to half her husband's property. In this case, where she was the one with a fortune, she should be offering Narcisse something to forgo his rights to half of it when they married. Philippe thought that deeding the entire Haut-Clair property to Alice unnecessary. She must have agreed to invest a lot of money in the coffee plantation on the Haut-Clair estate. But surely it would be in Narcisse's interests not to have a marriage settlement at all.

Half an hour later, Philippe received another telephone call from the hospital. His father was dead from a massive coronary; it was not unexpected, but with the surgeon in the air, on his way from Texas, it seemed like such a tragedy. He had loved his father. He wondered whether he should send his guests home; they were already arriving. He decided to turn it into a wake and get roaring drunk. He also decided that he would draw up the marriage contract as his father had asked. It was, after all, his father's last request.

Narcisse heard of Henri's death from his mother when he came home after his dinner date with Alice. She was in bed. The maids had gone home but he saw that her light was on and looked in. She was lying on her back, tears pouring down her face.

"We should not have let her go, that Alice. We should not have let her go," she sobbed.

"But Mama, Papa insisted, you remember, you know how Papa is – "he could not bring himself to say "was". "One could never say no to Papa."

"She killed him, that woman killed him, I know it, I know it."

"Mama, Mama," murmured Narcisse. He got her something to help her sleep and stayed with her until she dropped off. He called Alice early the next morning and told her the news. The funeral was to be on Thursday.

"I thought he was tired, that he should not have seen me, but you said he insisted. It's unfortunate and I feel terrible, as if it was my fault for going, but of course I know it wasn't. You had better spend the day with your mother," she said. "I'll see you tomorrow. But I would like to speak to Philippe, whom I have not yet met, and give him my condolences and tell him about my visit to your father. Would you please give me his number."

She called Philippe and expressed her shock that Henri Cantave had died so soon after her visit. She said what she had said to Narcisse, that she felt it was her fault for going. "You must understand that I did nothing to agitate him. He wanted to know my circumstances. Then he asked me how I felt about a marriage contract, whatever that is. You know, Philippe, he was kind to me, he was a nice man —" she paused as if suppressing a sob. She had decided to play the role with Philippe of a not very bright woman who needed protection. "So I told him what he wanted to know and I agreed to do as he asked. I showed him the financial statements I get from my bankers. He asked me if I was going to invest in the coffee plantation at Haut-Clair, and I said, I would, whatever Narcisse needs he will have, and I would pay to rebuild the château there, even if it costs millions, and all this to be left to our children. But I want to tell you something. My daddy, actually it was my step-daddy, left me a lot of money. He was a banker. I told Monsieur Cantave that, because I liked him, and because he asked me.

"But I don't like people to know about it, about the money, I mean. Once, when I was in Switzerland, I was nearly kidnapped. I never told Narcisse this. It was terrifying. The kidnappers knew all about me and the money. I was advised by the police to keep a low profile. And I have. So, on the island, I don't want it known – that I have money, I mean. And please, I don't want it known that I am going to invest in the plantation. I want people to think that Narcisse raised the money in Paris. It's better for him, too, for people to think he is an entrepreneur, you know, that he is a good businessman." Philippe listened to this carefully and accepted every word.

Needless to say, Alice had helped Henri Cantave to his rest. A minor adjustment to the medication; that was all it took. Henri was in her way. As always when performing these fatal acts, she recited to herself the words of Ayesha after killing a rival: "Where is her sin? Her sin is that she stands between me and my desire."

ALEYSHA
Hubris

7

Alice decided to visit Haut-Clair alone and asked the hotel desk to find her a car for the day; she would drive herself. She wore a white suit that she had bought for the tropics, dark glasses, and her large-brimmed straw hat. Around her neck she tied a blue and green Hermès scarf. She consulted her map and took an inland route, nearly getting lost twice.

As she drove across the alien island, she felt suddenly inexpressibly lonely and homesick. She thought about Manson; I had to shoot him, she reasoned, I could not bring him with me, and he would have been miserable without me. It was kinder than leaving him behind. She found herself thinking about Ottawa and winter as she drove along, and wondered if she would ever go back to Canada. Then with a sudden pang she remembered Theodore; the big lout had always been sweet to her. I miss him almost as much as the dog, she reflected, and I must put him out of my head.

Alice felt drawn to Haut-Clair in a way she didn't understand. She found the coffee merchant's place, turned off, and drove as far as she could, parking close to the place where Paul had left the Land Rover two days before. She ignored the sign and climbed boldly up the path, meeting no one. She came to the cliff and found the steps cut in the hard volcanic rock two hundred years before and worn by generations of bare feet. No doubt these people think they own the place, she thought as she climbed, and after two hundred years, they must have some rights. It was a long climb and she had to stop twice to catch her breath.

Thinking favorable thoughts about the people whose land she was in the process of making her own, she reached the plateau. Paul was right; land that had been cleared and productive two hundred years ago was now jungle. The life of the jungle was not on the forest floor, however, but in the light green canopy a hundred feet above her head. There she saw movement and sensed abundant life – parakeets, butterflies, even monkeys – although she couldn't see them.

Here on the forest floor all was quiet. On either side of her, tall trees rose some eighty feet or so before branching out. They must have a considerable commercial value, she thought – perhaps I shouldn't think like that before such beauty. It must be in my Ottawa valley lumberjacking blood. The bark had a pinkish glow in the diffused light. Rosewood! The lumber must be worth a fortune. And then she noticed another pair further on, and another. They were planted, she realized, over two hundred years before. They were not native to the island, but brought here from South America and planted to form an avenue. And a splendid avenue it was, the forest canopy above diffused a golden green light for a distance of three quarters of a mile. It was like being inside a cathedral with an aisle that stretched almost as far as one could see and then ended at what appeared to be the ruins of a house against a cliff face. On either side beyond the rosewoods the jungle was thick. I'll bulldoze the jungle for the plantation, but not all of it; the avenue I will definitely keep.

The footpath branched off to the right, but she didn't take it. Instead, she went up the avenue where the path was much less worn. The outlines of the plantation house were now clear; the walls seemed intact. There was no roof. Château Haut-Clair! It was cool in the avenue and she walked easily. She had gone about forty yards when she sensed that she was being watched. But she didn't sense any hostility; what she felt was awe. She felt suddenly supremely confident and at home, more at home than she had ever felt anywhere – the alpha lioness approaching her lair.

Haut-Clair stood at the base of a black cliff on a ledge of solid rock some twenty feet above the fertile plateau. The house had been built of coral and two hundred years of weather had turned the walls quite gray. But it still stood. The soft coral walls had crumbled in places, but the foundations, cut into the black rock of the mountain were solid. Black holes glared where there had once been windows, shutters long gone.

A broad set of steps cut into the rock led up to a vast portico. She saw, as she approached, parts of the skeleton of Dusseault, still nailed to the closed front door. The skull was missing but she imagined it, the black eyeholes glaring at her, the teeth in a grin. It seemed to dare her to continue.

Alice turned her back on it for a moment and looked back at the avenue and at the jungle, lying below the rock ledge and some thirty feet away. Yes, she was being watched, she was sure of it, an audience was closely watching her every move. Not to disappoint – to provide a bit of theatre – she turned back, faced the imagined skull and spat into one of its gaping black eyes. Did she hear a collective gasp of indrawn breath? One thing she knew: she was not going to enter her house by any means but the front door. She seized the handle, which turned easily, almost as if it had been waiting for her, pulled, and the great door slowly swung open, creaking and complaining. But the hinges held and it settled ajar with plenty of room for Alice to enter.

Her first impression was that the house was clean but totally and utterly bare. The floors were of marble. There was not a scrap of furniture, rug, or curtain. The building had no roof and no trace or remnant of anything wooden remained. She stood in a great hall that ended in a formal staircase. On either side were reception rooms, large, totally empty and clean. Someone sweeps the place, she thought.

On closer inspection, the rooms were not empty; there were snakes and lizards. The lizards were of the tiny green species she had seen at the hotel, perfectly harmless. The snakes were of several varieties, none of which she had seen before. She didn't believe that snakes were dangerous unless they were threatened. Perhaps it is they who keep the place clean, she thought. We can be friends. One large black snake lay across the lower step of the staircase.

"Move!" she commanded, clapping her hands. And it did, slowly slithering off the step. Now he knows who's boss, she said to herself as she mounted the marble staircase.

Halfway up was a landing. Two curved sets of stairs, one on each side, led to the second floor. One of these had collapsed, but the other was solid. When Alice reached the second floor she had reversed direction and was facing south. The layout was in the old colonial plantation style, similar to the hotel's, and on about the same scale. Corridors stretched east and west with openings to bedrooms, which, again like the hotel, themselves opened to the veranda. There were no doors, just openings. In front of her, the upstairs hall opened to two rooms larger than the others.

One would have been Gilbert's bedroom and the other Aloyshovna's. She walked through the right-hand one, which she somehow knew had belonged to Aloyshovna, onto the veranda. The overgrown jungle and rosewood avenue blocked a good deal of the original view. But to the east Alice could see the sea and she had a heart rending sense of *déjà vu*. Alice felt Aloyshovna's yearning, as she looked towards Russia, six thousand miles away, knowing that she could never return, that she would never again see snow nor hear the voice of the white-throated sparrow. Alice shook away tears; it is an emotional mirage, she told herself, it is no more than that.

"Aleysha."

A soft chorus rose up from below. At first she couldn't see them, and then she made them out in the avenue below as they moved their arms. There were about sixty altogether, men, women, and children, all kneeling, foreheads to the ground, arms still stretched out before them, as they raised themselves, remaining on their knees, and called out again in chorus, softly, gently, and reverently:

"Aleysha."

They resumed their prostrate position and held it for about ten seconds. She could see that they were not dressed in the silken robes of the Guinea people, but in worn and tattered jeans, shirtless and bare from the waist up.

"Aleysha."

Alice went to the railing. They raised themselves as they called her name. She could see that they had their eyes closed; none of them would look at her. *O, Ayesha, my queendom has come.*

"O, people of the Abu," she called out in English, "Why do you not look at me? Why do you close your eyes?"

There was a long silence. They held their prone positions on the ground for what seemed a full minute. She could just make out a muttering, some kind of conference. Then a young male voice.

"Because of thy beauty, O Queen."

"Who speaks? Please stand. The one who speaks, please stand."

A tall young man in the front stood up. He kept his head up and his eyes closed.

"What is your name?"

"My name is Abbah. I answered, O Queen, because I speak English and I am the chief."

"How do you do, Abbah. Your answer is pleasing to me. Please open your eyes. And bring me your priests. Ask the people to sit down and open their eyes and look at me."

There were more sounds of conferring, an instruction from Abbah in a tone of authority. Everyone sat and, in the forest's shade, Alice could see that their white eyes were open against their dark skin. Some of the children, too shy to look at her directly, were looking through their fingers. This made her smile and many of the people smiled back.

Two people were making their way up the avenue toward the stone steps. Abbah was leading an old woman. There was nowhere to receive them in state. That will have to be corrected, she thought, as she left the balcony and sat herself on the top step of the central staircase. I need a throne, she thought.

Suddenly Alice heard the sound of drums, beginning simply, then speaking with a complex syncopation, the beat rising and falling. She felt a moment of fear, and then recalled that Ayesha, the immortal white African queen, told Holly, the English scholar who manages to reach her kingdom, that she had no real power: she ruled through terror. They are afraid of me, she thought, and I must be careful that does not change.

The *mambo* wore a black robe that showed evidence of much repair and a necklace of large red beads. Her long hair was twisted elegantly about a pair of bones. Alice could not recognize the bones, and then it occurred to her that they were human femurs. At her bidding she sat quietly on the floor, cross-legged.

Abbah came up and made a rather exaggerated genuflection. That had better not have contained what I think I saw there – a hint of mockery, she thought. In the time to come, Alice would get to know Abbah well and, although he served her faithfully, she was never quite sure sometimes that he was not secretly laughing at her. As Paul had pointed out, after seven or eight generations, the entire Abu population was probably descended from Aloyshovna. Alice learned later that Abbah was directly descended from Aloyshovna's son on the male side and was the hereditary chief. He remained standing.

"Come closer. Climb the stairs."

Abbah slowly climbed up the steps, hesitating before each one, appearing to be waiting to be told to stop after each advance. This command came when Abbah was standing about six steps below her, his eyes about eight inches below hers.

"Move to the side and turn so that you can see the *mambo*." Abu did so, lowering his left foot to the step below to keep his balance.

"First, tell me, how is it that you alone speak English?" she asked gently.

"My father taught me to speak and also to read English. I have a book with your picture. I will show you. My father, I, Abbah, and my son to be born, and all our people – we – we are thy children, O Queen."

"God bless you, my son," said Alice. She got up, leaned forward, and kissed him on the forehead. "Tell the *mambo* and the people that I will come to stay. But before I move here, we must rebuild the house and restore the plantation. This will be done in the next year," said Alice. "Please ask the *mambo* if she will accept me as queen of the people."

Abbah translated. The *mambo* conferred with Abbah in their language and then he spoke.

"She says 'O mighty Queen, we have waited for generations for thy return. Sometimes we have heard you wailing in the halls of Haut-Clair and we have felt thy pain.'"

Alice wondered where Abbah got his archaic English – from the book? – and wondered again if he was mocking the situation. She looked at him shrewdly but there was no sign. He seemed to sincerely enjoy the flourish that he gave to the translation.

"She says: Thy pain is our pain as our pain was thy pain in the time of Dusseault. Now we want only to serve thee. It was prophesied that thou wouldst return. In the meantime thou livest inside us and within us."

It occurred to Alice that perhaps their ancestors ate Aloyshovna's corpse, as they might on her death eat hers: not at all

She's – Ayesha's – sort of immortality. Anyway it was time to get down to business.

"There will be work to do, hard work. But the people will be rewarded for their work. They will not be slaves. We will have tools and machines. Will your people object to working for their queen?"

"Nay, O Queen. It will be pleasure to work for our queen. We are poor. We need new clothes. We have no tools. All we have to offer is green coffee beans and they cheat us at the counting house. We need tools so that we can better cultivate the coffee tree. It was prophesied that when thou returned we would prosper, that the coffee plantation would be restored but without slaves. That thou would bring us oxen, elephants, and great birds made of iron such as we know they have in St. Anthony. But, O Queen, thou hast our loyalty whether the prophecy be fulfilled or not. We will work for thee if thou would only bring us machetes and hoes."

After this short speech he sat down. Alice was silent. She looked at Abbah and saw in his face an imploring look of such intensity that she dismissed her doubts of his sincerity. Extraordinary, she thought, the modern age has passed these people by.

She stood and said. "I will give you what you want and more." She came down the steps, not looking at Abbah, bowed gently to the *mambo*, took her hand, kissed it, and went out. To the left the ledge extended out from the mountain beyond the house. Alice walked over and inspected it carefully: it was a perfect landing pad for a helicopter.

"I shall return," she said, addressing the people below. "I shall return in an iron bird within two months." She turned and walked to the steps that led down to the forest. She held up her hand.

"I will be with you in spirit." She walked down the steps and entered the avenue, walking between the people who went on their knees and lowered their head, prostrate as before.

"I shall return," she murmured several times as she passed through them, patting the children gently on their heads, and left the forest the way she had come.

On her way back, Alice stopped the car at the coffee merchant's. He remembered her. She made him an offer for his house, land, and business, and left him thinking it over.

Driving back to the hotel she started making plans. Now that she had seen the place, she was quite excited about it. She decided to buy a small helicopter for her own transportation. Larger helicopters would be leased for contractors bringing in materials for the renovation of the house, and the "iron oxen and elephants," as the people called heavy machinery, that would be used for clearing the jungle. She didn't want to use St. Anthony firms; she didn't want island people to know too much about her business. The Abu could do much of the work under supervision.

That night she searched the Internet for contractors, wrote some emails, and made some phone calls. A couple of Florida construction companies seemed promising for the clearing and a Barbados firm of architects for the house.

Narcisse came to see her the next day and they had lunch at the hotel. They ordered a planter's punch each and when they came, he went down on one knee and offered her an old velvet box. Inside was a Victorian diamond ring with a large central yellow stone. She put it on her finger and smiled. Narcisse got back in his chair.

"My brother gave it to me this morning to give to you. He inherited it and says that as he will never marry, it should be yours. It was our great-grandmother's." Narcisse spoke tenderly about his father. He was upset by his death; it had taken him by surprise. Memories of his father had flooded back. He spoke of these and then asked about her visit to the hospital. He didn't mention his mother's suspicions. They ordered champagne with lunch.

"He wanted to talk business," she said. "I saw that it tired him, but he insisted and I agreed to everything he proposed, more to relieve his mind than anything else. I promised him that, once we were married, I would finance the coffee plantation entirely, and that I would pay to have the château rebuilt. He asked to see proof of my assets and I showed him bank and money market portfolio statements that satisfied him. I told him that you had offered to put Haut Clair in my name and he thought that fair, and made me promise to leave it to our oldest son. He was pleased; I believe because of my promises, he died a happy man."

"Yes, Philippe told me. Something about a marriage contract, it's normal on this island. Philippe said that our father wanted Haut-Clair put in your name. I already said I would give it to you anyway. You're the one who is going to spend a fortune on it. It will be entailed to our oldest son. And it was Papa's last request."

"I am so sorry it happened just after I saw him." Alice managed a tear.

"Listen," he took her hand. "No one blames you. But my mother – she is upset – I think we should have a long engagement."

The champagne came and they toasted Haut-Clair. A long engagement was not what Alice wanted after the hard bargaining session she had had with Henri Cantave over the marriage contract. "You know there are people whom I must consult about investing in Haut-Clair. Trustees. I have spoken to them about it – oh by the way, I went to Haut-Clair again, I will tell you about it – they are advising me not to invest until we are married. So it can't be too long."

"My mother will come around. It's rather a lot for her, me getting engaged and then Papa leaving us on the same day."

"Perhaps I should go away for a while. You spend time with your mother. Sing my virtues. I want to go to South America and learn about coffee growing. There's a man at the hotel who has invited me to Peru. He's sitting over there. I'd like you to meet him. And I want to see an architect in Barbados about the house. He specializes in restoring coral buildings. And then to Florida to see contractors about the plantation."

"I see you are all business. I am impressed. The funeral is tomorrow. Paul is going to bring you by the way. With Uncle Robert. Suppose you take your trip right after. Then there is Christmas, perhaps we should marry in late January." And they set a date. After their marriage they would rent a beach house while Haut-Clair was being restored.

"Who will give you away?" Narcisse asked.

"What do you say to Uncle Robert giving me away?" She was silent for a moment and thought of Bear. She imagined him at a lawn reception at the Cantaves downing Heinekens one after the other. "I told you I went to Haut-Clair. I met the Abu people. They like me, I think. I talked with the chief and told them we would restore the plantation, that there would be machinery to do the hard work; that there would be work for them and prosperity. They are extraordinarily poor, you know. I think not just the twentieth century passed them by, but the nineteenth. I feel almost as if they were my family."

"That would be fine with me. I am sure he will be happy to do it. I am impressed that you have befriended the Abu already. I was worried about how they would feel. What is the chief like?"

"He's young, not more than eighteen. He has good manners. He speaks a very old-fashioned English that it seems he got from books. Or a book."

"I look forward to meeting him. That's good, Alice, that we employ them. What a good idea. And you have made friends with them. You are quite wonderful."

"Narcisse, if I invest in it, I don't want it known. Certain people, such as Philippe and maybe your cousins may have to know, but the newspapers, the government, the public in general must think that you are using money you raised in Paris."

"If that is what you wish. It won't be a problem. More worrying to me is that I know nothing about plantations. Won't we need a cash crop of some kind as the coffee trees mature? It's five years, is it not? Surely we should get professional help, an agronomist, a manager." He looked worried.

"Suppose you leave it all to me. As I keep telling you, I have managed vineyards."

They were both silent for a few minutes. She thought of the underground drug factory on an abandoned farm, and on another farm the safe house for illegal immigrants. Yes, she had managed farms. Narcisse sat at the table with a vision of Alice supervising the crushing of grapes in France.

"You know," said Narcisse. "That would suit me very well. I'll just work on my research. You run the plantation. It's your money, after all."

"But remember, I don't want people to know. I want them to think I am the little wife who perhaps helps with the books."

"I understand. Philippe has spoken to me – you talked to him. He is very sympathetic toward you. You want everyone to think that I am the big businessman who raised the money. It is very sweet of you, he thinks. My mother may have her reservations but you have an ally in him."

They had finished eating when Hector dropped by their table. Narcisse stood up and Alice said, "This is Hector Gonzalez-Prieto who has invited me to Peru. Hector, I would like you to meet my fiancé, Narcisse Cantave."

"Please sit down," said Narcisse, "and join us in a glass of champagne. We have just become engaged."

Hector sat and accepted a glass. "I congratulate you both." He raised his glass then asked if he could take a closer look at the ring. Alice held out her hand, thinking that it would not surprise her if he took out a jeweler's glass as he bent over it. "Victorian setting, quite beautiful. Diamond is flawed but it is scarcely visible." He straightened up. "I understand there has been a death in the family. My condolences." Narcisse murmured his thanks. "You know," Hector continued, "I have invited Alice to Peru as my guest to learn about the coffee tree."

"She told me."

"She can learn a lot in Peru."

"I am sure. I think it's a good idea," said Narcisse. "We were just talking about Alice taking a little trip. My mother needs me to spend time with her. Which reminds me, I must go. I won't have coffee." He got up, kissed Alice on the cheek, and left. Alice and Hector went upstairs to the veranda for coffee.

"I am leaving the day after tomorrow in the morning." he told her. "I do not know if your fiancé knows of your interest in the coca plant. Do not protest, coffee trees take too long to grow. I know you are interested; Haut-Clair is so secluded. I was interested in the property myself, you know. I am traveling the West Indies looking for a property and I heard about it. That's why I am here, at this hotel. And, by coincidence, you are here. There would have been legal and local problems for me in any case. But we could be partners – I don't know how much capital you are planning to put in Haut-Clair – you could perhaps use a silent partner – one with knowhow, as you Americans say."

"It's worth reflecting on," said Alice. "Henri Cantave's funeral is Friday, tomorrow. I am taking a trip in any case. I was going to go to Columbia."

"Don't go to Columbia. You won't meet anyone there you can trust."

"Narcisse and I need a decent interval between the funeral and the wedding. I would like to visit Peru – I have never been there. Can we go to Cuzco, the Inca capital?"

"My dear, we have to go to Cuzco, our farm is in the province."

"I'll let you know tomorrow." She took a note of his flight number, got up, and said goodnight.

The next morning Alice avoided the Peruvian by going to the beach early and having lunch in her room. She knew no one in Columbia. She would go to Peru with him; she would learn all she could from him before making any decision about a partnership, but she shrank at any kind of intimacy. She didn't like him.

When the Cadillac came for her in the afternoon she sat in the back with the old doctor, Robert Cantave. He was courteous to her, acknowledging that the funeral would be a bit of an ordeal for her because his sister-in-law did not accept her and seemed to be offering his friendship. This amused Paul who teased his father for flirting with Alice. Soon they were all laughing and then, remembering that it was a funeral, were quiet.

"Paul, I went to Haut-Clair again yesterday. I went up the path and met the people. They seemed to welcome me as if I were Aloyshovna herself. But you know, if Narcisse and I do decide to farm there, those paths are too narrow to transport goods."

"They were built for two-legged beasts of burden."

"There is not even room for two people to pass. As you said, there must have been two paths, one for traffic going up and one for traffic going down, but the other is completely overgrown. As I say, if we farm there, we'll have to have another form of transport. I thought of helicopters. You flew helicopters for the US navy, didn't you, Paul? What do you think it would cost to run one?"

"Something that could move heavy goods? Like bulldozers? Suggest that you contract that out. A small one that only takes one pilot could be very useful. Put me on your list of applicants. I'm sure that the kind of work you offer would be a lot more interesting than driving a taxi. I'll try to work out a budget for you. I'm sure that I can help you in many ways." He looked back over the seat at her.

She remembered that the first time he drove her, he had hinted that he dealt in drugs. "The job might involve more than just flying," she replied.

"Good," said Paul.

They arrived at the church and drew up in front of it. Alice and Robert stepped out and were greeted on the steps by Narcisse and Philippe. She had not met Philippe in person and was introduced. He's a good-looking man, she thought, and obviously gay; he looks like he could be amusing. Yvonne was already inside. As they waited for Paul, a Cadillac limousine drew up. The Leopard contingent had arrived.

The first to emerge was Saba, the queen, dressed in black silk robes. She was recognizably Yvonne's sister. She was followed by her daughter, Zena, a startlingly beautiful young black woman. Her ancestor, Zena, who had led the rebellion, had been rumored to be Nubian, and her features were Eritrean, or Ethiopian, rather than West African. Herodotus makes it clear that, in his time, the pharaohs and priests of Egypt were Nubians. Zena's ancestress, the first queen of Guinea, was believed to have been a descendant of the pharaohs. Both women were, unlike the Guinea people Alice had seen, very black. It made sense. The Guinea men had taken Arawak wives because of a shortage of African women. But the original queen, also named Zena, would have had her pick of African men. Guinea was a matriarchy. Narcisse had told her that the queen did not always acknowledge the father of her children. She would choose one daughter as her successor, not necessarily the oldest.

Saba had chosen Zena. Her eyes immediately locked with Alice's and after a moment Alice felt obliged to lower her gaze. It's as though she has looked into my soul and did not like what she saw, Alice thought. The two women were followed by a man whom she assumed was Saba's consort.

Narcisse introduced his aunt Saba and Zena to Alice. Not sure if she was supposed to courtesy, Alice held out her hand, the women didn't take it, but made small polite bows, meeting her eyes. Saba's consort, Nguma, dressed in a beautifully tailored old-fashioned morning coat of black silk, did take her hand and said, in Creole, "I wish you many healthy children." She thanked him in Creole and said that she hoped to visit Guinea in the new year.

Saba took Nguma's arm and Zena took Narcisse's. Narcisse offered his other arm to Alice. Pretending not to see, she dropped back and took Philippe's arm. Alice noticed that Zena's face lit up when she looked at Narcisse. She will not be happy about our engagement, she thought. Paul and Robert came up behind. For the service, Alice sat in the front row on the right with Philippe, Paul and Robert. The Guineans sat on the left with Narcisse and his mother.

The Roman Catholic cathedral of St. Antoine was a fine old eighteenth-century church built of coral stone in a fourteenth-century gothic style. It was a long service with a full choir conducted in part by the Bishop of St. Anthony. After the service Narcisse came up to her, and said that his mother would like her to ride with them to the reception, so she got into the limousine with Yvonne, Narcisse, and Philippe.

The reception was in Yvonne's garden. Alice stood with the family and was introduced to St. Anthony society as Narcisse's fiancée. There was a choice of tea or a bar. After the last of the mourners had passed through, Alice left the family and headed for the bar to get herself a large rum and ginger ale. She took a sip and looking up, saw Narcisse a hundred feet away, with his back to her, in animated conversation with Zena. Paul, in the driveway helping his father into the Cadillac, was watching. "Wait a minute, Papa," he said. "I'll see if Alice wants a ride home."

As he walked toward Alice, Paul saw that the eyes of the two women were locked. There was an electric tension between them. All at once the lawn seemed like a giant chessboard and the path between the queens a diagonal. He had a sudden giddy feeling that neither of them was being protected; whoever had the first move could take the other off the board without risk.

But it was Narcisse who moved; following Zena's gaze, he noticed Alice standing alone. Paul could see but not hear him make his excuses and walk over to her. As Paul came up to them, he heard Alice say, "I'm tired. I would like to go home and pack. Would your mother mind?"

Yvonne and Saba, half-sisters, were seated together on a bench in an arbor near the orchids, their arms around each other, weeping and sharing a handkerchief. Narcisse said, "No, she won't mind. She knows that you are going away. I'll tell her that you have to pack. The will is being read after the reception. You don't need to stay for that. I'll come to the hotel after dinner to say goodbye."

Alice didn't want to stay for the reading of the will. Then they noticed Paul. "My father is not well," said Paul. "We're leaving now. Would you like a lift?" She gave Narcisse a kiss and left with Paul.

When Narcisse came to see her that evening to say goodbye, he told her that the will had appointed him heir to Haut-Clair as expected. Philippe would draw up the marriage contract on her return and it would become hers when they married. No money had been left to him to develop the plantation; that he had to find himself. Saba and Nguma had spoken to him about developing it and confirmed what Alphonse LaTulippe had told him in Paris; they were agreeable to its development and Philippe would negotiate the tax.

"What about the Abu? What do Saba and Nguma say about them?"

"Neither the Guinea people nor the government of St. Antoine recognize that the Abu even exist. They're not just considered squatters, but squatters without rights. They're our problem, and you, my good Alice, have befriended them already and offered them work."

"You're quite certain the government of St. Anthony has no say in what goes on at Haut-Clair?"

"Quite. You can ask Philippe about it if you like when you get back, but I can assure you that under the original treaty no one from St. Anthony, government agents included, has the right to set foot on it. You'll be seeing him anyway because he will be negotiating the terms of the royalties or taxes. I would prefer that you work that out with him. I have no head for business."

"Can you keep it secret from Nguma and Saba that this is being done with my money?"

"I think they know already. Philippe is their lawyer, after all, and can't very well keep things from them."

"Can Philippe keep it out of the newspaper?"

"He thinks so. Don't worry, Philippe understands that – sweetheart that you are – you want me to get all the credit."

"And your friend Zena, does she find me sweet?"

Narcisse laughed. "If she does, she didn't make it obvious."

"She doesn't like me. She made that obvious. She wants you for herself."

"Nonsense. We were friends as children, that's all. It is some kind of woman thing between you, I suppose. She has heard of the marriage settlement. I don't think she is happy about it, but Philippe has told them that they will just have to accept it, because you are financing the plantation. This all came up at the reading of the will. You know, Philippe was supposed to marry Zena, but he – "

"Is not interested in girls."

"No, I'm afraid not. And besides Zena never liked him and made it obvious. By the way, Saba is not well; she has cancer. Uncle Robert wants her to go into the hospital in Le Havre, but she refuses. She is treating herself, Zena assisting of course. It is a bad time all around for our family."

"I expect that interests you, though, the Voudon treatment."

"Very much. I hope to spend time with them in Guinea."

Alice was thoughtful for a moment. "Maybe I'll buy you a little sports car as a wedding present, make it easy for you to get over there, you could leave it at the trading post."

Narcisse looked at her, wondering whether there was an innuendo in this suggestion.

She smiled at this. "I'm serious. I'd like to buy you a car, I promised you one in Paris, didn't I? Go ahead, choose one, and I'll pay for it when I get back."

He wanted to come up to her room for some goodbye lovemaking before her trip, but Alice said no, not on the day of the funeral.

Besides, she said, she had to pack. The truth was that although annoyed with him for the attention he had paid to Zena, she was losing interest in him as a lover. And she knew that he wouldn't spend the night, that he would leave right after sex and go back to his mama. She just kissed him goodbye and he left. So, Alice thought as she went upstairs, Zena doesn't like the idea of Haut-Clair being mine and she wants Narcisse for herself. Well, maybe she can have him. He is starting to get in my way, we shall see – we shall see how it plays out.

8

Upstairs, dressed in pajamas, Alice began packing for the trip. If everything went satisfactorily in Peru, and there was no need to go to Columbia, Alice would go next to Barbados. After some emails and phone calls she had chosen a Barbadian architect, a firm experienced in restoring old coral buildings. Then she would go to Tampa to see a contractor about clearing a large tract of the jungle. The weather would be hot in all these places. It was most unlikely that she would encounter anyone in Peru who knew Hattie Brading, but the risk would be greater in Barbados and Tampa. Her modeling classes in Paris had succeeded in altering her posture and walk. Her hair was its natural black again – and she was not going to change it – but she would wear colored contacts in Barbados and Tampa. Wherever she went she had to dress fashionably to distinguish herself from Hattie. She had bought some good tropical clothes since she had arrived in St. Anthony and wouldn't be traveling as light as she would have preferred. The truth was that she had never been interested in clothes; dressing fashionably was a bit of a chore, but she had to do it.

She assumed that the possessions of the deceased Hattie Brading had been disposed of; she had not left a will. Her father would probably have just sent everything to the Salvation Army. So with the exception of her treasury bills, everything Alice owned was in the hotel suite. She wouldn't need her winter clothes. Since she was returning to the hotel in a few weeks, she could leave a couple of suitcases there.

She had finished packing and was sorting the suitcases into those that were coming and those that were staying when she came to the laptop computer case. Something wasn't right. The side pocket that was designed to hold the computer had two zipper clasps running on the same track. She always kept them both at the same end. Always. But the two clasps now met in the middle.

Someone had taken it out and put it back in. Recently. She looked about her. There were one or two other indications that her room had been searched.

There was nothing on the laptop computer. She kept everything encrypted on CDs that were in a side pocket. Her encryption code was an RC5-64, someone with a 450-MHz Pentium II might be able to crack it in a year. She wasn't worried about anyone getting at her files. She had her password memorized; it wasn't written down anywhere. But someone had evidently tried to look for information on her computer. With a growing sense of concern she took her computer out of the case and searched the pockets. There was one zippered envelope on the side that she never used. She opened it and there was the warranty for the computer made out to Hattie Braden.

"Damn! How stupid," she exclaimed aloud. Someone had her name: a search on the Internet would turn up news stories about her disappearance, about the headless woman in the lake, about her death.

It had to be Hector. She had set her heart on Haut-Clair, with its grand house, which she would restore to its earlier magnificence, its adoring people – part-time cannibals though they might be – and its tremendous economic potential as a producer of coca. She was looking into refining the coca into cocaine herself. No one could be permitted to get in her way. Hector wanted something from her: he wanted in on the cocaine plantation at Haut-Clair, and maybe something more. Could he be thinking of a bigger operation, Haut-Clair as a site for refining Peruvian coca? And now he could blackmail her into a partnership that he would control. This was intolerable to Alice.

Blackmailers are often murdered, and that this would be Hector's fate, she had no doubt. But they protect themselves, they seal an envelope, they leave it with someone, a lawyer perhaps "To be opened in the event of my death." The victim is informed; the blackmailer feels safe. Hector would do this immediately. He had a laptop himself – she had seen him working on it on the veranda. So he would, perhaps right now, be writing down what he knew, putting it in a file, and forwarding it to his lawyer or a trusted friend as an attachment to an email. As they were leaving the next morning he would probably delay making a paper copy until he got home.

How did he get in here? She looked at her own key, which was large and old fashioned; the locks on the rooms at Les Palmes could easily be picked. Probably it had happened while she was at the funeral. One night, strolling on the verandah, she had noticed that Hector sometimes slept with his sitting room door open. Although up to date in some respects, the hotel was not air-conditioned. Perhaps he had left the door open as an invitation to her.

She put on a dressing gown and walked along the verandah to his sitting room. The moon was full and in the west. The door was open and she could hear him snoring in the bedroom. She entered the sitting room and looked around for his laptop. Not seeing it, she looked in the bedroom and there it was on the bed beside him. He had fallen asleep with it on. Is there a battery? If I unplug it it should automatically go on battery. Moving like a cat she unhooked it – it stayed on, the battery was working – picked it up, and carried it back to her room. Because it was still on she didn't need his password. Had it been turned off, she would have hacked into it if it had taken her all night.

Alice could read Spanish quite well. She went to Sent Messages and found exactly what she was looking for: an email sent that night with an attached file. She looked up the recipient in Hector's electronic address book and found that he was indeed a lawyer. The email instructed the recipient to only open the file in the event of Hector's death. Alice opened the file herself. There it was: a short note identifying Alice LeBlanc as Hattie Brading and instructing the recipient to get in touch with the Sûrêté du Québec.

Alice went to her own computer and emailed her virus file, updated and improved, to Hector's email address as an attachment. Hector's computer then sent it to the lawyer with this message in Spanish: Please open this attachment pronto. She then deleted the message with the attachment that she had mailed to Hector in case he opened his computer in the morning. The lawyer's computer would probably not be opened until Monday. A telephone call between Hector and the lawyer on Saturday morning could give the game away. But who works Saturdays in South America? And they were leaving early. She would not let him out of her sight; Alice was a risk-taker and she liked her chances on this one.

There was one other thing: because the file that contained the virus had been sent from Hector's computer, questions would be asked on Monday at the lawyer's office. At some point over the weekend she would have to steal his laptop – not now though because then he would know it was her. She gave Hector's computer a new password so that he wouldn't be able to use it in the meantime.

She went back to Hector's room and just as she was replacing the computer on his bed and hooking it back up, he stirred. She took a couple of steps back, still facing him. He woke up and saw her; she took a step toward him so that it would look as if she had just walked in. She caught sight of herself in a full-length wardrobe mirror. The moonlight caught her from the side and with her black hair curling loose around her face, her dressing gown open and her top pajama buttons undone, she looked sexy. For a moment she was frozen, looking at herself. She felt a sudden pang and remembered Theodore, the horseman. I miss him, she thought suddenly, I shouldn't be in this room with this horrid little monster whom I am now going to have to seduce.

"Alice, what are you doing here?" asked Hector, closing his laptop and sliding it under the spare pillow.

Alice undid another button on her pajama top. "What do you think?" she whispered. "I'm lonely." Looking at him she undid another button. Her left breast was now almost entirely exposed. Hector was immediately animated. He sat up and then lay down again, his hand moving under the covers. Awful little man, he's masturbating, she thought. I don't want to touch him unless I have to.

"In the corner, in the corner," he pointed. In the corner of the room Alice could make out a tall narrow object that she soon saw was a horsewhip. She picked it up and looked back at him. He had turned over onto his side, his fat bottom exposed, his little hand still working. So that's what he wanted – she was greatly relieved and performed this task with zest. When Hector, gasping, reached orgasm Alice put the whip back in the corner.

"Not exactly what I came for," she remarked aloud. "But I enjoyed it." They exchanged sickly smiles and she left.

Alice had breakfast in the dining room. She did not want to go to Peru with Hector, but her business instincts told her that she had to. Hector entered the dining room and sat down at her table without asking, a revoltingly smug expression on his face. Alice made no reference to the night before, but asked him directly what she could hope to learn from him in Peru. Everything, he said, that you need to know about growing cocaine. Plus, he added with a wink, its refinement.

"I am to be your partner, after all, so I won't have any secrets from you. Nor will you have secrets from me. You don't, you know," he said, his voice oily with innuendo. "I am sure it has occurred to you that Haut-Clair is not just suited for the growing of coca, but because of its seclusion, for the refinement of the coca paste into cocaine."

All cards were now on the table. Almost. "We will have to agree to terms," said Alice.

"Oh, we will agree alright, have no fear of that, my dear. You will see, when we get to Lima – let's see, today is Saturday – we will go to the country on Sunday, I will show you a large coca plantation, I will show you seeds and a coca paste factory and we will come to terms. You will meet my nephew, Juan, you might like him; he is very good-looking for a *cocalero*, that's what we call them, the coca growers. Mind you, he grows coca on a very large scale and of course is from a very old Peruvian family. Mine. Oh yes, we will, we will agree, have no fear of that. With what I know about you, we will come to terms." He gave an unpleasant little laugh. "And Monday we will go and see my lawyer in Lima. I know you want to spend some time in Cuzco with the Inca ruins, but it will have to wait until later."

"I have ordered a taxi," she said. "We should share it. Are you packed?"

"My bags are already in the lobby," he said. His smugness told her told her that he had not yet talked to his lawyer. As long as the disgusting little man is smug, she thought, I'm holding the better cards.

Paul's wasn't the first taxi in line at the hotel entrance and Alice didn't ask for him, so he didn't drive them, but he saw them leave together with luggage and his curiosity was aroused. He questioned his friend the doorman and learned that the gentleman was Peruvian and the two were going to Peru together. This information made him all the more curious; he began to suspect what she was up to.

Hector owned several coffee plantations and on the flight he told her a number of useful things about coffee cultivation. She showed him the green beans that she had picked up when she went with Paul to find the path to Haut-Clair. He identified them as arabica, and thought that they were of the original African variety, from what is now called Namibia. She told him that she had tasted the coffee made from them and that it was excellent. As the coffee trees had survived in the wild at Haut-Clair for over two hundred years, clearly there would be no problems cultivating this variety. Hector would roast the beans and try the coffee when they got to his house in Lima.

"It will take five years. The other crop will take about three. It also takes time and time is money. Refinement on the other hand, we can begin as soon as we build the plant. You will have my help and that of my nephew. It is not something that you should risk on your own."

"Narcisse and I do not have a budget at present, Hector, but he has raised money in Paris and we should not be in need of capital."

"But you will need our help with the crops and building the refinery, and of course we can keep you supplied with coca paste. Then there is the marketing. You will need us for that."

"Maybe not. I have connections. Let's wait and see. I am sure we will come to an understanding."

"Where are your connections? Canada? Not a very big market."

Alice did not reply. He is going to be useful, there is no doubt about that, but I do not want him as a partner. I am certainly glad that he made that mistake with the zipper, she thought. Forewarned is forearmed. If I had to listen to these rotten innuendos without knowing what he knows and how he knows it, I might think him a narc – except they cannot possibly pick them this obnoxious. She picked up her book and ignored him for the rest of the flight.

Hector drank several vodkas with orange juice while Alice read. In Bogota there was an hour's wait for the flight to Peru. They went to the bar and he ordered another. They each carried their laptop cases and placed them on a spare seat at the table. The two cases were similar in appearance. Their other luggage had been checked through.

When Hector went to the washroom Alice picked up Hector's case and left the bar. She removed the address label, went to the airline counter and bought a one-way ticket to Le Havre on the next flight. She wrote a new label for the computer bag with her name on it, and the address as Les Palmes, St. Anthony, W.I. She attached this label and checked the bag.

Then she returned to the bar. Hector was ordering himself another drink. "I hope you will excuse my drinking so much," he said. "I am terrified of flying. It is unnatural that these big heavy aircraft can fly, what keeps them up? And don't talk to me about the airfoil effect. I simply do not believe it could work."

Alice smiled sympathetically. Their flight was called and Alice watched Hector pick up her laptop. She waited until he started to move off and then said, "Hector, I think you have my computer there."

He looked at the label. "Santa Madre, you're right. Then where's mine?"

They both looked around. "Perhaps you took it to the washroom," said Alice.

"Were you here all the time?"

"No, I went to the washroom myself."

"You didn't take your case?"

"Yes, I did, of course I did. When I came back, I didn't notice yours was gone – I supposed that you had it with you."

Hector was a bit too drunk to be sure what had happened. He rushed off to the washroom. "Please, Alicia, report it stolen. I'll meet you at the gate." He left and she went to the gate.

"Perhaps you checked it in Le Havre," said Alice when he came up.

"No, no, I remember taking it off the plane."

"Yes, I remember now, you did have it."

On the flight Hector was quite grumpy and suspicious. Alice was all innocence; they hardly spoke. They were met at the Lima airport by Manuel, Hector's manservant. He drove them in a small Cadillac to Hector's house, which was a two-story house of white-stucco at the top of a hill. It was built in Moorish style, surrounding a courtyard. In the center there was a swimming pool.

"Manuel will show you to your room. I'm going to take a siesta," said Hector. "I suggest that you do the same. Unless you would like to swim first."

"I shall siesta," said Alice, "and swim later."

Alice's bedroom was a corner room with windows looking east and south; it was misty out but she could see the port of Callao and the sea some miles away. When she woke up it was late afternoon. She put on a bathing suit, draped herself in a beach towel, and came downstairs. The inner court was elegant: the pool had shallow curved steps at both ends – there was no diving board – and water lilies. On the four sides of the courtyard there were flower gardens and palm trees in the corners. Alice swam ten lengths in a steady even crawl. Emerging, she heard Hector clapping his hands from a balcony above. "Magnifico, what a woman you are," he cried. "Now let us change and drink some good Peruvian wine."

He had definitely cheered up. "Do you know much about computers?" he asked, as they sipped chilled white wine. "There is nothing on it that I desperately need. It's just a piece of hardware really. I can replace it. What worries me is that it could have been stolen by an enemy, someone who wants information on my business. They would need my ID and a password to open it. There are people called hackers who can open these things. What do you think?"

Alice was pleasantly surprised by this candid request for help. She was evidently not suspected. She said, "If an enemy wanted your computer to find out your secrets, he would burglarize you. A laptop left lying around in an airport bar is a thousand times more likely to be stolen by a local thief who hangs around looking for an opportunity. I would be willing to wager a large sum that whoever stole your computer will have it wiped clean except for Windows or whatever program you have and sell it."

"My thinking exactly," exclaimed Hector, clapping his hands.

Alice knew full well that was a wager she couldn't win, if taken up on it, for she had every intention, as Hector's enemy, of hacking into Hector's laptop herself and finding out what she could about his business.

Hector began to talk about the Incas, mostly because he wanted Alice to know that he was descended from one of the Spanish aristocrat soldiers who had taken an Inca princess as his wife. Alice got rather drunk in case there was to be a distasteful sexual part to the evening, and affected a greater interest in Hector's family tree than she felt. At dinner they sat at either end of a dining table on a raised patio at one end of the pool under the stars. They were waited on by Manuel whose wife had cooked the dinner: the main course was a freshly caught sea bass, but Alice didn't touch it.

"Are you a vegetarian?" asked Hector.

"Not a strict one." Alice replied. "I eat fish now and then. But Chilean sea bass is an endangered species, it's over-fished."

"Peruvian sea bass, please, that is what we call it here."

"It was formerly called toothfish, actually, the name sea bass is a marketing gimmick. Who would buy something called a toothfish?"

Hector laughed and they were silent for a while. "A nuevo sol for your thoughts, Alice? That's the Peruvian currency in case you didn't know." Manual brought in fruit.

"Oh, I was imagining myself in a hockey rink." For some perverse reason, perhaps because she had drunk too much wine, Alice wanted to see if Hector could resist another snide reference to her nationality. "I was at school for a while in New Hampshire and we played ice hockey. I suppose it's the pool, shimmering like an ice rink, and the balconies above – for a moment it felt like I was in an arena."

"That is a Canadian sport is it not?" he asked, rising to the bait, and then giggled, as if he knew that she had done it on purpose. "You are quite the athlete. I saw you swimming and I am still smarting from last night. No little games tonight, I am afraid."

This was a great relief to Alice. "Let us try some of your coffee. Tomorrow you will see snow as we fly over the mountains to Cuzco. That should make you feel at home. I promise not to get drunk on the plane. The smaller the plane the less nervous I am. Because small planes are lighter perhaps. It's the big ones that I always feel are about to drop like stones. Cuzco, by the way, is the name of the district as well as the city. The district was the first Inca Empire. Manuel will come with us. He is a good driver. He comes from the district and knows the roads well. I keep a car at the airport at the other end. Roads are narrow and – uh – the driving can be treacherous once we leave the main road – which was built by the Incas, by the way. It leads to Machu Picchu, the most spectacular sanctuary of the Inca Empire. Undefiled by conquerors. I have been a number of times and don't want to go again, but perhaps after we have settled our business, you should go back to Cuzco and take a little tour.

"The plantation we are going to is on relatively low ground – for Peru. I think I have already mentioned that the variety of coca plant best suited for Haut-Clair is of the *novogranatense* species and the variety of the same name, *novogranatense*. The other *novogranatense* variety, *truxillense*, and the two varieties of the *coca* species that have commercial value, do better at higher altitudes. At our lower plantation in Cuzco the climate is hotter and drier; it's not very different from Haut-Clair. The altitude, at 1,000 feet is higher, but I am not worried about that.

"We have had success there with a variety of *novogranatense*. My nephew and I have developed a new strain. I am tempted to call it *novogranatense* variety *gonzalez*. But, you know, in this business one does not seek publicity. Rather the contrary. We will keep our seeds to ourselves and selected partners such as yourself. What makes a coca plant powerful is the cocaine alkaloid content. We are getting a content as high as the best coca grown at the highest altitudes. We think this variety can be grown further north in the West Indies, Mexico, perhaps even parts of the USA.

"We will pick up a bag of seeds for you and on Monday we will go and see my lawyer and formulate an agreement. I am not sure it will be enforceable legally, but we will know where we stand with respect to the other party. I do not break agreements and I am sure you don't either. Agreements can be enforced by means outside the law, as you know." He paused.

Alice said nothing.

"Terrible, really, how Western civilization overdoes things," Hector continued. "The leaves, chewed as they are picked off the plant, gave the Indians a lift, a bit of a boost that enabled them to climb mountains. The Coca Cola Company still buys a lot of coca paste from Peru. Nowadays they remove the alkaloid. They didn't always. It was a mild stimulant: "the pause that refreshes." In parts of Mexico, I believe, they still leave the alkaloid in. Perhaps that is why their president is so popular. But now we Westerners have airplanes to fly over the mountains, and we refine the coca plant to make a hard drug that drives people mad. It doesn't matter in the case of Americans; they are all mad already. Of course, by Americans, I don't mean us South Americans or Mexicans and Canadians who live in North America, I mean the people who live in the United States. I just make the paste. What the people I sell it to do with it is not my concern. If they sell it to Americans, so what? The USA has not been good to South America. I don't like the United States of America. I warmed to you a little, Alicia, when I discovered that you were Canadian."

"I am not a Canadian."

Hector ignored this. "What drew me to St. Anthony was that I was looking for a secluded, unsupervised place to start a small plantation and then refine the product. It is much, much more profitable refined. The refinery is much more important than the plantation – we will be bringing coca paste in from Peru long before your crop matures. The Guinea reservation seemed interesting; then I heard about Haut-Clair. I was in no position to proceed. I needed a local partner. It was a fortunate accident that I was staying at Les Palmes, Alicia, when you were. I investigated you and quickly found out your connection to the owners of Haut-Clair.

"These investigations led me to discover that your real name is Hattie Brading. So you see, my dear, I have a partner whom I can trust absolutely. Oh, and in case you get any ideas, my lawyer has a file with a great deal of information about Hattie Brading in his office. Sealed. To be opened in the event of my death."

This was a great relief to Alice. So far so good; he had not spoken to his lawyer. To make him feel comfortable in his advantage, she affected shock, was silent, then said, "You are rather an extraordinary man. But I can't understand how you know. It is disturbing. Please at least tell me how you found out. If I have left a track uncovered I must know."

Hector said, "I appreciate your concern and I will tell you. I picked the lock on your door and searched your room while you were at the funeral. I tried to open your computer and failed. But then I searched the pockets of your computer case. There is one I doubt if you ever use. Inside is the guarantee for your laptop made out to Hattie Brading. It is an unusual name. I looked for it on Google. She's dead. The headless body of a – "

"Stop! How stupid of me."

"You know we all of us make silly mistakes sometimes and it is the silly mistakes that get us caught out. Don't worry. Your secret is safe with me."

"I am in your debt, Hector. I will not forget it. I am sure that we can do business. So I admit it, I am a Canadian. I share your anti-Americanism. My ancestor, Henry Brading, was a Loyalist. Our property in Virginia was seized by the neighbors during the American Revolution. There was no compensation." In fact Alice was not anti-American at all and could trace the Bradings back only as far as her grandfather, who had died in prison in Kingston convicted of manslaughter.

"Really," said Hector, "how very interesting. You Canadians then are historical enemies of the USA. By the way, this is excellent coffee. Shade-grown, organic, I would leave your largest trees."

"I intend to."

Early the next morning as they set off in the Cadillac for the airport with Manuel, Alice said, "I have to go to a pharmacy. Is there time? Is there one on the way?"

"No problemo," said Manuel, and she realized that he understood English. He drove to a *farmacia* and Hector started to come in with her. She stopped him.

"To translate?" he asked.

"No, thank you," said Alice. "It is a woman thing, I would rather that you didn't come. I know the Spanish word."

Her purchase safely in her handbag, she got back in the car. It was Sunday and there was not much traffic so they were soon at the airport. The plane was small without a first class compartment. Alice sat by the window and Manuel sat a few seats behind them. After they took off, Hector pointed out the port of Callao, which Alice had seen from her room. The port seemed busy. She could see ships arriving and leaving and a huge cruise ship departing. It was December and North Americans who could afford it and had leisure were escaping their winter. It was early summer in Peru. The weather was clear and the view of the Andes spectacular. They were silent on the flight except for the occasional exclamation from Alice.

On arrival they disembarked and waited outside the airport for Manuel to pick them up in a yellow Lincoln Explorer utility vehicle with a manual shift.. They left Cuzco on the old Inca highway, which was smooth and solid, but soon turned off onto a narrow gravel road. The plantation that they were heading for was on the other side of a small mountain range. Alice, sitting behind Manuel, was exhilarated peering down the steep drop on the left as they climbed up and up, hugging the mountain. There were no guardrails. Hector on the other hand, she noticed, kept his eyes closed. The grade was steep but gave the Lincoln no trouble. When they came to a sharp curve, Manuel would honk and hug the mountain on their right. Occasionally there was an answering honk and an old truck would come roaring down on the outside track, in low gear, driving on the very edge of the precipice.

They descended into a broad valley, Manuel skillfully gearing down as they went. After driving on the plain for about half an hour, they went through a pair of formal white gates, up a long drive, and parked in front of a modern, California-style ranch house. Manuel disappeared around the back of the house as a handsome young man, looking quite South American with a moustache, jeans, and leather waistcoat, greeted Hector and Alice.

"Alice, I would like you to meet my nephew Juan, Juan Gonzalez-Sacramento. Juan, may I present Alice LeBlanc, our new associate in the Caribbean."

Juan was perhaps a bit too charming. He explained in excellent English that his cook was Manuel's sister. "My uncle tells me that you are vegetarian. We are going to have a specialty of the region, *pepe a la huan caina*. You will like it."

"But we must get back tonight, Juan," said Hector, "you understand, we cannot have a huge Peruvian dinner followed by a long siesta."

"*Entendido, tio*. It is a lunch, as the English say, and it is ready. You will have time for a short siesta while I show Alice around. Please come in."

Juan's wife, Pepita, and several attractive children joined them for lunch. The main course, *pepe a la huan caina*, turned out to be boiled potatoes with milk, cottage cheese, bread crumbs, and peppers of several sorts. Alice found it delicious and said so. The conversation was mostly about the coca plant. Hector was quiet and let his nephew speak. "We are harvesting seeds right now. I understand you are going to try our new variety in the West Indies, and I am to give you a bag of seeds – say four kilograms or so, about ten pounds. Right, uncle?"

"Yes. The details are not worked out but Alice I am confident will be our partner. She and I can work out the details about the refinery and the division of the profits with Alfonzo on Monday. Our lawyer and a cousin," he added, looking at Alice in his cagey way. "You are to take the seeds. I don't anticipate any problems with our agreement."

"Plant them when you get back," Juan continued. "December is a good time to plant. When the plants are two to three years old, you can gather your own seeds. The place is quite wild, I gather, so there will be wild bees to pollinate. You can start harvesting leaves after about a year, but you won't get many. Wait until the plant is big enough that it can afford to lose a few leaves. Here we harvest continually. Some farms higher up harvest only in certain months. We provide seeds to small farmers. Hector buys the leaves and turns them into coca paste. He has coca paste factories all over

Peru. Shall I take our guest to see your coca paste factory here, uncle?"

"By all means. I congratulate you, Pepita, on the *pepe a la huan caina*. You were quite right, Juan, there is now time for me to have a siesta. This northern woman," he said archly, "won't need one."

Juan and Alice got up and went outside to his Jeep. As he drove, he talked. "Coca harvesting is labor-intensive. A woman using her apron can gather, oh sixty pounds of leaves in a day. You don't let the plants grow too tall or the leaves become hard to reach. They can grow into a shrub thirty feet high. You don't want that. It's like pruning fruit trees: if you cut off the leader, you will get a bushier plant."

Juan took his hand from the stick shift and put it on her knee. Alice removed it. "Remember, soak the seeds first, remove the floaters, and put them in a seed bed for six weeks or so. Then you transplant them. Drainage is important for the coca plant, you – "

"I know most of this," said Alice, interrupting. "I have a Peruvian book on it. *La Cuidar y Cultivada de Coca Planta*. Do you know it?"

"An excellent book, but seeing and doing are also necessary." The hand went back on the knee and was again removed. "A good seed bed is very important. My wife Pepita no longer welcomes my seeds so I need to find other places to plant them." Alice found this remark sickeningly coy. He drove to a long shed near a stream on the edge of the ranch. Outside was a platform where Alice could see leaves spread out in the sun to dry. "We will watch them make the paste. It is better to see it done than to read about it."

They went into the shed. There were several large pits dug into the ground and lined with plastic. Several women were in the pit trampling the leaves. They gave Juan a warm greeting; evidently he was popular. She wondered which of them, how many of them, and how often had welcomed Juan's seeding organ. Alice herself was not the least bit interested; he was too smooth, too good-looking.

"There are four stages to making the paste. First we put the leaves in the pit, then add water and sodium carbonate." He gestured towards a wall where there were bags of the chemical and cans of kerosene. "Without the sodium carbonate the cocaine alkaloid would not dissolve in the kerosene, which we add next. That's the second stage. It's pretty simple. The girls know how to do it; no one supervises them. The leaves need to be agitated and for this we use the beautiful feet of Peruvian women."

One girl understood English and translated. They all laughed and looked coyly at the handsome Juan. Several of them took a break and lit hand-rolled cigarettes.

"So we soak the leaves and agitate them. After two days, we drain off the water and remove the leaves. That's the third step. Fourth, the solvent is added to a dilute acid solution. Dump in some more sodium carbonate and the cocaine alkaloid precipitates. Then it's filtered and dried." Juan handed her a lump. It was a whitish-brown putty-like substance.

"The next two stages, turning the paste into cocaine base, and then into cocaine hydrochloride, the valuable white stuff, are often combined. We don't do that here. It's illegal. Making paste is permitted. The paste is used in soft drinks and herbal teas. But frankly I don't think Uncle Hector sells his paste to people who use it to make soft drinks and herbal teas."

They went outside and got back in the Jeep. "What the girls were smoking is a blend of tobacco and dried coca paste. It gives them a lift. I will tell you something." Juan gave Alice a big smile and winked. "Hector pays us for the coca leaves approximately two per cent of the US wholesale value of cocaine. I rent that shed to him for peanuts. He makes a pretty good profit on the paste, much more than we farmers make growing the leaves.

"But what he is looking for is somewhere to refine it further. The next two steps involve more complex chemistry. He is looking for somewhere secret; we have the police, the army, and the United States drug enforcement people keeping an eye on us. I have not time to tell you everything. But the people we fear more than any government are the Columbians. They buy his paste. They are everywhere in Peru. Your place was on his list of possibilities. There is not that much money in growing coca, nor in selling the paste compared to the refined product, which is portable and untraceable. It is big business: it is estimated that over fifty billion dollars worth of drugs are sold in the USA every year. And three fifths of that is cocaine."

He lit a cigarette one of the girls had given him. "Want one?" Alice shook her head. "He is my uncle, but I tell you honestly, be careful doing business with him."

"I would rather do business with you, but let's get one thing straight. I am not interested in your dick," said Alice.

"I'm sorry, you are very beautiful and – "

"Forget it. Listen. I do not trust your uncle."

"Nor do I, and I am already in business with him."

They drove back in silence and walked around the house to the patio behind it. Alice saw that Manuel was sitting behind the house on the lawn behind the kitchen, drinking wine with a couple of cronies. His sister was not to be seen. Pepita brought out a big pot of strong coffee.

Alice said, "I'll bring Manuel some coffee."

Juan nodded approvingly. On her way over, Alice dropped a couple of tablets, which she had held concealed in her hand – tablets that she had obtained from the drugstore that morning – into the coffee and stirred it with the sugar spoon. Shortly afterward Manuel was not to be seen. Hector came out and poured himself some coffee.

"Did you learn anything?" he asked Alice.

"Yes, I did. A lot of it I had read about but it is another thing, as Juan pointed out, to see it."

"Ready to go? Where is Manuel?"

Pepita came out. There were some rapid words in Spanish, which Alice if she did not fully understand had anticipated. "I'll drive," she said to Pepita in Spanish. "Please get the keys."

Pepita looked at her. Alice had a way of speaking – in any language – that did not encourage questions or argument. She went to get them. Hector looked astonished. "But you do not know these mountain roads...."

"Come, come, of course I know the way. We just drove here. As for mountain roads, I am used to driving mountain roads on ice. I am Canadian, remember?" said Alice, staring Hector down. "I thought that you were anxious to get back. Big meeting tomorrow, you know."

Pepita came back with the keys and gave them to Alice, who turned and started walking around to the front of the house, swinging her bag, which was the heavier for the four kilos of coca seeds. The others followed. When they got to the car, she turned to Juan and Pepita, and kissed them both.

"Thank you so much for lunch and for the seeds. We will meet again. Perhaps you will both visit me in St. Anthony when our house is finished." The invitation was extended to both, but she knew that only Juan would come. She opened the rear door of the car with a flourish. "At your service, Hector," she said, giving him her most charming smile.

He stood there, somewhat flabbergasted, then laughed. "Of course, my dear. These American women, what can you do? Juan, I am disappointed with Manuel. Usually with wine he takes a glass or two, and that's it. Keep him for a day or two, maybe forever." He got in.

Alice closed the door, hopped into the driver's seat, called "Adios" out the open window, and drove off. She drove very fast, passing all traffic in sight, and then slowed down. There was a purpose to this; she wanted to leave the traffic far behind but didn't want to get too close to anything in front. She was looking for a gap in the traffic. That she was terrifying Hector was a bonus.

"Doubt my driving skills, Hector?" she taunted. She looked in the mirror and saw that Hector's face was wet. He was sweating, maybe even crying.

"Alice, I want you to stop. We can go back. Stay the night. Please, please." He had remembered that she was a killer, a useful bit of knowledge for blackmail purposes but it was a two-edged sword. She did not reply. She drove the big Lincoln SUV up the mountain pass and over to the other side driving carefully, skillfully, and very fast until she saw a car ahead. Then she dropped back.

"Alice, you know a complete file on Hattie Brading is at Alonzo's office."

"No, it's not. I destroyed it with a virus along with all his files." Alice had picked out several possible sharp turns on the way up. She would pick one when she could see there was no traffic coming towards her. There was no traffic behind them; she had seen to that. What she was about to do would be difficult. Years before when Charley was teaching her to drive, they had practiced controlled skids but she had never jumped from a moving vehicle. She decided she had to bring the Lincoln to almost a full stop, and if necessary reverse over the precipice.

'Then it was you who stole my computer. See, I believed you, I trusted you."

"You didn't trust me, you thought that you had me in your power, so you were safe. That was stupid and arrogant."

"Please slow down, I'll give you anything, anything." He collapsed in little sobs. He's like a little mouse, Alice thought, caught in a trap and not yet dead.

"I am slowing down, Hector. We'll take a moment to enjoy the view."

As they approached a sharp curve to the left, traveling in the outer lane, Alice braked and then pulled the wheel hard to the left with her right hand while opening the car door with her left. Hector's sobs turned to screams. *Ayesha, my queendom come* – at the last instant, she jumped with both feet and all her strength, carrying her bag, with its handle looped over her shoulder as the Lincoln skidded slowly sideways toward the precipice. It reached the edge going a little faster than Alice had calculated, paused for a brief, scary second on the edge, then went over, rear end first. But Alice, Hector's screams in her ears, went over the cliff, too, the vehicle's forward momentum overcoming the backward momentum of her jump. As the rear end went over first, she was tossed upward as well as forward and came down hard on the edge of the road, with her legs dangling over the cliff. She was badly winded but managed to save herself and the bag with its contents of precious seeds.

A car came along shortly and took her to the hospital in Cuzco. The woman driver gave her a severe scolding in rapid Spanish for speeding. It was one of the cars she had passed. She had trouble understanding most of it, but one persistent question, which included the word *pasajero*, she finally understood. "No, no, *solo*," she replied, shaking her head.

The woman did not come into the hospital, but left her at the door. Alice telephoned Juan's ranch immediately and got Pepita.

Her voice broke as she related what had happened. Then she went to the triage. The hospital decided to keep her overnight to treat her for shock. Late that afternoon two policemen came to her room. One of them spoke English. The Lincoln had burst into flames on landing. There was not much of Hector left to bury. They were sympathetic; there was no question of blame.

"I am sorry to have polluted your valley," said Alice.

The officer smiled at this. "Those SUVs, they are so heavy, they do not take the corners well," he said. "They have too much momentum and the center of balance is too high. That will be in the report. Perhaps you were driving too fast, but I do not like those vehicles. They burn so much *gaz*. Phew!"

The next morning Alonzo, Hector's lawyer, arrived in her room quite early. He was courteous, sympathetic, and spoke good English. If he had read Hector's file on Hattie, there was no sign. He asked her a few questions, explained that Juan was Hector's heir, and that he, Alonzo, was the executor. If she were planning to do any business with the estate, she should address herself to him.

After he had taken his leave and was at the door, he turned. "One thing, senora, one puzzlement, Hector's laptop. It was in the car, I suppose? It is not at his house. I looked for it there last night."

Alice replied, "It was stolen – at the airport in Bogota. He reported it. You can check. It may have turned up."

Alonzo looked thoughtful. "So it was stolen – at the airport – in Bogota. At what time?"

"Oh, about noon, while we were waiting for the Lima plane. We were in the bar. We each went to the washroom. I took the precaution of taking mine. He didn't."

"I see, I see. Well, that explains something." He was bluffing. Would anyone have noticed the time that the email arrived in the split second before opening the virus attachment? Alice doubted it. He gave her a long look with his large brown eyes and stood with his hand on the doorknob for a full minute, as if about to speak. Then he let the lid of his left eye fall for a split second – a beautifully executed wink – and left.

Juan Gonzalez-Balsells had never liked Hector Gonzalez-Prieto despite the fact that his uncle had been good to him. He did not like his personality. When he inherited the hacienda, which had been in the family for generations, Juan had been persuaded by Hector to put it into coca. His father, Jorge, a drinker and womanizer, had died young, leaving a lot of debts. The land was good, in Peru the best arable land on the sierra had been taken by the first settlers. But they were cattlemen and used the land for beef cattle so its fertility was not fully utilized.

Juan had studied agriculture at the university in Lima. It was clear to him that the land would yield a better return in cash crops. He was considering maize and wheat when his uncle Hector offered to buy coca leaves from him. This is happening in many parts of Peru; the price of coca and the ease of its cultivation are taking thousands of acres out of food crops.

Hector leased land from Juan near the small river that ran through the ranch. Coca paste needs a lot of water. The leaves are first dried, as Alice saw, and a shed was built there to shelter the plastic-lined paste pits. Hector used Juan's work force and paid them more than Juan could afford to pay. Juan soon realized that Hector was making much bigger profits on the sale of the paste than he was realizing on the leaves at the price Hector paid him. Hector, who had coca paste plants scattered in different parts of Peru, was a very rich man.

Whenever Juan approached him about renegotiating the deal, Hector would say, "Don't worry, you are my heir anyway, one day you'll get it all. Besides, I can't pay you more than I pay the other growers just because you are my nephew. There's a word for that," said his uncle. "Nepotism." Then he would start talking about the much larger profits made on the refined product.

"You think I have a bigger profit margin than you do? Do you know what those Columbians mark up the cocaine they make from our paste? Seven hundred per cent! And the US retail market is in the order of thirty billion dollars. Do you know that the people of the USA spend more on cocaine than they do on airline tickets? On gas utilities? On newspapers and magazines?" Hector would rant, and then deflect Juan's complaints by trying to interest him in the bold scheme of the refinery out of the country that he was not sure he had the courage to go through with on his own.

Neither Juan nor Hector thought that there was anything less ethical about refining coca into cocaine than in rendering the leaves into paste or growing the leaves. Nor for that matter in selling cocaine to the USA: it was up to the Americans to control the consumption of the drug in their own country. The government of Peru does not permit the refining of cocaine, but it cannot forbid the growing of coca without dire political consequences. It ignores the fact that only a small fraction of Peruvian coca paste actually goes into soft drinks and teas. Growing the leaves provides a cash crop for many people in poor rural areas.

Hector didn't want to break Peruvian law; Peru was his native land and he wanted to live there in peace. Also, it was unlikely that they could build a cocaine refinery in Peru without the Columbians finding out about it. This would result in his cold-blooded murder as an example to other entrepreneurial Peruvians. Hector wanted to refine the paste somewhere else, somewhere secluded where he would not have to bribe people and be at their mercy. His thoughts had turned to the Caribbean and he had visited a number of islands looking for a site.

When Hector came to St. Anthony he had been intrigued by Guinea and especially by Haut-Clair. When he found out that the property belonged to the Cantaves, he gave a junior in Philippe's office a handsome retainer to feed him information. On learning of his fellow guest's connection to the Cantaves, he decided to cultivate her. When he came across her reading a Peruvian book on cultivation of the plant, he thought his search was over. Hector's original plan was to get her more and more involved and then to suggest the idea of a cocaine refinery. When he found out about her past, he thought that he had her completely under his control.

The day after the car accident, which left Hector dead and Alice only bruised and scratched, Juan received a visit from his cousin, the family lawyer, Alonzo Gonzalez-Chavez. They were about the same age and were good friends. They went riding, as they usually did on his visits, but today they just walked the horses. They had much to talk about and did not wish to be overheard. Alonzo, who had been privy to most, but not all, of Hector's secrets, told Juan that he had not drawn up the will. It had been done in his office by one of his colleagues because Alonzo was a beneficiary.

"He left me the house, which was very good of him. Everything else is yours: a lot of cash securities. After we pay the taxes, you are a millionaire. I'll leave you a detailed list of your inheritance, including the coca paste factories that are the principal cash cows as the Americans say. In some of his activities, I was a junior partner. I can help you sort it out. But there is one thing we must talk about right away: the refining project. Are you interested in going through with it?"

"I didn't know that you knew about that. You are very discreet. The answer is, yes, I am interested, but I need to know more."

"In this total discretion is paramount. I have not discussed it with anyone except Hector until this moment. You know, Hector confided in me on most things, but not all – his personal life was always rather a mystery. For the refinery he had decided that that woman's plantation in St. Anthony is suitable. He has an agent in the law office of the Cantaves, and the property currently belongs to one Narcisse Cantave, but it will be hers under a marriage contract already signed, the moment they are married. My information is that she is very rich, and that she has undertaken to finance a coffee plantation there. The husband is not really a player. It is isolated both geographically and legally. They were negotiating. I think it looks promising. I want in for five per cent of your net profit plus my usual fees. What do you think?"

"I agree. If I am going to do this thing I'll want all the help I can get."

"Five per cent of this thing could be a lot more than I can spend." He laughed. "But you know, this woman! Incredible! I have to tell you something. Somebody destroyed the inbox file on our office computer. All our emails and files destroyed. It is not a disaster. We make paper copies. But she noticed – my secretary – she was just opening up the mail, you know, she sorts the emails for me – a lot of rubbish comes in at night – and prints the ones I should read. Well, there were two from Hector, one was titled a woman's name, an English name, Hattie something, she does not recall the last name, she opened it, there was an attachment marked 'to be opened in the event of my death', she did not see how she could print it without opening it, so she left it for me to decide. She saved it as a file. Then there was a second one, marked urgent, with an attachment from Hector, saying that this attachment must be opened immediately so she did and boom! All our files are destroyed."

"By a virus in an email from Hector."

"Yes. Now the woman, Alice, I went to see her at the hospital – she is okay by the way – some scratches, do you know she jumped as the car was going over the cliff, but not quite soon enough. She almost went over the cliff too, but managed to hang on to the edge of the cliff and pull herself up. They are treating her for shock, but she seemed pretty calm to me. She says Hector's laptop was stolen at the airport in Bogota."

"That's a bit strange. And then the car accident! She lives. He doesn't. I see now that she drugged Manuel."

Alfonzo reined in his horse. They were on a rise looking down on a pretty view of the ranch beside a stream. "Do you want to know what I think? He was blackmailing her. You know, we have talked of this before. In several ways Hector was not a nice man. He would blackmail people, not for money, but to get them to do something he wanted them to do. Business associates. There are a number of people who will not be at all sorry that he's dead."

They both dismounted. It was their custom to sit down on this spot, let their horses graze, and smoke cigars. "So it was not an accident, Alfonzo? Impossible to prove, but maybe that's the point. Incredible. Did you take a look at the place where the accident happened?"

They lit up.

"Yes. I looked at the skid marks. She turned the wheel hard left and went right into the skid. That was a new car, that Lincoln Explorer, it has – what do you call it?"

"Skid control, the brakes automatically release when you start to skid."

"Skid control. So to go into a skid, you can't just brake hard, you have to turn the wheel sharply. She did that. I saw the marks in the gravel."

"Did the police notice that?"

"No. It was not in the report. Mind you it would not prove anything. Still I rubbed out the marks with my heel."

"You what?"

"Juan, that woman is to be our partner. When you go to see her, you can tell her I did her a little favor. To let her know that we know." He laughed. "But we certainly must not hint that we might use that knowledge against her."

"What, afraid of her, are you?"

Alonzo laughed again. "That is one incredible woman. If we are going into business with her, we know these things about her. One, she has nerves of steel."

"Two, she is absolutely ruthless."

"And three, she has a past that she doesn't want anyone to know about. What was that name? Hattie. I think I will forget it. It seems that knowing it is fatal."

"I don't want to know about her past."

"Me neither. But, Juan, do you agree that her plantation is worth a look for what we want to do?"

"Yes, Alonzo, I will write to her, stay in touch, ask her how she is doing with the seeds. Then go and see the location in St. Anthony. She's rather attractive. She said to me that she would rather do business with me than Uncle Hector. She didn't like him, she told me." Juan shuddered. "I did mention that he was looking for a place for a refinery to her, you know."

"Did you? I don't know what Hector said to her. How far they got."

"I think she's interested. By the way, do you know if Hector ever tried the next stage, the base stage in Peru?"

"The answer is no. He was too scared of the Columbians," Alonzo replied.

"If we are going to refine cocaine HCl, Alonzo, we must decide, do we do the base stage here, and how do we get it to St. Anthony. We must explore all options, we may need a couple of landing strips, one here and one in Brazil."

"I don't think that we should go beyond the paste stage here in South America, Juan. I favor Guyana. Parts of it are not well policed. Fly the paste to Guyana and then perhaps by boat to St. Anthony. You know, the United States Coast Guard patrols the entire Caribbean with boats and planes. That's the part that worries me the most, do we use fast boats and make many small shipments? Fly it? And then we have to get the cocaine to the US."

"I like Guyana too. There are people refining it there, in the backcountry. Parts of Guyana have not even been explored. I know that Guyana and Barbados, two proud little nations, do not let the Americans stop ships in territorial waters. I don't know if St. Anthony has a coast guard. We have lots to work out before I go to see her," said Juan.

"No, I think we should put our cards on the table before she leaves the country. Maybe I should be the one to go to see her, tell her of my heroic scuffing of the tire marks, tell her that we are interested in being partners in a cocaine refinery."

"But there must not be the slightest hint of blackmail, Alonzo."

They both laughed and rode their horses back to the ranch, neither talking very much, both thinking about the scheme. Alonzo said goodbye and drove straight to the hospital, taking the fatal curve slowly when he came to it. He imagined the Lincoln going over, Hector screaming, his nemesis leaping from it, and shuddered. Unlike Juan, Alonzo had rather liked Hector; he had been amused by his eccentricity.

When Alonzo visited Alice in her private hospital room, he made a point of being agreeable and charming. He played with a cigar in his hand, but did not ask if he could light it. He told her about scuffing the tire tracks and watched her. She made no response, it was as if he had not spoken. Then he outlined the cocaine refining scheme.

"I would be a partner in a small way," he said. "Five per cent of Juan's net. When can you give me an answer?"

"Give me half an hour," said Alice. "Go outside and smoke your cigar."

When he came back, she favored him with a big smile. "I'm in," she said. "I'll build it, but I will need a set of plans and a list of the hardware we'll require as soon as possible. Tell Juan to come and see me at Haut-Clair. We will work out the finances. Can you get the paste to a safe port? Venezuela, Guyana, Surinam, it doesn't matter to me. If you can do that, I will take care of the transportation of the paste to St. Anthony by boat and of the finished product to the USA. We should arrange the financing in such a way that splitting the finished product on board fifty-fifty would be equitable. We each do our own marketing. By the way, I'm being released tomorrow morning. How about staying over and showing me around Cuzco?"

Alonzo agreed and they spent a pleasant morning together. He took an afternoon plane back to Lima and Alice rented a car and drove to the famous Inca ruin of Mach Picchu. She marveled at the power and splendor of this cliff-top citadel. She found the experience humbling and beneficial. I will be but an insignificant little queen ruling a tribe of maybe eighty. Not, Ayesha, that I am ungrateful for all you have done. She was reminded suddenly of something Ayesha had said to Holly, "My Empire is of thye imagination."

9

While Alice was away Paul and Narcisse met for drinks in a beach bar they used to frequent years before. The place had greatly changed. Narcisse looked around. "Remember when we used to come here and there was only a rough wooden shack and no stools? We had to stand."

"And there was nothing to drink but rum, Coca Cola and Banks beer."

The owner, a recent immigrant who had arrived from Pakistan via Canada where he had presumably picked up some capital, met them and escorted them to a corner table.

"You are the Cantave brothers, am I right?" he asked.

"Cousins, actually," said Paul.

"You look like brothers."

"How do you know us?" asked Narcisse.

"Ah, everyone know the Cantaves," he replied, "everyone on the island. I will send a waiter." And went away. They looked at each other and then at the broad expanse of tiled floor, the gleaming white balustrades, and the brightly colored parasols over each table. A single large palm loomed overhead.

"Well, the palm tree's still here and doing well, it seems. Frozen daiquiris, Paul, what do you say?"

"Why not?" This order was communicated to the white-jacketed waiter who shortly appeared.

"I think the change is good, on the whole," said Paul. "Tourism is good for the island and as we have so few beaches, we won't be swamped like Barbados. I hear that you are going to make a large contribution to the economy."

"To the economy of Guineas, I am not sure how much the rest of the island will benefit. I hear that you are to be part of it."

"Nothing's settled, and I'm not clear on who I would be working for. For her or for you?"

Narcisse smiled. "For both of us of course. We're not yet married so strictly speaking Alice and I are not partners yet. In law."

"You'll be running the plantation, so what is her role exactly?"

"Paul, I am interested in my studies, as you know, we talked before, and Alice is a business woman. She'll run the plantation. You will probably have more to do with it than me."

"But you are the financier, you are raising the money in Paris."

Narcisse was silent for a moment. The daiquiris arrived and they both took a sip, gazing at the pelicans in the bay, who would spot their prey and then plunge vertically with frightening precision into the sea and emerge with their gizzards full and heavy.

"Beats rum and coke, I would say," remarked Narcisse. "*Oui, je procure de l'argent pour la exploitation à Paris. Entre nous,*" he looked around. "Between you and I, and Philippe knows of course, it's all her money. I found her!"

"And where did you find her, if I may ask?"

"In Paris, in Hermes, where I was working. I sold her some scarfs and she took a fancy to me."

"But she's not a Parisienne? She's a Canadian, isn't she?"

"No, American, a rich American girl. Somewhat spoiled, has eccentric ideas."

"Like what?"

"Oh, about animals, for example, and humans. She professes to believe that humans are unworthy of their ascendancy in the animal kingdom. She thinks the human population should be reduced. Even sanctions murder, says it used to be part of the Innuit culture, kept the population down. The white man outlawed it. Big mistake, according to her. She said to me once that we are killer apes and not to kill is to betray the planet or something. And justifies this by quoting Kant, the German philosopher. Do you know anything about Kant's ethics?"

"I know the book, the Metaphysics of Ethics. Never read it – started to, but it's tough going. Had a professor at Boston College who amused himself by proving to us that his argument is circular, famously tautological."

"That's interesting, but I will not mention it to her – it would just get her going. Of course all this is crazy stuff. She was born rich, has never known any other life. Money she is good at, but in some areas she is not in touch with reality. She is as remote from the criminal mind, as those pelicans."

A few more questions and Paul realized that Narcisse knew nothing about her history. They had another drink – the first one had been on the house – went on to dinner, and did not talk about Alice again. On his way home Paul found himself thinking about her. He doubted that Alice had been born rich, and was not convinced that she was a stranger to crime, even to murder.

"While you were away studying at the Sorbonne," said Zena to Narcisse, "I was being educated but in a quite different way. I was sent to Haiti when I was seventeen, not to Port-au-Prince but to a remote rural area to study Voudon. Then I chose to go for three years to the University of Montreal to study philosophy. I put myself through, waiting on tables in restaurants and bars. It may surprise you, but those three years of Western education helped my understanding of Voudon, and my belief in it. To put it simply, there is both good and evil in the world, and the art of living is to accept both."

Narcisse was learning to prepare Voudon medicines and helping her care for her mother. At the same time, she was learning western psychopharmacology from him; he had brought his books to Guinea. Saba had begun a steep decline not long after Henri Cantave's funeral. Narcisse wanted to know whether Zena felt she was prepared to succeed her. Today he had finally managed to get her to talk about herself. Saba was sleeping. They were together seated on a large comfortable couch. The chamber they sat in was part of a warren of caves – partly man-made and partly natural – on the south side of Mont Noir. The caves were the community and political center of the Guinea reservation. Walls of bookshelves on four sides gave the cavern the rectilinear look of a conventional room. There was a large table at one end with a number of desks facing it, and there were scatter rugs made of dyed hemp on the floor.

Low-watt electric light bulbs hung above and candles had been placed here and there; not all of them were lit. In another part of the caves was a small hydroelectric installation, which took advantage of a powerful underground mountain stream. He remembered seeing it as a boy when Saba had brought him and Philippe here. He had sometimes seen things that he knew he was not supposed to see, such as Saba's mother's workshop. He remembered shelves of glass bottles and jars – it seemed to him thousands of them, with bizarre and scary contents such as spiders, snakes, and strange bloated fish, sometimes alive and sometimes not. And what appeared to be human parts, he recalled, not with a shudder, which was Philippe's reaction, but with a certain excitement.

It was a few days before Christmas. Alice had bought Narcisse a little sports car as an engagement present and he used it to drive to Guinea to visit Zena and her mother almost every day. Alice had found that if she telephoned Narcisse from abroad at his mother's during the day, he was not there. Zena connected to the Internet by a landline; the phone number was not listed. So Alice could not call him in Guinea even if she was disposed to. When she did get through to him at his mother's house, early one morning while he was still in bed, she told him that she would not be back in St. Anthony for Christmas and gave a date in January about a week before the wedding date. The reason she gave was that she was not yet comfortable with his family – meaning his mother – nor they with her. She thought that Narcisse's mother would find her first Christmas as a widow more tolerable with just her two sons. In the future there would be many a family Christmas. With little ones, said Narcisse. She hung up rather quickly after that.

In the cavern, Zena broached the delicate subject that had been hovering in the background since Narcisse had returned from Paris. They were speaking Creole. "When I came back from Montreal I found that I was immensely glad to be home with people whose values I shared. If the World Bank would come here – and I doubt if they know we exist – they would find that our average dollar income from what we earn to be zero. But our people eat well, mostly fruit, and all sorts of vegetables, yams, breadfruit, squash, peas, leddos, lentils, roots of several kinds, and fish from our lagoon. Most families keep chickens and pigs. The huts are comfortable enough for this climate, for we live most of our lives outdoors. We have our music and dancing, in bad weather we meet in these caves and party. And our religion and its ceremonies center our lives. But certain things we do need to import and we love our silk clothes." She paused and looked at Narcisse.

"But the treasure is running out."

"You know our secret. Of course you do, it's why you came back to the island. We found the pirate's treasure, and we have spent it. Slowly and carefully, but we have spent it. You see to us, who consider capital evil, after all our ancestors *were* capital to their white owners, to have *not* spent it, would have been wrong. But the treasure is about to run out, Narcisse, as you know."

"I know, and that is where I, the mulatto capitalist pig dog entrepreneur come in."

"Yes, and Saba wants you and I to discuss it before the Council meets with you, although I believe old LaTulippe in Paris talked to you about it. My mother is going to die, Narcisse, and I will be queen. I am not looking forward to it. There is something I have to tell you before we discuss business and get it off my chest, Narcisse. I would like my first child to be yours. Its paternity would be secret, but you and I would know. Please, don't give me your answer right now, but it is not a request that men are permitted to decline in Guinea." She smiled at him.

Narcisse said nothing but he found his eyes exploring the round curves of her body. It suddenly dawned on him that his little cousin had grown up.

"Now back to the business in hand. We are in a bit of a moral dilemma. We just need a small cash income every year for bales of silk and for hand tools. To get it we have decided that it is acceptable for our land south of Mont Petit to be farmed for profit by a Cantave and for us to receive a royalty. Philippe, as you know, has discussed the idea of putting Haut-Clair back into coffee with the authorities in Le Havre. They have no legal right to put up any obstacles, and acknowledge that under the treaty they have no right to tax either the property or its income. Philippe will negotiate our royalty, or tax, with you. You will require outside capital.

"But now, now," Zena's Nubian features became transformed with anger, "now, Philippe says that Haut-Clair is to belong to this woman you are supposed to marry under a marriage contract. What folly! He says she has money, a lot of it – your father told him. But she doesn't want it known, she says she is afraid of kidnapping! Maybe it's kidnapping, maybe it's something else. The night Uncle Henri died the woman –"

"Zena, her name is Alice LeBlanc."

"And that is all that is known about her." Neither of them spoke for a minute. "And all that there is to know. I investigated Alice LeBlanc over the Internet. There was someone of the right age born in Boston, and that fits. Same birthday."

"How do you know her birthday?"

"Never mind, I do. But there is no other trace of her. To make a long story short, she has not left any trace anywhere of her existence. People with money get it from somewhere. But there is no trace."

"Zena, so what? Is your family history on the Internet? I think the money came through a stepfather, a banker in Paris."

"Do you know the name?"

"No, and I'm not happy about this interrogation, Zena." Narcisse's indignation stemmed from his own inner doubts. "Why are you suspicious of her? It looks to me that you *have* established that Alice LeBlanc is her real name. What more do you want? She is going to finance the plantation at Haut-Clair. There is an old English proverb: do not look a gift horse in the mouth."

"Philippe originally said that you were the financier, that you raised the money for the plantation in Paris."

"It's all her money. As you said, she doesn't want it known. But I did raise the money in Paris. I found her! She will be good for the island, you'll see, and she'll be good for me."

But Zena could see from his face that he was worried, that he shared her concerns. "I'm sorry, Narcisse. Clearly you are infatuated; you believe that you love her. That should be enough for me. But don't marry her. It will lead to disaster. Mama and I have invoked the Voudon goddess Oshun and she could not have given us a sterner warning. And Oshun also told us that she's barren, Narcisse, she cannot have babies. That night she visited your father

- who knows what went on in that room? And she emerged with Haut-Clair as good as in her possession. *If* you marry her. I implore you not to marry her."

"My dear Zena, if I don't marry her, we cannot develop the plantation, and your people need the royalties. You owe it to them to let me marry her. Where else would we get the money?"

Zena suddenly relaxed. He won't marry her unless she let him; he just said it. Narcisse continued to defend her but Zena could tell that he was wavering. He seemed to be torn, to be trying to convince himself. "She says it was Papa's idea, the marriage contract. It was his last wish; he telephoned Philippe just before he died. Why would she lie? And Alice loves Haut-Clair. We will have children, Cantaves, who will inherit it."

Narcisse paused and looked at her. Had Zena not just said that Alice could not have children, that she, Zena, wanted a child by him? Her eyes were wet. He embraced her to comfort her but something had changed in his feelings for her. He felt a sudden sexual excitement. Zena began to kiss him passionately. She began to remove his clothes and they made love.

Afterwards, Narcisse said, "My darling, my darling, I cannot refuse you. I will marry her for her money, and then when the plantation is going, and the Leopards are getting the royalties, I will come and live with you."

Narcisse, like most men and women, wanted to have his cake and eat it too. Zena asked him, "Will you really do that? Marry her for her money, then leave her and come and live with me, and give me a baby? Then one day, would our baby inherit the title to Haut-Clair? The Leopards do not recognize the paternity of the queen's children."

"Haut-Clair belongs to the Cantaves, to me, according to the laws of St. Anthony. If I formally recognize the child as mine, he or she would inherit. The Leopard customs are not germane, as Philippe would say."

Zena was satisfied, she pulled a blanket over them both, and they slept arms around one another. When Narcisse woke up, Zena was fully dressed and was kneeling beside the couch, offering him a cup of tea. He got up and dressed.

"My mother is sleeping. I haven't told you this before but Uncle Robert recently gave me morphine to ease the pain. She does not know she is taking it. Are you shocked?"

"No, I didn't mention it, but I knew. I think it only sensible. Why should she suffer?"

"It won't be long now."

"You'll be queen."

Zena reflected on this for a moment and then said, "What is that woman, I mean, Alice, what is Alice going to do about the Abu? I hear that they worship her. They think she is a goddess called Aleysha and they have accepted her as their queen."

"Why, she has just befriended them. They are going to work for her, they know how to cultivate coffee." Narcisse spent all his time in Guinea and had not yet visited Haut-Clair. To him the coffee plantation was a big headache and he was content to let Alice handle it.

"They don't know how to cultivate it. They know nothing at all. The trees grow wild. Well, as long as she pays us our royalty, she can do with them what she likes. If she wants to use the Abu as labor, let her go ahead. It can only improve them. Those people are – "

Zena got up from the couch, and looked down at him with a fierce expression on her handsome face, "They are squatters, savages. You know there is ancient enmity between our peoples. We are descended from Africans who intermarried with the Arawak. But the Abu, they took Dusseault's Carib concubines as wives! Cannibals! Of course, they do not come after our people, not any more, for they know what happens to them when they do. We turn them into the walking dead!"

Alice spent four days touring Cuzco and then returned to Lima. She called on Alonzo at his office and flew to Barbados to meet with the architect, bringing with her photographs and a floor plan. He foresaw no serious problems to restoring the plantation house if given a sufficient budget. He agreed to come and see it early in the New Year. She visited a few houses that he had restored and spent

Christmas there in a small hotel in Bridgetown. From Barbados she flew to Tampa. When she discussed her plans for the plantation with the contractors in Florida, she made it clear to them that the Abu must be employed in the work.

"It is not just a Third World country," she explained. "History has completely passed these people by. I am doing this project for profit – I must make that clear – but also I am doing it for them. Leave them out of your budget; I will meet their payroll. You will train them to use the machinery as well as to do the manual work. The cost of training them, I assure you, will not equal the work that they will do, so the difference will be in your bottom line."

She had said more or less the same thing to the architect, but in the case of the house, she was her own prime contractor. He was going to recommend a few skilled Barbadian workers who would stay in an airport hotel near Le Havre and be flown in daily by Paul.

Alice was making no financial commitments until after the wedding. But she wanted to have her plans in place. Paul's recommendation was that she purchase a five-seat Bell helicopter with pontoons and seats that could be removed for cargo. She went to look at one. The contractors would charter a larger chopper for heavy work – such as bringing bulldozers in and hauling timber out – and this would be included in their budget. The sale of the lumber they would remove would partially offset expenses. A timber surveyor would visit Haut-Clair and give an estimate for the whole project.

She visited the Tampa Bay book stores, both new and rare, and picked up several books that dealt with the religion of Zarathustra, also known as Zoroaster. The day before she was to leave, she read in the *Tampa Tribune* that the Ottawa Senators were in town to play the Lightning. Impulsively she went to the Tampa Forum; she hadn't seen a hockey game all winter.

Waiting at a stall to buy a Lightning jacket – for it would be chilly in the rink – her eye was attracted to the bright red, black, and gray colors of a Senators jacket. Not quite in time to look away, she realized that the wearer was Charley, strolling along with a much younger woman on his arm. For a fraction of a second their eyes had met with a mutual shock of recognition. As she turned away, she caught the attention of the sales girl and asked for the jacket. Out of the corner of her eye she saw Charley drop the arm of his companion and walk over to stand just beside her.

"A Lightning jacket, Hattie?" he exclaimed boldly.

She turned and looked at him levelly through her blue contacts. "I beg your pardon?" she asked in a faint southern accent. She gave him a surprised blank look, then nearly burst out laughing. She saw the fright at the back of his eyes and realized that he thought he was looking at a ghost and was bravely confronting it; she knew him so well. She stared him down and watched the fright dissolve into embarrassment.

He blushed and said, "Sorry, madame, you look like someone I used to know," and walked away. She left during the third period even though it was a good game and the score tied. She did not want to risk seeing him again, not just because of the risk. The encounter had left her bruised and homesick.

"You look like you've seen a ghost," Charley's girlfriend had said when he went back to her.

"That's exactly what I thought I saw, someone who's dead. My granddaddy taught me if you see a ghost go right up to it and call it by name. Then it will run away. But it was a real woman, she didn't run away at all. She looked just like Henry's daughter, a girl I used to coach, drive around, and babysit. But it couldn't even have been her ghost. Blue eyes. This dame had blue eyes. A woman can change the color of her hair, but she can't change the color of her eyes. Not even a ghost can do that!"

"You ever hear of colored contact lenses, Charley?"

"Huh?"

Alice returned to Les Palmes in January. Narcisse took her to dinner and they decided that she would start looking for a beach house in the morning. He made love to her in her room at Les Palmes, and then went home to his mother. Annoyed at first, she realized that she was losing interest in him anyway. But it was imperative that they get married so she could take possession of Haut-Clair under the marriage settlement; after that his existence might pose a bit of a problem. After Narcisse left that night, she found herself thinking of Theodore, the horseman. She wished that he was the one lying next to her sleeping in the empty half of the queen-sized bed.

In the morning Alice found an email from Juan Gonzalez-Balsells. He had conferred with Alonzo and felt that they were close to an agreement. He wanted to see the site and complete the negotiations. He hoped to visit St. Anthony in May. She replied that she looked forward to his visit. The most important unknown was the volume of paste they were going to be processing. They couldn't finish their plans until they knew this.

She had picked up Hector's briefcase at the St. Anthony airport. She had set the password herself the night before stealing it, so she had no need to hack into it. From certain files she found she was able to estimate how much coca paste Hector was producing each year. She transferred some of the files she found, took a hotel rowboat out to sea, and slipped the computer over the side.

Narcisse called in the morning. "Mama has offered us the little guest house at home. There's no kitchen, but that's all right, we'll eat with Mama. She has a really good cook, Tia. She does good island vegetables."

"I don't need her cooking. They don't like me, Narcisse, your mother, and your cook, and all the women in your family. I want a house of my own. I'll get my own cook. There are some lovely old beach houses to rent around here, where the planters used to come in the hot weather. I'm calling an agent."

The hotel manager recommended a real estate agent named Ann Sutton. She first took them to a house up the coast to the north that was for sale, not for rent, but she thought that Alice should see it because it was a bargain. It was built on and into a cliff and was called The Thirty-Nine Steps. The previous owner, a retired homosexual American naval officer, had had no family. Although the American had built the house only fifteen years before, it looked as if it had been there forever. He had had a taste for gothic and had brought a stone carver from Italy to embellish the tall square cliff side of the building with gargoyles and fake turrets. But the interior needed some work. Ann thought that if someone fixed it up it could be sold at a profit.

Thirty-Nine steps had been cut into the coral cliff to give access to the beach, which was some twenty-five feet below the terrace in front of the ground floor. The house had three floors on the cliff side – all of the bedrooms with a view of the sea. Driving in from the main road, the car went past an open field where a farmer kept a few cows and then through a luxuriant tropical garden to the front door of what appeared to be a quaint one floored castle.

"Would I be able to keep a helicopter in the cow pasture?" Alice asked Ann as they drove up.

Ann laughed. "I don't suppose the cows would like it, but the farmer can take them somewhere else. There's no lease; he doesn't even pay to keep them there. There shouldn't be a problem. The land belongs to the house. You'd have to get a permit to land the helicopter."

The commodore's will had directed that the place be sold with everything in it, the proceeds going to a local orphanage. He had cut his own throat on the drawing room carpet after almost decapitating his young lover. There were supposedly bloodstains under the new carpet. Narcisse had been in Paris at the time and hadn't heard the story. The house had been for sale for some time but no one had shown any interest. Alice made a low offer, what Ann called a "stink bid."

Narcisse told her that Philippe was anxious to get the agreement between the Leopards and himself signed, but that he had stalled, waiting for her. "I think you should sign it after the wedding. It seems silly for me to sign it and then make it over to you. Let's invite Philippe to lunch."

When Philippe heard about the house, he told them amusing stories about the commodore and the famous parties he gave there for the gay crowd. Philippe became quite animated with wine and began to flirt with the waiter. The restaurant wasn't busy and he kept getting up from the table to engage the waiter in tête-a-tête conversations. Narcisse was embarrassed, but Alice didn't mind. We'll see how clear his head is when we get down to business after lunch, she thought.

"When do we get down to business?" Narcisse asked Philippe after one of these excursions.

"Over coffee. It is the French way," Philippe said to Alice. "The island has been English for two hundred years, but we mulattos keep some of the French habits. We like to have a good lunch, enjoy our wine and food, and then over coffee: business. Whereas you English like to get the business over with and then enjoy yourselves." Alice had noticed this difference in Canada, but said nothing.

After a cup of coffee, Philippe was suddenly sober and all business. "The Leopards want a property tax of $12,000 US a year starting right away, plus twenty per cent sales tax on the gross revenues when it comes into production. They insist on the right to visit Haut-Clair at all times to see that the operation is being run to their liking, and their own accountant is to examine the books whenever they choose."

Narcisse smiled, shrugged, and looked over at Alice. "Sounds rather businesslike for people who dislike capitalism."

Philippe laughed. "They are the terms I suggested and they're negotiable."

"Tell them that I have spoken to our people in Paris," Alice replied, "and they might agree to the ground rent but will not accept the other conditions. No way. And if we don't invest, there's no revenue at all. We're putting in a lot of capital and there will be no revenue for five years. Yet we will pay the property tax monthly from the day we sign. The price of coffee is unstable; it depends on the weather in Brazil and so many other unknowns. Your people would be better off asking for a higher property tax in place of a sales tax when the coffee trees mature. Then there would be no need to visit the plantation nor for anyone to look at the books. We don't want them on the property."

"How can you justify that when the whole project is at the sufferance of the Leopard Society? Of which, by the way, I am now a member."

"Take it or leave it," said Alice. "We won't compromise. My trustees are adamant. It must be in the agreement that they are not permitted to visit the property."

Philippe knew that the Guinea people needed the money and there were no other investors in sight. He doubted whether the trustees existed. "I have to tell you that Saba knows it's your money. I had to tell her. I am their lawyer. But I did stress that you don't want it known on the island. I don't see a problem as the only people in St. Anthony they ever speak to is our family," said Philippe. "What you propose is a lot simpler and I think in their interest, if the property tax were to be higher. I will talk to them. You and I can negotiate. What I'll do is ask them what they need for their silk, their tools, etc. And the property tax will be based on that, on their needs. I'll check and see what they spent the last few years before they finished doling out their treasure."

"We must have the right to fly in helicopters, Philippe. They must agree to that. There's no road to Haut-Clair. There are cliffs on all sides. I understand that aircraft are forbidden over Guinea. We would undertake not to fly over the rest of Guinea, that is not to fly north of Mont Petit nor over the lagoon."

A week later Philippe came back with a proposed new property tax of $25,000 a year, with an allowance for inflation but he told her they insisted on the right to visit the property. Alice accepted the tax proposal but refused the right to inspect the property, saying she would not invest at all if this clause were not dropped. Instead, she and Philippe offered them something they had not asked for: a trust fund to guarantee the property tax. Philippe came up with the idea that she might put a million dollars US into a trust that he would administer. The income from the trust, which was to be invested in US treasury bills, would be available to the Leopards, to make up any shortfall in the tax paid. If the tax were paid, the income would then go the settlor – Alice. The trust would be dissolved and the funds returned to the owners of the plantation when the coffee trees had matured and Philippe's accountant certified that the plantation was earning twice the property tax. Philippe specifically put in the deed that in the event of a change of ownership, the funds remained in the trust, and Alice did not object. Under the terms of the marriage settlement, Haut-Clair would revert to the Cantave family in the event of her death and Philippe set it up so that in these circumstances the fund remained in place.

Tying up $1,000,000 for a maximium ten years was not a problem for Alice: in return the Leopards agreed not to set foot on the property. It guaranteed her privacy and shouldn't in the end, cost her a cent. Alice signed the draft but nothing would be final until after the wedding. Philippe suggested that Alice make a will, but she never got around to it.

Alice and Narcisse were married on a Saturday morning in late January. The wedding was small because it was so soon after the funeral, with only family attending. Philippe was best man and Dr. Robert Cantave, visibly not well, gave Alice away. Ann Sutton acted as Alice's matron of honour. Saba was now too ill to come and Zena used the excuse of caring for her mother to stay away. So it would not appear that the Guinea people were shunning the wedding, Nguma attended. Alice decided against inviting Abbah on the grounds that the less the Abu knew or thought about her marriage, the better. It took place in the chapel of the church where the funeral had taken place.

The reception was in the garden of The Thirty-Nine Steps. Alice's low offer had been accepted and she moved in three days before the wedding. Sara, Alice's new housekeeper and cook, supervised a cold lunch served by a butler and a maid. Sara had come strongly recommended by Ann Sutton. Hire Sara, Ann told Alice, and all household problems will be solved. She is an excellent cook, will hire the other staff for you, run the house, and keep accurate and honest accounts. Sara didn't live in; nor did any of the other servants.

Alice dismissed the landscapers hired by the estate to keep the garden. She brought Abbah from Haut-Clair; together they would start a coca seedbed, and maintain the garden. She wanted him to learn all about the cultivation of coca, and she wanted to discuss her plans with him. He was a bright lad and his status with the Abu made him an ideal lieutenant. She taught him to drive the Jeep. He taught her the Abu language. On the ground or terrace floor above the sea, there was a boat room where two windsurfers and a skiff were stored. They were light and could be carried down the steps but she didn't expect to use them. Opposite there was a bedroom with a private bath. Here Abbah would sleep when he stayed over.

Alice also wanted to learn more from Abbah about the religion of the Abu. She was not religious herself – aside from appealing to Ayesha in times of stress, as non-religious believers are inclined to do – believing with Ayesha that "The religions come and the religions pass, and civilizations come and pass, and naught endures but the world and human nature". But as the people considered her a goddess, she wanted to know if they had other gods. She needed to know if she had competition.

Abbah himself brought up the subject at breakfast on the first morning that he stayed over. Narcisse was in Guinea with Zena. He had brought his copy of the book, *She*, from Haut-Clair to show her. It was the same edition that she had found in the library as a girl. He said that an old missionary, who had taught his great-grandfather to read as a boy, had given it to him, and it had been passed on, along with the English language and the ability to read from father to son. He showed her the portrait of Ayesha, which she remembered, and pointed out the likeness to herself. He also had a portrait of Aloyshovna in his cabin, he told her. He marveled at the resemblances and said that the Abu believed that Aloyshovna, Aleysha, and Ayesha were the same.

"Do you have other gods and goddesses?" she asked.

"Oh, yes, Aleysha, there are many, there are the gods of the sea, and of the jungle."

"But are they powerful?"

"Only Ngai is powerful. He is the lord of them all."

"Of me, my Abbah. Do you believe he is lord over me?" She stood up from the ground where she had been demonstrating the planting of the coca seeds and looked down on him severely.

He was afraid of her suddenly. "O, Aleysha, you are my queen, I do not know how to answer that."

She smiled down at him. Alice had been studying the religion of Zarathustra, the first prophet, who had taught that there was only one God, and had managed to persuade the people of his tribe in Central Asia of this by explaining the concept of the trinity.

"Abbah, the god Ngai is female and her other name is Ayesha. I am her daughter sent to you from heaven."

"Then who was Aloyshovna if you and Ayesha are not the same?"

"She is the Holy Spirit. You see, my Abbah, we are all three one and yet we are three. Ayesha is the Mother of all things, I am her Daughter sent to care for you, and Aloyshovna is the Holy Spirit. She is the spirit of the sea and of the jungle that you confuse with minor gods. We are all one. There is only one God."

This argument had worked for Zarathrustra and it worked now. A light came into Abbah's eyes and he almost fainted. "So there is just one God, Ayesha is the Mother, you are the Daughter, and all the gods of the jungle and sea and mountains, the spirits of the trees and the animals are the ghost of Aloyshovna. I see, I see."

They sat down together under a palm tree and she taught Abbah what she had learned about the Zarathustran or Zoroastrian religion as if it was her own, making a few adaptations (as Jews, Christians, and Moslems had done before her). She asked him to preach her teachings to the *mambo* while she learned the Abu language from him. Her message was not complicated: "I am Good but I am not all-powerful", she told Abbah. "Opposed to me is Evil. Evil is the Big Lie. I am the Truth. There is evil in the world and we must fight it."

"I wish to be good, O Aleysha, like you. What must I do to be good?"

"Think good thoughts, say good words, do good deeds."

"But how do I know what is good and what is evil?"

"Ah, that you must decide for yourself. But each time you make the right choice, good is stronger and evil is weaker."

"So each of us has the power to strengthen good and weaken evil?"

"Yes, my Abbah, and one day good will triumph."

"And my queen, who is good, will triumph over her enemies who are evil?"

"Yes, my Abbah."

The cows were moved from the meadow and one day Paul arrived from the airport in the brand new Bell helicopter and landed on the field, with the Barbados architect and an assessor from the Florida contractor's office, who was preparing an estimate. Narcisse Cantave was in Guinea, deeply involved in his studies with Zena. They picked up Alice and flew to Haut-Clair.

The Abu had been awed by their queen's first appearance; Aleysha's second appearance was equally sensational. An iron bird dropped out of the sky as promised. Abbah had gone ahead the day before to prepare the people for her return and they all turned out. There was to be a feast.

Alice disembarked alone and the helicopter took off again. Both the contractor and the architect wanted a good look at the site from above. As the helicopter rose above the jungle, Paul watched Abbah, dressed like a young prince in a gold shirt and red jeans, leave the avenue of rosewood, with the Abu prostrate on the ground behind him in worship, and greet his queen. The assessor saw this too, but he was more interested in the trees.

"So the rosewood's not for sale," he muttered, shaking his head. "Any idea what that's worth? Four hundred thousand, easy, maybe more. And she has asked me to leave the largest trees so the coffee will be shade-grown. But here," he waved a plan that Alice had given him, "She wants to clear cut 90 acres. What for? Is she planning some other crop?"

Paul shook his head. "Dunno."

"Okay, take me down. I get the picture. I will have to complete this on foot."

Alice had bought sixty plain gold-plated lockets with gold silver alloy chains in Florida, enough for the entire population. A small photograph of Alice had been placed in each. She was in a pose similar to that of Aloyshovna in the portrait that Abbah had of her, which he had taken her to see. For Abbah and for the *mambo*, she had brought ornate lockets of pure gold. These were presented first.

Then the people came up, by families, as Abbah called their names. He passed the lockets to Alice from a brown leather suitcase. Alice placed one around the neck of each of her subjects as they kneeled before her. Several mothers brought babies and Alice put a second locket in the mother's hand.

The helicopter returned just as this ceremony ended. A dozen bow bucksaws, a dozen axes, and a dozen machetes were unloaded. They were all brand new and were examined by the Abu with great interest. The architect toured the house, taking notes; Alice accompanied him discussing business. Abbah tagged along, listening. The Abu returned to their village to prepare the feast. When the timber assessor returned, the two visitors got into the chopper with Paul and left.

Alice was then led to the Abu village about a quarter of a mile from the bottom of the rosewood avenue. A crescent of mud and straw huts formed a half-circle around a huge black iron cauldron simmering over a fire. An old woman was standing on a stone platform stirring with a long iron spoon. Taking Alice's arm like a dutiful son, Abbah escorted her to an old French wooden chair, that still had remnants of gilt on its ornate carvings: a throne. Abbah sat at her feet. Near the fire were the drums; they started their intricate rhythms and the people began to dance.

They were a slender and good-looking people. Both men and women were naked above the waist. Their jeans were old and tattered. They did not appear to have needles or know how to sew. I will get them new clothes, Alice thought, and needles and personally give sewing lessons. After the dancing, Abbah stood and apologized that they had no meat that day. This apology was directed to the whole assembly; it was ceremonial and was given at most of the Abu feasts. The queen did not eat meat, he reminded them. A fish soup, a sort of gumbo rich with vegetables was served to Alice in a porcelain bowl. She ate it to be courteous. The Abu people ate out of wooden bowls, sitting in a half-circle on the ground in front of her.

When everyone had finished eating, Alice stood and made a short speech in Abu. The forty acres near the village, where they had their gardens, was not to be touched. The original plantation, roughly a square mile of arable land, one-eighth of the plateau, would be gradually restored and planted in coffee and coca. She would need their help; they would be taught to use machinery. All timber of commercial value in the area to be cleared was to be piled to await the large load-bearing helicopter that would carry it to the docks of Le Havre. The rosewood and the existing coffee trees would not be touched. Nor would a large number of tall trees in the area earmarked for the coffee plantation. Then it would be slash and burn; the potash would enrich the soil.

She was going to bring them new clothes; if there was anything else they needed they were to speak to Abbah and he would bring the request to her. She was going to bring artisans from Barbados to teach pottery and cabinet making. She was going to bring in tropical birds from Tobago and release them in the forest. The Abu were to undertake not to catch them and eat them; she was going to bring wild boar and deer to Haut-Clair. Alice, a vegetarian as a rule, was of the opinion that as in some circumstances it was acceptable to kill humans, so in others it was acceptable to kill animals. Hunting was acceptable; at least the beasts had a sporting chance. She didn't mention it in her speech, but told Abbah to tell the people privately that she was sorry not to be able to provide human flesh at the present time but would do so from time to time in the future.

The tools – the bucksaws, axes, and machetes – were gifts from Aleysha in exchange for the work done and were common property. Alice had bought the goat farm of the coffee merchant and closed down his business. His goats joined the small Abu herd. From now on the coffee beans would be brought to a store in the Abu village that Abbah had set up. All goods in it were free to the population. New colored jeans and shirts were to be brought in. People were to take what they needed.

Then the dancing recommenced. After the feast, Abbah and the *mambo* led Alice to a sacred grove and they sat together under a giant banyan tree. She had learned enough Abu to ask her how she felt about the Zoroastrian teachings that she had asked Abbah to pass on as her own, and she nodded slowly and sagely. There is only one God, she said, you are the Daughter, Ayesha is the Mother, and Aloyshovna, the spirits of the trees and the sea, she is all minor gods, and you three are one. She looked at Alice for confirmation, and Alice got up and kissed her on the forehead.

She told her that there would be much dancing and singing at services just as before, and there would be new songs and bright new clothes. She walked away and thought of Ngai. If he exists, I may be in trouble, she smiled to herself, and then suddenly saw Zena's strong Nubian black face before her and shuddered.

Abbah led her to the village vegetable gardens where seedbeds of tiny coca plants and coffee trees had been prepared under his supervision. This was the time of year that the Abu gathered coffee beans from the trees that were growing wild on the former plantation. This year a good proportion of the crop was to be used as seed. Abbah had instructed them to set aside some of the largest and healthiest cherries from the better trees. These had been washed, the flesh pulped, and the seeds extracted by hand. They were now in the ground and would be transplanted to an intermediate seedbed in May.

The work on both the coca and the coffee seedbeds had been carefully done and Alice was pleased. After inspecting the seedbeds, Abbah led her to the top of the cliff overlooking the sea to the east where the steps had been cut into the cliff. The south and east faces of the plateau were cliffs a thousand feet in height in places. The place where Dusseault had had his slaves cut steps into the hard volcanic rock two centuries ago was only about two hundred feet high.

Alice stood at a lookout with Abbah beside her and admired the view. Directly below was a small cove, created by an arm of coral stretching out and almost surrounding it, invisible from the sea. Alice could see from where she stood that the water was deep, that a small ship could rest at anchor. There was a beach and she could see the Abu dugouts drawn up on it. The Guinea people kept to their lagoon way to the north; the Abu fished in the open sea.

Alice left Abbah at the village and returned to the house to wait for Paul. She reviewed her plans. They would not be getting a good yield from the coca plants for three or four years and it would be six before they could count on a decent harvest from the cultivated coffee trees. Alice didn't have a cash flow problem; the income from her money market investments was more than she was spending. It looked like she would not even have to dip into capital for the renovations and the plantation.

Alice didn't enter the cocaine business with her Peruvian associates because she needed the money. She was attracted to the spectacular profits that would ensue and to the danger. She also looked forward to working with her father again, she felt that she owed him a job, and she wanted to impress him with the scale of her operation.

She knew that so called "fast boats", cigarette boats and light weight narrow hard bottomed inflatables were used to bring cocaine to Haiti, making the four hundred-mile trip across the open sea from Columbia in ten hours. They didn't always go in a straight line and often they traveled at night because they were harassed by United States Drug Enforcement Administration helicopters who raked their rubber hulls with machine gun fire, sometimes stranding the crew in the shark-infested waters, and sometimes picking them up. There was also considerable action closer to St. Anthony in the Virgin Islands.

St. Anthony as the northernmost of the Lesser Antilles, was not much further away from what was at one time called the Spanish Main. Bringing paste from Guyana meant traveling from South America through the whole archipelago rather than on the open sea. A fast boat was likely to be spotted; they needed a vessel that was above suspicion and that would not look out of place on the less-traveled Atlantic side of the archipelago.

Haitian officials took a big cut of the profits for permitting the cocaine trade to continue, enabling them to maintain their big houses in Cité Lavalas. One advantage of Haut-Clair was that no one would have to be bribed. As part of the original treaty the British had made with the Leopards, goods brought in to Guinea – and Haut Clair was legally part of Guinea – did not go through customs and no duty was paid. Goods leaving and arriving at Haut-Clair would not be inspected either. The produce and earnings from the plantation would not be subject to any taxes. Alice had her own warehouse built at the airport where materials for the reconstruction of the plantation house could be stored before being transported by helicopter. Anything arriving by ship in Le Havre would be transported to the warehouse. Packing crates wouldn't be examined. But Alice was not going to take any chances with the coca paste; she would have her own boat and keep it in the cove.

Philippe began confidential negotiations on Alice's behalf with the government of St. Anthony concerning the helicopter and a coast guard vessel. The idea was that the Haut-Clair plantation would provide both to the St. Anthony Coast Guard for free. Narcisse vaguely knew that these negotiations were going on but did not take much interest. Philippe spoke only to Alice, who had already bought the helicopter and was looking for a coast guard vessel.

On behalf of the Leopard Society Philippe arranged with the government of St. Anthony for his cousin Paul to patrol the perimeter of the island in the helicopter. Saba, hovering close to death, and thinking of other things, agreed to this in a private interview with Philippe; she had tended not to question Henri's advice even when she was in good health and didn't question Philippe's. Zena was not present at this interview and knew nothing about it. The helicopter was considered part of the St. Anthony Coast Guard. Paul wouldn't be paid for this; it was a service that the Haut-Clair plantation provided to Guinea and to the island. Paul's US Navy experience impressed the authorities, and of course it helped that he was a Cantave. The government of St. Anthony was pleased to get the patrol at no cost. The little nation was concerned about its sovereignty. US Drug Enforcement Administration – DEA – boats moved in and out of its territorial waters without permission. Paul's job was to let them know that the St. Anthony authorities knew they were there.

He sometimes flew tourists along the coast in the course of his patrols. This enabled the helicopter to almost pay for itself. Deliveries to Haut-Clair took only an hour or two a day. The tourists always wanted a closer look at the lagoon, but Paul would explain that flying over Guinea was forbidden. This prohibition of course included the plateau of Haut-Clair.

Having established the helicopter patrols, Alice asked Philippe to propose to the government and to Saba that Haut-Clair provide the island with a coast guard vessel at no cost. It would fly the flag of St. Anthony, patrol the coast, and carry out rescue and salvage operations. The salvage operations would permit it to range far and wide from the island. Any boats salvaged on the high seas would be the property of the St. Anthony government and would be towed into the harbor at Le Havre. The government was pleased; the current coast guard consisted of an ancient tugboat. Alice, who was considered a young and not serious woman in upper government circles, had Philippe explain to officials that she felt badly about not paying duty and taxes, and wanted to do something for the island. This explanation was accepted. A coast guard cutter would enable St. Anthony to further protect its sovereignty. The plantation would pay all the maintenance and running expenses and keep the vessel in the cove below Haut-Clair. Saba agreed to this arrangement. Philippe added these services to the contract between Guinea and the plantation.

On Saba's death later that year, Zena succeeded her mother. When she learned of these arrangements she was furious with Philippe, whom she had never liked anyway. She did not see any benefits to her people and was suspicious of Aleysha's motives. But everything had been signed by her mother and there was nothing she could do, other than stipulate that the boat not be permitted in the lagoon where her people fished.

A few weeks after her marriage Alice looked on the Internet for breeders of giant schnauzers, and emailed several to ask if they had salt and pepper giant puppies with white chests. She specified that the tails and ears of the puppies not be cropped. It is standard to crop them, indeed it is a condition if one wants to show them. One of the kennels she contacted was the place not far from Ottawa where she had bought Manson. She didn't see that there was any risk in doing this.

But the owner of the kennel, unbeknownst to Alice, was a police officer with connections to the Angels, and one who had a particular grudge against Hattie Braden. René Lachapelle, who had begun his career as a dog trainer with the Sûreté du Quebec, or SQ, had risen to the rank of inspector in the division that dealt with organized crime. And dealing with it was exactly what he did. In police forces everywhere are those who appreciate that crime pays – particularly if organized – and share in the profits. René was a perceptive officer of this sort; he had left his scruples in his mother's womb. He got away with it because he was a good detective and because he had only one direct contact with crime: "The Deacon" Kane of the Quebec chapter of the Hells Angels Motorcycle Club. And he confided in no one.

His payoffs were always in cash, left discreetly in prearranged places. He invested the cash in several little businesses, which were owned by numbered companies. His favorite was a large dog breeding kennel and training center near Lachute. The kennel specialized in the breeding and training of giant schnauzers and Dobermans. He was chief trainer and paid himself a good salary. The SQ knew about this job. He worked there in his spare time and there was no objection. But aside from his mistress, Monique, no one knew that he owned the place. She lived in a farmhouse beside the kennel and ran it; everyone thought that she owned it.

One February morning five months after the Song affair, which he had been asked to look into by his private client, the kennel received an email asking if it had any salt-and- pepper giant schnauzers with white chests. The black schnauzer is much more popular than the salt and pepper, and for show purposes white on the chest is not considered *chic*. So the request was unusual. Furthermore the inquirer specified that the ears and tails of the puppies not be clipped. A few years before Lachapelle had brought in salt-and-pepper puppies from a kennel in California. They had not sold quickly. One, with a large expanse of white chest, had been bought by Hattie Brading from Ottawa. Monique had dealt with her; the young woman had not even noticed René. She was attractive and sexy; René was of the view that attractive sexy women had no business not noticing him, and was slighted. When he helped her load the cage with the puppy in it in the back of her VW bus, he took the liberty of running his hand down her *derrière* for which he was rewarded with a swift kick in *les testicules*. So he remembered her, yes, indeed, he remembered her. He had her investigated and found out about her connections to the Bandits. At the time of her disappearance he was putting together a case against her involving money laundering for a gang in Lachute. At the time of the Song affair he had given her a lot of thought.

When Song and Hattie disappeared, René was asked by the Angels to bring them all the information that the police had on the case. The Deacon, who called him at his private phone at the kennel, sounded furious. Because one of the missing people was a Hells Angel and the other a daughter of a member of the Bandits in Ottawa, there were ramifications outside the district, and his interest in the case was not remarked upon by the SQ.

The SQ was investigating both disappearances. The neighbors had reported that the couple had often been seen swimming and canoeing together and that they never wore life jackets. There had been a fierce storm that night; the canoe had been found tossed up on the shore at the other side of the lake quite far away. The life jackets and paddles had been washed up nearby. Song had been seen and heard driving through North Hatley in the heavy rain.

The water was hundreds of feet deep on the west side of the lake; strong currents near the bottom made dragging the lake with a grapnel problematic. No body had been found but it was possible the bodies had been swept away in an underground river. A discovery was made outside Song's rented cottage: the chopping block by the woodpile had bloodstains on its underside. The bloodstains were explained when the headless corpse of a woman popped up from the bottom of the lake six weeks later. The DNA of the blood on the chopping block matched that of the lady in the lake. The Ottawa police found some bloodstains in Hattie's bathroom that matched. There was no record of her fingerprints and no other record of the DNA of Hattie Brading anywhere. The SQ came to the conclusion that Hattie had been murdered by the Korean.

By coincidence, the RCMP and the Ontario Provincial Police had succeeded in making a major bust at a Bandits drug lab at about the time of the couple's disappearance. Hattie's father, Henry Brading, who was out on bail, promptly arrived in Sherbrooke to identify the body. He positively identified it as that of his daughter, pointing out a distinctive birthmark on the right calf. Henry had the body cremated promptly. The head was never found and the case was closed. The Deacon continued to bother René Lachapelle about the case. He allowed to René that a lot of money was missing. He wanted the police to find Song. The Bandits told the Deacon that they had been robbed; they blamed the Angels and the Angels blamed Song. The Bandits killed an Angel and a gang war broke out.

This distracted everyone except Inspector René Lachapelle, who had a festering hatred for Hattie Brading. What started him thinking that the police had got it wrong was the dog. What had happened to the dog? It seemed to him that the body of the lady in the lake might not have been Hattie's. Perhaps Hattie had planted this woman's blood on the chopping block and in her bathroom in Ottawa. Odd that the Ottawa police had found no fingerprints at all in her apartment. If Hattie had murdered Song, and not the other way round, of course Henry Brading, if he knew about it, would have shown up promptly, made a positive identification of the corpse, and had it quickly cremated.

And where was the dog? He asked in the village and was told that she always brought her dog with her. It was unthinkable that the giant schnauzer would have allowed his mistress to be attacked. If the dog had been killed, where was the body? And where was the head? Police had assumed it was with the fishes. But why cut it off in the first place? Snooping around the property by himself, he found an abandoned well. He lifted the lid, dropped a stone, and listened to the clunk when it struck something solid which rang like concrete, a long way down. Maybe Song's body was in the well with the dog's. Thinking that he would look a fool if he had the well dug up and nothing found, except for sharing his suspicions with the Deacon, he kept them to himself. Besides it was evident from the gang war that a lot of money was missing; if Hattie had made off with a fortune there was a possibility of blackmail.

So when the request came in for a giant schnauzer that matched the coloring of the dog that Monique had sold Hattie six years before, and specifying that the tail and ears not be cropped, he thought immediately that it might be her.

He supposed from the Deacon's concern that a lot of money had been taken, and he preferred having a chunk of it to giving her away to the police. Clever woman, he thought, if I am right. She made just one mistake: how could she have anticipated that a simple request to a kennel for puppies, would be acutely interesting to the owner, a policeman in the pay of the Angels, whom she had once kicked in the groin? Perhaps she did not know that requests for white chested salt-and-pepper giant schnauzers with their ears and tails intact were rare.

He telephoned the kennel in California and established that they had salt-and-pepper puppies with the white patch. He asked if they had had their ears and tail clipped yet, and the reply was negative so he asked that they be flown to Mirabel airport right away; he would pick them up himself. This kennel, which was owned by a retired couple, had no website or email, so Alice LeBlanc had not contacted them. He made a firm order for two. He then replied to the email, stating that the kennel had salt and pepper puppies in stock. He put Monique's name on the reply. Where would they like the puppies delivered?

Narcisse Cantave was spending more and more time in the Guinea part of the reservation. The truth was that he had begun a serious affair with Zena. He now believed that he had always loved her and that his marriage had been a mistake. But he was not yet ready to break with Alice; he needed money for his laboratory.

The next time he came home to The Thirty-Nine Steps, Alice asked him to make some sketches of his requirements for the laboratory at Haut-Clair for the architect. Narcisse was silent for a minute.

"What's the problem?" she asked. "Don't you know what you want?"

"Alice, I think I can pursue my work better with my aunt Saba and Zena. Saba is an original source of the traditional healing arts of Voudon and of South America. She is familiar with all the botanical and zoological ingredients and the potions. I can better pursue my work there, with a teacher, than on my own. She and Zena are willing to share their secrets with me. I am a relative, after all. It's fascinating what they do – many of the medicines that they concoct for their own people are not known or understood by Western science.

"Don't forget that on my mother's side we have both African and Indian ancestry. When the Arawak came from South America, they brought medicinal plants with them in their canoes. This is a tremendous opportunity for me. I know Western science and I can apply it to the knowledge that my aunt has. I will make important discoveries and justify to my father – " He paused.

"I know my father's dead but I still sense the presence of his spirit. I want to prove that I did not waste my time in Paris. They have a laboratory over there, they don't call it that, but I do even though it needs some western equipment. It would be cheaper for you to give me money for equipment that I could set up there, than to build me a lab at Haut-Clair. For example," he took a glass test tube containing a white powder out of his pocket, "this powder contains the ingredients used to induce the zombie state – something that is done in their society as a stage in punishment for bad behavior –"

"A zombie? Your cousins make people into zombies?" Alice was almost amused.

"The reasons for making people into zombies are complex, Alice. Don't judge what you do not understand. In many of your United States, do you not have the death penalty? Well, this is morally superior. The deceased is dug up from his grave and enters a new life in bondage. Slavery is in some ways a better way to treat a convicted criminal than putting him in prison. Or her. In your country, in the United States, you have several million people, whose only crime may be a liking for marijuana, in prisons being buggered, becoming addicted to harder drugs, and learning to be criminals. And the prisons are incubators for AIDS, tuberculosis, hepatitis – "

"And slavery is more humane?"

"It can be a more humane way of dealing with people who have committed crimes against the society they were born into. In Africa criminals were legally enslaved for a number of different reasons. Take the case of the slaves on the *Amistad*, the only slave ship for which we have accurate information. We have it because of the court case. In his movie Stephen Spielberg insulted the African people by supposing that there was no law in that part of West Africa that is now Senegal. There was a civil war going on at the time that the *Amistad* slaves were bought; some of the slaves were prisoners of war, but most of them had been convicted of crimes.

"Where do you put convicted criminals? There were no prisons in Africa. These men were legally enslaved under African law: for murder, for debt, for adultery, for theft. Victims were awarded the perpetrators as slaves by way of compensation. Often they were sold, not always to Europeans. But by the seventeenth century the European slavers usually offered the most in cash or goods. The abolitionists in Massachusetts, who argued in the courts that the slaves on the *Amistad* were not legally enslaved, were wrong, and their assumption essentially racist. They had been legally enslaved under African tribal law.

"Don't get me wrong. I do not approve at all of the way the white man treated African slaves after they bought them and took them across the Atlantic. In Africa the slaves were simply domestic servants and were well treated."

"You said something about turning criminals into zombies?"

"That is another African way of dealing with crime. It is more of a private arrangement between the family that has been wronged and a *bokor*, or sorcerer. This is what the ancestors of the Guinea people practiced in Africa. But here, on this island, the pharmacology has become more sophisticated. The Africans, as I just said, intermarried with the Arawak, who had come from South America and brought with them exotic South American plants for medicinal reasons. Here, the zombies can be put into a permanent submissive mental state, with most of their faculties intact, in which they accept their lot as a slave. Sometimes some faculties are enhanced. There appear to be formulae that result in side effects where the zombie is over-sexed or aggressive, or – there are variants." He frowned.

"And that powder in your hand can turn someone into a zombie? Right away?"

"Yes. Within seconds. The first symptom is extreme drowsiness, then unconsciousness, and then the heart actually stops beating. Western medicine would pronounce the person dead. Sometimes they are dead – it depends on the dosage. If the dosage is accurate, they are pronounced dead but then – other things can happen."

Alice, looking at the vial, couldn't conceal her interest. "How much would you have to give someone to knock them out? And how do you give it to them?"

"This batch? It doesn't take much. You would give it to them with food. Exposure to a mucus membrane will do it, the tongue, the skin if wet. Bokors in Haiti will sprinkle the powder where a victim might put his wet feet. If you wet the tip of your finger and put it in the vial, you'd get a dose, probably a light dose if it were only the tip of your finger.

"It could be used as an anaesthetic in the west, and variants as medications for psychiatric disorders. The chemistry would have to be exact and the dosage calculated. That is one of the things you see that I could work on in Guinea. Right now the potency and purpose is largely guesswork." He put the vial back in the breast pocket of his shirt.

"How long do they stay unconscious?"

"It depends. When they stop breathing they are often buried alive. The family of the zombie believes that they are dead. But one night, it can be after several weeks, I believe, the wronged family, the family of the zombie's victim, who made the arrangement with the *bokor*, might get the *bokor* to dig them up. They are revived and passed into slavery. That this is done in Haiti is well documented.

"But you see, even I, who has made Western psychopharmacology my study, do not yet know the chemistry. I don't know exactly what is in this glass phial for example. I know the ingredients, and how it is prepared, but I don't know the chemistry; it has been cooked and the ingredients altered. I'm sending this vial to a colleague in Paris for analysis. That is why I brought it from Guinea. You see, Alice, if I had modern Western equipment in Guinea, I could do the analysis myself. If the lab were at Haut-Clair I would be going back and forth all the time.

"It's just one of a number of preparations that I need to study intensively. Matieu in Paris might not do all that I would like to do. And he might take all the credit. Perhaps I won't send it to Paris but to an independent lab in the USA. Have them analyze it without knowing what it is. It could be expensive. So you see, don't you, that I need a laboratory here, on this island, and it would be so much easier to have it in Guinea, in the cave there, where the *mambo*s and *bokor*s do their work, than," he smiled at her, "in our beautiful plantation house. I would commute, that is all."

Alice rather doubted the sincerity of his devotion to his vocation. He is just making excuses for hanky-panky with his Zena, thought Alice. But she didn't really want him at Haut-Clair anymore. She was bored with him. They would keep the beach house and meet there occasionally. Perhaps she could send Zena a venereal disease – it was worth looking into. How the black queen felt about sharing him she did not know or care. Still, she felt that Narcisse should be punished for his infidelity.

The life she looked forward to at Haut-Clair was a solitary one. If Narcisse spent all of his time in Guinea, she would not miss him.

But she didn't trust Zena. If Alice were to die, Haut-Clair and all the riches that she planned to enjoy there would revert to Narcisse, and then perhaps to Zena. On the other hand if Narcisse were to die first Zena could not profit from her death.

Narcisse was blind to the fact that Zena and Alice were rivals, as deadly to one another as two queen bees in a single hive. He thought that they could be friends. Narcisse wanted Alice to learn more about Voudon; he wanted her to get really interested so she would provide him with the lab he needed – in Guinea.

So he said to her now, "I would really like you to witness a Voudon ceremony. Philippe has recently helped Zena's brother, Shanguma, who is a *bokor*, to set up a *hounfor* or temple, in Le Havre. The idea is to make some money for the Guinea people by summoning spirits and allowing paying tourists to witness the event. It's a closed ceremony, guests by invitation only. It's not to become simply a tourist attraction; visitors have to be serious. It's a religious ceremony. We can get in, no problem. There's one tonight. Zena will be there and will be participating. I would really like us to go, would you come with me?"

Alice thought for a moment and said, "Yes, I would like to. The more I can learn about this island the better." She saw it as a scouting expedition.

―――∞∞∞―――

As it happened Theodore McLeod and his new friend, the forensic psychiatrist, Dr. Bernard Levinson, were preparing to attend the same Voudon session at the invitation of Michael, the waiter from the hotel. Michael was born in Guinea and was one of those who had chosen to leave the reservation. He still had friends there, one of whom was Shangomo. He worked as doorman and greeter for Shangomo's *hounfor* ceremonies.

By another coincidence, René Lachapelle of the Sûreté du Québec, who had just arrived on the island with two giant schnauzer puppies, also planned to attend. He had not yet made contact with his customer, Alice LeBlanc, because he was making some discreet inquiries about her. His invitation came from a contact he had made with the St. Anthony police.

10

Alice, concerned as always with keeping a low profile, told Narcisse that she wanted to sit somewhere in the back of the tent. The *hounfours* took place in an old circus tent that was perfectly round. A visiting American circus years before had not been able to pay its hotel bill; the hotel had seized the tent and rented it out. The guests sat at tables as in a nightclub. On each table was a bottle of St. Anthony rum, water, limes, ginger ale, glasses, rapidly melting ice, and a small candle. The guests served themselves. They had paid a large fee for admittance and the rum was free. Most of the guests were white but tonight there was a large party of black Americans.

Shangomo sat at a long table with about a dozen Guinea people. He looked quite African, distinct from the other Guineas with their mixed Indian and African blood. Zena also stood out as distinctly black, yet exotic with her Nubian looks. She sat at another table with the young initiates who all wore white dresses.

On the far side of the tent from the entrance was a flap through which the Guinea people passed, coming and going from Shangomo's table. Alice sat alone at the back about halfway between the guests' entrance and the flap. Narcisse had gone off to talk to his Guinea cousins. To his chagrin, Alice had declined to go with him. She was there to observe and didn't wish to be noticed. She found herself feeling a strong hostility toward Zena and the Guinea people. When she looked at them in their silk clothes, she thought of her Abu people and their tattered jeans. Soon, she consoled herself, with the cocaine money, they would all be living in stone houses with hot and cold running water.

Sitting alone, austere and beautiful, wearing a plain black evening dress and a pearl necklace, she didn't seem to be aware that she was in fact being noticed. Her features were barely discernible in the dark tent. Seated at a distant table, straining to see her face, was her former lover, Theodore McLeod.

Theodore, on catching sight of her, thought that she was Hattie. He knew that she couldn't be because Hattie was dead. He only thought it was her, he knew, because he was drunk. He and Bernard hadn't left the beach bar that afternoon but had continued to drink the rum punches that Michael had cheerfully brought them until dinnertime. But he cautioned them to please remember that they would be at a religious ceremony deserving of respect. They had dined well at the hotel on flying fish, West Indian vegetables, and white Bordeaux. When they arrived at the *hounfour* he showed them to a good table near the front, which he had saved for them.

Theodore kept looking at the woman in black. I see her everywhere, he thought. It is a fantasy, I'll leave it as a fantasy and not go over there and make a fool of myself.

"Do you know her?" someone asked. An astonishingly beautiful woman, tall, young, and black, in a white silk gown, was standing at their table looking down at him. Surprised by her sudden appearance, he looked over at Bernard who gazed back at him quizzically, curious to see how Theodore would handle this apparition.

"The woman in the black evening dress. You have been looking at her and I wonder if you know her," said Zena.

"She – she looks like someone – I used to know," said Theodore.

"Will you sit down?" asked Bernard, raising his great bulk from his chair. He graciously pulled out an empty chair for her. "But you are not Quebecoise?"

Zena laughed and sat. "I learned my English in Montreal. You have a good ear."

"Thank you," said Bernard.

"It's a chess game!" cried Theodore suddenly. "You are the black queen and she the white! But she wears black and you wear white, you are both witches. The rest of us are merely pawns."

"But you are a knight, surely," said Zena, "a white knight, and your friend here – "

"I rather fancy myself as a bishop, but it can never happen. I'm a Jew. My name is Bernard and my companion, the wild Canadian hockey player, is Theodore."

"Bernard, you at least make sense," murmured Zena.

"It is your strong island rum, poor chap, he's not accustomed to it."

"Jews can be bishops. Why not?" asked Theodore. "Was not Disraeli prime minister of England and a favorite of Queen Victoria?"

"That was secular," replied Bernard. "Besides he was elected not appointed."

"You think she is a white queen, the woman that looks like the woman you knew? And where was that? Who was she?" asked Zena.

"'It was long ago, in another country, and besides the witch is dead,'" quoted Theodore.

"'Wench' is what Marlowe wrote," corrected Bernard.

"The wicked witch is dead, the wicked witch is dead,'" chanted Theodore. "She's dead."

"People rise from the dead," said Zena. "*Par ici*. Bernard, your rum soaked friend will be quiet, I hope. This is a religious service."

"Quiet as a mouse," said Theodore. "I promise."

Suddenly, from the temple at the centre of the tent there was the sharp crisp beat of a small drum, its rhythm disconnected, disconcerting.

"That is the *cata*. I must go."

They all looked up and saw three men with drums of different sizes seated around the center post of the temple. The *cata*, which had just started up, was the smallest.

Alice also had a visitor at her table. In another part of the tent René Lachapelle was sitting quietly by himself. Unlike Theodore he identified her positively. He had planned to get in touch with her the next morning, but as she had appeared at the *hounfour*, he went over to her table. He stood above her for a moment, looking down, a cigarette dangling from a corner of his mouth. She looked back up at him, did not like what she saw, and looked around for Narcisse.

"You don't remember me, Hattie, do you? May I sit down?"

She shrugged indifference. He stubbed his cigarette out on the ground, sat down, and lit another. "I brought two puppies for you, both salt-and-pepper with white throats. Ears and tail were not clipped. You bought Manson from my kennel? You don't remember me then. I didn't breed them myself; I got them from California. They're in a kennel outside Le Havre. Don't worry, they have each other, I would not leave a dog alone. They are social creatures, like us." He had the effrontery to put his hand on her knee.

"Have a drink," said Alice, removing the hand and digging her fingernails into his flesh. "And pour me one. Straight up."

René poured the drinks. "You know, Hattie, I have a day job. I learned to train dogs while working full time for the SQ. I'm an inspector. Rather bad luck for you." He produced his card and passed it over. Hattie glanced at it. The background was blood red. His name and the words Surêté du Quebec were printed in black. "The job took me to North Hatley last September. To a cottage on the east side of Lake Massawippi. Above it, where the old farmhouse stood, there's an abandoned well. I dropped a pebble in it. Long drop." He raised his eyebrows. "Then a funny sort of clunk. Like when you drop something on concrete. No odor that way. I can understand why you shot the dog. Manson would have missed you and you could hardly take him with you on a motorbike."

René knocked back his rum in one shot, and pushed back his chair. He could see Narcisse making his way back to the table. "But, of course, that is only conjecture on my part. I told no one. Still, one call from me and the well would be dug up."

The *cata* started its strident staccato. René got up, leaned over, and spoke quietly into her ear. "The dogs will be expensive: two hundred thousand dollars each. American dollars. I am staying at the Miramar. Call me tonight or early in the morning."

"I'm sure they're worth it," said Alice evenly, her face white and taut. "I'll call on you tonight late and we'll get the business done. I want to see my dogs. *Au revoir*."

"*Bon. Cette nuit. Au revoir*," René nodded to her and then to Narcisse, but didn't wait to be introduced.

"Who was that?" asked Narcisse sitting down, looking at her curiously. "He seems to have made you angry."

"That is the man who has brought me two giant schnauzers from Canada. He didn't breed them himself. He got them from California and I am angry because he is asking too much money for them. Shhh. The ceremony is starting."

The *hounfour* was in the center of the tent and consisted of a sloping wooden roof with five supporting posts, one at each corner and one in the middle. The middle one, the *poteau mitan,* was ornate and had vegetation growing out of it, as if it were alive. The raised wooden floor, or deck, was about twenty-five feet square, one side narrowing and extending to the flap entrance used by the Guineas. The drum ceased and in its place one heard a rattle from the darkness at the end of the passage.

The temple was dark. The only light was from the tiny candles on the guests' tables. A girl ran out of the darkness, spun first to the left and then to the right, visible only because her silk dress was white. She placed four large candles around the *poteau mitan* and lit them. Zena came out bearing two clay jars that she put down between the candles, where they could be plainly seen. She spun twice clockwise and then anti-clockwise, her white gown billowing out and revealing in silhouette her striking female figure. She then took a handful of grain from one of the jars and pouring it carefully, used it to draw a symbol on the floor.

"She has written the symbol of the first spirit to be invoked," whispered Narcisse to Alice. "Probably Eleggua, the messenger."

The other jar held watered rum. Zena presented it to the four corners of the temple and then poured libations to the *poteau mitan,* to the drums, and to the entrance. The young initiates, also in white, filed in. Shangomo appeared from the darkness and led them in a litany.

"He is invoking in order the *orishas* from the Voudon pantheon," Narcisse whispered.

There was an armchair near the passage and Shangomo sat on it. From his robes he produced two doves that perched on his fingers. Two men ran out with a two-handled cast-iron brazier filled with glowing charcoal, which they placed before the *poteau mitan* where the three drummers, dressed in yellow silk, were seated. The *cata* recommenced its staccato beat.

Zena stood by the drums, moving intermittently to the irregular beat, shaking the rattle heard before offstage. As the initiates reached the main platform, the second drum, larger than the *cata*, came in and the girls, who ranged in age from thirteen to about twenty, began to dance. This drum produced a rolling rhythm, to which the beat of the smaller drum was syncopated. Zena joined the dancers. All of them faced inward dancing not for the audience, but for the *poteau mitan* and the burning embers.

Then the third drum came in like thunder. This is not a show, thought Theodore, sobering up, they aren't doing this for us; it is a religious service. He took a long drink of water to sober up some more and concentrated on what was happening in front of him. The dance was a powerful movement of shoulders and arms, feet flat and pounding on the wooden platform, the effect monotonous and powerful. Zena, the *mambo*, sang out in a powerful contralto what was unmistakably an invocation, wordless and imploring.

"She is calling a spirit," whispered Bernard.

After about thirty minutes, with the audience lulled into thinking nothing was happening, the big drum, or *maman,* suddenly broke into a different beat, as if taken over by a different drummer, and then back to a violent syncopation with the other drums. One of the young women froze, cringed, spun like a top, and then went wild, hurtling about the stage, falling, leaping, crashing – she had been mounted by a spirit.

In one of her wild gyrations she grabbed a live coal out of the brazier with her bare hands and put it in her mouth, then ran around the perimeter of the temple, her eyes wide, staring at the audience, the red burning lump of charcoal like a third eye glaring at them. Spitting it back into the brazier, she seized one of the doves from Shanguma's hands and bit off its head. She turned in a circle in front of the other initiates, the blood of the dove spurting on to their white dresses, just below their waists. Then she leapt off the stage and seizing the hands of one of the black American tourists, a huge man built like a football lineman, swung him like a doll in a circle around her. Just as suddenly she dropped him and he crashed into a table. Zena came down onto the floor and chased the spirit, or *loa,* back into the temple with her rattle. Everyone in the audience was now on their feet.

"The *orisha* who has mounted her is Oya," said Narcisse. "She is a great witch and the guardian of the gates of death. She is the spirit of female power and the source of thunderbolts and tornados."

Soon two other *hounsis*, or initiates, were possessed and the stage became pandemonium. Zena, now appeared to be trying to calm the spirits, tossing water and rum on them as libations and shaking her rattle at them in rhythm with the drums, taming them back into joining the dance. Gradually the *loa* subsided, the tempo of the dance slowed, and the three girls who had been mounted collapsed utterly in heaps on the floor.

The drums ceased. Zena extinguished the four large candles. The girls were slowly revived and the stage cleared. One or two guests began to applaud, then, confused and uncertain, stopped, realizing that applause was not expected. The guests slowly resumed their seats, and having sat, quickly poured themselves large rums. Everyone was rather shaken. The large American who had been swung about was unhurt. He sat calmly in his seat looking astonished and relieved.

"I would like to meet the girl who was first possessed. The one who picked up a coal and put it in her mouth. Do you think that you could bring her over?" Alice asked Narcisse.

"I'll try." He got up and left the table.

Alice glanced over at René, who met her glance and waved, a cigarette in his hand. He smokes a lot, she thought. Theodore, whom she had never noticed, had stopped looking at her. Since she had encountered Charley, she made a point of not looking directly at strangers, fearful of making eye contact with someone who might turn out not to be a stranger. This aloofness gave her a regal quality that had the unwanted effect of drawing attention to her.

Several of the initiates had been staring at her and when Narcisse asked the one who had been possessed by the *orisha* Oya, to come over and meet his wife, she agreed with alacrity. But when she arrived at the table, she was shy and could not look Alice in the eye. Alice asked to examine her hands and mouth, and when she did this, the girl looked away, frightened. Her hands and mouth were not marked at all by the coals. The girl quickly excused herself and ran back to her friends.

Narcisse chuckled. "That's odd. One who has been possessed by the fearless spirit Oya seems afraid of you."

"I suppose," said Alice, smiling, "that Oya was enough for one night. But she was unmarked. I wonder how they did that. Ice cubes perhaps."

The Miramar was further north on the coast than Les Palmes, so Theodore dropped Bernard off on the way, said goodbye, and continued on in the taxi. When he got to the hotel, he went to a little square bar on the patio behind the hotel that faced the sea. He sat down with the sea to his left and ordered a Banks beer. There was no moon. He thought about Hattie. It was odd; that was the second time that he thought he had seen her that day.

A man came and sat on his right facing the sea, so that the two of them took up a corner with a post between them. Theodore looked at him for a moment. "Didn't I see you tonight at the voodoo?" he asked.

"Yes, I was there, amazing, amazing, I'm a good Catholic, but I begin to think, what did your Hamlet say, there are more things on heaven and earth than dreamt of in my philosophy. Don't I know you? Tell me, are you Canadian?"

"Yes."

"And forgive me if I am mistaken, were you ever with the RCMP?"

"Yes. But not anymore."

"I have you now, *quelle scandale*. Let me introduce myself, René Lachapelle, of the Quebec Sûreté. I saw a picture of you somewhere – at the office perhaps – I don't think your picture was in the papers. The big Bandits bust last summer. Good piece of undercover work, but you didn't get credit for it, did you? But I forget your name."

"Theodore McLeod. It was a fluke and the girl was murdered. The force dumped me in fact. Suspected of cavorting with the enemy. Honorable discharge, generous severance, but dumped all the same. I'm glad someone thought I did good work." There was a silence as both drank their beer.

"That woman you spoke to – I was looking at her when you went up to her – "

"Looked a lot like Hattie Brading – I was startled myself. That's why I went over. Curiosity. It's not her, of course. *Ca va sans dire.* She is dead. No question. I was involved in the case. But it was such a resemblance – I had to get closer, made up an excuse. This woman is American. Blue eyes, and how shall I put it? More classy than Hattie. Hattie seemed to me – *oh, je sais pas – une gamine* – how you say in English – a rough diamond."

"How did you know Hattie?"

"I trained a dog for her a few years ago. I didn't really know her. I was many years in charge of the dogs at the SQ."

"I knew that dog, Manson, a giant schnauzer. I wonder what happened to the dog."

René was silent for a moment; looking for the answer to that question had brought him to where he was tonight. He chose not to comment. "You see, I work sometimes at a private kennel training dogs. That's how we met. How long are you here?"

"I leave tomorrow morning. My two weeks are up. I enjoyed myself. Tonight was something I will never forget."

"Tonight was a memorable evening – for both of us. I expect to leave tomorrow myself. Depends on some business. I have an open ticket. Maybe I will see you on the plane."

René finished his beer and left Theodore alone with his thoughts. So, thought René on his way up in the elevator, I am already beginning to earn my $400,000, perhaps I should ask for $500,000. Poor chap, I wonder if he is in love with her. He watched television until the phone rang.

That night, pretending that she had been turned on by the Voudon ceremony, Alice had Narcisse make love to her until he was exhausted (and rather fed up with her demands). He was tired and she suspected that he had made love to Zena the day before. When she was certain that he was sound asleep, she slipped out of bed and searched for the vial of powder he had showed her that afternoon. It was on the chest of drawers in his dressing room. She checked the cork and carefully put it in her knife holster, which she strapped to her calf. The knife held it firmly in place. She took a pair of Narcisse's gloves out of a drawer.

Then she telephoned the Miramar. Speaking English with a French-Canadian accent in a low voice, she asked for René Lachapelle.

"*Allo?*"

"Do you have a car?"

"Is it Hattie?"

"Yes."

"I have a rental in the lot: a black Suzuki four-wheel. It's not locked. You will meet me there?"

"Give me forty-five minutes."

"Come alone."

She put on a bikini bathing suit, picked up a pair of her own gloves, and put them in the bag. She put on black slacks and an open black jacket over the bikini. She put a small flashlight in the pocket of the jacket. Going downstairs to the linen closet she found a Miramar beach towel that had come over with other linen from the Cantaves when they moved into their new house. Then she went down another flight of stairs to where Abbah was sleeping in the bedroom next to the boat room. She knocked gently on his door. There was a sleepy "What is it?"

"It's Aleysha. I need you, get dressed." He joined her in the boat room in less than a minute. "Listen carefully. A dangerous enemy of mine has arrived on the island. An evil man. Are my enemies your enemies?"

"Yes, Aleysha. I will kill him for thee."

"What would you do with the body?"

"I told thee, Aleysha. We Abu eat our enemies."

"There must not be a trace of him. It's a crime on St. Anthony to kill your enemies. If they find the body or any part of it they would come after us."

"Nay, Aleysha, there will be nothing left. What we don't eat we will feed to the gulls. The bones we burn. We use the ashes for —"

"But they might find the teeth. You must take the skull to sea and sink it."

"Yes, Aleysha. But first we eat the tongue and the brain."

"What I am going to do, Abbah, is turn him into a zombie."

"Oh, yes, canst thou do that, Aleysha? That means we can keep him fresh until we cook him."

That's interesting, thought Alice. Narcisse told me that the Guinea people think their zombies turn into spirits. "You will then drive the body to Haut-Clair. He is quite big, will you be able to get the body up the path?"

"I will get help, that will be easy, the people will be pleased. We have not had meat in our stew for a long time. And I will tell them that thou hast the power of a *bokor*, that thou can turn men into zombies. That will please them but not surprise them. Dost thou have many enemies, Aleysha?"

"Put on these gloves and come. We'll take the Jeep. Bring your knife."

Abbah and Alice parked the Jeep on the road near the entrance to the Miramar where it could not be seen. They sat in it for a few minutes with the lights off. She had said forty-five minutes and they had deliberately come fifteen minutes early. She wanted to be sure that she was in the Suzuki first, in the driver's seat. There was a hedge between the road and the hotel grounds, but they could see the parking lot over it. She pointed out the Suzuki to Abbah. After five minutes there was no sign of a night watchman.

"Watch from here, don't get out of the Jeep unless I flash my flashlight. I will only do that if something goes wrong. I will distract him; the window will be open. Kill him quietly with your knife and we will walk slowly back to the Jeep. But I don't think it will be necessary. If I don't flash my light, you'll see me drive the Suzuki, that's the black car you will see me get into, out of the parking lot with the zombie beside me. Follow me to the beach but don't drive onto the beach after me. Leave the Jeep on the road and come on foot."

She walked up the driveway to the parking lot. There was no moon. Electricity in St. Anthony was expensive so there were few lights and their wattage was low. She went up to the Suzuki, opened the driver's side door, and got in. She took the vial out of the sheath, removed the cork, and put it between her thighs. She took her arms out of her jacket so that it hung loosely over her shoulders.

Policemen are punctual and five minutes later René got in on the passenger side. He was dressed smartly in blue blazer and white duck trousers. He immediately lit a cigarette using the dashboard lighter, his hand resting briefly on her knee. I won't remove it this time, she thought.

"If you're going to smoke, please open the window."

He did. "What's the matter? Did you forget that they drive on the left-hand side or afraid I might drive off to a deserted beach and have my way with you?" he asked, leering at her over the lit cigarette. He took out a police automatic and put it on his lap pointing at her. "You will forgive me if I take the precaution of pointing a loaded gun at you. You are a killer and one has to be careful with killers. Any trouble and I'll shoot you. I'll tell them that I was attempting to verify that you were who I thought you were before informing the local police when you attacked me. I'm sure you are armed. I have already introduced myself to the St. Anthony police – they know that I am looking for someone, but they don't know who."

Alice looked nervously at the gun. "I think I will have one of your cigarettes. I am not armed. You can search me."

"I believe you." He passed her the pack. They were filtered Gauloise. She shook off her jacket, exposing the top of her bikini. As she had planned, René's eyes were not on her hands. She extracted two cigarettes, put one in her mouth, wet it, and then dipped the filter end in the powder in the open vial between her legs. She put that one back in the package, being careful not to touch the powdered end, which she left sticking out a little over an inch. She put the other one in her mouth. Pushing in the lighter, she placed the package of cigarettes on his lap, her hand almost touching his crotch.

"If you shoot me, you won't get the four hundred thousand," she said. "Will you? Tell me, what assurance will I have that you will not come back for more?"

"It's true, blackmailers have been known to do that," he said. "Perhaps you could have me arrested for blackmail?" He laughed as picked up his gun and pointed it at her. "This is the deal. I won't ask for more and you won't have me, oh, conveniently killed by contract, as a woman of your means can easily afford. When I get back to Canada I will email you a bank account number, one that I have offshore. You will wire four hundred thousand American dollars to it."

"I can pick the dogs up from the kennel early tomorrow?"

"Here's the address." René passed her a card with the name of the kennel and stubbed out his cigarette. "I told them Alice Cantave had bought them and that you would pick them up. I leave tomorrow."

"How do you know I will not have you killed?"

"There is an envelope – to be opened in the event of my death – with the SQ."

"Sounds good." All he is offering is his promise not to blackmail me again, she thought, which is worthless. Does he think me stupid?

"There is one small extra. Something I just thought of. Sex. Now. In the car. A blow job, while I hold the gun and smoke a cigarette. It will be only the once, kind of like a handshake, a seal on the deal." He laughed. "Take off your top."

René took out the poisoned cigarette, put it in his mouth, and gasped. He looked at her stupefied as she took his gun, and then collapsed, unconscious. Alice picked the cigarette up carefully and put it in the ashtray. She took a handkerchief, wiped everything she might have touched, and put on her gloves. She carefully placed the vial back in the knife holster. She reached into his jacket pockets, found the car keys, started the Suzuki and drove off. Coming out of the entrance, she turned left and glanced at Abbah, who started up the Jeep.

Abbah did a U-turn and followed the Suzuki to a deserted stony beach quite far north on the coast. Alice turned off the lights, drove onto the beach, and stopped. Abbah parked the Jeep on the road. The beach was never used. A coral reef had broken up only recently and the beach consisted of sharp coral stones that were hard on the feet. No one would want to sunbathe or picnic here. Nor would anyone want to swim while the tide was going out. There was a fierce rip tide – a swimmer could be caught in it and carried out to deep water where there were sharks. Live coral reefs, a scratch from which would bring infection, lay close to the shore. But there was a passage, a way to swim out. Alice had been here before. On her first helicopter ride with Paul they had landed here. It was a desolated, lonely spot. She stopped the Suzuki and got out. It was low tide; the tide was just starting to come back in.

Alice had planned that René's body would not be found and that his death would appear to be a faked suicide, making it unlikely that a death certificate could be issued for seven years under the law of St. Anthony. There were to be three clues that he had walked away from the scene: his shoes, his gun, and his cigarettes would not be found.

"We are going to have to undress him," she said. "Down to his underwear." They stripped him and put him in the back of the Jeep. She felt his pulse. There was none but if Narcisse was correct he was alive.

"He is muscular but soft," said Abbah. "He will be good eating. Do you know what sort of food he ate? If they eat a lot of fish or meat they do not taste so good. Do you know, O Aleysha?"

Alice ignored this question. "He can hear what you say, you know." Abbah looked down at René as if he were going to ask him, then thought better of it. "You know what to do. Deliver him to your people and then drive back. Wipe his mouth carefully. It's poisoned." He nodded. "I know it's late but I want the Jeep and my things back at the house before daybreak."

"But you, Aleysha?"

"I'm going to swim home. Before I enter the sea, I am going to toss you the shoes. You are to destroy them. That's important, that the shoes are not found."

She stripped down to her bikini, aware that Abbah was staring at her body, and left her clothes and bag on the sand for him to pick up. Then she put René's clothes over her arm, passed Abbah her gloves and the package of filtered Gauloise, and then and took the poisoned cigarette carefully out of the ashtray. She turned to Abbah and kissed him quickly on the mouth.

"You are a good boy, Abbah, I am pleased with you." She undid the knife holster strapped to her calf and passed it to him. "You must be very careful with this. You see the glass vial beside the knife? That contains the zombie magic. Be very careful with it. Do not open it. You must bring it back with my clothes tonight. I am taking his gun. I'll drop it into the sea." She slipped René's smart black loafers on her feet, dropped the clothes in a pile on the beach just above the high water mark, and walked into the sea, taking the shoes off, just before going in. She threw the cigarette into the water, and then she tossed the shoes, one by one, back to Abbah who caught them neatly.

Since the tide was out the water was low; she would have to be careful of the reefs. The sea was calm and she made it to deep water where she dropped the gun. She thought suddenly of sharks. They didn't like the reefs, she had been told, so they didn't follow the tide in. From the air, on the jaunt with Paul when they had landed on the stony beach, she had seen them, not far from here, on the north end of the island. They might be cruising further out. She swam close to the island; she didn't dare stray far from the reefs. It was a longer swim than she had thought. To stay close to the reefs she couldn't swim in a straight line, but had to swim around them, being careful not to get too close.

She swam about five miles before she saw the house. She had been swimming a breast stroke, because sharks are attracted to splashing, but now, so close to home she broke into a crawl, and arrived at her own beach utterly exhausted. So exhausted that on entering the house, she couldn't manage the stairs, and had only enough strength to take off her wet bathing suit and collapse on Abbah's bed.

Where he found her naked under his sheets in the dim light of dawn. She awoke to see him standing there, not knowing what to do. She looked at him tenderly for a moment, got out of bed, undressed him, and took him to bed. "Don't worry," she murmured, running her hands over his young body, "Narcisse always sleeps till noon. You know that."

But Narcisse got up early that morning because he had an errand to do. He had decided to send the glass vial not to Matieu in Paris, but to the States for analysis in a laboratory where no one knew him. The lab would be told nothing about the contents. But he could not find the vial nor could he find Alice. The servants had come in but no one had seen her. He went downstairs; perhaps Abbah had seen her. Opening the door of his room, he found them both in bed, naked and fast asleep.

He let out a startled cry and they both woke up. Alice, grabbed the sheet to wrap herself in and got up, leaving poor Abbah to hide his nakedness by rolling onto his stomach and burying his face in his pillow. She picked up her knife and sheath from the top of the chest of drawers where Abbah had put her things, checking that the vial was still tucked in beside the knife. Not having specific instructions as to what to do with the cigarettes, Abbah had brought back the half empty package of Gauloise. These she took too and led Narcisse into the boatroom.

"This is the end of us!" Narcisse declared, who although very angry, saw his way clear now to leave her for Zena. "I want a divorce and I want it right away. I'll see Philippe and see what we can do to get Haut-Clair back from you. I'm leaving you."

"Hold on," said Alice, knowing he would go to Zena. "Zena and the Guinea people still need the coffee plantation, they need me. Look, that was an accident. It never happened before and won't happen again." She put on a beach robe, one of several hanging in the boat room, and slipped the sheath, with the knife and vial, and the Gauloises into the pocket. "Let's talk this over like adults. We'll go upstairs and have a cigarette. A time like this calls for staying calm."

When Narcisse collapsed on the couch of their little sitting room after putting the cigarette Alice had given him to his lips, she quickly poured a third of the powder onto the glass top of the coffee table in front of him. She then took her knife and neatly divided this third of the powder again into three, and placed the knife beside it. She placed the vial back in the knife holster and put it back into the pocket of the beach robe. She carefully picked up the cigarette, went into the adjacent powder room, flushed it down the toilet, went back into the dressing room, and screamed.

Sara was first on the scene. She brought water and tried to revive Narcisse. She noticed the powder on the table. "What is that stuff?" she demanded.

"It's something he got in Guinea," Alice stammered. "He was dividing it and I think he got some on his fingers. Maybe he licked his fingers. I don't know, I was in the bathroom. Get a doctor, get Dr. Cantave."

She looked so upset that Sara, who liked her, gave her a quick hug. They stretched Narcisse out on the couch, Sara went to call Dr. Cantave, and Alice went into Narcisse's bathroom with the vial, emptied the contents of four bottles of vitamin pills down the toilet, flushed it, cleaned the jars, put the remaining contents of the vial in one, which she put in the pocket of her beach robe, and carried the others into the sitting room. She put the empty vial on the table, the three empty jars on the floor beneath it, then went to her bathroom, showered, and got dressed.

If he were to die, Zena would believe it was murder. I am afraid of that woman, Alice thought. She has strange powers of intuition; she knows things without being told. I don't want her here. She called Philippe. "Narcisse has collapsed. He had some strange powder he had got from Zena. He was going to send it to somewhere in France for analysis. He was dividing it, and somehow – "she began to sob. "Somehow – I think – he must have got some on his finger and then, I don't know, absent mindedly licked his finger – without thinking. I have sent for Robert."

As she was hanging up the phone, Dr. Robert Cantave arrived. Alice explained about the powder again. "There's no heartbeat," he said. "I know something about that potion. I don't believe he's dead. I have seen such cases in Guinea and I believe that he's in a state of suspended animation."

"A zombie!" said Sara. "The poor man."

"I'm going to call Zena. Saba is very ill, but only she or Zena could help him now." He got up and went to the hall to telephone.

Through the window, Alice could see Abbah working in the garden. "Sara, perhaps if we gave him coffee," she said.

Sara looked at her. "Coffee won't help him, child." She put a motherly arm around Alice. She hadn't had much sleep and her eyes were still red from the long swim in salt water; she looked terrible. "But I'll make some for the rest of we. You, child, have not had breakfast, you better come along with me." With her arm around Alice, she led her out of the room.

Philippe arrived while Alice was having breakfast. He studied the scene – his unconscious brother, the powder, the knife, and the little jars under the table. "I can't believe Narcisse would be so careless." Then he sat down and wept.

Sara brought him a cup of coffee and he slowly pulled himself together. "What's to be done, medically, Uncle Robert?"

"I have sent for Zena. Paul has gone to fetch her. Saba is too ill to come. I don't think Western medicine can help him. I'm going to recommend to Alice that Zena take him to Guinea and that she treat him there. There are legal implications, I believe. What do you think, Philippe?"

"There are." said his nephew. "I think we must declare him *non compos mentis.*" Alice came into the room and Philippe embraced her.

"You should get some rest," Dr. Cantave said to her. "You've had a nasty shock. We are thinking that Zena should take Narcisse to Guinea to treat him."

"Over my dead body," declared Alice, fearing that Zena might cure him. "She has done enough harm. He goes into a western hospital." She started to shake with rage and exhaustion. "That bitch, that bitch, that black bitch!"

"Let me give you something," said Dr. Cantave, looking in his bag. He shook eight green pills into her hand. "It's valium. You haven't taken anything else? Take two now, two after four hours, and you can take more after that but you probably won't need to. If you do need more, call me. Go and get some rest."

Alice left them and went to bed. When she awoke, Narcisse was gone. The family had taken him to Guinea.

Theodore looked for his bar acquaintance of the night before in the airport that morning and didn't see him. He bought a bottle of duty free over-proof rum, and finally got around to writing his aunts a postcard. I love it here, he wrote, but my severance pay is running out. I doubt if I will ever be able to afford to come back.

ALEYSHA
Nemesis

11

Not long after Narcisse Cantave's collapse, the roof was finished on the château at Haut-Clair and Aleysha moved in as she had planned. She put the beach house up for sale. She was the primary contractor on all the renovations and it was easier to supervise the work if she was living on site. Paul would fly the Barbados foremen and skilled workers in daily from their airport hotel. They supervised the Abu. The foremen and everyone else, including Paul, now addressed her as Aleysha.

Although Narcisse Cantave appeared to be unconscious, Zena talked to him earnestly and at length. She was certain that he could hear and understand her. She had a physical relationship with him; she felt that he needed to be touched and in time had gentle sex with him. She tried different cures, with no success. She sent for a famous *bokor* from Haiti who tried some magic that was new to her. The problem, according to him, was that Narcisse was too Westernized. The zombie magic was not just chemistry; part of it was in the culture and worldview of the African people. The *bokor* could not reach Narcisse.

Zena quietly vowed a terrible revenge on Aleysha if he died. Two weeks after she and Paul brought Narcisse to Guinea, her mother died and she had her hands full dealing with the funeral and her own coronation. Paul's father, her uncle by marriage, the good doctor Robert Cantave, had a fatal heart attack at Saba's funeral.

Under the laws of St. Anthony, if a person is *non compos mentis*, the court commits the care of the person to a friend who is then known as his or her Committee. Philippe believed that as Zena was the one looking after Narcisse, she should be Committee of Narcisse's person. For the first time, he was in conflict with Aleysha, but he truly believed that his brother had a better chance of recovery under Zena's care. He felt at times as if he was the ping-pong ball in a match between the two queens.

Aleysha found her own lawyer and surprised Philippe by going to court. Their strategy was for her lawyer to argue in court that she should be his Committee, not just because she was his wife, but because he stood a better chance of being cured by western doctors. In fact, she planned to put him in an institution in Albania, where they would simply maintain him in his present condition and not even try to cure him.

The case was heard in midsummer; Aleysha won and was appointed Committee. But there was another problem: there was no precedent for removing a person from Guinea with a court order from Le Havre. If Zena refused to give him up, there was nothing Aleysha could do. Zena was bound by the laws of the Leopard Society; she believed that Aleysha had deliberately turned Narcisse into a zombie, but under her law she could not exact revenge unless he died. So the conflict between the two queens in the mountains of St. Anthony was at a stalemate.

The St. Anthony police had come to the beach house and questioned her. René Lachapelle's car and clothes had been found on a beach. The police suspected either a suicide or a faked suicide and were investigating. She told them that she had first met him at the *hounfour*, that they had arranged payment, and that he had told her where to pick up the dogs. She had not seen them before she picked them up; she had seen photographs of them and looked at their pedigrees on the Internet. She hadn't known that he was a police officer. She was surprised that he would commit suicide. He was all right when he talked to her at the *hounfour*. She said that he had told her that he was a good Catholic, and that he was not sure that he should be witnessing a voodoo ceremony.

She didn't know why he flew down here with the dogs instead of having them shipped. Perhaps he needed a holiday, perhaps he was stressed about something at home. Could he have had cancer? Could they not do an autopsy? His body was not found, they told her. That beach was a dangerous place to swim when the tide was going out, one could be caught and carried out to sea, they said. If he had gone to the beach directly from the *hounfour*, the tide would still have been going out. No one at the hotel remembered him leaving. It was possible that sharks had got him. There was no trace of his remains. Aleysha said she was sorry about his disappearance, but she was upset by her husband's sudden illness and she would like to be left alone.

On the island of St. Anthony in the absence of a body, a court must adjudicate the fact of death. There was a difficulty in this case because the circumstances of René's death resembled a couple of suicides on island beaches that had turned out to be faked. His clothes were found but not his shoes. The beach was stony and the court found that suspicious. He had been carrying a licensed gun when he went through customs – he had told the police he was looking for a fugitive but gave them no information. They had established that he was an inveterate smoker. No gun and no cigarettes were found with his clothes. The court would not issue a death certificate. It would do so if he did not make an appearance for a period of seven years.

Because of his final insult of demanding fellatio, with his gun pointing at her, she had rather hoped that he would be tossed into the simmering stew alive. Narcisse had explained to her that zombies, although totally immobilized, even when buried alive, are conscious of what is going on around them. But Abbah told her that this was not their custom; he had been hung upside down, and his throat cut to drain the blood, exactly as pigs are butchered. Then the flesh was cut up, seasoned, and put in the stew. The intestines and other undesirable parts were fed to the gulls and the bones were burnt. Abbah had personally taken the skull out to sea and sunk it, so that there was no possibility of a positive identification from dental records.

She attended the feast. The feasts and the religious services were much the same, except at the latter there was food, of course. It began with her seated on her throne at the village and the people prostrate before her, chanting her name, Aleysha, Aleysha, Aleysha, to the beat of drums. Then, on a signal from Abbah, they began to dance and, from time to time, bowing and curtsying before her. In the center of the village the stew simmered in the cauldron, stirred occasionally by an old woman who stood on a platform with a long spoon, as the froth fell hissing into the fire. Aleysha ate only fruit.

Incest is forbidden in all human societies, and sexual relations between mother and son are not practiced even by the highly sexed bonobos, mankind's closest relatives among the other apes. The Abu believed Aleysha to be an incarnation of Aloyshanova, from whom they were descended, and Abbah the incarnation of her son. But they did not object to Abbah's relationship with Aleysha. Today many consider interracial sex and homosexual sex acceptable but the new puritanism forbids what it calls intergenerational sex. The Abu did not share that prejudice. Abbah was seventeen and Aleysha infinitely old in their eyes. They saw it as a wonderful thing that the hereditary high priest and chieftain should mate with the queen. They hoped for a child.

Aleysha had settled in the great bedroom at the top of the stairs that she believed had been Aloyshovna's. Abbah had a small guest bedroom down the hall. He still saw himself as a servant; sex was now simply part of his duties as priest. He worshipped Aleysha in every way that he could. The Thirty-Nine Steps had been sold to an American. She seldom left the plantation now.

But after a couple of weeks, Aleysha decided to call off the affair with Abbah and sent him back to live in the village. He was not happy to be so dismissed from this part of his duties, but accepted the wishes of his queen. She told him, and he passed it on the Abu, that he was to mate with her once a month until she was pregnant.

The snakes, which had not left of their own accord, were allowed to remain. They curled up on the marble-topped tables and the new marble floors and slept. The giant schnauzers, a male and a female, whom she named Solomon and Sheba, grew quickly. She had picked them up in the Jeep with Paul and flown them to Haut-Clair the day she moved in. They were not allowed in the house and slept outside by the front entrance. They guarded it so ferociously that only Aleysha could use the front door. From the beginning, they were completely devoted to her. Had she not rescued them from cages, airplanes, and kennels, and brought them to paradise?

From their position at the front entrance of the house they had a view down the alley of rosewood trees, which she trained them to patrol. They had excellent hearing. Anyone who climbed up the cliff from the west would be challenged. They accompanied Aleysha when she inspected the plantation and when she visited the village they played with the children. Giant schnauzers, not related to the gentle German schnauzer, are a cross between Bouviers and Great Danes; they have been bred for generations to be aggressive with strangers. But Aleysha made sure that they knew all the Abu people and they often wandered down to the village on their own to play with the children.

Paul Cantave brought Juan Gonzalez-Prieto to Haut-Clair by helicopter one Sunday morning in May. Aleysha had ruled that Sunday was a day of rest on the plateau of Haut-Clair, and no work was being done on the house.

The religious services were held on Sunday mornings. Aleysha would walk down to the village in a scarlet silk dress with a long train, wearing her crown and most of her jewelry. Abbah would come for her with a huge black umbrella or parasol and escort her down the avenue, keeping the rays of the sun from reaching her white skin, and carrying her train over his arm. Solomon and Sheba were being trained to walk on either side at heel, but they were still puppies and were on leashes that Sunday morning. When they got close to the village the children would come up and play with the puppies. Some of them competed to carry her train, jockeying a bit for position. Abbah would keep order.

The new Sunday clothes had arrived and the Abu, men and women both, were arrayed in brilliant colored skirts, jeans, shirts, and vests. On hot days, most still preferred to be bare breasted.

When she arrived she would assume her seat on the old French armchair. Here the dogs were being trained to assume the heraldic *couchant* position on either side of her. The people would make their obeisances as they had when she first laid eyes on them, kneeling and prostrating themselves, their arms moving rhythmically, first outstretched before them their hands touching the ground, and then, as they straightened up, over their heads. Aleysha never let the worshipping go to her head. They clearly enjoyed doing it, and who was she to spoil their fun? But she was careful to maintain a stern expression. As Ayesha had told Holly, I have no real power, I rule by fear.

The *mambo* then performed a little ceremony in the Abu language. Aleysha could follow it and was pleased to see some respect paid to the teachings of Zarathustra. Abbah told her that the adjustments were not radical.

Then she would rise and sing a hymn. She had always had a good voice. She was teaching them to sing along with her and the hymn she always sang was William Blake's "Jerusalem." She had changed the word "England's" in the line "And did those feet in ancient time walk upon England's green and pleasant land" to "Aleysha's". And the word Jerusalem she changed to Persepolis, the great Persian capital and center of Zoroastrianism, that was destroyed by Alexander the Great. The Abu did not understand the words, except for Abbah, who had quickly learned them and sang with her in a fine tenor, but they were learning to sing them and they loved it. When it was finished everyone was smiling. The drummers were improvising a few syncopated beats here and there and each time it got better. Blake, who was never ever wholly in his own skull, would have been completely knocked out of it by the performance.

And, of course, the Abu had their own songs. Aleysha had found in the books she had bought in Paris a few of Zarathustra's hymns, translated into English. These she was slowly translating into Abu, trying to adjust the words to their complicated rhythmic speech. These she would teach them when she was satisfied with them. Abbah was helping her with this task.

Then Abbah asked if there was anyone who had a grievance against another. There were always a few petty grievances. Aleysha was a good queen. She listened carefully to both sides. If she had trouble understanding Abbah would translate. She would make suggestions for resolution of the conflict. Occasionally, she had to make a judgment in someone's favor. No one ever questioned one of her rulings.

Then she would stand, curtsy to the *mambo*, and with Abbah carrying the umbrella, she would depart. And so it was this Sunday morning, that Juan, standing on the steps of the half-renovated plantation house, saw her, bejeweled and dressed in scarlet, walking up the avenue, under a huge black umbrella carried by her devoted Abbah. He had heard the singing and was now flabbergasted by the sight of her and turned to Paul, who was standing beside him, for an explanation. Paul played this beautifully and just looked at him blankly as if everything was normal, which it was at Haut-Clair in those days.

Juan was staying at Les Palmes. Paul had picked him up there in the Jeep, which Aleysha had more or less given to him, and was to bring him back later that day. Aleysha didn't want him staying overnight. Paul also brought along a few bottles of champagne. As a rule Alyesha did not drink, and ate only the fruit, vegetables, and nuts that grew on the plantation. But today they were having flying fish, freshly caught that morning, and cooked by Oku, the Abu fisherman who had caught them.

Aleysha had been training servants. Two young Abu girls had been helping out in the house and they were to serve the lunch on a long refectory table in the kitchen. The dining room was not ready. Paul was to sit in on the meeting because she wanted him to know what was going on and to talk knowledgeably about the cutter to Juan. He understood that Juan was to be a partner not in the boat but in its cargo. Aleysha had not told him what the meeting was about, but he had a pretty good idea.

Juan and Aleysha, who had been corresponding by email, were close to an agreement and had decided to conclude it face to face. They were going to build a cocaine refinery on the cliff above the inlet. The coast guard cutter was to pick up coca paste at a tiny harbor at the mouth of a river in Guyana near the Venezuelan border. They could refuel there and that was the excuse for landing. There would be no problem bringing the paste to St. Anthony. They could have unloaded it in Le Havre and shipped it in bond to Haut-Clair, but Aleysha and Juan supposed that the DEA had spies at the Port of Le Havre. The cutter was going to anchor at Haut-Clair's own little harbor. The helicopter would bring the sacks of paste up the cliff on pallets.

Taking the refined product to Florida would be more risky, but Aleysha felt that a St. Anthony Coast Guard vessel was not going to be stopped by the US Coast Guard or the US Drug Enforcement Administration. Philippe had asked the St. Anthony government to offer the services of the vessel to the DEA. Aleysha's boat would be part of the vast Caribbean network of drug law enforcement. The presence of the boat in Florida coastal waters or anywhere in the Caribbean or the Atlantic, could be explained by saying that they were in pursuit of a suspicious vessel and maintaining radio silence. If things went seriously wrong, the cocaine could be weighted and dumped.

When Aleysha and Abbah reached the top of the avenue that Sunday morning, the schnauzers, having been let off their leashes on the way back, bounded forward barking aggressively at Juan. They took an instant dislike to him for standing near the entrance. Paul, whom they had long since accepted, was able to calm them. Nonetheless they growled fiercely at Juan before going to their places on either side of the entrance.

Juan was Aleysha's first guest at Haut-Clair. She went upstairs to change into something less formal and when she came down explained to Juan that Paul was her assistant and indispensable, which was news to Paul, and that he was her husband's cousin. She explained that her husband was a scientist who took little interest in business. He was at his laboratory that morning on another part of the island. Oddly enough, she told him, his field was psychopharmacology. He wouldn't be joining them; Paul would sit in at the meeting.

The three of them first went to the cliff site where the refinery would be built and looked down on the cove where Aleysha planned to keep her boat. They then returned to the house and sat down in the large drawing room to the left of the main staircase. This room, which was stunning in its elegance, had just been finished; it had not been used before. It was furnished with French Empire reproductions and Aubusson carpets. The Flemish tapestries hanging on the walls were originals. Snakes made themselves comfortable on the cool marble tables. Juan managed to ignore them.

"It was a ruin when I first came. The walls were standing, that was about it. I enjoy restoring it and I like living here," said Aleysha. "Shall we get down to business?"

She outlined the scheme to Paul, who had suspected what was going on but had not been officially brought in. The discussion became technical. Both Juan and Aleysha had studied the process and Juan had brought a detailed engineer's plan for the plant that had been drawn up in Mexico. They were going to combine the process of making cocaine base from the paste with the refining stage. The paste wasn't coming just from Juan's hacienda, but from other paste factories he now owned in different parts of Peru.

The process varied depending on the variety of coca plant. Potassium permanganate is dissolved in water and added to the coca paste that has itself been dissolved in an acid solution. Undesirable alkaloids and other material are extracted. The potassium permanganate breaks down the alkaloid ciscinnamoylcocaine found in large concentrations in *E. novogranatense* varieties. If the coca paste has a high concentration of this alkaloid and potassium permanganate is not used, then crystallization of cocaine HCl will be difficult. The solution is allowed to stand for about six hours. Then it is filtered, and the precipitate discarded. Ammonia water is added to the filtered solution and another precipitate is formed. The liquid is drained away and the remaining precipitate is dried in the sun or with heating lamps.

"Paul, you'll be helping me supervise building this plant and so will Abbah. You'd better get him. He's in the kitchen." Paul dutifully fetched the lad. Aleysha had bought him a cotton suit. He sat down and took an immediate interest. He had been fascinated by the architect's plans for restoring the house. Here were plans for a new building. He made a good impression on Juan by asking tough questions about the electrical requirements. For obvious reasons they didn't want to bring in an electrical contractor. Paul had a good grasp of electrical problems and also impressed Juan by answering Abbah's questions.

They decided that it would be better to dry the cocaine base in the sun; heating lamps would consume a lot of power and were only going to be used as backup. They were going to install a gasoline-driven generator. The gasoline would arrive in drums by boat and hoisted up the cliff by the helicopter on pallets. Paul was already bringing in gasoline in drums by helicopter for the house generator.

The cocaine base is then refined into cocaine hydrochloride (HCI) by dissolving it in acetone, and the solution is again filtered to remove undesired material. Hydrochloric acid diluted in acetone is added to the cocaine solution. The addition of the hydrochloric acid causes the cocaine to crystallize out of the solution as cocaine hydrochloride. The crystals are then dried in the sun or with heat lamps and fans. The remaining acetone can be recycled. Aleysha was adamant that there should be little chemical waste; recycling it added to the cost, but the profits would be so enormous that Juan did not object.

Aleysha thought that with the experience they had obtained building the house the Abu people could build the factory and warehouse with Abbah, Paul, and herself supervising. She wanted the two men to give their opinion. After studying and discussing the plans for about an hour, they were both fairly confident they could do it. Aleysha hoped to have her father on the island for the last stages of setting up the plant. She told them she was bringing someone in that could be trusted, but she didn't say who it would be.

Aleysha then explained the coast guard credentials to Juan. Up to this point she had told him that she would supply the boat, but had not told him that it would be flying the flag of the St. Anthony Coast Guard. The cutter was to drop off the cocaine at pre-appointed times at two separate satellite co-ordinates inside American waters during periods of relatively calm water. These would change with every shipment. The cocaine was to be wrapped in plastic bundles and placed in submerged containers kept afloat by a small visible buoy. In an emergency, the buoy could be cut and the container would sink.

Juan had his own contacts in the US. Half the cocaine was to be his for supplying the paste; he had Cuban American partners who would market it. Aleysha's territory included Canada and the American south extending to California. Neither he nor Aleysha cared to know the details of the other's arrangements within their zones. Aleysha was confident that her father, despite working under a new name and identity, could sell her share through motorcycle gangs. She didn't mention this at the meeting. The money laundering she would organize herself.

Paul and Abbah were asked to leave while Aleysha and Juan ironed out a few financial details. This done, she rang a little silver bell and the maids brought in champagne. Aleysha and Juan became quite merry. Aleysha showed him around the downstairs rooms – none of which, aside from the room they had been sitting in, were yet finished – and explained her plans. The dining room was to be furnished with eighteenth-century English furniture, with animal studies by Albrecht Durer hanging on the walls. The paintings were already there, on the floor leaning against the wall.

They ate at the long refectory table in the kitchen. The two maids and Oku sat at one end and Paul and Abbah joined Aleysha and Juan at the other. The maids got up from time to time to serve them. The champagne continued to flow but stayed down at their end. Aleysha did not want her people to become interested in alcohol. She knew that they grew marijuana and she was going to encourage them to chew coca leaves when the plants were bigger. She figured this would allow them to work harder. Aleysah didn't drink as a rule and it seemed to Paul that the alcohol was going to her head. Paul observed that Abbah was quiet and rather unhappy, and he supposed that the lad was jealous of Juan.

After lunch Aleysha took Juan out to show him the progress that was being made on the garden. Paul stayed in the kitchen showing Oku how to make coffee using a filter. Suddenly Abbah ran in, grabbed a large knife, and ran out again. There was an outburst of savage barking from outside. Paul ran quickly after Abbah and disarmed him as they came across an awkward scene. The two schnauzers were snarling and glaring at Juan, and were barely under Aleysha's control. It appeared that Juan had tried to embrace her. Now he looked terrified. Aleysha laughed at the sight of Abbah appearing with the knife and at his quick disarmament by Paul. Juan started to apologize, mumbled something about the bathroom, and went into the house through the kitchen door. Aleysha calmed the dogs, gave Abbah a kiss, thanked him for his efforts, and sent him back to the kitchen with the knife.

"My fault, I suppose," she said to Paul. "I didn't mean to encourage him, but these Latins..." She laughed. "Please take him back right away. Tell him I forgive him and to phone me tomorrow before he leaves. I'll have to stay here to hold the dogs."

"What's going on with Abbah?" asked Paul. "He's jealous and upset."

"Oh, I know he's upset," she said. "I have sent him back to live in the village. He and I, well, it was a – "she paused, looking for a word.

"Mistake."

"Yes, and it was an accident, the way it started." She smiled at Paul who was looking at her oddly, wondering how an adult woman could accidentally start an affair with a nineteen year-old boy. But she misunderstood his look. "Now, don't *you* get any ideas."

"Don't worry," said Paul. "I would as soon sleep with the cobra in your dining room."

"That's not a cobra! The one in the dining room?"

"You sure?" Paul was laughing at her.

Aleysha was miffed. "Well, maybe one day you'll find it in your bed."

Clearing the ground for the refinery began the next day.

12

Forty acres of the plateau had now been cleared and planted with coca and coffee trees, and more acreage was added every month. The Abu had learned to use the tools their queen had brought to them and they worked peacefully if not very hard. The more industrious ones had been conscripted to work on the refinery. Ayesha had rather lost interest in the plantation; her own crop of coca was now looking very small compared to the coca they were to be bringing in from Peru. She was more interested in the formal garden that was being created in front of the house. The gardeners were all women.

If the Abu had a complaint, it was that Aleysha did not use her powers as a sorceress more often to bring them the human meat that they liked in their stews. Wild pigs had been brought in and released in the jungle. The Abu were supposed to hunt them with bows and arrows but this was not working out. They were afraid of the pigs and had not mastered the use of the expensive bows she had brought them.

They started hinting about wanting Aleysha to bring them more human flesh to Abbah. He told them to be patient: Aleysha would reward them in due course. When he mentioned this to her, she was at a bit of a loss. She only killed her enemies and those who were in her way; she was not going to cold-bloodedly kill to feed her people. She told him to organize archery contests. Winners would be awarded silver cups.

The Abu had been making primitive pottery from a clay deposit that Dusseault had found on the plateau years before. Aleysha had a pottery wheel brought from Barbados, and the Barbadian woman who came with the wheel stayed a few weeks to teach the Abu how to use it. Her husband knew cabinet making and he taught this craft to certain of the Abu who had shown skill with carpentry tools in constructing the house.

She brought in the tropical birds she had promised from Tobago. There were no cats on Haut-Clair. The only pets the Abu had were monkeys; they would catch baby monkeys in nets and bring them up. The Abus revered the monkeys and would not eat them, although they were often a nuisance, disturbing and robbing the gardens. Given their taste for human flesh, Aleysha found this odd, but it pleased her.

She was lonely at times. When thoughts of Theodore entered her mind, she tried to dismiss them along with other troublesome nostalgic memories of snow, of pine, birch, and maple trees, and of northern birds. She was comforted by her dogs and absorbed herself in work. She was trying to make contact with her father. If she was going to refine cocaine for the North American market, she also wanted to manage its distribution. She needed a tough, clever, experienced partner whom she could trust, but there was a good chance her father was angry with her.

She regularly checked the Bandits website, which she herself had originally set up. He had received a relatively light sentence. His lawyer had argued that although he was a member of the Bandits, he was not involved in any criminal activities. There was no proof that he was. He had attended the meeting at the underground facility near Alexandria by special invitation because one of the items on the agenda concerned his daughter. The site was owned by a series of numbered companies whose trail disappeared offshore. He swore that he had never been there before and none of the Bandits dared contradict him. The two junior members who had undertaken to take the rap if the lab was ever discovered had done so. There was a good chance that he would be out after a year and a year was almost up.

One day in late May she found the following item on the website: "The Bear, currently a guest of Her Majesty's government, amuses himself learning computers and playing chess on the Internet". There was an email address for him at the Kingston penitentiary. She suspected that any messages that she might send him would be monitored by the police or the prison authorities. Her father's positive identification of the decapitated woman's body as Hattie's, as reported in the Montreal papers last fall, indicated to her that he knew she was still alive.

Using a brand-new Hotmail address with a false name and address, she sent Bear the following message : <Qg3>. It was the final move in a famous chess game that he had taught her as a child: Lewinsky versus Marshall. Black on his 23rd move, Qg3, sacrificed the Queen in checkmating Lewinsky's king. The answer came back almost immediately: <?>. She replied with the opening move: <d4e6>. An hour later he came back with the next move. They played the game out. Contact had been made. Henry had several chess games going over the Internet. If his emails from prison were indeed monitored, this chess game would have no more significance to anyone spying on his correspondence than any other. When he got out he would know where – in cyberspace anyway – she could be found.

One day in June two weeks before he was due to be released, Henry "The Bear" Brading had an unexpected visitor – none other than Deacon Kane of the Hells Angels Motorcycle Club, Quebec Chapter.

Their conversation took place in a long narrow room. A counter with a divider ran down the middle. Prisoners sat on one side, their visitors on the other and they spoke into microphones and wore head-sets. Four prison guards were assigned to the room, and they paced up and down. Today, because of the Deacon, there were two extra guards.

"You're not doing me any favor by coming here," said Henry. "A visit from you is not good for my reputation. But I did not want to offend by refusing to see you. Why did you come?"

"Thought that you might like to have a ride back to Ottawa when you get out. With your daughter not around to provide one."

"I have friends, thank you, Deacon."

Pause, two or three beats. "I'm your friend, Henry, you know that. I'm the guy who fixed Hattie up with Angel Eyes, remember. So where is she?"

"Where is who?"

"Your daughter, Henry."

"My daughter's dead. You know that. For a club executive you ask dumb questions. I don't appreciate your humor, Deacon. I don't see why you're being inquisitive about her afterlife. How the hell would I know where she ended up? She was a good girl so I suppose she's upstairs." He pointed towards the ceiling.

Deacon snorted. "She was not a good girl, Henry. You know that. But I think the Hells Angels chapter downstairs has not yet set eyes on her."

Henry said nothing.

"So where is she?"

"I think you better be leaving, Deacon."

"Okay, just so you know that when you get out of here, we're going to be staying in touch."

"Yeah? Well, thanks." Neither man wanted to risk offending the other by getting up first. Finally they got up together.

"Maybe, Henry, after you get home, you can come down to Montreal, have a few Heineken with me."

"I'll think about it. See yuh, Deacon."

"*A bientôt*, eh, Henry?" They nodded curtly and the Deacon turned away. Henry walked heavily as he was escorted back to his cell; the Deacon, who was also escorted, with almost equal weight walked back to his cut-down Harley in the parking lot. Each of them pondered the meaning of this less than nourishing conversation.

Henry was aware that there were a number of people who might suspect that Hattie was still alive somewhere in the world, and that her father probably knew where. This suspicion was going to make his life difficult after he got out and was one more reason to be annoyed with her.

When he was out on bail he had established that she had taken almost half of his assets. But then she had sent the $125,000 for the lawyer and the guys who were taking the rap. She had betrayed him and the Bandits to the police, but in trouble herself, perhaps more serious than he knew, she could be excused for striking some kind of deal. Where was the Korean? She may have killed Song or they might have robbed the Angels together. The Angels' extreme anger before her body was discovered – which had cost the lives of several of his friends – indicated that a lot of money was missing. The Deacon appeared to be offering him some kind of deal if he turned her in, and if he didn't cooperate, kidnapping and torture were the probable alternatives.

Charley was a pretty regular visitor while he was in prison. He was living in Henry's house and taking care of things. He hadn't been at the meeting where they all got busted. He told Henry that he'd seen her, or someone who looked just like her, at a hockey game in Tampa that winter.

"You know, Henry, it looked just like her except for the red hair. I wasn't sure it was her. This dame was well dressed and classy – Hattie, you know, never cared about clothes. But when I got close to her, I saw she had blue eyes, and she looked right through me. And she had a southern accent. So I turned away. But when she first saw me, she did a double take, you know. And then the chick I was with, Sally, she tells me that chicks can change the color of their eyes with colored contact lenses. Did you know that?"

"Everybody knows that, Charley. Except you, I guess."

"Well, I know now. I didn't tell no one except you, and Sally forgot about it. Sally didn't know her anyway. But you know what? I think it was her. In Tampa. What would she be doing there? Well, I can see her going to a Sens game, in fact that's a clue that it was her, isn't it? But in Tampa?"

"Good that you didn't tell anyone. Don't tell no one. She's dead, Charley, remember that. Even if she isn't."

"Sure, even if she isn't, she is, as far as I'm concerned, and if she isn't, which she is, of course, Henry, I'm glad because I was always fond of her, you know, what a dream she was in goal, but I'll shut up about it, as I have. Just thought I would tell her dad, that's all." Charley would keep his mouth shut. Henry knew that.

Lonely and depressed in prison, he had realized that he loved his daughter. She alone carried his genes, the last of the Bradings. He had no other children. He had never really thought about her much at first, other than recognizing that she did a good job taking care of the house. He had taken her in because it looked good on his record to be a single parent. But he had seen right away that she was both cunning and ruthless, qualities that he admired, and she had been a huge help to him in business. Thing about family, you can trust family, he had always thought, but now he had his doubts.

The work that she had done for him after she had grown up was nothing less than brilliant. They had always been allies, partners. It had never occurred to him that she had her own ambitions regarding serious money. Whenever she needed money, he let her take it; she had only taken what she needed, she had never been greedy. So it was a shock to him when she took half of everything liquid, on top of liquidating a few properties first. But perhaps she considered half of everything to be rightfully hers, in which case, she was not really stealing it.

He had a feeling that he was going to hear from her before he got out. After all, he had positively identified the decapitated woman, whom she had no doubt murdered, as Hattie. He had pointed to a birthmark on the corpse and told the police that it was the body of his daughter. She would know, wherever she was, that he had done that, not just for her, but for them.

So he waited. He knew she couldn't write to him or phone him. He spent his time in prison learning to use a laptop computer that he had got Charley to bring him and playing chess. He had posted on the club Internet site that he had an email address. She would look there if she wanted to get in touch. His mail was no doubt read. She would figure that out and use some kind of code. If it were to happen, it should happen shortly before he was to be released.

A few days after his visit from the Deacon, there it was in his email. A stranger with a Hotmail address wanted to play chess with him. Opening move: <Qg3>. That is not an opening move. He knew right away it was Hattie. He queried it and she came back with the opening move of the Lewinsky/Marshall game.

Two weeks later he was out and back in his house in Ottawa. Charley had got in a few cases of beer. A few friends came by, including an old girl friend. Henry had a good time his first night home.

The next afternoon he went to the Vanier library, got on a public computer, obtained a new Hotmail address under a false name and postal address, and wrote an email to his daughter as follows:

<Am in Ottawa. Where are you? Heard you were in Tampa. Bear>

He did not expect an immediate reply. He had a lot of things to sort out. His complex business affairs had suffered not just from his own absence, but also from Hattie's. The big computer in his basement had been destroyed by a virus. But there were printouts. He got in touch with a computer guy who was also a bookkeeper, whom he had known for years and who owed him a favor; they were able to sort out what was left his assets.

They also found quite a lot of laundered money that belonged to other Bandits. As the Bandits all thought that Angel Eyes had murdered Hattie and stolen their money, they decided to split it rather than return it. He began selling his real estate, his cars, bikes, the computer – everything owned – he planned to move to Florida where he had connections. He was going to need a new identity, maybe several, and he knew people in Florida who could get them for him. He wasn't going to build his life around his daughter.

He knew he was being watched and followed. He and Charley both took to carrying guns and Charley watched his back. Charley had noticed the tail and offered to do something about it, but Henry said no, they'll just send someone else. He was sure it was the Angels.

One morning, a few days later, he went into a public computer coffee shop in Ottawa to see if there was a reply. There was:

<So Charley did make me. Give him my love. Got to see you face to face. Big things brewing. Big money. Need you. H>

He replied: <What makes you think I'm not totally pissed off? Where and when?>

He waited a few minutes in case she was online and then went about his business. That afternoon he checked for messages at the library.

<Go to the west coast of Florida. When you have a new ID and a cell phone and a new email address, email me. I'll call you>

He got one more message giving a new email address and that was the end of the correspondence for a while.

Sally, the girl who had gone to Florida with Charley, hung out at a biker's bar in Ottawa. Charley had dropped her not long after their return and she didn't like being dropped; she much preferred being the one doing the dropping. But it had not been a big thing with Charley and she was not broken up over it. That summer she took up with another member of the Bandits, one Tony Battaglia. Tony's brother, Leonardo, was the one who had called the big meeting about Hattie Brading that had resulted in the bust. Leonardo had not got off as lightly as Henry and was still in prison.

When Henry got out in late June, ten months after the big bust, she heard Tony talking about it to some of his friends. Poor guy, they were saying, probably lost everything with the Angels' big computer scam.

"He's okay," said Tony. "He's got real estate. He's no friend of mine, anyway. Leonardo thinks he killed our cousin, he and his daughter, Hattie. Well, she got hers. The Angels cut her head off with an axe."

"Who got her head cut off?" asked Sally.

"Hattie Brading, Henry's daughter."

"She's still got her head," said Sally.

"Whatta ya mean, she's got her head?"

"I saw her in Tampa. Last winter. Charley and I went to see the Sens play the Lightning. She was at the game. Charley recognized her, she had her hair dyed red. And she got blue eyes. Stupid Charley, he said, can't be her, he said, she has blue eyes. Hadn't heard of colored contacts."

"You sure?"

"Hey, is it a big deal? I dunno, maybe it wasn't her. But it was funny because Charley knew her since she was a kid. He knew her real well. And he thought it was her. Except for the eyes. And the hair. Ask him."

"If she's alive and living in Tampa, I can think of a few people that would like to know that."

Tony Battaglia didn't ask Charley. As it happened he was thinking of leaving the Bandits. He wanted to move to Montreal and was looking for an in with the Angels. And so it happened that the Tampa chapter of the Hells Angels got a photograph of Hattie Brading; they were asked to circulate copies of it and to look out for her. Several tall redhead lookalikes in the Tampa Bay area had unpleasant experiences with the Hells Angels as a consequence, but none of them of course was Hattie.

13

Progress was being made at Haut-Clair. The renovations of the house were to be completed by September, a year after Aleysha's departure from Canada. The cocaine refinery building, situated on the cliff above the inlet, was nearing completion. The construction foremen from Barbados, flown in daily to supervise and train the Abu workers, had gone home long ago; the Abu were now working directly under the supervision of their queen. Gravity-fed fresh water from a mountain spring fed to a modern plumbing system that included a septic tank. This water was now being piped to the refinery.

Reproductions of late eighteenth-century and Empire-style furniture, and some genuine pieces, had arrived from Paris. Gilt-framed mirrors, marble-topped tables, armchairs, sofas, gold and marble clocks, and Aubusson carpets, distributed sparsely and elegantly in the halls of Haut-Clair, brought the house to life. Aleysha had indulged in period tapestries from Arles and Bruges. The kid from Vanier had good taste.

Paul had convinced Aleysha that his US navy experience qualified him to advise her on the purchase of a cutter. Aleysha had appointed herself commodore of the Guinea Command of the St. Anthony Coast Guard.

It was the opinion of the government of St. Anthony that Aleysha was buying the boat mostly for her own pleasure. In official circles she was considered a spoiled rich woman. But she had volunteered it for rescue operations for free, supplementing the aging St. Anthony coast guard vessel. Local fishing boats got into trouble occasionally, and tourist craft more and more frequently. It was an offer they couldn't turn down, and they accepted that her generosity was motivated by a desire to compensate the island for the fact that neither she nor the coffee plantation were required to pay taxes. And any boats brought in by salvage operations were to be the property of the government. By offering to assist the DEA in looking for drug smugglers, St. Anthony earned some goodwill with the United States. Objections to DEA vessels stopping boats in St. Anthony's territorial waters had irritated the American authorities. Now this practice would, if not cease altogether, certainly be curtailed.

The Leopards objected whenever the old St. Anthony coast guard vessel operated off the coast of Guinea without permission, but the time spent obtaining permission hampered rescue operations. This vexing problem now appeared to be solved because the new boat was officially a Guinea boat, the objections of the new queen, Zena, notwithstanding. The government of St. Anthony had agreed that the boat would fly the flag of the St. Anthony Coast Guard, and to carry its papers. Its status was the same as that of the helicopter. Zena, who had never liked Philippe, even as a child, was to prove less docile than her mother. But in the case of the coast guard it was too late. The boat was to be under Aleysha's command as was the helicopter; Zena, the queen of Guinea, had no control over either. Saba had signed the treaty.

Using the Internet, Aleysha had located an old 95-foot Canadian Coast Guard cutter, the M.V. *Bamfield,* which had seen service in the stormy waters off the west coast of Vancouver Island. It had been decommissioned, sold at an auction, found its way somehow to the southeast coast of Florida, and was now for sale. Paul had taken a flight over to Florida to a marina on the Indian River Inlet to have a look at it.

"It's seaworthy, Aleysha," Paul said to her one June morning on his return. "It's not fast, but can do 20 knots. Has a range of 1,500 miles cruising at 12 knots. She could weather a hurricane, that one. She was built for bad weather. It's been for sale for a while and it's a bargain. It takes a crew of six, an engineer, a cook, first mate, and the captain. Ten. But that was for rescue operations. It could be sailed by a skeleton crew of three. For a long voyage you'd need more for shifts. It was designed in the States and is known as a Cape Class cutter. The *Bamfield* was built in Canada and has relatively new twin Deutz diesels, not the originals."

"I want to see it," said Aleysha. She had taken to arraying herself regally every day, even when she was supervising the construction crew, the plantation workers, or the gardeners. This morning she sat on a cushioned gilded-iron armchair of throne-like proportions on the terrace in front of Haut-Clair. An awning protected her from the sun. The schnauzers sat at her feet. Today she was wearing white denims and a scarlet silk top and like Theodore in his undercover days, was dripping with gold. She wore gold bracelets, a gold necklace, and was seldom seen now without the gold coronet on her head. The effect was stunning, but Paul couldn't help wondering if she was not a bit mad. He never commented on her appearance. It was just before lunch and they were sipping mint juleps that Paul had made.

"Are we going to re-christen her?"

"Re-christen her? Come, my Paul, we are Zarathustrians here – or sort of. I have modified the religion a bit because I am the goddess around here. I suppose I have not explained it all to you. Let's see where should I start? The elements, Earth, Fire, and Water are sacred. They must not be contaminated with a dead body, for example. Bodies can't be buried or cremated or committed to the sea. The Abu don't eat their own as you know so we are going to dispose of the dead in a new way: Vultures! I am getting a nesting pair from the Parsees in India – they are Zarathustrians. The dead there are carried to a special place and left out naked for vultures to eat. Clean and neat, eh, from an environmental point of view? Which is my point of view, always, the point of view of Gaia. The bones are then tossed somewhere, I am not sure about that part. But we do have a cave available.

"Look up there". She stood up and pointed. "See, there is a shelf and beyond it a cave. I have been there, I climbed up."

"But it's sheer cliff!"

"I'm a good climber. There will be a problem with the bodies. That's where you and your whirleybird come in. Dear Paul, I would be lost without you."

"And what do the Abu think of this idea?"

She frowned. "I have convinced Abbah but I am afraid the old priestess baulked. Rather put her foot down, actually. She has been good about so many things that I am letting her have her way for now. She is very old – she has not long to go, and when she does, why, she'll be the first, thus sanctioning the process."

"I see," said Paul doubtfully. "To get back to the boat, how about we call her the Aleysha?"

She nodded agreement. "Excellent choice."

Paul was still looking puzzled. "But I am still not clear on the religious bit. Who is Ayesha? I was talking to Abbah about it. He showed me a picture in a book and let me look through it. It was very old, he got it from his father. It was the book my grandmother told me about. Remember, I mentioned it to you when we went to the museum?"

Aleysha nodded and Paul continued. "He treated it like it was a Bible or something. *She* by an Englishman named H. Rider Haggard. There were pictures of her, portraits by a Victorian artist, Maurice Greiffenhagen. Now he could never have laid eyes on Aloyshovna Dusseault. Yet the portraits could be of her and you're a dead ringer for both. You know this book?"

Aleysha smiled at him. "I know it well."

"All about an immortal white goddess in Africa named Ayesha. It's just a novel, a story made up by some Victorian Englishman."

"It is not just a novel, my Paul, it's an epiphany." She gave him a long look. "You may know her as Gaia"

"Gaia is a theory," exclaimed Paul dismissively. "So what's with Ayesha, Aloyshovna, and Aleysha? And who the hell is Alice anyway, really? Who is she really?"

"Were you brought up a Roman Catholic, Paul?"

"Sort of."

"Remember the Trinity?"

"Yeah, but I never understood it."

"You don't have to understand religion, my Paul, for it to ease the burden of life. Their religion means a lot to the Abu."

"And that's what you are? Their religion? Still, I don't get it. What's with the Trinity?"

"Ayesha is the Mother, I am the Daughter, and Aloyshovna is the Holy Ghost."

"Father, Son, and Holy Ghost. Aren't we getting a little close to blasphemy here?"

"All religions are blasphemy, my Paul, to other religions. The trinity is older than Christianity. In the teachings of Zarathrustra, which the Abu and I follow as well as we can, when the Lord

Varuna was seen as the one true God, named Ashura Mazda - see Zarathrustra invented monotheism, which the Abu are learning to practice, it's good for them - Mithra, his twin brother became the Holy Spirit, and, later, in another aspect, the son of Ahura Mazda, the Son of God."

"I see. It's good for the Abu that they become monotheists. The Lady my Goddess is a jealous goddess." Paul managed to get just the right level of sarcasm in his voice, or so he thought. He was good with her and knew it, he knew that he amused her and could get away with a lot of stuff if he kept it light. But this time he had gone too far.

"Of course." She was suddenly angry. "Don't worry about it, okay? Fly your whirlybird, help with the boat, make a ton of money, and amuse me, okay? Don't worry about it. Listen, it's fun being a queen and a goddess. If you were a girl you would understand. Okay?"

"Okay. Thanks for explaining the theology to me. One more thing, according to the book, Ayesha was immortal, are you expecting – "

Aleysha relaxed as suddenly as she had become angry. She was thoughtful for a while, and then said, "I always pitied her for that. Death is a friend, everybody's best friend in the end." She laughed. "And I from time to time make the introductions. We are killer apes, Paul, the chimpanzees do it, maybe once in a while, but as for us, the homo sapiens, the wise apes, it is what we do best, to not recognize that is to deceive ourselves. Now if there is nothing left in that cocktail shaker, please make some more." She looked at him and smiled.

Paul stared at her for a long moment, wondering if she was mad, thinking of his cousin Narcisse, and then of his uncle Henri. He pushed these thoughts out of his mind and changed the subject. "To get back to the boat: who's going to be the skipper?"

"Me. Who did you think?" asked Aleysha rhetorically and yawned. *"L'état c'est moi, le dieu c'est moi, le diable c'est moi, la maison c'est moi, le terrain c'est moi, les Abu c'est moi, et le bâteau c'est moi."*

She is crazy, thought Paul. "And for crew, me and Abbah?"

"We will have to train a couple of the Abu as sailors. Abbah will have to stay here to run the place while we are at sea. Juan may want someone to come along, I don't know yet."

Henry Brading disappeared suddenly and completely. The Deacon was pissed off. He gave hell to those who had been keeping his house under surveillance but there was little he could do. The Tampa tip had come to nothing.

Going to see Henry in prison had been a mistake. He had hoped that he could do some kind of deal with him, make it clear to him that he would be rewarded if he co-operated and that he faced torture and death if he didn't. But all the visit had accomplished was that Henry had been warned. The Bandit leader had taken a powder, as The Deacon's father used to say. And Henry was the only lead to Hattie that he had.

There was no trace whatsoever of the Korean, Song "Angel Eyes" Hang-sen. Every chapter of the club worldwide was on the lookout for him, as were the police. The Deacon was almost alone in suspecting that he was dead, that Hattie had killed him and taken the money.

"You know who you might go and see," said a friend of his one day with whom he was commiserating, "René Lachapelle. He went there, didn't he? To the cottage where she was killed. Or according to you, he was killed."

"He's disappeared. Someone was after him; faked his suicide in the Bahamas or someplace. So I heard but maybe he did commit suicide. You know cops, suicide is common. I talked to him last fall. He was the one who put it in my head that Henry maybe was lying, that the body in the lake was not his daughter's."

This conversation got him thinking about René Lachapelle and he went to see René's widow. But she had nothing useful to tell him. He had left her, she said, and she was relieved; she had begun to hate him. He had taken early retirement, and gone to live with his girlfriend, Monique at her kennels near Lachute. When the Deacon roared up to the kennel on his Harley, causing an echoing roar of loud barking, he was told that Monique had sold out after René's death. No one knew where she had gone, not even her lawyer. So that was a dead end.

The Deacon went to Ottawa to have another talk with Colin, the Angel who had been surveying Henry. Charley O'Donnell, who was Henry's best friend, was living in Henry's house, he was told. Henry had made over the house to him. Charley might know something. Colin, wanted to get back in the Deacon's favor and offered to find out what Charley knew and the Deacon decided to help him.

Henry hadn't actually told Charley anything except that that he was leaving. Best for your own sake, you don't know my new name, nor where I'm going, he told Charley. But Charley was curious and looked in Henry's bag that night while the Bear was asleep. Maybe he would turn up and surprise him one day. He looked at his airline tickets, and wrote down his new name and the Miami address on the Florida driver's license.

The way Charley died was not pretty, and he had the added anguish of knowing that he had betrayed his best friend.

For the early morning flight to Miami, Aleysha cut her hair short, donned a red wig, and put the blue contacts back in. She wore white ducks, a blue and white horizontally striped top, and put on a French sailor's beret, complete with red pompom. This outfit she gaily wore on the plane. She looked pretty good and Paul could not suppress the dangerous thought that sleeping with a cobra that looked like that might have its compensations. They didn't sit together; Aleysha flew first class.

They were planning to complete the purchase of the cutter and bring it from Indian River Inlet, a hundred and fifty miles north of Miami, to St. Anthony, a distance of well over a thousand nautical miles. They were to pick up a third crew member, Aleysha told Paul, but she didn't tell him who it was.

Aleysha rented a car at the airport. "You drive. You've been there before," she said. "I'll sit in front with you, that is, if you don't mind sitting beside someone who makes a cobra look like a fairy princess." Good Lord, thought Paul, I believe I got to her.

It was a lovely day and they enjoyed the drive up the coast. Arriving at the marina, they went to the office and met Ralph, the white-haired old gentleman who owned it and the *Bamfield*. They walked down the quay and Aleysha ran ahead in her eagerness to look at the cutter, which they could see moored at the end. Paul stayed behind and walked with the old man.

"You two together?" he asked, frowning at Paul.

"Oh no," he laughed, realizing that the old man thought that they were a couple and didn't like to see a white girl with a black boy. "I work for her."

"You were with the navy, as I recall."

"Yes, sir."

"What's she going to do with it?"

"She's buying it for the St. Anthony Coast Guard," Paul replied.

Aleysha was admiring the *Bamfield* from the quay. Ralph went on board. Paul stood with her for a minute. "I like her lines," she said.

"Why not? It's Canadian. By the way, people don't consider boats female any more" said Paul.

"Listen, will you can that Canadian bullshit. I don't find it funny. And this boat is female."

They went on board and Paul went down to the engine room. On his last visit, he had borrowed the manual and made a photocopy. Since then he had been studying it. Ralph called down the stairs: "We'll start her up and take her for a spin."

Paul stayed in the engine room for ten minutes and then joined the others on the bridge. "Runs like a clock," he said.

"I bought her on spec," said Ralph, "because she was in such beautiful shape and it was a bargain. Couple of Canadians brought her down here, got in some kind of financial trouble, and had to sell her. She's a bit of a tub. Not built for speed. But she'll do twenty knots."

They left the inlet and went out to the open sea, Aleysha intensely watching Ralph at the wheel as he opened up the throttle. "So she's going back to coast guard duty?" he asked.

Aleysha nodded. "May I take the wheel?" They cruised down the coast for about fifteen minutes with Aleysha at the wheel. She did a few manoeuvres with both men watching.

"She likes you, she answers to you well. She's your boat," said Ralph, smiling at Aleysha, who looked every inch a French sailor with her white ducks, striped shirt, and beret.

"And I like her," said Aleysha and turned the boat around to go back. As they went through the gap to Indian River, Aleysha surrendered the bridge to Ralph and studiously watched him land the boat. Paul threw the lines to a couple of men waiting on the dock. She asked Ralph a few questions about landing a boat this size. Then they walked up to the office. Paul stayed outside as she negotiated.

They then proceeded in two cars to a lawyer's office. Aleysha took her laptop. Paul waited in a coffee shop downstairs. "Everything's done," she said as she joined him. "She's mine. The lawyer let me use his phone line to pick up my email and something's come up. We're going to have to go to Key West right away. We'll take the cutter. Ralph's agreed to come with us. He knows an anchorage, I don't want to tie up at a marina. He has a brother there he likes to visit. I'd like more time with him on the boat anyway."

They went back to Ralph's marina. Paul took the rental to the nearest local agent and returned in a taxi. It was about four in the afternoon when they left. Cruising at fifteen knots they would get in around four in the morning. Paul went to one of the two aft cabins around eleven, leaving Ralph and Ayesha on the bridge. There was one longitudinal bunk and two transverse bunks against the aft bulkhead. Paul took the single bunk.

In the middle of the night he woke up suddenly, not sure where he was. It was pitch black. Then he remembered and at the same time became aware that there was someone in the room.

It was Aleysha. "We're anchored off the harbor at Key West Bight," she said. "I rowed Ralph in to shore. Before that we filled up. The fuel tanks are full."

She turned on a reading light above the lower transverse bunk. Paul watched her undress. With one hand on the upper bunk, she took off her bra and kicked off her knickers. Naked and looking at Paul, she put the beret with the red pompom back on her head.

"What do you think, Paul? How do I look? You ever fancy sailors? You were in the navy, weren't you, big boy?"

He was lying on his back, his head turned towards her. She came over to his bunk and went down on her knees, looking first at his eyes and then at a small tent that had been erected in the center of his blanket. She reached under the sheet, grasped the pole that held the tent up, and then released it.

"Not bad," she said and brushed her breasts over his face. Then still on her knees, her head held high, she put her right hand behind his head and drew it towards her. Paul did with his tongue what he was expected to do. After about a minute, she tore off the covers and mounted him. Her lovemaking was violent, ferocious. He came; he was quite sure she had not, and she quickly got off him and went to the head to shower. In the shower she masturbated and thought of Theodore. She called his name out aloud as she came. Paul heard the name and never forgot it. Gift of God.

When she came back, she said, "That will never happen again. I didn't come. At least not with you. That cobra remark got to me. I just wanted you to know that I can have you anytime I want. In future I'm sleeping in the skipper's cabin." She yawned and got into the lower bunk opposite, turned off the light, and within minutes was fast asleep. Paul, on the other hand, could not get back to sleep.

14

Paul was woken by the sound of Aleysha's cell phone ringing. "Hello," she said and listened briefly. "Okay. You're sure they don't know you're on to them. We'll trap them."

There was another pause while she listened. "I'm on a boat anchored offshore outside the harbour of Key West Bight. I just bought it. We want them to follow you. But we don't want them to be able to identify our boat in case they've got friends. I've got a plan. Call me back this afternoon around five and I'll give you the exact place where I'll pick you up. We don't want to waste time looking for each other. Don't try to shake them" Pause. "There's two of us and with you, that's three. You'll bring handguns – got silencers? A Kalashnikov? Okay but we can't let them see it." Pause. "It's in your suitcase. Good. Mind, we we're not going to shoot them. But it's a good idea to let Deacon see it. He might rush a handgun. We won't have to use them either, I hope. I want those fuckers alive, but yeah, we'd better have them." Pause. "Okay." She sat up and holding the phone in her left hand, covered herself with the sheet. "What you'll do is take a taxi to Key West Bight, the harbor there. Call me on the cell phone from the shore." Pause. "Yeah. Bring all your stuff – we'll be going to sea." Pause. "An island in the Caribbean, you'll see. Hey, Bear, I'm going to make it up to you big time."

She glanced at Paul, pulled at the sheet, and listened. "Look for a Zodiac, a rubber boat with an outboard engine, one of those rigid-hull inflatables, we'll have MOBY DICK painted on the side – that's not a hundred per cent about the name – I'll let you know when you call me back at five – and I'll be driving, wearing a French sailor hat with a red pompom. The Deacon will notice me for sure."

She covered the phone and said to Paul, "Look the other way."

Then back to the phone. "Unh-huh. Exactly. But we won't kill them. I'll drug them. I'll explain when I see you. It'll be good to have you on board, Bear, if you'll forgive the pun. And you'll forgive me everything else when I tell you what I'm up to. How the hell did they find you? What? Charley's dead? Back home in Ottawa? But you never told Charley?" She hung up."To Paul: "Good, you're facing the wall. I'm getting dressed."

Paul was thinking, okay, I met Alice and she was one tough chick, then I met Aleysha and she is unbelievable, but this one, this Ottawa girl, she's something else. He heard her getting dressed and then heard something he thought that he would never hear: Aleysha burst into tears. He turned around. She was dressed in the same clothes, the white ducks and the horizontally blue-and-white-striped top, sitting on the bed. The beret with the red pompom covered her face.

"The fuckers, they killed Charley," she sobbed. "They tortured him and then they killed him. The fuckers, the bastards, *calice, tabernac, maudits têtes de marde*. Killing's too good for them, they're not going to die easy."

Her sorrow turned to rage and then she was quiet. Paul sat up, swung his long legs on to the floor, but he covered himself with the sheet. "That's the third member of our crew, the man you just spoke to?" he asked gently.

'My father."

"And who was Charley?"

"My father's best friend. And mine."

"And these guys? Who are they?"

"Hells Angels. From Montreal. You were right, Paul. I'm Canadian."

"And they're after your dad?"

"They're after me."

"Okay, I don't want to know any more, but I'm with you, come Hells Angels or high water." He looked into her sea-green eyes. She has me in thrall, he thought. I know she's evil, that she's one bad girl, but I would do anything for her, I can't help myself. Besides, I mustn't forget, she's going to make me rich. "I just want you to know that no matter if you think I'm a lousy lay, you can count on me. 'Live pure, speak true, right wrong, follow the queen – else, wherefore born?'" He paused. "Alfred Tennyson."

They both laughed. "You've got the right stuff, Paul. And you're not a lousy lay – I just didn't want you to have the satisfaction of knowing you had given me an orgasm. I'd rather sleep with a cobra." She laughed. All was forgiven. "About these guys, we think there's only two of them, but we're not sure. Bear, that's my father, hasn't let on that he's seen them. I was meeting my father. He's coming to Haut-Clair. He is going to be – uh – head of marketing for the organization. We settled on Key West to rendezvous but he was followed. We figure that if he comes aboard, they'll follow. We're setting a trap. I'm bait. They want to grab me and torture me and rape me, or whatever, until they get their money back. At this point they can't be sure that I'm alive.

"But I'm going to show myself. I've met this guy, the Deacon. He started this – he set his man to spy on me – on Bear's gang, the Ottawa Bandits. It's a long story. But he has a temper and if he gets a look at me, he'll go apeshit. I don't think he'll think about a trap. They'll figure that we'll leave in the morning. And if we get away, they'll never find us. Just west of here it's open sea – the Gulf of Mexico. We could be going anywhere. They'll watch to see if we keep a lookout. In the middle of the night, they'll sneak aboard. But I don't think we'll use our own boat. Tell me, Paul, is there anything wrong with my thinking?"

Paul was silent for a couple of minutes while she looked at him. He was thinking of kings and queens and how royal lineage got started – with someone common, coarse, cunning, and ruthless. And how such people find that they can only trust members of their family. Like Saddam Hussein. He thought of Narcisse Cantave. Then he answered. "No. I don't see anything wrong with it. I don't know them, but it's what I would do. Following us to sea in another boat or a plane would be –" he paused.

"Problematic."

"Calling the police –"

"Futile. The police would believe us, not them."

'But what's this about using another boat?"

"I don't know that it's necessary. There's a boat moored nearby with no one on it. The *Moby Dick*. We're going to paint its name on our Zodiac. When we go in to get Bear they'll see the name. Before they come out to get us, they'll call someone, tell the Angels the name of the boat. I know we're changing the name of this boat, in fact, the new name has already been registered. But if they have the name *Bamfield*, they'll trace it and they'll find the island. Does that make sense to you?"

"Yeah. So we're going over to the *Moby Dick* tonight?"

She got up. "Get dressed, Paul. First you're going to paint the name MOBY DICK on our Zodiac. Then we'll take it into Key West, have a late breakfast, pick up supplies, including maybe duct tape. The *Moby Dick* is an old wooden yacht, kind of a classic, but in poor shape. It's got a sign on it, the name of a yacht broker. You're going to go and see them and ask about it. But you don't want them showing it to you. What I want you to do is find out the security arrangements. Find out if we can sneak on board and have the use of the deck for the night without anyone knowing. We don't need keys to the *Moby Dick*, we don't have to go inside, but we can probably break in. When those boys climb over the side – no the stern, we'll leave a rope ladder there, make it easy for them – there'll be three of us waiting with guns."

At the door she said, "Paul, you have three things to forget. One, what I just told you about me being Canadian and the Hells Angels, two, that I fucked you. And three, that you saw me cry."

"Heard you cry," he said. "I didn't watch."

Paul had been seduced. The *Bamfield* had a captain's cabin with its own head – a complete bathroom and shower, just forward and lower than the wheelhouse. Aleysha could have slept there. As for Paul he was tired and had just looked for a place to lie down. There were two cabins aft that slept three each for a crew of six. There were two cabins forward on the same level as the bunk-houses, one for the engineer, which would be his, and the other for the first mate, which would be Henry's. And further forward next to the galley, the cook's cabin. Paul's job was engineer, but the cutter had engine alarm modifications that allowed bridge control and monitoring. Most of the time he would not be needed in the engine room and could stand watch.

Paul painted the name MOBY DICK with white latex paint in small letters on both sides of the Zodiac. Then they went into Key West and did their errands. Aleysha bought Paul white ducks, a blue boating jacket, and a white shirt. He went to the ship-broker, whose office was downtown with no view of the harbor, and told them he was on a yacht in the anchorage off the Bight and expressed an interest in the *Moby Dick*. He chatted about security on the Bight and learned that there wasn't a watchman on the *Moby Dick*. Someone from the broker's office checked her with binoculars early every morning.

At four that afternoon Aleysha drove Paul over to the *Moby Dick*. Paul climbed up a rope ladder on the side. They'd brought beer, sandwiches, duct tape, etc., and Aleysha passed them up, and then followed. They found that there was an unlocked window. Paul went through it and opened the door of the cabin

"Stay out of sight for now but I want you working when I bring my father on board." Paul wondered if she was trying to impress her father with the fact that he was only an employee or if she had to put some distance between them after sex the night before. "So when you see us coming get a mop and pail and swab the deck. It'll look better if anyone's watching. I'll get Bear. Remember, when he comes aboard I want you looking busy."

"Aye, aye, captain."

The Zodiac came back after about an hour. Aleysha's father was agile for a big man, coming over the side like a sixteen-year old midshipman, swinging a large black suitcase. Paul put down his mop, clicked his heels, came to attention navy-style, and saluted.

"Knock it off, will ya? This is my father, Bear. This is Paul. Give us a hand. They saw us. And within half an hour they'll be on the Bight watching the *Moby Dick* with binoculars, if they aren't already."

Aleysha who hadn't had much sleep the night before, went down to one of the cabins for a nap. "Take it easy on the Heinekens, guys. We have to be real sharp tonight. But go out on deck. Show yourselves."

The two men went on deck with a couple of cans of Heineken. Paul soon learned that taking it easy on the Heinekens was something that Henry was not interested in. He soon went back to the cabin for a six-pack. But it seemed to have no effect on him. "Hattie – I got to stop calling her that – what do you call her?"

"Aleysha."

"Aleysha," he rolled the name with his tongue. "It'll take me a while to get used to that. Anyway she had a late night last night, eh?"

"Yeah. I went to bed. She and Ralph, the guy she bought the boat from, they brought the boat to Key West and got in around four."

"There's no moon tonight, that'll help. Hattie's lucky. Luck follows her around. Mind you, she thinks of everything. You must have noticed that."

Paul nodded.

"She tells me that you were in the United States Navy. Hear they don't allow booze on board – that true?"

"True," said Paul. "Speaking of the navy, I think I'll get back to the mop and pail." He did.

Henry sat down on a deck chair. "So you're the engineer, I'm the first mate and she's the skipper. But you're not American?"

"No. Citizen of St. Anthony."

"That's where we're going, right?" Henry looked over at the *Bamfield* a quarter of a mile away. "A coast guard cutter, eh? There was a time in my life when the sight of a coast guard cutter was very bad news. Bad news indeed. So she's changing the name to the *Aleysha*. I'll do the name painting. We'll just sling a rope over the stern. I can stand on that. I paint motorbikes. That's what I do for a living."

Paul doubted the last statement. "ST.ACGC ALEYSHA is what you'll have to paint. Calling it the *Aleysha* was my idea."

Henry was still looking at the cutter. "The St. Anthony Coast Guard Cutter *Aleysha*, right? How do you like working for a woman?"

Paul looked up. "She's okay. She's fair and she pays me well. Also, I'm promised a cut of the business. I trust her to make good on it. On land I don't see that much of her. I fly the helicopter, run errands." He shrugged.

"That's right, you're a helicopter pilot. She told me. Maybe you can give me a lesson on the radio. I've been put in charge of the radio and I don't know how the goddam thing works. And don't worry, you'll get your cut. We Bradings are men of our word. Even the women." He laughed his big booming laugh and finished another beer. "Remind me to save a couple of cans for the Deacon and his pal." He scrunched up the can in one giant hand, glared at Paul with tiny sea-green eyes, and put it in the side pocket of his jean jacket. There were about five flattened tins in there already. "Don't believe in throwing stuff in the sea. Sea's for fish."

"You an environmentalist, then?" Paul asked, amusement showing in his face. Brading seemed a most unlikely member of the green movement.

"You mean like do I go on demonstrations? Hah, hah, hah, hah, hah, hah," he roared, his laughter booming over the ocean. "That's funny. You're okay, Paul. Hah, hah, hah. You're funny." He does look like a bear, thought Paul, all bushy beard and uncombed hair. And the eyes were Aleysha's and not really tiny; they just look that way because of the size of the rest of him.

Late that night a rowboat slipped out from the harbor of Key West Bight and entered the Gulf of Mexico. Deacon Kane had bought it that afternoon; he was sitting in the stern and his pal Colin was rowing. The sea was calm and there was no moon; there was a light onshore breeze. Several ships were anchored offshore. They could make out the stern light of the *Moby Dick* about three quarters of a mile ahead. They had scouted its location from the Bight earlier that night. There was a slight swell and Colin was promptly seasick.

"For God's sake," whispered Deacon, "if you're going to be sick, do it quietly."

Then the Deacon was sick. Stretched prone on the afterdeck, watching through a telescope, Henry had trouble muffling his laughter.

"For God's sake," whispered Aleysha, "if you're going to laugh, do it quietly."

But the two men couldn't hear Bear's laughter for the sound of their own retching. They paused until they had somewhat recovered and pressed on. They rowed slowly and quietly, the Deacon every once in a while whispering "left" or "right" as required. Then "Steady, we're there."

Colin turned, moved quietly to the front, grasped the rope ladder, and tied up the boat. With a gun in his belt, another in a holster at one side, and a large knife sheathed on the other, he began to climb the ladder.

On the deck, Paul, dressed entirely in black, stood motionless beside the cabin on the side shaded from the moon, holding the Kalashnikov. It wasn't loaded. Behind him Henry held a little tray on which stood two cans of Heineken, open and dusted with a white powder. Ayesha lay prone on top of the cabin, a Beretta with silencer in both hands stretched out in front of her, and trained on the stern of the boat. Beside her was a powerful electric flashlight.

When the Deacon heaved himself on board, Aleysha took her right hand off the gun, flicked on the light, and put it back. Paul stepped out so that he was about ten feet in front of the two Angels, pointing the Kalashnikov at the Deacon's navel, standing to the side so that Aleysha would have a clear shot if necessary. Henry stepped forward with the tray and offered the Heinekens to his guests. "Now, Deacon, let's talk this over. Have a beer."

Aleysha shot the Deacon's baseball cap off his head. Too small for his huge head, it had perched on the top of it precariously. "Reckon I will, Henry," said the Deacon, picking up one of the cans and taking a long pull. Colin acted in unison.

Both men choked and spluttered. The Deacon cried out "By God, Henry this isn't beer – "

Aleysha snapped off the light before they collapsed on the deck. It had been on for no more than five seconds. If anyone had been looking they would have seen two guests being offered drinks. Henry was on his knees taking the Deacon's pulse. "Hattie, he's dead."

"No, he isn't, he's a zombie. Don't touch their mouths or their hands. This stuff stops the heart, but doesn't kill. No kidding."

She carefully picked the cans up by their bottoms, wiped the tops against their mouths, and then threw them overboard. "Depends on the dose. They could be dead, but I don't think so."

"Done this before, have you?"

"Couple of times."

Aleysha had a jug of water ready to rinse their mouths and hands. Henry strapped duct tape around their hands and feet. "Just in case they wake up."

Paul put down the Kalashnikov, ran to the bow, shinnied down the *Moby Dick*'s anchor line, untied the Zodiac, and began to row it to the stern of the yacht. He chuckled to himself over the seawater in the cans. Henry had simply not been able to save two cans of Heineken for his guests. Paul had never met a man with such an appetite for beer. When he got to the stern he set the little rowboat adrift and, using ropes, they lowered the Angels into the rubber boat.

They winched the Zodiac aboard the M.V.*Bamfield* with the two zombies stretched out supine on its rigid floor. It was secured on the roof of the main cabin, and with some difficulty, they carried the two heavy unconscious men to the lower bunkhouses. Henry took them under the arms and Aleysha and Paul each took a leg. The men appeared to be dead but Aleysha told the others that not only were they alive, they were conscious of what was going on around them. Narcisse had told her a bit about the zombie state. Being unsure of the dosage, Aleysha told them that there were five possibilities for the two men: one, they could recover completely and suddenly; two, they could recover completely but slowly; three, they could recover certain brain functions but remain disabled for some time, perhaps for life, four, they could remain alive but in their present condition for life, or five; they could die. Narcisse Cantave was currently in the third condition.

Each zombie was placed in one of the two lower bunkhouses, on the single bunk. Both Angels had pissed their pants.

"Leave it," said Henry. "It'll dry up."

"It shouldn't happen again," said Aleysha. "They're in a state of suspended animation."

"Like a hibernating bear?" asked Paul.

"Sort of. I'm not an expert. I don't think we'll have to feed them."

"Deacon could lose some weight. But suppose they shit?" asked Henry. "I'm not going to deal with that. We going to put them in diapers? Reckon that's woman's work, huh, Paul?" He roared with laughter.

"You forget I'm the skipper," said Aleysha. "Let's go up to the wheelhouse. We have some things to talk about."

"I'm kidding," said Henry. "Whether they shit or not, they're my responsibility, I'll look after them." Their relationship had changed. Aleysha was now dominant, but Henry didn't seem to mind. He was having too much fun.

When they got to the wheelhouse, Aleysha pulled out some maps and said, "We should all get some sleep. All we have is a skeleton crew here. Early tomorrow we leave for St. Anthony. Sleep is going to be a problem. Cruising at twelve knots, it should take us about ninety hours. Of course, we could go faster. The question: do we go with one sailor at the wheel and watching the radar, a second keeping watch, checking the radio, doing the cooking, checking the zombies, and minding the engine, while the third sailor sleeps? Or do we anchor at night, two sleep and one keep watch?" She looked at Bear who looked at Paul.

"What's the US navy think?" asked the Bear.

"This is a ship," said Paul, "that's usually sailed by a crew of ten. None of us is that familiar with it. I think it's crazy enough for just the three of us to sail it. I recommend we anchor at night. So it adds – what a day and a half to the voyage? What's the rush? And I don't recommend we go any faster than cruising speed. It's June – we should have good weather. But there's an off-season hurricane coming, Hurricane Alice, I kid you not, that's what they're calling it. It's due in about eight days. We have time. Our little cove has protection from the southwest and we should be okay. All we have to do is get there."

Aleysha studied the maps. "So we do about two hundred and twenty-five miles a day, depending on where we anchor. If we have to go out of our way to anchor, it might stretch into eight days."

"Worst-case scenario, this boat could ride out a hurricane." Paul looked at the maps. "I dunno, I think we should stay away from the Bahamas – there are lot of reefs. I say we sail the coasts of Cuba, Haiti, and Puerto Rico. There's clear channels on that route – the Nicholas Channel, the Old Bahama Channel, hey, we're about two hundred and fifty miles from a marina off the north coast of Cuba, the Nauticas Jardinas del Rey."

"They sell Heineken in Cuba?"

"They sell it everywhere, Bear, you know that," said Aleysha. "Okay, we leave before daybreak with no lights. First thing we do after we get to sea is to take down the Stars and Stripes. But we'll keep it: it might come in handy. From then on, we fly the flag of the St. Anthony Coast Guard."

Half an hour after this conversation, Henry arrived at the wheelhouse with the contents of the two Angels' pockets: coins, billfolds, an odd collection of little objects like marbles and an old rabbit's foot that could have come from the pockets of a nine year old boy, and an address book. This Aleysha scooped up right away and looked through it carefully. Under S she found SQ and there, under the scratched out name of René Lachapelle – that he was connected to the Angels was news to her - a new name had been written in: Pierre Morin. There was a phone number and a private email address marked confidential beside a password. So, she thought, an offer of, say $25,000 to Morin, purportedly coming from the Deacon, should buy her the destruction of René Lachapelle's sealed envelope. She got out her computer, got a Hotmail address in the name of deaconkane – it happened to be available – and made a discreet offer.

One week later, the ST.ACGC *Aleysha*, proudly flying the flag of St. Anthony – a red cormorant on a field of white – that at a distance had a potentially useful resemblance to the Canadian flag – purred into the little cove on the southeast coast of the island and lowered anchor. The sea was calm inside the cove, away from the relentless swell of the Atlantic Ocean. The hurricane was expected the next day.

Aleysha herself appeared on the short deck before the wheelhouse. It was late evening and a few Abu in their dugouts were bringing in their day's catch. Others were gathering their fish and placing them in baskets for the long climb up the steep cliff. When they saw Aleysha they began their chant, Aleysha, Aleysha, Aleysha, those on the shore going down onto their knees, prostrating themselves, arms outstretched at the last syllable. Dressed in white, she took off her French sailor's cap and waved to her people.

"Holy Mother of God!" exclaimed her father, standing with Paul on the rear deck. "Who the hell do they think she is?"

"The daughter of Ayesha," Paul answered. "I'll have to explain to you about the Trinity. Don't laugh, it'll hurt their feelings and hers. She takes this seriously. I think."

The cargo of zombies had remained in a state of catalepsy throughout the voyage, requiring neither food nor drink. Henry now carried each of them in turn up the steps of the boat in a fireman's grip and they were hoisted up to the Zodiac with the winch. The plan was for Paul to climb the cliff and fetch the helicopter, which was on the landing pad beside the house. He would then lift the Zodiac off the roof and deposit it in the Abu village. After the zombies were unloaded, he would return it to the cove and fly back to the airport.

"Okay," he had said to Aleysha the night before. "I'll do it. Then I'm going to take the copter back to the airport and take a few days holiday. I think I know what's going to happen next and I don't want any part of it, although I suppose I'm already an accessory or something. Your father know what's happening?" Henry had been downstairs cooking dinner. "Sometimes I think you must be a psycho."

"As in psychopath?" Aleysha had asked, furious. "Listen, you want psychopaths, take a look at people who drop cluster bombs where kids can play with them. Take a look at people who go into supermarkets and buy little pieces of pigs all cut up and wrapped in cellophane. Those guys tortured my – and Bear's – best friend to death. Treating them as protein is to do them a favor. I am seeing to it that their lives aren't a complete waste."

Paul thought about this conversation as he beckoned Oku to give him a lift to shore. Abbah had come down the cliff and greeted him. He looked thrilled at the sight of the ship as were all the

Abu, none more so than Oku. Those who had not been down in the cove fishing could be seen waving from the top of the cliff. Abbah got into Oku's dugout and went out to the *Aleysha*. Paul began to climb the path up the cliff. He was about halfway when he heard Abbah calling out excitedly from the deck of the ship to the Abu on the shore. There was only one word he understood: "zombies." He thought of his cousin Narcisse and found himself suddenly retching. When he recovered, he continued on his way up, thinking to himself: If Narcisse dies, I will betray her.

"Can we sit in the kitchen?" asked Henry from his Louis Quinze armchair, waving a can of Heineken – Aleysha had got in a good supply before leaving for Florida – looking around at the tapestries and Aubusson carpets. "I appreciate that it's good stuff, money well spent – my money by the way. I remind you that aside from the money you stole from me, it was me that set you up with the Korean."

"I thought it was the Deacon's idea," said Aleysha.

"Well, regardless of who thought of it first, I deserve the credit for knowing that you would outwit the little bugger. Anyway, all is forgiven, I didn't have such a bad time in prison, learnt computers, played chess, and met some interesting people. There were a few punks in there who I had to beat up occasionally. And I had nothing to do with the queens, I want you to know that. As my daughter." Henry was on about his twentieth Heineken and was getting sentimental. "Anyway, can we sit in the kitchen?"

There was a huge carved oak armchair at one end of the refectory table with room for Henry's great bulk. Aleysha had always known that if Henry ever came to Haut-Clair that he would sit in the kitchen and had ordered the chair especially for him. She was surprised at how long he had lasted in the drawing room. Instinctive Brading good manners, she supposed, smiling to herself.

"Ah, this is better. You'll find me here, anytime you need me. Near the beer fridge." He laughed his big booming laugh. Aleysha had installed a second fridge just to hold the Heineken.

"Don't get too comfortable on this island. You're in charge of North American sales remember. But would you stay until the cocaine refinery is completed? The building is finished, but we haven't installed the equipment. You know about that stuff. You can tell the Abu what to do. They've learned a few skills. Abbah knows that you are my biological father and he'll tell the others. I want them to get to know you."

Henry frowned. "I've never built a cocaine refinery." He seemed surprised that there should be such a gap in his knowledge and experience. "Do you have plans?"

"Oh, yes, detailed plans drawn by an engineer in Mexico."

Just then there was the sound of drums. "There's a big celebration down at the village tonight. A feast. We're expected. There's something else. I don't know how to say this. Abbah thinks they will want your seed. He's going to talk it over with the *mambo*."

"That would be the chief witch," said Henry.

"Yes. If she gives it her okay, you're to choose one of the girls and make her pregnant. Can you do that, Bear? It's important to them." In fact it was important to her. She could not provide an heir and needed an excuse to stop her monthly matings with Abbah.

Henry frowned again. "I'll consider it. I take parenting seriously, as you know. I am proud of you and I think that I have had a lot to do with your success. I'll take a look at the girls."

"That's generous of you, Bear. We have to change. Have you any clean clothes? I bought a whole set of denim pants for the Abu, all different sizes and colors. There are a couple of pairs that would fit you. I ordered them specially. They're red – any problem with that?"

When Aleysha came downstairs she was wearing a long white silk dress, a diamond tiara, two emerald and diamond bracelets, and a diamond necklace with a large emerald pendant. Her hair was back to its natural black and with the contacts removed, the jewelry set off her eyes. She went to the kitchen where she found Bear wearing his freshly laundered jean jacket and his new red denim trousers. They were a good fit. His body hair was so thick that one had to look twice to see that he was not wearing a shirt. Aleysha was carrying a thick gold necklace, which she put around his neck. Henry had packed twenty-four Heinekens into a cooler that he had found in the pantry.

They set off together toward the drums. It was a dark night with the hurricane threatening. The wind howled and whistled through the trees. They could see a bonfire blazing, the huge black pot, and the woman standing over it on the pedestal, stirring the contents with the long spoon. When they reached the clearing they could see that the Abu had set up a separate table for Henry to the right of the throne. As soon as they sat down, the dancing commenced. The people now all had new colored denims, red, orange, yellow, blue, and green, every shade of the rainbow – and they were mostly topless. They had not been seated long when Aleysha was brought a dish of fruit and Henry a large porcelain bowl of stew. He ate with great gusto and dutifully regarded the half-naked dancing girls.

Midway through his second bowl, he turned to Aleysha and remarked, "This is good. What kind of meat is it?"

"I think they're saving Colin for another occasion. What you are eating is the Deacon with local vegetables," replied Aleysha.

Henry's mouth dropped open. Aleysha could see by the firelight a small chunk of the Deacon on his tongue. He closed his mouth and eyes and chewed for half a minute, then swallowed and let out a huge roar of laughter. "You're not kidding me, Hattie, are you? The Deacon, he's good, mind you, there's spices, I taste peppers, coriander, and I think a little nutmeg ...."

He let out a great whoop, put down his bowl and cried: "I love these people." Taking a young girl with exceptionally pretty breasts by the hand, he joined the dance. Like many large people, Henry was light on his feet and danced like an angel.

Bear didn't come back to the plantation house for two days. That night the hurricane hit the island from the south. Aleysha made her way to the cliff to check on the cutter. The cove offered good shelter from the southwest and the anchor held. The St. Anthony Coast Guard Cutter *Aleysha* rocked securely on the backward swell.

15

The cocaine refinery was completed by September. It had now been a year since Hattie had left Canada and nine months since Alice had arrived on the island. Aleysha was pleased with the progress she had made in her new life. It was good to have her father around. He got on well with the Abu people and proved an excellent foreman in the assembly of the refining equipment.

Aleysha forbade the consumption of cocaine in Haut-Clair, but the Abu had taken to chewing the leaves of the young coca plants. This gave them energy and they worked harder. It meant that it would take longer before there was a commercial harvest, but Aleysha didn't mind. The income that Haut-Clair would receive from the rendering of Peruvian coca paste into the refined product was many times what the plantation would have generated from the coffee and coca crops.

Henry didn't object when Aleysha forbade him to bring beer to the village. He agreed that it was not a good idea to introduce the Abu to alcohol. He was doing his best to impregnate the Abu girl he had chosen, and did not think alcohol would be good for the baby. He did his drinking in the plantation house kitchen, chatting with his daughter, and sometimes Paul, who on these occasions would sleep over.

One night when they were alone, Henry questioned his daughter about her love life. "I'm doing my bit for the population," he said. "I don't see where you're headed with men. You ought to have a baby and not by either of those guys."

Juan had made another visit to Haut-Clair and Aleysha had yielded and admitted him to her bed. Once. He was good-looking but not much use in bed; it was no wonder to Alyesha that his wife had given up on him. The dogs continued to dislike him and so did Henry.

In the case of Abbah, Aleysha explained to her father, it was simply a case of a monthly mercy-fuck. The boy was devoted to her and broken-hearted when she cut him off as a lover. He was head priest of the Abu and she couldn't afford to have him sulking. She explained this to Henry. But Henry didn't think he was suitable for his daughter.

"Find yourself a real man," he said. "A guy I can get along with, drink beer with, talk about hockey, and so on. You're not in love with either of these guys. Girls are supposed to fall in love with guys like – guys who are like their fathers. When are you going to find a guy like me and fall in love?"

Aleysha was silent for a long moment. Henry thought he saw her eyes soften a little but wasn't sure. "I did fall in love once," she admitted. "And I think maybe I still am – it's over a year now."

Henry plunged into thought for a full minute. "Not the goddam Korean?"

"No."

Henry's mouth fell open. "The goddam Mountie," he said softly.

"You know who he reminded me of? Charley. He was a lot like Charley, tall, blond, tough, but gentle. A hockey player. Of course he was bigger than Charley and more sophisticated. You would have liked him, Bear. He liked beer, and you know what, when he was a teenager he was a member of the Bandidos. A Nomad. He didn't think the Mounties knew. They didn't have a chapter in Winnipeg and he just wanted to wear their colors."

"But then he became an undercover narc?"

"Not when I knew him, but he had been, out west somewhere. He's from Winnipeg. When I knew him he was at a desk job but you know all that – "

Henry was no longer listening. He was on his feet headed for the fridge and another Heineken. "Holy mother of Jesus, you're in love with the goddam horseman who sent me to prison."

"He didn't send you to prison, Bear," replied Aleysha. "I did."

Aleysha decided that the *Aleysha* could be sailed with a crew of four if everyone learned everyone else's job and the ship anchored at night. There were four private cabins. Aleysha, Henry, and Paul had found themselves undermanned bringing the ship to the island from Florida, but not by much. A round trip to Guyana would take less than a week cruising at twelve knots.

The plastic bins of cocaine paste would be stored in the large cabin underneath the Zodiac, officially known as the Rescue Room, and in the two large crew cabins. Abu carpenters removed the Rescue Room windows and replaced them with wooden panels, removed the bunks, and created additional cargo space elsewhere on the ship.

Aleysha would sail on every voyage as captain. Paul was to be first mate. Oku begged Abbah to let him join the crew. Aleysha agreed to enlist him and he was asked to choose a friend who would make up the fourth. Abbah himself would not be part of the crew – as chief he could hardly leave his people. He would stay behind and supervise the plantation and the refinery. But he did learn how to operate the boat, and taught Oku and his chum, Obah, the English terms that they needed for their work.

When training was completed, they took the cutter into Le Havre. The crew of the other coast guard vessel, a former tug, came aboard and were shown around; the prime minister and a number of dignitaries were invited and served tea. Oku and Obah wore sailor suits.

Henry came along, and was introduced as captain. Aleysha had sent him into Le Havre for a tailored officer's uniform, a haircut, and a shave. Officials were told that he was a retired officer of the Canadian Coast Guard who was training the crew. He managed to abstain from Heineken and ostentatiously held his teacup with his pinky pointing up. Paul had several decorations and badges from the US Navy and wore them. He took a certain amount of good-natured joshing about this from his cousin Philippe, who was among the guests. Aleysha wore her French sailor's outfit with the red pompom; she was aware that the St. Anthony establishment considered her a rich spoiled flibbertigibbet and it was a reputation that she wanted to maintain.

In November the ST.ACGC *Aleysha* took its first trip to Guyana, a journey of six hundred miles that took about two and a half days, anchoring for one night in the harbor of Ville de Saint-Pierre in Martinique. They skirted the Lesser Antilles on the Atlantic side, out of sight of land, passing even to the east of Barbados, the easternmost island of the West Indies. There is a certain amount of yacht traffic to Barbados that Aleysha wished to avoid. There is more traffic on the Caribbean side because the Atlantic seas are heavier. They seldom saw another ship except at a distance. One freighter on its way to Europe crossed their path, but nothing shared their southbound course. Aleysha was aware that they were probably being observed by American DEA satellite surveillance, but was confident that once the identity of the ship was established, reconnaissance would cease.

Oku, who had no formal education and had never been off the Haut-Clair plateau except in his little dugout canoe, was fascinated by the ship's navigational tools. He had spent his lifetime observing the stars, and when Paul taught him navigation he seemed to intuit the whole process, including the computerized mathematics. Everyone had to learn to run the engine, how to use the radio, and take a turn at the wheel and understand the navigational aids, such as the GPS. Aleysha insisted that every member of the crew learn to use a sextant in case the modern technology broke down.

Henry, who would soon be returning to Florida, had come along on this trip to make five. Aleysha wanted him to be familiar with all phases of the operation, and she felt that an extra crewmember might come in handy on the first trip. He took a full watch. Aleysha spent her spare time on the roof of the wheelhouse on the lookout known as the 'monkey's island.' She enjoyed being up there even in rough weather, calling out "Land to starboard one o'clock," and "ship to port nine o'clock." *O Ayesha, this is the life for me, thankyou, thankyou.* Her presence up there with field glasses was consistent with their story – if anyone questioned their presence so far from St. Anthony – that they were looking for a suspected drug smuggler. They wore their uniforms when on deck and when Aleysha was on the monkey's island, she changed her French sailors' beret for an officer's cap, partly for the eyeshade but mostly to look official.

It was night when they navigated the small river mouth on the coast of Guyana and anchored in the estuary. There were no lights to be seen and they had turned their own lights off as soon as Aleysha sighted land. In the morning they were able to see the dock and Juan standing on it with two longshoremen. They brought the ship in and the plastic tubs of paste were loaded by hand. Everyone pitched in except Aleysha, who supervised. The *Aleysha* was not designed to carry cargo and the load had to be balanced and secured. They also refueled, the ostensible reason for putting into port.

Juan had told Aleysha that he wanted to come along on the way back and she agreed, but made it clear that there were to be no attempts at hanky-panky with the captain. He was allotted the cook's cabin, which was empty; everyone shared the cooking. The Abu preferred sleeping on deck.

On their arrival back at the cove, the paste was loaded on pallets and carried up to the refinery by helicopter. Henry supervised as the refinery went into full production. Juan, satisfied that everything was going well, flew home. He would return to sail with the boat on its first smuggling voyage to Florida.

Henry would pick up the first drop off the coast of Florida. He had taken a trip there in November and bought a beach house and a fast outboard ostensibly for fishing near Jacksonville. He had contacts in Florida and IDs in several different names. Regardless of the papers he carried he was generally known to bikers in Florida as Mister Henry. He also bought a local motorcycle shop from an old friend.

He had chosen Jacksonville because of this friend. Richard "Judge" Hogarth and Henry had worked together at Hogarth's motorcycle body shop about the time that Aleysha's mother was carrying her. Henry had been required to leave Ottawa rather suddenly because of an execution that he had participated in. He didn't have proper papers, but he showed Mr. Judge, as everyone called him, what he could do with a paintbrush and got hired, no questions asked.

The two became friends. Mr. Judge did not belong to a motorcycle club because he didn't think it was good for business to show any partiality. The Bandits didn't have a branch in Jacksonville, so Henry joined the Nomad chapter, and this meant that, like Mr. Judge, he was welcome everywhere. He learned the manufacture of crack from his boss as well as a number of other things.

It was this body shop that Henry bought from Hogarth over twenty years later. Mr. Judge had invested in Jacksonville real estate and made a lot of money. He had kept the motorcycle shop, but he didn't really have time to run it anymore. When Henry turned up and offered a little more than it was worth, he sold.

Mr. Judge was always on good terms with the young men who came to his shop. Many of them were not joining the established clubs; they disliked the initiation procedures and the authoritarian attitudes of older club members. So as a retirement hobby, Mr. Judge decided to start a new motorcycle club and call it Sons of Beelzebub or the SOBs for short. When he had enough members signed up, he built a clubhouse at his own expense. He looked forward to opening clubs all across the country. As a businessman he wanted to see the different chapters prosper and felt obliged to find the boys a solid source of income. He had grown to look down on crack; he had seen it ruin the lives of too many kids. It was inexpensive and addictive. He was looking for a source of good cocaine when Henry turned up.

"This being Florida," he told Henry, "and the Caribbean being right next door, there's a lot of it coming in. There's competition. Frankly, I don't want to have anything to do with it directly, but my boys need the income. We have opened six new chapters, two more in Florida, one each in Georgia, Louisiana, Alabama, and Texas. We're spreading right across the states, all young guys. There's a new generation out there."

"What about the competition?" asked Henry. "Do you know who they are?"

"Some of them, yeah," and Mr. Judge named a few and described where they operated.

SUSAN

16

Three months after opening an office as a private detective in Winnipeg, and the day after the hurricane hit the south coast of the island of St. Anthony, Theodore told his secretary/receptionist that he didn't have enough work for her and that he had to let her go. She was a tall, leggy girl who looked just right for the part and worked at it. Looking right for the part that is, she had little work to do for Theodore. She spent her time reading Sam Spade and Philip Marlowe detective novels and looking disdainfully at her boss – who had not lived up to expectations – waiting for something to happen.

The little work he did get he didn't like. It involved spying on people's spouses and looking for hopelessly lost dogs. The former disgusted him and the latter depressed him. Bizarre displaced people would come to his office claiming to have inside information on long forgotten crimes. This information they wouldn't share unless he gave them money. He grew his hair long, donned his gold jewelry, and took to hanging out in Winnipeg hotel bars, as he had as an undercover operator, except instead of telling strangers that he was looking for dope, he passed out his private detective business card. It seldom worked.

Sixteen months after his trip to St. Anthony, and a year after Henry left the island for Florida, a well-dressed American came to see Theodore. He placed a business card on the desk. It read:

Reinhold Woppler
Drug Enforcement Administration
Office of Personnel
2401 Jefferson Davis Highway
Alexandria, VA 22301   *800 DEA-4288*

Theodore looked at it for a moment, his eyes drawn to the words "Office of Personnel" and observed, "I notice that you guys leave out the word 'law.' It's like you were forcing people to take drugs. What can I do for you, Mr. Woppler?"

"Work for us."

"Just like that?"

Woppler nodded. "DEA Special Agent. Undercover."

"Where?"

"In the US where your mug isn't known. Fifty thousand a year plus expenses to start. Green card, of course, possibility of US citizenship."

"The last item would be an option?" asked Theodore.

"The green card is not optional, but you can keep your Canadian citizenship if you wish. We know about you Canadians, fought with the British in the American Revolution, War of 1812, still stubborn, wouldn't join the Iraq coalition, still assholes, but reliable. You are the only immigrants who won't take out American citizenship, but I suppose there is an historical excuse." Woppler grinned again.

"The job is mine just like that? No application forms, no medical examinations?"

"We know all about you. All that we need to know. There are papers to sign. Come down to Washington. Get a hotel room, call me from there, and we'll fix a time. As soon as you've called me, destroy this card. I'll come to your room with your supervisor. Here's expense money." He peeled off ten one hundred US dollar bills and held them out.

Theodore looked at the money: the Yankee dollar, so that's how it works. Who can say no when you need the money? "Okay," he said. "I accept. Do you want a receipt?"

"Yes," said Woppler, as Theodore took the money. "Keep your apartment, your phone, and your business. We'll pay the rent. Leave a message on your machine that you're out of town. When you get to Washington, give me copies of your keys. Someone will forward your mail. We'll fix it so everyone thinks you're still here. You'll have to fly back now and then."

Theodore signed, noting that the receipt already had his name on it and stated that he had received $1,000 in cash from the

Personnel Department of the Drug Enforcement Administration for expenses.

Both men stood up. Woppler extended his hand, they shook, and Theodore walked him to the door. "See you," said Woppler and was gone.

The man accompanying Woppler at the hotel room door in Washington wore mirror glasses and had an ankle holster under the trouser leg of his well-cut suit. He watched Theodore notice it as they came in.

"You got good eyes, I'll give you that. But you got cop written all over you, except for the long hair. My name's Marlowe, Ken Marlowe."

They shook hands. Theodore got his jewelry out of his suitcase, put it on, and swaggered a bit. "It's called casting contrary to type. No one thought that even the Mounties were dumb enough to put a guy who looked so much like a cop undercover. Of course I had to develop a flamboyant personality. Bored the shit out of myself sometimes. I dunno. It worked in Canada."

He gestured to Marlowe to take the armchair in the corner of the room, shook hands with Woppler, and pulled out the desk chair for him. Woppler sat down and opened his briefcase. Theodore picked up the phone book, sat down, put it on his lap, and waited for Woppler to pass him papers.

"You've lived in the USA.before, according to immigration. Hockey player."

"Binghamton Senators. One of the coaches was kind enough to tell me I'd never make the NHL. So I quit. Joined the Mounties. Nice town, Binghamton, New York. I like the United States. Can't stand Canadians who are anti-American." He then remembered that Woppler, who seemed to have a sense of history, had remarked – with a friendly smile – that Canadians were assholes. "I figure the English-speaking people of North America are one people. Still, when you kicked out the loyalists, you lost a good part of the population that had any common sense."

"Speaking of loyalty," said Woppler, with a slight smile, "you have to take an oath. There must be a Bible in the drawer."

Marlowe was quiet while the oath was sworn and the documentation was completed. Then he tossed a handsome leather briefcase on the bed.

Theodore examined the contents. "My name is James Smith and among other things I'm a card-carrying fan of the Florida Panthers. Do I get tickets?"

"Jimmy not James. You'll see that you were once a Nomad member of the Bandidos, Jimmy." This was said with powerful innuendo.

Theodore was speechless. "You know?"

"We know." Marlowe grinned.

"Gee, you guys are good. The Mounties never found out. I grew up in Winnipeg. I was young, I had a Harley. I was really into it. I'm not much of a joiner, but I wanted the colors. They didn't have a branch there so I joined the Nomad chapter. Hell, you guys, it's possible to belong to one of those clubs and never commit a crime. I knew a Hells Angel in Binghamton who was a florist. Hold on – you're going to ask me to infiltrate a motorcycle gang?"

There was a slight nodding of heads. Theodore thought for a moment and continued. "The busts I did for the Mounties were not related to motorcycle gangs. If that's what you want me to do, I'll do it. But I don't like the things you sometimes have to do before they trust you. I don't like the way many of them treat women. But some of those guys are okay."

"Bullshit, but if you really think that, it could help you. Yes, we want you to hang out with bikers. The less-established gangs, the ones that are trying to get in on things like dope racketeering, are less demanding. They just pretend they're tough. But they would love to get in on a big deal. You spend time with one of those and then maybe cross over to a more established gang. Play it by ear, buy a little cocaine now and then. If you're offered crack let us know, but the pure imported stuff is what we're after with you. When the time comes – it might take six months – when you have a good idea where it's coming from, let the right party know you have a major buyer. You know what to do, you've done it before."

"Yeah, I have. But not with bikers."

"In Ottawa you never had any direct contacts with the Bandits, did you?"

"No. Just the woman. I didn't know she was involved with them. But one of them was spying on her and found out who I was. You know about that of course. I was a clean-shaven short-haired Mountie. Hell, I even walk differently when I am undercover. I'll take my chances. Where are you sending me?"

"Florida. We assign undercover agents to a state rather than a city. You are free to move around. But Florida is a key state in the cocaine business. Most of it comes in there. We have a lot of undercover people in Florida."

"Good. Nice warm climate. Better and better."

"You have written instructions on how to draw expenses that you will memorize and destroy. First thing you do is get yourself a chopper. The bike is already authorized: pay what you have to but get as much credit as you can. When things happen, you'll be abandoning it."

Theodore looked through his papers. "Okay, flashy it is. High profile. I don't see a badge here. That's good. I don't want one."

"No, you don't make arrests. And if you get caught, we don't know you. If you set up a successful sting operation, you get a bonus – size of which depends on what you have achieved – wired to the bank account of the second ID, which you will assume immediately. Your life may depend on it. Then you go underground for a couple of months. Disappear. Eventually we offer you a desk job. Understood?"

Theodore nodded.

"Here's a Miami cell phone. You're responsible for keeping up payments, Mr. Jimmy." He took out a pen, picked up the hotel memo pad, tore off a sheet, and wrote out a phone number. "Memorize this phone number, tear up the paper, and flush it down the toilet. I know the phone's goddam computer will remember the number, but do it anyway. When you call, call me Ken. Never mention my last name. One more thing." He passed over two thick brown envelopes. "Here are two more IDs. If the second gets blown, you have a back-up."

Theodore took them and asked, "What if I run into other agents? How do we know each other?"

"There's a password. It changes. I'll let you know when you call in once a week. Right now it's "Do you think the Marlins will trade for a pitcher?" The answer is, "Yeah, Lopez."

Theodore put the two envelopes in his briefcase. Unknown to him, imbedded in the leather case was a tiny electronic transistor that sent out a radio signal to a global positioning satellite. The DEA would know where he was at all times and did not want him to know that. It was calculated that the kind of agent who would turn might throw out everything else, but would keep the expensive briefcase.

When Theodore – or rather Jimmy Smith – arrived in Jacksonville, the first thing he did was to go shopping for a motorbike, a project he planned to spend some time on. He visited all the bike dealers and custom shops and talked to people; he enjoyed looking at the machines and he was making contacts. One of the shops he visited was called Hogarth's, but now belonged to a Mr. Henry.

Henry Brading had never laid eyes on Theodore McLeod, but with his daughter declaring herself in love with him, he was on his mind. He knew a number of things about him: in his late teens he had been a Bandido Nomad, he had been an undercover narc for the Mounties, he was Canadian and would have a Canadian accent, he was a larger more sophisticated version of Charley, and he had been a professional hockey player. Henry knew that he had resigned from the Mounties and had dropped out of sight. This Jimmy Smith who came into the shop wearing a Bandido Nomad badge, had something of Charley about him. If Theodore had not been on his mind, he would not have made the connection. But he started wondering.

So when he came in the second time, Henry made a point of spending some time with him and got him talking about hockey. Then he offered him a deal on a Harley that Henry would customize especially for him. The deal Henry offered was a real bargain. There was something in the way Jimmy negotiated that made Henry suspect that he was not spending his own money. He sold

Theodore the bike and introduced him to the Sons of Beelzebub. If he is going to try anything, thought Henry, let it first be with me; then I'll use him. But he still wasn't sure.

Theodore didn't recognize Henry; he had never been on the Bandits' case. Hattie had told him the time and place for the bust, but he was not in on what happened afterwards. He had seen photographs of Henry but the Bear had had shaved off his beard and cut his hair. Theodore had followed the case in the papers after he left the force, and was glad to learn that Hattie's father had not been convicted of anything serious. He read that Henry had made the positive ID of the headless woman; after that he never gave him a thought.

Jimmy Smith had been enjoying the good life provided for him by the DEA for about six months when his employers started to get impatient. It takes time to gain trust, he told Ken Marlowe. Be patient; something's cooking at the SOB clubhouse, I can smell it.

Henry liked Jimmy; he had all the requirements of a first-class Canadian son-in-law: they drank beer together and talked hockey. He became convinced that he was dealing with an undercover agent, and that this agent was Theodore McLeod. He racked his brains trying to figure out how an undercover DEA agent and the owner of a cocaine refinery could get back together. Maybe he could turn Theodore.

Business was good. The refinery was going at near capacity and the SOBs were now taking nearly all the cocaine that came into Henry's possession. One day Theodore made his big pitch about cocaine, and Henry hesitated. He decided to be cautious and test Jimmy by sending him to someone else. "I can't help you myself," he said, "but I can tell you where to go. Just don't mention my name. I expect a cut." His friend Judge Hogarth had told him the names of some of the competition. Not long after that there was a big cocaine bust in Jacksonville, and some of the SOB's competition was eliminated by the DEA.

As soon as the bust was made Ken informed Theodore by cell phone. He assumed his second ID and took a taxi to the airport.

He took the first flight out of Jacksonville, which was non-stop to Chicago. He was sorry to leave the bike behind, there was a little owed on it, so he assumed Henry would repossess it. The value of the bike, less what he owed on it, was all that he could leave Henry as his cut.

But Henry Brading's cut was of a different sort. After the DEA caught some of Henry's competitors in Theodore's sting operation, and made a number of arrests, some of the survivors went looking for Theodore. Although Jimmy Smith had not mentioned Henry's name, a Son of Beelzebub informed them that Henry had sponsored him and that they were often seen together. Some of Henry's competition in the cocaine trade had suspected for a long time that Henry might be the source of the SOB's cocaine. They had no evidence – just a hunch – but now that his pal Jimmy Smith had turned out to be a narc, they suspected that Henry had sent Jimmy to them, knowing he was a narc. They didn't hesitate. Jimmy Smith had completely disappeared and someone had to pay for the bust. So they arranged for Aleysha's father – that jovial, clever, wicked bear of a man – to be rubbed out, erased from the book of life.

And with him went Juan, the South American aristocrat who had chosen to be a cocaine smuggler. The Sons of Beelzebub had expanded into states that had been allotted to him and the Cubans in his network were complaining. He had gone to Florida to discuss the matter with Henry. The two were out night fishing when a "fast boat" came by without lights, cut its motor, turned on a search light, riddled Henry and Juan with machine-gun fire, and stayed just long enough to see Henry's boat sink into the sea.

Aleysha received the news when the telephone rang very early one morning. It was Alonzo. She was up, having had a fitful night of bad dreams. The dreams were of darkness, terror and impotence – she had never before had nightmares and their effect was compounded by the certain sense that she had been sent them, that someone – her nemesis Zena – was sending her the dreams like emails.

Alonzo was upset. In his grief he blamed her, accused her of indiscretion, and was insensitive to the grief that the news was bringing to her. It was too much. She hung up

She wandered about the house, poured herself a stiff rum, and lit a cigar. One of the maids when she came up from the village found her in the morning in her nightgown in the kitchen weeping and a bit drunk. The girl went down on her knees.

"O, Aleysha, what has happened?"

"My father has been murdered."

The evening that this maritime drive-by happened, Theodore was watching television in his Chicago hotel room. He was bored. He did not think it wise to be seen in public for a while and had not left the room for two days. He was reflecting that he knew no one in the city who could lighten up his exile, when he remembered Bernard Levinson. He found him right away in the phone book.

"Don't stay at a hotel, for God's sake, come and stay with me. Tell me what you've been up to. I have news for you, by the way."

Theodore took a taxi to Bernard's house, which turned out to be a mansion in the Park Ridge district. It was six o'clock and Bernard told him to leave his bag at the foot of the stairs, his Filipino butler would take care of it. "And," said Bernard, "Luis has learned to make a pretty good rum punch. Come into the study. What do you say to a planter's punch? For old times sake?"

"What do I say? I say yes," replied Theodore

The hall was oak-paneled. Two Tang horses stood on Chinese tables against the walls. There was a full suit of Japanese armor in one corner. Theodore found himself stopping to look at Impressionist paintings, each one cleverly lit with its own single beam from somewhere above: Manet, Renoir, Monet, Sisley.

"I'm a very lucky man," said Bernard. "I didn't earn all this by listening to the sad stories of screwed-up people and trying – without much success – to help them. My grandfather was a banker. I became a psychiatrist in order to try to overcome the guilt. I had no brothers or sisters and neither did my dad. So I inherited a bank. Not understanding banking, I sold it. Come into the study."

Luis brought in a large crystal jug filled with rum punch. There was a big bucket of ice on the tray with limes and maraschino cherries.

"Thank you, Luis. Luis also cooks for me and he is very good at it as you will see."

"I like to cook for you, Mr. Bernard, you are so fond of your food," said Luis cheerfully as he left.

"So, tell me, what's been happening? What brings you to Chicago?"

"Flight," said Theodore, and told him everything.

Over a dinner of soup, sole, crème glacées, and a couple of bottles of Australian Chardonnay, they chatted about the world and the island of St. Anthony in particular. "I told you that I had news," said Bernard. "Let's see, we met there about two years ago. Well, I've been back there several times. I like the island. Unlike Barbados, which is a modern little nation, not Third World at all, St. Anthony still has its old-fashioned West Indian character. The summer after we met, I went back and bought a house. I'm on my way there on Tuesday – what is this, Sunday? – day after tomorrow. Now if you are looking for a place to lie low, it's ideal. I'm going for three months, and you're welcome to come and stay with me. There will be a few houseguests, but mostly I go there to work. I am writing a book on the psychopathic state, you remember, we talked about such people. I mean it, quite sincerely, you are welcome to stay the whole three months."

It was tempting, but Theodore hesitated. "It's appealing," he said, "but I am not in a position to repay such hospitality."

"Come on," said Bernard. "I'm Jewish. It would give me infinite pleasure to make a Christian feel guilty. But you can take me out to dinner now and then and buy me drinks at Les Palmes with your DEA bonus. Give me the police officer's view on psychopaths. It's a big house, there's lots of room. We can go whole days, scarcely seeing each other. It's right on the beach, on a cliff, with thirty-nine steps cut into the rock going down to a private beach, a little bay with cliffs on both sides. In fact, that's the name of the house, The Thirty-Nine Steps. Do you know the book?"

"Yes," said Theodore. "John Buchan. He was at one time governor-general of Canada."

"Ah, that settles it then. The Canadian connection. You're coming. How about a glass of port, and we watch a couple of films about psychopaths?"

They went to the library and Bernard took out DVDs of the films, *Body Heat* and *Double Indemnity*.

"These are two films with almost identical plots," he said. "We'll play the more recent one first. Maybe you saw it, with William Hurt and Kathleen Turner? Made in 1981?"

"No, I don't think so."

"I would not ordinarily give the plot of a film away, but as our interest is academic, I will. You'll be able to watch Kathleen Turner play the character Matty Walker, a classic over-controlled psychopath, knowing what she's up to. She plays what we call the *omega* role, that of women who use their sexuality to delude, manipulate, and sometimes even murder men. She is an example of cognitive evil: she has the ability to maintain secrecy, to engage in misdirection, that is to distract people from what she is actually doing, and she abdicates any moral responsibility completely. Over-controlled psychopaths remove obstructions and eliminate adversaries who block their paths, and they do not look back."

When it was over, with Ned, her lover, the William Hurt character, going to prison for murder and arson, and Matty, wealthy and relaxed on a Hawaiian beach, Theodore, leant back in his armchair and laughed. "What an idiot. I saw right through her from the beginning. Mind, you warned me. She even says to him, did you notice? 'You're not very smart. I like that in a man.' He still didn't get it. So, if the next movie is the same story, I would like to see it another night. Can we bring it with us, and watch it in St. Anthony?"

17

When Theodore left Winnipeg to work for the American DEA he had traveled light, for the DEA was paying him to keep his apartment and his office. He would rather have given them up and pocketed the rent money, but it was clear that he was to do things their way. One of the things he took was the photo of Hattie that he had printed from the RCMP Drug Law Enforcement computer files two years before. He had scarcely looked at it since, as it brought back painful memories, but going through his files, he came across it. She was looking down at her dog outside her father's house in Ottawa. The picture appeared to have been taken with a telephoto lens from a parked car some distance away. It was winter and the snow was piled high along the side of the road. She was smiling and looked beautiful, her features clear in the brilliant winter light. Memories of her flooded his mind. He put it in the back pocket under the lid of his suitcase and took it with him.

Theodore was comfortable in Bernard's house and at ease with his host. He found that Bernard was interested in all phases of police work. They had numerous discussions about the criminal mind; Bernard questioned him relentlessly about every criminal he had ever met. It was Bernard's life work to determine if the mind of a psychopath or any criminal was different from that of someone who obeyed the law. Were they insane or evil? Did they just choose a life strategy that disregarded the law? Bernard seemed to regard Theodore as a file folder from which he could extract data. Bernard was particularly interested in their childhood, and here Theodore could not help him. But he was glad to supply facts from his experience and felt a bit better about enjoying Bernard's hospitality. I am singing for my supper, he would tell his host, who would just smile and ask another question. Theodore himself was interested in the possible existence of evil as an entity and Bernard was enlightening on the topic.

Bernard worked mornings on his book. They would have two or three rum drinks before lunch and would retire afterward for a siesta or nap as is the custom in the tropics. Some mornings Theodore would borrow Bernard's Jaguar two-seater and tour the island. One morning he visited the museum in Le Havre. Theodore liked museums where whole rooms were furnished in the style of a period of long ago. He liked to stand in these rooms and dream himself back in time. He was in this kind of reverie when he suddenly became aware of the miniature portrait of the Russian Aloyshovna on top of a little writing desk. It's uncanny he thought, it's Hattie. And it's on this island that I thought I saw her. Was I seeing a ghost?

When he got back to the house he went to his room and looked in the flap of his suitcase for the picture of Hattie. He took it out and, yes, the resemblance was striking. He carried it downstairs and showed it to Bernard over rum punch.

"In the museum in Le Havre," he told Bernard, "there's an eighteenth-century miniature painting of this very woman." He enjoyed astonishing his friend. "A woman I once loved," he declared dramatically. "Perhaps the only woman I have ever loved."

"Oh," said Bernard slowly, "was that the one who was murdered? I mean, not Aloyshovna, I have noticed that portrait myself and I know a little of her history, but was not the woman you loved involved in crime? I seem to remember – "

"Really, Bernard, your mind runs on one track."

"Was she?"

"Well, a little bit of money laundering perhaps for her father. She kept his books. As you say, she was a victim of a crime. She was murdered."

Both of them were looking down at the computer printout of Hattie, which lay on the table between them when Sara, who never underestimated the speed at which the two gentlemen consumed their rum punch, brought the second round. She looked down at the picture, as people do, instinctively following the gaze of others when it's focused on the same object. She almost dropped the tray.

"Why, it's Miz Alice. Miz Alice in winter, in snow. Did you know her, Mr. Theodore?"

"Who?" asked Bernard. "Did Mr. Theodore know who?"

"Why, Miz Alice, from whom you bought the house, Mr. Bernard."

"I never met her."

"I worked for her. All of we at The Thirty-Nine Steps worked for Miz Alice. She was good to us too."

"Hold on," said Theodore. He picked up the picture and passed it to Sara after she had put down the drinks. "Take another look. It can't be the same person. The woman in the picture is dead."

"She not, Mr. Theodore," said Sara looking closely at the picture. "Miz Alice not dead. She over at Haut-Clair, at the plantation. Her husband dead, I just heard this morning. Poor Mr. Narcisse Cantave, he got sick here one morning early, two years ago, poisoned by his own experiments. It took two years, but now he dead." She put the picture back on the table.

Theodore took a deep swallow of his drink. Bernard picked up the picture. "You say this is a picture of Alice LeBlanc whose house this was? I never met her. I dealt with her lawyer, a Philippe Cantave." Theodore was thinking, she's alive, she's here, it was her I saw two years ago. "But Theodore, the woman you knew, it says here, is called Hattie Brading."

Sara looked at the two confused men. "Only one way settle it. You go see her at Haut-Clair. But it not easy to get to. You go see Mr. Paul, Mr. Paul Cantave he fly the whirleybird for Miz Alice. Used to land it right behind the house, when she live here, on the meadow in front of the Steps but now he fly out of the airport. You go there after lunch instead of sleeping. Settle it." She looked at them severely and left.

On hearing of Narcisse's death from Philippe, Paul called the DEA in Florida from his office at the airport. He told them everything except his name. He had promised himself that if Narcisse died he would betray Aleysha. He had money put away and planned to disappear after the funeral, which was to take place the following morning. Philippe told him that Narcisse was to be buried in the Guinea graveyard, near the lagoon. The Cantaves were traditionally buried in the Roman Catholic cemetery in Le Havre, but their mother had agreed to this request of Zena's. The widow was not consulted and could not, under the treaty, have had his remains taken from Guinea if she had wished to do so.

Zena had loved Narcisse Cantave. All her life she had loved his sweet face and ingenuous nature. They had spent much of their childhood together. When her aunt Yvonne married Henri Cantave, she went to live in Le Havre. The life she was expected to live there, as a suburban matron, was very different from the simple rustic life she was used to in Guinea and she was often homesick. Henri was sympathetic and encouraged her to make frequent visits home. After the two boys, Philippe and Narcisse, were born she brought them with her on her visits to Guinea. Her sister Saba's oldest child, Zena, was four years younger than Narcisse and the two sisters often took the children for picnics on the beach. They learned to swim and to fish in the tranquil waters of the lagoon.

Zena could remember one particular evening when she was eight. The three children had gone out in a dugout not far from shore and Narcisse caught an odd looking fish that looked like a balloon. They had had difficulty getting it into the net. It was about sixteen inches from head to tail and almost round. When they got it in the boat and killed it, about a gallon of water had spilled out of its mouth into the boat, which Philippe hastily bailed with a half coconut shell kept in the boat for that purpose. It was late in the afternoon and they were being signaled to come back to shore. It was time to go home.

They had caught several other fish, but her mother was only interested in the one that had puffed itself up with seawater. "They do that whenever they feel they are in danger. They make themselves bigger," Saba explained. "I can use this fish. Please let me have it, Narcisse."

The children were responsible for the fish they caught; they cleaned them on the beach, carried them home, and, with some help, cooked them for supper. But Saba wouldn't let anyone else touch the puffer fish and cleaned it herself. It was a female and she cut out the eggs, or roe, and then the liver. Zena had watched her do it.

When they got home, Zena had followed her mother into the cave as the other children gathered around the fire outside to cook the other fish they had caught. Saba put the liver and roe in a stone pickle jar and sealed it with beeswax. "The liver and eggs of this fish are a dangerous magic," she told her daughter. "The flesh of the fish has a softer magic – your aunt and I will eat it – but it's not safe for you children."

Zena remembered watching her mother and aunt to see if any magic happened when they ate the fish, and what she observed was that they seemed unusually cheerful and excitable. They played games with the children after dinner with what seemed to her an almost embarrassing childish merriment. What on earth would happen if someone ate the other parts, she wondered?

Years later when she was apprenticing with her mother, she learned that the liver and roe of the puffer fish were used in concoctions that cast serious spells on members of the community, people whose behavior would be judged criminal in the west. These people were turned into zombies and lived out their lives as slave laborers. She had learned only recently from Narcisse that western science had isolated the chemical found in the liver and roe of the puffer fish, and had their own name for it: tetrodotoxin.

In Guinea there were ways of mixing in other ingredients that altered the personality of the zombie. For example, although Saba frowned on this practice, an aphrodisiac that permanently increased the zombie's sex drive could be added to the concoction. A violent person could be changed into a gentle zombie. Should the person who was to own the slave want a warrior, a gentle man could be made ferocious.

The victims of these potions at first appeared to be dead; so profound was the state of suspended animation that the heart stopped. Western doctors would declare them dead. People in Haiti were buried alive with full Catholic ceremony, family members weeping and moaning above ground, the victim, immobilized, listening below. Three nights later the *bokor* would come to the grave and the body would be dug up. The family was often unaware that the victim was taken away to a life of bondage in another part of the island. In cases of murder, the body of the killer would not be dug up; the punishment for murder was to be buried alive.

Zena's exposure to Western ideas at the University of Montreal had not weakened her faith in Voudon. On the contrary, she believed that the values that guided her people's lives were superior to the consumer culture of the West. In Guinea people wanted no more than they needed and they were, it was evident to her, happier than people in the West. And they were happy, she believed, because they were good. They needed to be protected from Western culture, and if the political philosophy of her parents and the other Leopards could not be considered democratic – and was dictatorial in banning Western books, radio, and television – that bothered her not one bit. She saw her mother as similar to Plato's philosopher king – but who came to wisdom without study, perhaps because the society she grew up in was ingenuous.

The people of Guinea were not exposed to contagious diseases and illness was rare. They would use Western science and medicine but only in the context of their own culture. Some of the medicines her mother used – for example, iodine and acetylsalicylic acid, which she found in plants and tree bark in the forest of Guinea – were used in the West. The medicines that the Arawaks had brought from South America particularly interested Narcisse: a few of them had yet to be discovered by Western medicine. Zena acknowledged that some of her mother's medicines were placebos and her cures the consequence of people's belief in the strength of her magic. But even Western doctors admit that many illnesses are psychosomatic and that many cures appear to take place through faith. She had observed her mother cure cancer in some instances simply by invoking the subject's faith in her ability to do so. But it did not always work.

When Philippe had called her and told her that Narcisse had been taken ill, she instantly knew that Alice, or Aleysha as she was coming to be known in Guinea, was somehow responsible. Zena had made her way down the valley on foot to St. Anthony to wait for Paul's taxi. She said nothing to Paul about her suspicions; she sat in the back of the taxi and scarcely spoke to him. He was Narcisse's first cousin and a distant cousin of hers, but she knew that he worked closely with Aleysha in whatever she was really doing at Haut-Clair and she didn't trust him.

She took Narcisse back with her to cure him, without any real confidence that this could be done. Zena had had another reason for wanting Narcisse with her in Guinea: she feared for his life under Aleysha's care. It was a difficult time for Zena. Saba was ill with cervical cancer; she was in constant pain. Zena was getting morphine from Dr. Cantave and had persuaded her mother to take it. Dr. Cantave wanted her in a Western hospital but Saba refused to go. When she died, Zena, as the new queen, had to deal with a backlog of hearings that had been postponed because of Saba's illness.

The potion that Zena had given to Narcisse for analysis had a number of ingredients that Narcisse suspected were not active and not necessary. He had asked her to make the potion strong in tetrodotoxin believing that it would be easier for a lab to isolate; it was the other ingredients that he was interested in. He knew exactly what had gone into the potion but it was possible that there had been some synthesis and certainly oxidation during the cooking process.

The tetrodotoxin from the liver and roe of the blowfish was a strong poison that could easily kill a person. In Japan certain parts of the fish – prepared by specialized cooks – are considered an exciting delicacy, the excitement derived partly from the risk, partly from the flavor, and partly from the narcotic effect that most poisons – such as certain mushrooms – induce. Artists and writers have been known to die from the experience. There is no cure known to western science.

The Haitian *bokor* who had tried tried to cure Narcisse thought that he might have managed to bring him out of his catatonic state if Narcisse had been a native of Guinea, or a Haitian of rural background; some faith in the zombie snake god was requisite. Before leaving he had told Saba and Zena that even if Narcisse did recover, he would be both mentally and physically handicapped. Saba had thought otherwise and the two women had refused to give up. The one person Zena wished she could consult through all of this was Narcisse himself. She was certain that he could hear them deliberating; if only he could speak.

During those two years, Zena devoted herself to finding a cure. She studied Narcisse's books and did experiments using Western science. She never did find a cure but she developed a profound knowledge of the poison, its different blends with the different side effects, and the correct dosage to achieve such effects. During those years her hatred for Aleysha intensified, but as long as he lived she had to respect the laws of her people; she could take no action against her.

And then, after being in this state for over two years – possibly as a consequence of a new medicine – Narcisse died. It was time to punish Aleysha for his murder. Zena was also convinced that Aleysha was encouraging cannibalism among the Abu, and she suspected her of manufacturing and smuggling drugs. As queen, she needed no proof, and needed no trial to proceed with Aleysha's punishment.

She resolved that Narcisse would be buried in the graveyard at Guinea. She called Yvonne and discussed it with her. Yvonne agreed. Philippe called Aleysha with the news and told her that the family wished the funeral and burial to be in Guinea. Aleysha had never been north of Mont Petit; she feared and mistrusted Zena, but she could hardly refuse to attend her own husband's funeral.

* * *

When word of the maritime drive-by reached Haut Clair, Aleysha knew grief. She had mourned the death of her dog, Mansfield, but that had been her own decision. And this was different: it was for a human being. She took to taking long walks with her dogs in the forest along paths that had been cleared for them, and to listening to Bach, Beethoven, and Brahms. At the service on Sunday she was noticeably depressed. The Abu were in mourning themselves – Henry had been popular in the village. She took to spending time with the young woman Henry had impregnated and playing with the baby.

Paul, who had been fond of Henry, was surprised by the depth of her grief, which appeared to him to border on despair. When the time came to inform her of the death of Narcisse, he watched her closely. For a long while she said nothing and then came a long sigh.

"He is to be buried in Guinea," he told her. "The family expects you to attend." There was a long silence.

"I will go of course," she said with a look of foreboding.

Paul, suffering from remorse for informing the DEA of the cocaine operations on hearing that Narcisse had died, flew her to Guinea in silence. Zena had given him special permission to land the plane. Abba had wanted to come with them but Aleysha had forbidden it. As they came in to land, they saw the Guinea people stretched out along the shore. The whole community had turned out. She was famous, notorious even, in Guinea, but except for the Cantave family and those who had been at the hounfour, none of them had ever laid eyes on her.

Paul landed on the water near the shore, dropped down onto a pontoon with a paddle, and brought the copter in to shore. Then he helped her disembark with ceremony and the reverence that he felt for her at that moment.

"I fear a trap," he said to her as he let go of her hand on the beach.

She gave him a long look. "Fate cannot harm me," she said, "I have dined". And set off along the beach to Zena who awaited her.

The service, which took place in the graveyard, was a bizarre blend of Voudon and Roman Catholicism. A priest had come from Le Havre and participated in the ceremony.

After the service, the people all drifted to the beach. It was very hot. Many of them took off their clothes and went swimming in the lagoon. Paul stood quietly in the shade at a distance and watched Zena, Aleysha, and Yvonne approach the shore. After the service Yvonne had gently linked arms with both women. All three were dressed in black silk. Zena walked right into the water wearing her dress and beckoned Aleysha to follow. Aleysha kicked off her black sandals. Everyone was watching them and the crowd was mesmerized as they swam together slowly, side by side, out into the lagoon. As they were coming back in, Paul noticed Yvonne stoop suddenly and sprinkle a white powder onto Aleysha's sandals. He looked about him – if anyone else had seen this there was no sign.

Paul started to run but he was too late. The two queens emerged from the lagoon, their black silk dresses clinging to their wet bodies. From a distance, except for the skin color, they looked identical, like two queens in a chess set. Paul, hurrying towards Aleysha watched, horrified, as she slipped her feet into her sandals. As the two walked together up the beach, Zena held back a little and was ready to catch Aleysha when she fell.

Some people ran up to help carry her unconscious body, while others brought forward a waiting coffin. Aleysha was placed inside it and then the coffin was swiftly carried into the forest. The crowd followed in complete silence as the coffin was taken not to the graveyard where Narcisse was buried, but to the old pirate graveyard near the beach. Two men were already there digging a grave in the sand. The lid was placed over Aleysha's coffin and it was lowered into the ground. Philippe stood with his mother as everyone bowed their heads. The priest came forward and said a few words. The gravediggers shoveled sand over the coffin.

Paul wanted only to get away. A feast was planned but he didn't stay. He took a dugout canoe and paddled out to his helicopter. Squatting on one of the pontoons he burst into tears. He knew what he had to do – return that night and dig her up. He didn't want to return to Haut-Clair without her, so he flew to the airport.

He found two visitors in the St. Anthony Coast Guard office. One of them he recognized as the man who had bought The Thirty-Nine Steps.

"Dr. Bernard Levinson," said Paul. "You may be just the man I need."

Bernard introduced the other man as Theodore McLeod.

"Ah," said Paul, "the gift from god. I am afraid that you have come too late."

Theodore said, "I want to show you a picture."

Paul looked at it for a long moment before saying, "It's her. In snow." He began to weep.

"What is it, man?" asked Bernard. "What's happened?"

Paul sat down at his little desk, put his head in his hands, and tried to pull himself together. "There's something we have to do. Tonight after dark. She's in deep trouble, maybe dead, I don't know. I don't think she's dead. I think we can save her. They buried her – they buried her alive."

Bernard and Theodore were aghast. Bernard said, "If she's buried alive, we must go at once."

"No. No. She's a zombie. She won't suffocate."

"What?"

"And they'll stop us. They won't let us take her. They have their own laws there; we wouldn't be allowed to take her. She'll be all right. We have go after dark. Come back here tonight. Late – say midnight and we'll go get her. Bring shovels. Now please leave me."

"I don't think so," said Bernard. "I think you better come with us. I think you need a mild sedative."

"But I'll be flying."

"Trust me. The effects of what I will give you will have worn off by tonight. In the meantime you need rest. Come back to my house. You are suffering from shock. I'm a doctor. Let me take care of you."

Paul went with them to the Thirty-Nine Steps, a house he knew well. They talked about Aleysha. Although what he had done that morning did not seem to matter that much anymore, he was still wracked with guilt. In the shock of what he had witnessed he realized that he loved her. He couldn't bring himself to speak ill of her to Theodore. He could see that Theodore loved her in a way that was to Paul wondrously ingenuous. But he played along and told them of the good work she had done, how she had helped the poor people of Haut-Clair, and then been turned into a zombie by a jealous rival. But Bernard looked at him curiously as if he knew there was more to the story.

It was decided that they needed an inflatable rubber boat with a small silent electric motor. Theodore volunteered to go and get it. Paul told him where he could find one and he left.

"I may be gone awhile," he said. "I want to take another look at the miniature, and I'll bring the picture of Hattie with me."

This left Paul alone with the good doctor, who then gave Paul a sedative, and rather unscrupulously added a smidgen of a truth drug to it. They were alone for two hours, and Paul, who wanted it all off his chest anyway, told Bernard everything.

Late that night they flew the helicopter to the far side of the lagoon and landed on the shore. They inflated the rubber boat and made their way silently into the lagoon, crossed it, and pulled it up onto the sand. None of the Guinea people lived near the beach. It was swampy in places and there were mosquitos. Carrying two shovels, Paul led them to the old pirates' graveyard. If anyone was awake and knew what they were doing they gave no sign. The digging wasn't hard. The coffin had not been buried very deep in the sand and about three feet down their shovels hit its wooden lid.

They freed it without difficulty and lifted it out; they could feel some movement inside. Bernard started to pry open the lid but it was suddenly pushed up from within and Aleysha leapt out. Seeing Theodore, she embraced and held him. She seemed to have lost the power of speech. She was still wearing the long black dress and it was still damp. Bernard and Paul saw that the tips of her fingers were bloody and the nails broken. The inside of the coffin lid was scratched and marked with blood. Theodore picked her up and carried her to the boat as the others replaced the coffin and shoveled the earth back over it. They left the grave just as they had found it.

Bernard gave her fresh water to drink. He washed her feet in the sea and rubbed them with rum. When they got back to the helicopter, they deflated the boat, and taking off right away, flew west over the ocean towards the tiny British island of Sombrero, a journey of about an hour. Theodore sat in the back with Aleysha on his lap holding her in his arms. He made her drink a lot of water; Bernard said it would help to flush out her system. She was trembling and held on to him tightly.

No one spoke until Paul noticed the lights of a large ship, traveling east. "It's a US navy destroyer, Spruance class. Could even be the Spruance, which is based in Florida. I served on one of those. It carries two Sea Hawk helicopters, that's the navy version of the Black Hawk, and it's what I learned to fly. They're sometimes used for what they call drug interdiction. They have a crew of four and they're armed with machine guns and missiles. Its course is a bit too northerly for Le Havre and it's not going to the Azores. I know where she's going. I'll have to drop you off, refuel, and get right back. It could be that all hell's going to break loose."

"What are you saying?" asked Theodore.

Paul was silent for long moment. Then he said, "It would take too long to explain. You take care of Aleysha and I'll try to make peace with the United States Navy."

Aleysha had stopped trembling and was fast asleep. Suddenly she cried out in a loud voice, "O, Ayesha, Ayesha, why hast thou forsaken me?"

Bernard turned around sharply. "What was that?"

Theodore was looking down at her. "I don't know – a dream. She's fast asleep."

Bernard was thoughtful. "Whoever it was has not forsaken her entirely. She can speak. At least in dreams."

Paul looked over at him and said nothing. The airport of the island of Sombrero was now beneath them and he landed the helicopter. Bernard hopped out. "She's fast asleep," he remarked as Theodore handed her down. "What'll we do? She has no papers."

"I think I can fix that. I'll phone from inside. Meantime, I'm her husband, we're all Americans, and you're her doctor."

"Right."

Paul gave Theodore his briefcase and Bernard his medical bag; it was all they had brought with them. He looked long and hard at Aleysha as she lay asleep cradled in the arms of the big psychiatrist. Suddenly he reached over and kissed her cheek. As he straightened up, his eyes were moist.

He looked at Theodore. "She was my boss. She planted coffee trees to help some poor people on the island. But then she was persuaded to grow coca plants. She was doing it for the Abu. They were so poor. They had nothing. That ship, they're on their way to shoot up the place. I've gotta try to stop it."

"Good luck. Don't feel so bad, you've saved her life," said Bernard

"Maybe, but it doesn't make up for something I did earlier today. I must hurry," said Paul, looking around. "Doesn't look as if anything is open. Damn. I wonder if I have enough fuel. Maybe I'll just head straight for the destroyer. They'll have fuel. It's not as if I don't know the drill."

Theodore went inside the little airport building. There was only a night watchman. "Nothing open here, suh. But I can open up the duty free. Do that anytime, night or day. Immigration officer, she don't come in till eight. But there's a little hotel over there will take you in. Just knock hard and wake 'em up."

Still carrying the sleeping medicated Aleysha in his arms, Bernard watched Paul take off and approach the destroyer. He wanted to see him safely landed on its deck. Theodore, crossing the road to the hotel, looked back, stopped, and also watched. Suddenly a missile shot out and hit the little helicopter, which burst into flames and fell into the sea. What had happened was this: the doctor's great knee had accidentally disconnected the radio when he had turned around to talk to Theodore. Knowing that the airport in Sombrero was closed Paul had not used the radio. Now as he struggled to reconnect, the missile struck.

Theodore stood silently and waited for Bernard, who was very angry. "You saw that? Trigger-happy bastards."

"You know? I worked for those guys. No more. I'm going to call them as soon as I can get hold of a phone and give them hell."

The hotel was an old plantation house. The three of them took one large room. Theodore got on the phone to Ken Marlowe.

"Sorry to wake you up, but do you know what just happened?"

"We're all awake here, thanks to you. What are you doing in Sombrero?"

"How do you know where I am?"

"We always know where you are. The DEA are going into St. Anthony tomorrow morning, that was you that called it in?"

"I know nothing about it."

"Big drug bust, cocaine plantation and refinery. That wasn't you then that called it in? Didn't give his name. I didn't speak to him myself. I just assumed it was you. We knew you were on the island."

"How? Oh, that goddam GPS tracking disc. I found it months ago but I put the goddam thing out of my mind. Listen and listen up good. The US navy just shot down the St. Anthony Coast Guard helicopter. He was trying to make contact. A missile. They blew him up."

"No, oh, no. How do you know this?"

"Saw it. He had just flown us over here."

"Oh, no." Theodore heard him swearing under his breath. "Oh, well, stuff happens."

Theodore was so disgusted he almost hung up but remembered why he called. "Listen, I need a favor, another passport. In the name of my wife." He paused, thinking of a name. "Name of Susan. I'm using the second ID." Pause. "Well, now I have a wife. Trust me, I need this, I'll explain later, right now I have to go. Send it to the American consul here in Sombrero. You'll need a photograph? I'll email you a digital passport photo in the morning from the consulate." Then he hung up. He thought of leaving the phone number, but then realized, they will know that, they know everything.

"What did he say about the helicopter?"

"'Stuff happens.'"

"Shit! Stuff happens, collateral damage, they think that if they can dismiss these things with a catchy phrase, it's as if it never happened. No remorse. All government is psychopathic."

They had laid Aleysha out on one of the beds. She was still in her black dress, but it was now quite dry. "She'll sleep until morning. We could put her in a hospital, but we can take better care of her ourselves. I'm the doctor and you're the nurse. She's been poisoned. It would be a big help if I knew precisely with what. But I believe the principal ingredient is tetrodotoxin. No known antidote. But water weakens it."

Theodore thought for a moment. "Do you remember the *houdon* we went to two years ago? The gorgeous black witch? She spoke to us."

"I do remember her. I've been thinking about her too. Paul said she did this. When I get you two settled in Chicago, I'm going back to the island and I am going to go to see her. It's Voudon; it works best on people who believe in it. I doubt if Hattie believed in it. So it's a simple case of poisoning. I have books at home on it. I think the best thing we can do now is force her to vomit, give her an enema, get her to drink lots of water. It's probably too late to do much good but maybe we can help her system flush it out. Listen, I can do it by myself, you don't have to help. You go and sit in the lobby with your rum. I noticed a pop machine. I'll have mine later." He opened up his medical bag and set to work. Theodore left.

As he worked on her he thought about Paul – looks like he called in the DEA and then regretted it. When Susan was tucked up in bed, he called in Theodore from the lobby. They sat quietly sipping their rum and Coke and talked about Paul.

"I liked the guy, "Bernard sighed. "I suppose they thought that he was a terrorist with a bomb or something. It's dusk in America today. All cats are gray. Terrorists, drug runners, they're all the same to our government, our armed forces." They were both silent a moment. "Of course, you are an American yourself now - perhaps only temporarily. But your wife – "

"She's not exactly my wife – "

"You just asked the US government to make her your wife. She's going to need a lot of care. Maybe for life. Are you up to it? From what you've told me, it would not be wise for her to return to Canada and resume her old identity. What you and – uh – Susan – better do is to come to Chicago with me."

"I owe you so much already."

"Then you can do me a favor. As her husband you can let me treat her."

"You are interested in her? Professionally?"

"Very much."

The next morning the Sea Hawk choppers flew low over Guinea and saw nothing of interest. The people stared and then the choppers were gone as suddenly as they arrived. On the other side of Mont Petit their interest perked up: coca crops. One of the Sea Hawks was equipped to spray herbicide and proceeded to do so. The other looked for the reported coca refinery.

That morning Abbah, worried that Aleysha had not come back and that there was no sign of Paul, had gone down to the *Aleysha* and got out the rifle that was kept in the wheelhouse. He was worried about her; he was afraid that the Guinea people had captured her and was considering a rescue operation. Carrying the rifle he went to her office in the plantation house to see if she had phoned. There were no messages. Trouble was he didn't know how to use a gun. When he heard the choppers he went to the window, still clutching the rifle. Someone on the Sea Hawk spraying herbicide saw him and radioed its armed companion, which flew up to the house. When the DEA agent on board saw Abbah with his gun, he told the pilot to open fire and he released two AGM-114 Hellfire missiles. One hit the roof, the other Aleysha's bedroom. Neither was near the office. The walls of the château were made of coral, but everything else was wood and the plantation house was shortly in flames.

To be fair to the DEA, they were accustomed to raiding in Columbia, where it was necessary to strike first and to strike hard. They did not know that they were up against one boy with a rifle that he had never learned to shoot. Abbah, seeing the flames engulf the staircase, ran for the back stairs, then thought, I have time to save something, what shall I save? He went back to the office and scooped up Aleysha's laptop. He had learned to run all sorts of machines but the computer was a mystery to him. He knew from the amount of time she spent on it that it was important to her, and he saved it and himself, getting out just before the roof collapsed.

The agents now spotted the cocaine refinery and landed to verify the contents. Two of the crew got out and were immediately and savagely attacked by the giant schnauzers. One of the men remaining in the Sea Hawk opened up with a machine gun, killing both dogs and wounding one of his own men. The other quickly checked the refinery, came back, and yelled, "Affirmative." He helped his wounded colleague back into the chopper. It took off, circled above the refinery, released two missiles, and destroyed the building.

The other chopper had now finished spraying and the two circled the cutter in the cove. They identified it as belonging to the St. Anthony Coast Guard and radioed back to the mother ship for instructions. They were told to leave it strictly alone and return to the ship. Word had reached the destroyer that the helicopter had belonged to the coast guard.

The Abu came out of their hiding places and did their best to fight the fires. Many were crying from the smoke and from sorrow. Where was Aleysha? Had these evil men taken her away from them? Abbah could not comfort them; he didn't know the answers himself.

In Chicago Bernard, Theodore, and Susan settled into Bernard's large and comfortable house. Luis was told that Susan was a patient and that she and her husband would be staying indefinitely. He wasn't surprised; it had happened before.

Theodore told Bernard that she had a father in Ottawa and together they tried to locate him on the Internet using local directories. They had no success. But Bernard had not expected to find him. Paul had told him that Henry was working for his daughter distributing cocaine in Florida. Still determined to keep the extent of her criminal activities from Theodore, Bernard did not pass this on; instead, without telling Theodore, he hired a private detective in Florida to look for Henry. Two weeks later he received a report that a man answering to Henry Brading's description, known locally as Mr. Henry, had gone missing one night with his boat and was presumed dead, lost at sea. Again, he did not pass this on. It appeared she had no other family and Bernard made no more attempts to find any. Theodore, of course, had never suspected that Henry Brading and his friend, Mr. Henry, were the same man, nor had he mentioned Mr. Henry to Bernard.

Susan appeared to be deficient in some capacities and not in others. Bernard was interested in this; he was not a disciple of the notion that the human mind contains the structures of thought at birth, and that these have specific locations in the brain. Bernard thought that the brain was a *tabula rasa*, that if one part was damaged another could be trained to perform its function. Susan appeared to have lost the power of speech, and was suffering from aphasia induced not by physical brain damage, not from an injury, but by chemicals, by poisons. In addition, she was suffering from shock, from the extreme trauma caused by being buried alive. Bernard believed she could learn to speak again.

Her physical coordination had been damaged. She could move about and perform the basic functions of eating, drinking, and eliminating. She ate well. Theodore would take her for long walks in Park Ridge. He took her to a matinée at the Pickwick Theatre. She seemed to have forgotten her table manners but they came back within a few days. She was anxious to please, to figure out what was wanted from her and provide it. This encouraged Theodore and Bernard greatly; perhaps she would regain all her faculties. She was affectionate to both of them and Bernard found her efforts to please touching.

Theodore and Susan shared a big double bed in a large guest room with its own bath. Bernard asked Theodore if she was interested in sex, and he replied shyly that she had a powerful sexual appetite. They watched television but Bernard could see that she didn't seem to understand what was going on. He played her classical music and found that she loved it. She would sit for hours in the living room listening to opera. Bernard showed her how to play the compact discs herself, and after he showed her the opera section, she never listened to anything else, never looking at the labels. She listened only to opera.

Theodore assumed Bernard's professional interest in Susan was simply in the effects of the poison and the trauma. But Bernard was interested not just in the way she was now, but in the woman she had been before and the transformation. He didn't believe that she was simply the clever computer expert who had swindled a motorcycle gang. What had really gone on at the plantation? He had gathered from Paul that she was known as Hattie in Canada, Alice in Le Havre, and Aleysha on the plantation. Could she be a multiple personality? He thought not. What Paul had told him about her indicated a pattern of behavior which intrigued him: the omega role-playing over-controlled psychopath. Paul had told him that she had had a good relationship with her father. She had gone to some trouble to bring him to Haut-Clair. He concluded that she had not been abused as a child, at least not by her father.

That suggested to him that she was one of those whose psychopathology had begun in her imagination. He wondered how old she had been when she first killed. Susan was cooperative and compliant so he attempted conventional psychoanalysis, placing her on a couch in his office and trying to get her to talk about her past. But it was hopeless: her powers of speech were limited and she did not seem to want to remember anything about her past.

Bernard had a speech therapist come daily to the house. An educational kinesiologist also came regularly and taught both Theodore and Susan muscle testing and balancing. She chose goals for herself in physical activities and learned exercises that helped achieve those goals. Theodore and she worked together on this when the E-K instructor wasn't there. Her mental skills slowly improved. Bernard once suggested that she choose remembering as a goal. This was a mistake – all she could remember was the coffin and her frantic attempts to escape from it. Further back she would not go deliberately but certain memories came back. Research informed Bernard that zombies were subject to progressive limb paralysis. He carried out certain tests and resolved to repeat them on a regular basis

They seemed happy together and in love. Bernard decided that he could safely leave Susan in Theodore and Luis's care. He wanted to go back to his house in St. Anthony, pick up the manuscript he was working on and connected files, and return. He also wanted to find out all that he could about his patient's past life and he wanted to talk to Zena.

Back at The Thirty-Nine Steps, he began his research with a friendly interrogation of Sara while she was serving him breakfast. People on the island believed that Aleysha, or as Sara still called her, Miz Alice, had been turned into a zombie by the Guinea people, rescued by Paul Cantave, and killed when the US navy shot down the St. Anthony Coast Guard helicopter by mistake.

"They was growing coca over there and the United States government found out about it. So they went to turn themselves in. That's what we think. They wanted to stop the destruction and bombing that was to take place. But Miz Alice and Mr. Paul they got shot down." Sara began to cry.

"Now, Sara, one more question. How could I find Zena, the queen of the Guinea people? I met her once before and would like to see her again."

"You must go and see Mr. Philip. Mr. Philip Cantave he take care of all their business this part of the island. Go see him."

Bernard knew Philippe from the closing of his purchase of the house, and he telephoned him at his office and told him that he wished to meet Zena, that his interest was in the medical aspects of Voudon. Philippe invited him for a drink at his house at six and said he would see what he could do.

They sat in the garden behind Philippe's pleasant bungalow where they were served drinks by an exquisitely handsome black butler called Andre. Using the house to broach the subject, Bernard got Philippe talking about Aleysha, which he was not at all reluctant to do. But he was not about to tell Bernard everything he knew; he was after all present when his mother and Zena had drugged Aleysha and had her buried alive. He was an accessory and he had to protect his mother. He had only learned of the extent of the cocaine operation when he went over to inspect Haut-Clair after the DEA raid. It was his first visit to Haut-Clair. Aleysha had asked him to visit before but he had always declined; he was conscientious in his work for Guinea and for Haut-Clair but he had no interest in going to either place.

He was shocked that Aleysha had used Haut-Clair in this way and, despite her cruel punishment for his brother's death, had no sympathy for her. He felt betrayed. He had managed to persuade Zena and the St. Anthony government that he had known nothing about it – which was true. He now believed what he had previously dismissed as nonsense: that she had deliberately turned his brother into a zombie.

"Alice, or Aleysha, or whoever she was, is dead. There is no question about that." He paused. "It appears that she has died more than once. A couple of years ago, a certain René Lachapelle, an officer of the SQ, the Quebec provincial police, came to this island, and brought her two dogs that she had bought over the Internet. He delivered them in person. Then he mysteriously disappeared. It looked like a fake suicide.

"The authorities here would not issue a death certificate because there was no body. His clothes were found near his car on a deserted beach. A beach with sharp stones, his shoes were not found, nor his gun, nor his cigarettes. Our court thought that quite possibly he had faked his own suicide. That has happened here with tourists a couple of times. There was something fishy about the whole thing.

"But now we believe he was murdered. By her. It seems that he was blackmailing her. For murder or murders she had committed in Canada. He had left an envelope with the SQ, to be opened in the event of his death. But without a death certificate, they could not legally open it for seven years. Someone in the SQ was bribed to destroy it, but he didn't. He took it home and kept it. But this corrupt officer was very recently caught. The internal investigators raided his home and found the document in a wall safe among other things, and opened it. The SQ sent a copy to our police who have looked into it. They now think that Alice LeBlanc murdered him. An officer came to see me a few days ago and gave me a copy of Lachapelle's statement and I'll make you a copy. It's in French. It's in my office upstairs. I'll go and fetch it."

He came back within two minutes and passed Bernard an envelope. "Another drink? André!" he shouted. "The police dug up the well as the blackmailer had suggested and they found the body of the man who they had previously believed had murdered Hattie Brading, together with the body of her dog. She had killed her own dog. It appears that she also killed and decapitated a stranger whose body her father identified as hers. Hattie Brading and Alice LeBlanc were one and the same person. Now what's left of her is at the bottom of the ocean."

André brought the drinks. Servant and master exchanged sly smiles. I don't think that boy is really a butler, thought Bernard. "It's a bit of a scandal for the Quebec police – a blackmailer in their midst. They are not going to reopen the case now that she's dead. Nor will the St. Anthony police. There is more. She killed my brother and I have every reason to believe she murdered my father."

Bernard then brought up his request to meet Zena. Bernard didn't intend to tell anyone that Aleysha was still alive, but he wanted to meet her and, as a doctor, persuade her to tell him exactly what was in the potion.

"I have a feeling she won't want to see you, but I'll try," said Philippe. He reached for the phone and dialed a number. "I'll call her. You can speak to her yourself." He spoke into the phone.

"There's a doctor here, Dr. Bernard Levinson, who has a house on the island, an American. He is a psychiatrist, a forensic psychiatrist." A pause. "Yes, forensic. He is interested, as Narcisse was, in your medicines. He wants to come and see you." There was a pause as he listened to her answer. "I see."

"Well, the best thing I can say about her answer," he said when he had hung up, "is that it was unequivocal. In no circumstances will she see you. Perhaps I should not have mentioned the word forensic. It seemed to put her off." But Philippe had mentioned it on purpose. He wished to give Bernard the impression that he was doing his best but he didn't want Dr. Levinson sniffing around Guinea. Bernard stood up to leave.

"One more thing about Alice, which is what I called her." Philippe got up and saw Bernard to the front door. "The helicopter crashed outside St. Anthony's territorial waters. Officially she was lost at sea. I am getting the Coroner to ask the Minister of Justice to issue a death certificate in the name of Alice Cantave. All her property on the island reverts to the Cantaves. As for any other assets," he shrugged, "I neither know nor care about them."

Bernard had a superficial knowledge of several languages. His German was better than his French, but he could make sense of the document. It related what René knew, that Hattie was still alive, and what he thought that she had done. It was chilling reading. Bernard had thought that Theodore's tale of computer theft from a motorcycle gang was somehow an oversimplification; he had had an intuition that Hattie was not the innocent Theodore supposed. When he first met him, he had thought that there was something odd about his story; that he had been set up by a woman, but didn't know it. And Theodore had made a remark – "I do not think that I have ever met an evil woman" – that struck him at the time as naive. But now that he knew more of the story it did not seem to him that – whatever crimes Hattie, or Alice, or Aleysha had committed – she had betrayed Theodore nor seriously exploited him

He had one more thing to do and that was to visit Haut-Clair. He set out the next morning in his car, stopped at the little coffee trading post – the coffee merchant had stayed on as a gatekeeper – asked directions, and received dire warnings. He found the steps up the cliffs, the avenue of rosewood trees, and the ruin of the plantation house. He was looking over the ruins of what appeared to have once been valuable furniture and works of art when a young man came up behind him.

"Good morning," he said. "My name is Abbah. I am chief of the Abu."

"Good morning, Abbah. I am Dr. Levinson. I am the man who bought The Thirty-Nine Steps – perhaps you know that house. What a terrible thing – this destruction."

"I was upstairs at the time. I had a rifle with me and they saw it. I did not even know how to shoot it. And then they shot Aleysha out of the sky, she and Paul. I heard."

Bernard looked into the Abbah's deep brown eyes, but didn't respond.

"But they could not kill her. Nay, not Aleysha. I know that. Paul they could kill, and me if I had not been lucky. But they could not kill her. I know that. Thou knowst it, too, I see it in thine eyes that she is alive. If I go and get something, can thee bring it to her?"

Bernard continued to look into his eyes. What he saw in them was love and faith. He couldn't bring himself to refuse what the young man had asked, but he remained silent.

"Wait, wait here, I'll get it."

Bernard turned and left the ruin. It was too depressing. He started to walk back down the avenue, and a few minutes later Abbah came running up to him, carrying a laptop computer in a black case.

"Please bring it to her. I saved it from the fire. I only had time to save one thing and this is what I chose. Tell her I hope I made a good choice. Tell her the people know she will return again."

Bernard opened the case and saw inside a laptop and a CD.

Bernard returned to Chicago the following night. After breakfast he tested her for progressive limb paralysis and he observed deterioration even in the short time he had been away. Then he presented her with the laptop. "This was saved from the fire by a young man," he said.

"Abbah." She looked at them and smiled.

"That was the young man's name." Bernard was pleased that her memory was improving and her powers of speech.

She opened the computer, turned it on, and started slowly to press keys. Bernard left them and went to his study to wrestle with his problem.

Her life was in his hands. Should he turn her over to the authorities? And if he did, could he reasonably argue, as her psychiatrist, that she had a mental disorder? He thought not. She was currently impaired, but that was not germane, she had been in full command of her faculties when her crimes were committed. It was merely something that should be taken into consideration if she were sentenced.

He ruled out the notion of a multiple personality. She had changed her name from Hattie to Alice because she was on the run, and Aleysha was a name the Abu had given her. Susan was a name Theodore had given her, without time to give it much thought. There was no indication that she had changed her personality under the first three names. Under all three she had been a cold-blooded murderess.

If he was to let her go, he reflected, and if he was correct in thinking that she was no longer dangerous, there was no need to tell Theodore about any of this. Bernard had told Theodore of the discovery of Song's murder. But Theodore believed the Angels had done it to punish Song for letting himself be fooled by Hattie, at such great cost to themselves. According to Theodore's version of events, the lady in the lake had been murdered by persons unknown. It had nothing to do with Hattie; her father had been clever enough to take advantage of it and had somehow faked the DNA evidence.

His main interest had always been the psychopathic mind, and the possibility that psychopaths could be treated. He did not think the character of men and women could be changed, but he believed that they could be persuaded to adopt new goals and values. For this he needed to know their history. Had Hattie chosen at an early age, perhaps because of cruel treatment, or perhaps even because of one shocking disappointment, to shut down her ability to love? Could something as simple perhaps as the very early betrayal of a friendship by another child, pushed her to a strategy of total selfishness? Or had she had a normal childhood, but fantasized a role for herself as a killer, and then grown up to act out her fantasies? Had she lacked at birth, as Chomsky might put it, a structure in her brain for moral thought? Another possibility was Dr. Birbaumer's hypothesis that certain areas of the brain – in the case of psychopaths the part that produced a concern for others – in some individuals were deprived of an adequate blood supply?

He reflected, not for the first time, on what she had said to Paul about killer apes, something about not killing was to betray the planet and then justifying this with a reference to Kant's ethics. Bernard himself had no doubt that the human population explosion was a threat to the planet. So she believed that for the sake of the planet, everyone should adopt this ethic. He got up and looked up the quote: So act that the maxim for your action could be enacted as a law for all mankind. She had her ethics; psychopaths had none, other than to act in their perceived self-interest. To her, murder was not evil. Should a psychiatrist consider this world-view the rationalization of a psychopath? He thought not. No, it deserved to be taken seriously. He thought again of Janet Malcolm's statement that the concept of the psychopath is an admission of failure to solve the mystery of evil, and finally, he pondered Michael's remark: "In the Voudon religion, good cannot exist without evil and evil cannot exist without good. You must not confuse them but you cannot always tell them apart."

It was time for a decision. His diagnosis was that she was an omega-type female over-controlled psychopath, recovered as a consequence of the shock caused by the tetrodotoxin. She was no longer a threat. And in his opinion the consideration that overruled all others was that, without question, she had paid her debt. She had been judged and found guilty by the queen of the land in which she had chosen to live. She had been executed according to the law of that country. She had already met justice and paid for her crimes. Even though she had been rescued from death, she was to endure in her zombie state a punishment for life, and with the progressive limb paralysis the prognosis was not good.

Bernard went back to the breakfast room determined that he would do what he could to see that her last years were as comfortable as possible. He found them both still sitting and laughing. Could it be, he wondered, that she has found what she had once lost, the ability to love? Was that what it was all about?

"She knows how to work the computer very well. She seems to be finding millions of dollars, and she doesn't want them, they are in the name of Alice Laporte. She says that Susan is her name, so they can't belong to her. But I tell her that was her name before she married me."

"That's true, my dear," said Bernard, putting his hands on her shoulder. "That's your money."

"But what would we do with all that money?" grinned Theodore.

They seemed so happy, he finally laughed with them and impulsively answered Theodore's question. "What should you do with all that money? Why, why don't you buy a vineyard in California and live happily ever afterwards?"

They did buy a vineyard in California, but it would not be truthful to say they were entirely happy. Susan never fully recovered. She could speak but could only express simple thoughts: What did Theodore want, What could she do for him? Theodore cared for her there to the end of her days, which as it turned out were not many, a thousand or so. She worked in the vineyard silently, slowly, and conscientiously, as long as she was strong enough, and at home she continued to look at him with adoring spaniel green eyes. She was amorous in bed. He wondered occasionally if he had not just found himself a slave, and a sex slave at that.

But the paralysis of her limbs progressed rapidly and she was soon crippled and then bedridden. One night Theodore heard her whispering softly in bed, *"O, Ayesha, let me die."*

He asked her gently, "Who is Ayesha?" She didn't answer but that night her wish was granted. He had her remains cremated, took them to Ottawa, and tossed them off the bridge over the Chaudière Falls. It was spring and the water was wildly turbulent; in an instant they were gone.

He invited his aunts to come and live with him. Some time later he married a young woman who worked in the vineyard, but he never forgot Hattie. To the end of his life, Theodore believed that she was a good Ottawa girl who had stolen money from criminals in order to help poor people in the Third World.

Epilogue

Philippe Cantave was the last of the Cantaves. He did not want children and because of his sexual preferences, knew there would be none. He didn't know what to with Haut-Clair – the mere thought of it made him shudder. He did have a talk with Abbah about cannibalism and Abbah told him that in memory of Aleysha the Abu had decided to forgo human flesh. They were working on their archery and had been able to shoot the occasional pig. They waited patiently for her return as good Christians await the return of Jesus. The new coffee trees, unharmed by the species selective chemical spray of the Americans, matured and the Abu prospered, chewing the leaves of the surviving coca plants, as they worked in the fields.

Philippe decided that he should get over his reluctance to visit Guinea and one day called on Zena, and was shown about the caves. On his way back he stopped at the little café on the north coast. While ordering a cup of coffee he found himself struck by the appearance of the girl who brought it. He saw a family resemblance – of course! This was the café to which the office had been sending a remittance for years – the girl was Paul's daughter. There was another living Cantave beside himself! Emma, now seventeen, confirmed that Paul had been her father. He introduced himself to her as her cousin and asked to meet her mother. He stayed for lunch, invited them both to Haut-Clair, and drove them there that afternoon. They climbed the steps together, walked about, and met Abbah. Emma was enchanted by the place despite the ugly ruins of the château and the refinery. Philippe explained that there were funds to put it back in shape. All that was needed was a Cantave who was willing to work at doing so.

He looked hard at them both. Emma's mother was the first to realize that he was offering it to them. Abbah, who was smitten by Emma at first sight, urged them to accept. He told them that one day

Aleysha would return but no one took this very seriously. Philippe took them home, went back to his office, checked the million dollar trust document that guaranteed revenue to the Leopards, and deeded the plateau of Haut-Clair to Emma Cantave.

The ST.ACGC *Aleysha* also now belonged to Emma, who with Abbah, Oku, and Obah took it out in all sorts of weather and one day cruised into the harbor of Le Havre with a full crew of ten. Philippe had arranged for the authorities to come aboard and the sailors demonstrated their mastery of the vessel with a series of well-executed manoeuvres. The government accepted them as members of the St. Anthony Coast Guard. After a number of rescues and a few salvaged ships the reputation of the Abu did an about face. A story about the ship and its crew in *The Saint Anthony Sun-Times* brought them local fame.

Emma set up a website and began to sell Haut Clair Shadegrown Coffee directly to retailers worldwide. This enterprise prospered. Ayesha's jewelry was found among the ruins; Abbah kept them for when she would return.

The people of Guinea and the Abu continued to ignore each other's existence. Abbah and Zena never spoke. If Zena continued Narcisse's research she did not share it with the Western world of corporate-controlled patent protection. Emma and Abbah were to marry and to have a little girl whom they named Christina. She was to grow up and marry Henry Brading's son, Henry, Ayesha's half brother.

Their daughter was to be born in the year 2033 and she was named Aleysha.

Acknowledgements

The debt to Henry Rider Haggard's *She* is obvious, but there are other authors and books to whom I am in debt: Wade Davis for his account of psychopharmacology, Voudon, and zombies in Haiti in his book, *The Serpent and the Rainbow*; Wayne Wilson for his book, *The Psychopath in Film*; Stephen King for his book *On Writing*; Yves Lavigne for his book on the Hells Angels, *Hells Angels: Into the Abyss*.

About James Lovelock's Gaia, it is a theory named after a Greek goddess rather than the goddess herself, as both Narcisse and Paul point out to our protagonist. But Lovelock himself has said that if people want to jump aboard and consider her a goddess, he has no objection.

I am indebted to Bill Hutchison for finding errors in the book regarding computers and international banking, and for pointing the way to corrections. Clay Evans, of the Canadian Coast Guard, Bamfield station, who recently completed a book on coast guard vessels, *Rescue at Sea*, kindly helped with a detailed description of the coast guard cutter on which the Saint Anthony Coast Guard Cutter Aleysha was modeled.

Andrea Knight edited the fourth draft approximately of this book and was a big help. She respected the story, as I did, to use Stephen King's simile, as a fossil found in the sand, and only pointed out errors and flaws in my telling of it

Gord Naunton designed the cover. Tammy Flynn Seybold painted the miniature portrait of Aloyshovna (the original is actually about six inches high and hangs in my living room in a gold oval frame). Maurice Greiffenhagen drew the portrait of Ayesha on the cover in sepia ink for the November 1, 1888 Longmans Green edition of *She*. The portrait on page 12 is also by him from the same edition. Denise Wey drew the map.

Several scraps of poetry are acknowledged in the text. The verse Hattie chants as she paddles up the Ottawa was not acknowledged and was written by Wilson Macdonald

J.B.

For information about the author please go to
www.ayeshamyqueendomcome.net

ISBN 1-4120-3776-X